VICKY PETERWALD
SURVIVOR

MIKE SHEPHERD

ACE BOOKS, NEW YORK

SF

57142101

An imprint of Penguin Random House LLC
375 Hudson Street, New York, New York 10014

VICKY PETERWALD: SURVIVOR

An Ace Book / published by arrangement with the author

ISBN: 978-0-425-26658-8

PUBLISHING HISTORY
Ace mass-market edition / June 2015

PRINTED IN THE UNITED STATES OF AMERICA

10 9 8 7 6 5 4 3 2 1

Cover illustration by Scott Grimando.
Cover design by Diana Kolsky.
Interior text design by Kristin del Rosario.

Penguin
Random
House

CHAPTER 1

H ᴇʀ Imperial Grace, the Grand Duchess, Lieutenant Commander Vicky Peterwald cinched in her five-point restraint harness as tight as she could. Beside her, the man sworn to protect her life with his own, Commander Gerrit Schlieffen, did the same. Only then did he begin to activate the myriad of controls and systems of the loaned shuttle.

Vicky was careful not to touch anything.

Kris Longknife could probably land the shuttle herself from orbit, while dodging lasers all the way down. Vicky winced; she'd been raised to be traded off for some advantageous marriage by her dad, the Emperor. Her training had consisted mainly of looking pretty while learning needlepoint and the Kama Sutra for both defense and offense.

In the world she'd been raised to expect, she would be back in the passenger compartment of the shuttle, seducing her husband into the five-hundred-mile-high club.

Today, Vicky's partner would either dodge the threatened lasers aimed at them, or both of them would die.

And Vicky couldn't do a damn thing about it.

Then again, if they survived the next couple of hours, Vicky just might save a couple of planets in the Emperor's crumbling Empire from economic collapse, starvation, and cannibalism.

Maybe.

If she was lucky, and could pull a political miracle out of thin air.

Too bad she had no idea how she might do that.

"You want to turn on the electronic-countermeasures suite?" Commander Schlieffen said.

Vicky looked at the collection of gauges, dials, and lights in front of her. Most were a duplicate of those in front of the pilot's seat. There was a light gray panel identified as made by Singer. Vicky pointed at it.

"You mean this?"

"Yep. The admiral wasn't kidding when he said he was giving us his most expendable shuttle. You need to warm up the ECM system if it's going to do us any good in a few minutes."

During her three years in the Imperial Greenfeld Navy, Vicky had learned to stand communications watches on the bridges of battleships. They usually had a couple of specialists standing the ECM watches. As a boot ensign, Vicky had rotated through one watch at the ECM station.

She hadn't learned much.

However, as limited as her education was, she *could* recognize an on/off button. She pressed it. The lights on the gray board slowly flickered to life.

"That old system isn't worth much," the commander said, glancing from his own board. "Still, if you hold down the update button on the central screen, it might give you a tutorial."

"Might?" Vicky said.

"Some versions did. Others were too old and too limited to store that in the system. Give it a try and see what happens."

Vicky held the identified button down. The small central screen on the gray box began to scroll instructions. The Grand Duchess *had* learned to read. Today, what she read told her the system could identify threats that were in its database, prioritize them, and provide a limited amount of distraction.

"I wonder when the database was last updated?" Vicky asked.

"There should be an option in the menu for that."

Vicky found the option and activated it.

The system went down.

She rebooted the light gray box and went to the update option again.

It went out to lunch . . . again.

The third time, it updated.

"This shuttle isn't in very good shape," she observed dryly. "As the plane captain told me."

Vicky raised an eyebrow. "This wreck has a plane captain?"

"Actually no," the commander admitted, flipping a switch several times before the data strip above it came to life. "But a second class petty officer was told two hours ago that this wreck was his to captain. It's in as good a shape as it is because he and the best half dozen Sailors he could lay his hands on spent their time getting it fit for a drop. He hopes."

"I can only imagine what it must have looked like four hours ago," Vicky said dryly.

The commander flipped a switch slowly, a half dozen times, frowned, and said, "I doubt it."

Vicky was trying to get a report on the number of reloads of chaff the ECM system had. She'd interrogated it three times and gotten three different answers when the commander announced, "You better say any prayers you know. I'm about to activate the antimatter reactor."

"Now I lay me down to sleep," Vicky muttered.

"Is that the only prayer you know?"

"You may have noticed, we don't do a lot of praying at the Imperial Palace."

"Then I guess my 'God help us' will have to do."

The commander threw a large double switch between them. Nothing happened.

A few breathless seconds later, several strip gauges lit up, and lights began to dance up and down them.

"Is that good?" Vicky asked.

"You're still here to ask," the commander said. "It appears that either I, or my dear mother, still has some pull with the Big Man."

"I suspect it's your mother," Vicky answered.

"No doubt."

Together, they watched the gauges as their dance settled down to a placid wiggle in the green zones of all six strip gauges.

"I believe we're ready to drop," the commander said.

"I do have a meeting to attend with an old friend."

"Assuming he doesn't carry through with his threat to have us shot out of *his* sky. Do you affect all your old flames like that?"

"Most. You seem to be a nice exception to the rule."

"Our relationship hardly has the blush off the rose," the commander said.

"I hadn't noticed any blushes on your part."

"Or yours, Your Grace."

"Shall we quit stalling and see if this contraption can get away from the station?"

"Why not? I don't want to live forever."

So saying, Commander Schlieffen reached above his head for the red bar with RELEASE in yellow letters and pulled it.

The shuttle did not depart the station with the grace of a falling angel. Instead, the aft tie-down released their rear to dangle. The spin of the station pressed them tight against their seats.

The commander yanked again, harder, on the release.

Reluctantly, their forward tie-down came loose. They drifted away from High St. Petersburg station with the deck canted down to the right.

"That wasn't the best launch I ever made," the commander observed, half to himself. "Nor was it the worst. Now, let's go see if the mayor of Sevastopol really intends to kill us."

CHAPTER 2

B EFORE the mayor of Sevastopol could have his go at killing them, they had to get away from the station. That proved
exciting.

"Damn," the commander said, as the shuttle began to spin.
"I've got a stuck thruster."

Vicky was close to graying out before the commander got
the thruster off-line.

"Let's try that again," he said as he slowly backed them away
from the station using long, low burns from the four thrusters
he found trustworthy. This time, there were no surprises.

"Who's tracking us?" he asked, as they crossed the ten-
klick threshold from station control to orbital control.

"I've got five search radars on us," Vicky reported crisply.

"Can that Ouija board tell you which are ground-based and
might have fire-control radars slaved to them?"

"Not a clue."

"Well, I could hope."

"I like a man who can hope," Vicky said.

"I have many admirable qualities," he muttered, firing the
main retro engine. "Some of them don't even require a bed."

"I could like the ones that don't," Vicky purred.

"Variety from a woman is nice," he said, eyeing his readouts. "Consistency, however, is very appreciated from rocket engines. Ours, at least for now, appear to be demonstrating a delightful degree of reliability."

"That can, at the proper time, be quite nice," Vicky agreed.

Their verbal foreplay abruptly ended as the radio squawked. "Unidentified shuttle. This is Petersburg Orbital Control. You are not authorized in our space. Return to the station."

Commander Schlieffen glanced at his comm unit and toggled a switch. "Petersburg Orbital Control, this is shuttle November, X-ray, three four niner. I have filed a flight plan for a descent to Sevastopol Bay shuttle-landing area. I am on descent."

"Shuttle November, X-ray, three four niner, be advised. Your flight plan was rejected. Return to station."

Vicky glanced at Gerrit. He pulled a flimsy from his shipsuit pocket. A large header at the top of it identified it as a flight plan. Even larger print, in red letters, read REJECTED.

"Orbital Control, this is three four niner. I have an approved flight plan here. I'm on my way down."

"Three four niner, I have a flight plan for you that was rejected. It shows a time stamp of one hour, fifty-six minutes ago. Cease your burn and return to the station."

"Sorry, Control. Shuttle three four niner is committed to a deorbiting burn. I'll see you in thirty minutes."

"Shuttle November, X-ray, three four niner, be advised that Petersburg reserves control of its space to our sovereignty. I am authorized to use deadly force to protect our sovereign space."

Gerrit glanced at Vicky. She shrugged, as much as her five-point restraining harness allowed.

"Orbital Control, I understand your politics. Be advised, I have the Grand Duchess Victoria Peterwald on board, and I am committed to descent. Again, we'll see you in thirty minutes."

A new voice came on the radio. "We know who you have on board, and we will see you in hell."

The transmission ended in a determined click.

"Was that the mayor?" the commander asked.

"I think so," Vicky said. "It's been a while."

"Touchy fellow, don't you think?"

"He was much nicer the last time we met. But then, he wanted an official, Imperial-approved city charter. Give a guy what *he* wants, and he never calls back for a second date."

"I'd call you back for a second date," the commander said, helpfully, hopefully, even a bit consolingly. Vicky wasn't quite sure which to choose from. Distraction was probably the overriding content of his answer.

The main engine was not firing smoothly.

There were coughs in the flow of reaction mass to the engines. The deorbital burn was not only uneven, it seemed to pull to the right, then left, then right again, with no particular pattern.

The commander concentrated on doing some of that nifty pilot stuff.

Vicky checked her board.

"We got fire-control radars scanning us," she said.

"They locked on?"

"Not yet."

"So they aren't serious yet."

"Apparently."

"I hope this crazy dance we're doing is causing them as much trouble as it's causing me."

Vicky left the commander to do his piloting thing and eyed her board. The fire-control radars were still in scanning mode. In a few minutes, as they began their fiery reentry, radar would become useless.

The problem was surviving until then.

One of the scanning radars locked on.

"They've got a lock," she announced in a low, firm voice. Admiral Krätz would be so proud of his student.

"I'm going to initiate a bit of a turn. When I tell you, release chaff."

Vicky rested her thumb on the chaff-release button. "Ready."

"Hold it, hold it," the commander said softly, mostly to himself. "Now."

Vicky depressed the button firmly once, then let up. The shuttle, responding to the commander's firm hand, began a shallow pull to the right.

The solid tone of the fire-control radar went back to an intermittent beeping as it found itself suddenly with two targets and unable to determine which was its intended.

"Lost you," the commander chortled.

A moment later, the solid tone was back.

He swung the lander to the left softly. Again the tone broke up, then, a few seconds later, was solid again.

"You weren't sure where I was there for a second, were you?" the commander said to the distant men intent on tracking them for the kill.

Vicky said nothing.

Twice more, the commander did his dodge. Twice more, the tone broke briefly, then came back. The second time, he had Vicky release chaff.

Each time, the threatened lasers remained silent.

When firebugs began to flow over the shuttle's tiny windows, the commander seemed to relax a bit.

"We're entering the atmosphere. They can't be sure where we are in all this static. Let's really make them unsure. I'm going to take us through some wide, gentle S turns to bleed off energy and be unpredictable. You get ready to squirt out chaff."

"Ready," Vicky said.

The gee force was climbing as the atmosphere slowed them, still, Vicky kept her finger on the button. As the commander readied to edge his control stick over a fraction, he whispered, "Pop chaff."

Vicky shot a packet of chaff into their fiery slipstream. The bits of aluminum instantly burned away into droplets and fell behind. They showed as one track; the shuttle as another. Vicky could imagine the picture facing the radar operators: two flaming balls. Either one might be a lander.

Meanwhile, the commander slid the actual lander off to the left.

The commander made four more shallow S turns but didn't task Vicky with spiking any of the others with burning aluminum.

The threatened lasers held their peace all the while.

"What happens when we clear out of this reentry phase?" Vicky asked the commander when he seemed less intent on his flying.

"They'll track us. You'll use all the chaff we have aboard. There isn't nearly enough. They either burn us out of their sky, or they let you come down and talk to them."

The commander glanced at Vicky. "I sure hope Your Grace

has a nice dog and pony show ready. As much as I find your body delectable and desirable, I don't think they'll be much interested in a striptease."

"I suspect you're right," Vicky said.

Too bad she had no idea what she might say to enlist Mannie and his fellow mayors in a program of whose details she hadn't the foggiest idea yet.

CHAPTER 3

THE threatened lasers never fired. The shuttle-landing ground in the middle of Sevastopol Bay was not blocked with shipping. The commander brought the shuttle down in a spray of cooling water.

Then they sat there.

The radio stayed silent. No tug appeared.

"Does this expendable shuttle Admiral von Mittleburg loaned us have any ground-mobility options?" Vicky asked.

Commander Schlieffen tapped the main screen and ran it through several menus before answering. "Yes, it appears it does have auxiliary waterpower."

It took him a bit of time to activate it, but soon he was steering them toward a shuttle ramp.

"No pier we can dock at?" Vicky asked.

"Nope. We got to go up that ramp."

"I don't see any tug waiting," Vicky noted.

"Hmm, neither do I."

"Will I have to dive off this thing and swim for shore?" Vicky asked. She was willing, though not looking forward, to starting her plea for cooperation while dripping wet.

"I think we have motors on our landing gear," the commander said.

"I've never seen a shuttle use them."

Gerrit studied the screen as more instructions scrolled down.

"They haven't been standard on most shuttles in a while. I did this once back in my Academy days. Let's see if I do better this time," he said with a grin.

Vicky checked her harness. She couldn't make it any tighter.

"Could you lower the landing gear?" the commander asked.

Surprise of surprises, the landing gear lowered when Vicky pulled up on the lever between them.

"Do it again," the commander ordered. "The right main gear hasn't locked down."

Vicky recycled the landing gear. On the second try, the right main gear locked, but the left didn't. She recycled the gear four times before all three gears dropped and locked in place together.

"I hope the motors are a bit more reliable," Gerrit mused.

The nose gear bumped onto the ramp. There was a grinding noise, but the nose began to rise from the water. There was more grinding as the main gear engaged and pushed the lander from the water and up the ramp.

At least, they did for a moment.

"Help me with the wheel. The left main wheel motor has dropped out."

Vicky grabbed the control wheel that she'd been careful not to touch and helped Gerrit haul the nose wheel off to the right. The yaw to the left damped down, but it was clear the shuttle could not make it all the way up the ramp.

"Engage the brake," the commander ordered. "Let's get out of here before this wreck drifts back down the ramp and heads out to sea."

Vicky popped her harness. Three of the five restraint points broke loose. The ones around her waist and between her legs stayed locked in place.

She hit the release again, and nothing happened.

Beside her, the commander was wiggling out of his harness. The top two of his restraint points hadn't popped. She tried to do some wiggling up, but she really had gotten the harness tight.

The brakes groaned.

Gerrit freed himself and came over to feel around between her legs. On another day, that would have been fun. "Get me out of this, and you can feel all you want between my legs tonight," Vicky offered.

"Promises, promises," he said, working on the release.

"I've kept my promises," she pointed out.

There was a snap.

"Ouch," Vicky said. "That pinched."

"I'll kiss it and make it all better later. Let's get out of here before we have to swim for it.

They exited the forward hatch. There were chocks slung beside the door. Vicky grabbed one, the commander grabbed the other, and they each raced for a different one of the main landing gears.

They got the chocks in place about two seconds before the brake gave up the ghost, and the lander slid back. Back onto the chocks rather than into the bay.

A pickup truck drove up, with a tug not far behind. Three men in coveralls got out of the truck. The senior of the three held a life buoy with a long length of rope attached.

He seemed disappointed that he hadn't gotten a chance to use it.

Tossing the buoy in the back of the truck, he ordered the other two to hitch the lander's nose to the tug. They did.

The foreman approached Vicky. "We'll tow the lander to a parking spot on the ramp. You got a credit chit to pay for the tow and ramp rental?"

Vicky was about to open her mouth, but the commander got there first. "Nope. No credit chit that hasn't been canceled. Guess you'll have to throw it back."

"Don't you think I wouldn't," the man grumbled, "but I got my orders to deliver you two to City Hall, so hop in. Maybe while I'm there, I can get someone to impound the lander for lack of payment."

"I doubt if that wreck is worth enough to pay your charges," the commander said, and opened the passenger door for Vicky. She settled in the middle slot, with the gearshift nearly in her lap.

When the commander settled in beside her, she cuddled up close to him with her legs well away from the gearshift.

The foreman chuckled softly as he got in, started the engine, and reached for the stick.

It was a very quiet drive to City Hall.

CHAPTER 4

―――――

T HE man in coveralls deposited them at the curb in front of a new and gleaming glass high-rise.

"You been here before?" the commander asked.

"Nope. City Hall was a mite bit smaller last time I visited."

Many people hurried by them on the street. Many more crossed the gray cobblestoned courtyard as they entered or exited the building.

None so much as glanced at the two Imperial Greenfeld Navy officers in green shipsuits.

With a slight bow, the commander directed Vicky to head inside. He even opened the door for her when they got there.

The ground floor was a marbled foyer full of potted plants and busy people going about their business. None offered to help two Navy officers.

There was an information desk.

No one sat behind it.

No one continued to sit behind it for a full five minutes while Vicky watched it, and busy people ignored them.

"Computer," Vicky finally said. Her computer was made of the same self-organizing material as Kris Longknife's Nelly. Unlike Nelly, it did not talk back.

It also did not offer suggestions.

"Can you connect to this building's net?"

"Yes, Your Grace."

"Do so, please."

"I am connected to the public portion. There appears to be a much larger private net behind a firewall."

"Can you get through that firewall?"

"No, Your Grace."

"Can you locate the office of the mayor of Sevastopol?"

"Yes, Your Grace."

"Guide us there."

"You will need to take the bank of elevators that services floors fifteen through thirty."

No one interfered with their boarding an elevator. They shared it with many busy people. Some got off. Others got on.

None so much as made eye contact with Vicky.

"Their welcoming committee seems very well organized," Vicky observed dryly.

"Very well organized," the commander agreed. "One has to wonder if they've been practicing for days."

A young woman, arms full of paper files, almost laughed at that, but she covered her mouth and turned away before Vicky could say anything in response.

They got off on the thirtieth floor.

Down the hall, at a corner office, they found an unmarked door that Vicky's computer insisted was the mayor's office.

The commander opened the door.

A young woman studied her computer screen intently. She did not look up.

"Do you have an appointment with the mayor?" she asked, eyes still on the computer.

"I suspect not," Vicky admitted.

"The mayor is a very busy man. He only sees people by appointment," she said, eyes still only for the screen.

Vicky could have mentioned that Mannie had waited on her the last time they met, but she chose not to argue with the gatekeeper.

She also did not show any willingness to go away.

The woman finally glanced at Vicky. "I may be able to slip you in later in the day. Please be seated."

There were plenty of seats in the outer office.

There was no one sitting in them.

Vicky decided that she would not sit in one either.

There were three doors out of the waiting room besides the door she'd come in.

She remembered a story she'd read when very young. It involved a man and two doors. Behind one was a gorgeous woman.

Behind the other was a man-eating tiger.

Today, Vicky faced three doors.

Might there be a half-naked hunk behind one of them?

Alas, more likely one only led to the restroom. The other might shield a broom closet. The third led to the mayor.

Vicky studied her three doors. Was the light fooling her or did the carpet leading to one of them show more wear?

She picked her door, praying to any interested God that a lot of people hadn't beaten a pathway to the head.

The commander stepped in front of Vicky and opened the door.

"You can't go in there," the secretary said, coming out of her chair.

Vicky had chosen well.

CHAPTER 5

MAYOR Manuel Artamus's office was quite spacious. His expansive wooden desk had a magnificent view, but his back was to the windows. Vicky doubted he ever swung his chair around to gaze out over the city he managed.

Facing him, and behind Vicky, were two walls paneled in light wood. On them, eight large screens showed people working hard at their desks.

None of them looked up as Vicky walked into the office. That none included Mannie.

Vicky sized up her situation. If she addressed Mannie at his desk, she'd have her back to the eight other people. If she turned to face them, Mannie got her back, something she doubted he'd care for.

She covered the distance to the side of Mannie's desk and turned so she could face him and them at the same time.

Commander Schlieffen moved to cover her back.

She had plenty of time to do this; the important people of the planet of St. Petersburg continued to ignore her. It was tempting to see how long that could go on, but Vicky wanted to know what was going to happen next too much to just wait around and twiddle her thumbs.

Also, she had promises to keep to a certain commander.

"Having a busy day, Mannie?"

"I don't have any slow ones," he said, not looking up.

"You were having a pretty slow one the day you hit Kris Longknife up to talk me into giving you a royal city charter. How's that working out?" Vicky said, playing her single ace.

"It's on the wall there," Mannie said, glancing up at the framed charter. Metal seals hung from it. Kris Longknife's staff had researched what a mediaeval city charter looked like. When Kris Longknife's gang staffed out something, it came on parchment and with silver seals.

Vicky would give her right arm just now for a staff like that.

But Vicky's glance at the framed charter had included the eight city mayors keeping busy in their offices around this globe. On the wall behind most of them was a charter just like the one Mannie had.

Vicky took a few steps toward the wall of screens, studying the charters. "My dad was not at all happy to learn I'd signed that charter. Who'd you get to sign the other ones?"

"Nobody looks at the signatures all that closely," Mannie said, now leaning back in his chair and eyeing Vicky. "We forged your signature and Kris Longknife's on all of the other seven."

"If it works for you," Vicky said with a shrug.

"It's given us the cover we need to keep our heads down and stay out of the shitstorm sweeping your father's so-called Empire. We're not going hungry here," had force behind it.

"I know. You're doing well here on St. Petersburg. You got the Navy to keep my darling stepmother out of your hair, and you have Navy contracts to keep jobs going on your factory floors. It couldn't be better."

"So why are you here?" didn't give Vicky any cover.

The Grand Duchess chose to dodge the question. "How are you set for crystal? You need it for most of your high-power industry and communications. You need it for those screens you're talking to me through. How long will your stockpile last?"

Mannie looked at one of the screens. A middle-aged woman frowned for a second, then tapped her desk. Numbers began to flow on a screen embedded in Mannie's desk. Vicky could just barely make them out. Mannie, however, studied them intently. A frown grew on his face as he did.

On seven screens, a lot of men and women frowned at what they saw.

"We can buy more," the woman who'd done the work said.

"At a price set by my stepmother's family," Vicky pointed out. "Are you prepared to pay that piper? Their charge isn't just an arm and a leg. They demand a chunk of your soul to go with it."

"There are other sources," the woman said.

"Yes," Vicky said. "Presov is just a few jumps away from here. I recently visited them. Their miners are getting zero supplies, neither food nor spare parts. In three to six months, they'll be unable to produce a gram of any kind of crystal. In six to nine months, they'll be in economic chaos. By early next year, those who haven't managed to beg, steal, or borrow a ride off that bejeweled mud ball will be eating each other."

"It can't be that bad," the woman on-screen said.

"Computer, deliver to them the workup you did for me on Presov. Toss in the analysis of Poznan as well."

Vicky turned to the screens. "The executive summary won't take you long to read. Both end the same. I may be off by a few months, plus or minus, for either planet. They all end in the total collapse of civilization, starvation, and, well, whatever else happens when people have nothing to eat."

"We knew it was bad out there," a young mayor said, a man in a three-piece suit with ruffles at his throat, "but there's only so much room in our lifeboat. If we overload it, we all end up drowning, along with everybody else."

"Or you can expand the lifeboat," Vicky said, turning on the young man. "You need crystal for your lifeboat, so you include Presov. Poznan has resources you could use as well. Not as critical as crystal, but still nice to have. You're already trading with the Navy colonies. You expand your safety net to include more."

"Why should we?" an older woman demanded. "We keep our heads down, and your loving stepmother and the rest of the bloodthirsty Bowlingame family look for easier prey. When all this is over, we will have saved ourselves and our own."

"You dodged a bullet when their Security Consultants showed up last time," Vicky pointed out, almost delicately. "You sure they won't show up again? This time they'll be bigger and badder, having fattened on easier prey."

Vicky paused for only a second. "They don't like the Navy. They're trying to take it down, or better yet, take it and its ships over. You sure that if you stay small, you won't become next year's prey? That if you do nothing, this tragedy will ever end well?"

"That's strange talk coming from a Peterwald Grand Duchess," the older woman snapped.

"And one who has a rather high price on her head," the man with the frilly shirt added.

"True on both counts," Vicky conceded.

"Are you planning on going rebel on your old man?" Mannie asked. "What are you looking for? Us to be your power base?"

"No, no, and no," Vicky said quickly.

"Then may I ask," Mannie said, coming to his feet, "just what the hell are you doing here?"

Vicky had been asking herself that question for way too long. She opened her mouth to give them the only answer she had.

CHAPTER 6

"HAVE any of you read the file we have on Princess Kris Longknife?" Vicky asked.

Her answer was a collection of shaking heads.

"It's interesting reading. My dad's in a lot of it."

"Why'd she have to save his neck?" someone asked.

Vicky ignored that question and went on.

"I don't know how many of you were aware or remember those six rogue battleships that showed up in the Wardhaven system and threatened to blast them back to the Stone Age."

Some of the heads on the screens nodded. Others shook from side to side.

"No one ever found out where the ships came from," Mannie said.

"I found out," Vicky said, and suddenly had their full attention.

"They were our ships. My father sent them. Navy reunions have had a lot of unexplained empty chairs at their tables of late, haven't they, Gerrit?"

The commander nodded solemnly.

"How do you know?" the older woman demanded.

"I overheard my father arguing with an admiral shortly

after the affair. I didn't know what I was hearing until I shared it with Kris Longknife. Her and a few of her friends. One of them lost her husband of three days blowing up those battleships."

"Oh my God," someone said softly.

"But what is important for us here and now is that back then and there no one had any idea what to do about the incoming battleships. Wardhaven had been maneuvered into sending its fleet off on some wild-goose chase, and there was a caretaker government. No doubt my father's fingerprints can be found on a lot of that."

"Son of a bitch," came from one screen.

Vicky wasn't sure if it was a reaction to the revelation or a reference to her father. Once again, she tossed it off to bore in on her point.

"What matters to us here and now is that Princess Kris Longknife returned to her squadron. She'd been relieved of the command of one of the fast-attack boats. Tiny things, ships with no real chance against battleships. She declared herself the commander of the squadron. No one knew what to make of her actions. But while their government diddled, she and many others used her princess card as a pretense to rally a defense not one of them could have produced without her."

Vicky stepped forward to face the eight screens. "I'm nothing. But I'm also a Grand Duchess. I can keep being nothing, or I can be the tiny grain of sand that causes an oyster to produce a pearl."

"I understand the oyster considers that grain of sand an irritant," Mannie said.

"I don't doubt that," Vicky said.

"Let me get this straight," said the elder woman who wanted to wait until things blew over. "Are you rebelling against your father?"

"That is not my intention at this time. I pray it will never be my intention," Vicky said with all the sincerity she could manage. She really meant the words. However, getting enough sincerity around anything a Peterwald said was always a problem.

The man with the frilly shirt was up from his desk and leaning into the camera so that his face filled the screen. "Are you trying to tell me that a Peterwald is doing something good for altruistic reasons?"

"Yes," Vicky said back as blandly as she could.

"There's got to be a first time for anything, folks," Mannie said. "Remember, people, I was there when she signed the first city charter. Her neck may not have been on the line, but a good bit of her skin was in the game."

He came to stand beside Vicky and stared hard into her eyes. "I don't know where she'll be coming from next month, and surely not next year, but right now, I really do think we have a Peterwald in our lap who cares about starving people and parents who look at their children and the stew pot. And vice versa."

Mannie leaned back against his desk. "Where's the Navy in all this?".

"They loaned me a shuttle to come down here to talk to you," Vicky said without flinching.

"A shuttle that damn near fell out of the sky," one mayor said.

"I didn't have any trouble flying it," Gerrit lied through a smile.

Vicky really owed him tonight.

"We've got a lot of out-of-work ships drifting around behind the station," Mannie pointed out. "We're harvesting a bumper crop. We can afford to risk some of it to help these other planets, and we *do* need that crystal."

The consensus was building, slowly, with every nod.

Vicky kept her mouth shut and let the mayors of St. Petersburg talk themselves into what they knew was a good thing. But a good thing that only she could offer them a chance to grab for. She felt a strange feeling, sitting in silence while all those around her struggled to meet some high bar they thought she'd set.

Dad always bragged about what he'd done, what butt he'd kicked in this or that meeting. Vicky found herself kicking no butt and not really doing much of anything. Still, around her, *because of her*, things were being done that neither they nor she thought possible.

This was a change from everything she'd ever known, ever even thought feasible.

But there was more going on. Somewhere deep inside her, something was happening. That dirty, naked savage, willing to do anything for a morsel of food was changing, metamorphosing into something entirely different. Vicky was none too sure just what the changed her would be like, but she kind of liked it.

For maybe the first time in my life, I feel good about something I'm involved in, and I really like it.

CHAPTER 7

A N hour later, Mannie ticked off their action plan on his fingers.

"We will send a trade delegation to Presov to see about swapping food for crystal. We'll include industrial agents not only to check out the quality of the crystal but also to see what goods and services, parts and supplies they need. Maybe we'll carry some of what they likely need with us as well," he said, half to himself.

"Considering the quality of civil discourse no doubt now existent on Presov, we'll need a cruiser to protect our merchant hulls and a Marine detachment to protect our negotiators. Possibly our food and supplies as well," Mannie said, glancing at Vicky.

She replied with a confident smile she didn't feel.

On the screens, eight people nodded. Mannie then added, "It would be nice to have a certain Grand Duchess present to provide irritation and some cover for this."

Grand Duchess Vicky Peterwald nodded. There were a few scowls from the screen, but they weren't too bad. Not at all as bad as she might have feared.

"Your Grace," Mannie said. "In your official Navy capacity,

I expect you to arrange with the appropriate admiral for the necessary escort, both cruiser and Marines."

"That I will do," Vicky said, having no idea how she would.

"Then I think we are done here," Mannie said. "Your Grace, no doubt several people would like to have dinner with you tonight. Shall I have my chauffeur pick you up at eight?"

"That will be fine." Where she would be at eight was anybody's guess. That she had nothing to wear but a green shipsuit, now in need of a washing, went without saying.

The screens snapped off as the mayors no doubt returned to their busy day, which had gotten much more busy.

"I'll arrange for your stay," Mannie said. "The Imperial Suite at the Hilton has had few uses of late."

"You know, of course, that my credit chit has been canceled," Vicky said.

"So I was advised by our spaceport. We of St. Petersburg recognize a certain debt toward the Navy of unspecified monetary value. Your necessary expenses will be charged against that."

"No doubt you've heard this from a woman before, but I really do have nothing to wear," Vicky said, enjoying, for a moment, sounding just like any other girl.

"I also received a report from the spaceport that there was no luggage aboard your shuttle. Once you're settled into your suite, I'll have my grandmadre take you on a shopping expedition. Commander, we have tailors who can meet your needs."

"I will need to stay at Her Grace's side. My orders are that no one gets to her except over my dead body. From a personal interest, may I ask how secure she is on St. Petersburg?"

Mannie winced. "I'd like to say as safe as that pearl in a clam, but as we all know, that pearl is not safe at all. I suspect at least one of my fellow mayors will be sending a report to your stepmother. My net may even be compromised. Likely, a copy of our meeting will be on its way to Greenfeld within the hour. One of the few advantages of these troubled times is that news travels much more slowly, what with the lack of shipping using the jump points."

"I suspect my dear loving stepmama will pay extra for premium communications service," Vicky pointed out.

"And with the standing price on her head," the commander

pointed out, "any local freelancer is likely to already be moving into position for a shot."

"Which is why you will find my best agents waiting outside," Mannie said. "The Imperial Suite was not a casual choice for your stay, Your Grace. Your father, our Emperor, requested and required that all Imperial suites throughout Greenfeld have bulletproof glass. Your suite will not only tuck you way up and out of sight, but also behind glass strong enough to stop a rocket grenade."

Mannie paused, then smiled at Vicky. "We play no more games, Your Grace. You are a pearl of great worth, and you'll be treated as such."

"Thank you, Mannie," Vicky said. It was one of the few "thank-you's" she'd ever said that she truly meant.

Mannie actually cracked a smile. Then his worried face was back. He turned to his desk. "I have work to do. A lot more than I expected this morning when I came in with a full to-do list. So, if you will please go make yourself imperially beautiful, I'll get back to work."

"Will I see you at eight?" Vicky asked.

"No doubt," Mannie said without glancing back.

CHAPTER 8

VICKY hardly had a moment to step into the hall and take a deep breath and exhale before she was surrounded by a team of eight agents. Vicky did her best to look beautiful while Commander Schlieffen and the Special Agent in Charge did their bulls-suddenly-locked-in-the-same-pasture male thing.

It didn't last overly long.

At the elevator, they were joined by two female agents. The ride down was uninterrupted and longer in length.

They stepped out into a lower parking level. Five large black, passenger vehicles waited with motors running. Vicky was escorted to the fourth one in line as the agents with her joined those waiting in the cars.

She was asked to fasten her seat belt. She did.

Then the ride got exciting.

In the screeching race up three floors of parking, her ride changed from fourth to second to third in line. This game of musical cars continued when they hit the street. She wondered about the wisdom of her being in the lead car or the trailing car, but while driving five minutes to the Hilton, her car changed its place in line at just about every block.

"Are they taking this too seriously, or am I at this much risk?" Vicky asked the commander.

He smiled. "I don't see a problem."

The hotel was much like the City Hall. She was taken to the lowest parking level, then whisked up an elevator to the top floor.

"I have the shower while you talk security," she declared, and was lathering up nicely in a spectacularly luxurious shower a minute later. The needlelike hot water washed off the tension of the morning, leaving her pink both in skin and mind . . . and delighting at the thought of sharing it with the commander when the time came.

Said commander came into the bathroom as she was getting out of the shower.

"All measures have been arranged," was all he got out before she threw herself on him, wet and willing. His shipsuit was already in need of washing, so getting it wet certainly was a minor thing. She wrapped her legs around him as he stumbled back into the bedroom.

"Things are a bit different from the ship," he managed to mutter as her tongue explored his mouth.

Things were. No doubt she weighed more.

And there were two female agents across the bedroom.

One turned beet red.

The other, maybe a bit older, ushered the younger out and closed the door firmly behind them.

The commander fell backward into a large, fluffy bed. Vicky quickly lost herself in fulfilling all the promises she'd made him. She added some extras as a special reward for his outstanding performance in the hours since they'd docked at High St. Petersburg station.

It was a very pleasant hour and ended with her showing him just how delightful the shower was.

CHAPTER 9

VICKY'S computer announced the arrival of Mannie's grandmadre. "She has clothes for you. The Senior Agent in Charge also has clothes for the commander."

The bathroom offered fluffy robes. The commander helped Vicky into one, then quickly slipped into the other as she went to meet their public.

Grandmadre had brought Vicky a simple business suit and skirt in soft earth tones. Everything, from bra to skirt, was exactly one size too small.

"I may have erred a bit when asked your sizing," the commander admitted.

His set of dress greens fit him perfectly.

"I know just the store for you," Grandmadre assured Vicky.

That store was their first stop. It was small and quiet but as modern as any on Greenfeld. Vicky's measurements were quickly taken by lasers.

The store also had an amazing quantity of merchandise. Apparently, what was in the store could be augmented by a quick run across the street or a duck down the alley.

The staff ducked and ran a lot.

The senior of the two female agents insisted Vicky add

ballistic protection to her ordered clothes, a recommendation supported by her own Senior Agent in Charge and Commander Schlieffen.

A beige suit that actually fit was quickly produced . . . with protection.

Vicky sighed as she put it on. She'd always been well rounded. Now her curves had padding.

The commander assured her she looked very cuddly.

A similar power suit, this one in red, was just as quickly made for her, armor and all.

Vicky balked when they tried to add ballistic protection to a simple black dress.

"First off, there's not all that much dress here for you to armor," Vicky pointed out.

"We were hoping you'd choose something more conservative," the female agent said.

"I'm not," Vicky said flatly.

The look on the agent's face caused Vicky to offer a compromise. "Computer, do you have a copy of that new dinner dress uniform I wore at the palace not too long ago. The one I proposed that Admiral Heller authorize for all female Navy officers?"

"I do."

"Provide it to them."

The computer did. The entire sales staff quickly congregated around a hologram table where her diminutive self modeled the dinner dress uniform. From the sounds of their comments, they liked the design.

From the moans of the seamstresses, there was no way they could duplicate it anytime soon.

"We lack the cloth. We haven't had any cloth of gold in months," one pointed out.

"Those colors. We'd have to dye them ourselves," another groaned.

"How did they get that skirt to fall that way with ballistic-resistant cloth?" a third asked.

"They didn't," Vicky said. "That dress was not armored."

Vicky and the agent were back to a standoff.

"I will not go to dinner tonight looking like a brick outhouse," Vicky said. She'd learned that expression during her Navy time and found it useful.

Vicky got her simple black dress.

As her purchases were bagged, the commander shook his head. "We have got to order you some of that spidersilk under-all armor that they have in the U.S."

"Why don't we have any here?" Vicky asked.

"Restrictions on sales of it outside the U.S.," Gerrit said. "We'll have to smuggle it out."

"Please have someone do it," Vicky said.

Grandmadre returned Vicky to her suite a good four hours before Mannie was due to pick her up.

Vicky put it to good use. The commander voiced no complaints.

CHAPTER 10

―――――

T HE mayor of Sevastopol voiced delight in Vicky's appearance when he met her at the door at eight o'clock sharp.

There were eight large, identical, vehicles waiting for Vicky
in the lowest parking basement of the Hilton. Again, they played
shuffle car, but this time it was a lengthy drive that took them
out of the city.

The dinner meeting that evening was at an estate high in
the hills overlooking the city lights and enhanced by the spar-
kle of a newly risen full moon on the bay. Surrounded by crop-
lands, pasture, and woods, the uniformed and armed troops
walking the perimeter had clear lanes of fire.

The commander voiced approval.

"We've had need of a secure meeting location a time or
two," Mannie admitted. "This used to belong to the head of
State Security for our province. I doubt there will be time for a
tour this evening of the lower basements. I would have thought
dungeons had gone out with the horse-and-buggy whip."

"When I was a little girl, General Boyng, the head of State
Security, used to give me the loveliest dresses," Vicky said
dreamily, then added cynically, "With bugs on them so he could

record my daddy's conversations with me. I did not weep when my father had him killed," she finished dryly.

"None of us did," Mannie agreed. "It just would have been nicer if the destruction of the black shirts hadn't taken the entire Empire down with them."

"Yes, change is difficult. You seem to have managed it better than most."

"Yes." Mannie smiled at the praise. "We had the black shirts tamed and half replaced when your father chose to demolish the rest."

They entered what might have passed for a hunting lodge on old Earth five hundred years ago. A wood fire blazed away with cheerful snaps. A dozen men and women awaited Vicky.

She was introduced to each one of them individually. Spouses had not been included in tonight's invitation.

Colonel Mary White was introduced first. A tall, athletic woman, she'd been an explorer of the southern continent out in the back and beyond of Sevastopol when the need had arisen for a soldier. She'd mustered ranchers and distant farmers who had been allowed hunting rifles even under the old regime. A few retired Navy hands strengthened her organizational skills, and, suddenly, Sevastopol had an army.

"Now we're standing up a National Guard. On old Earth, there's an animal called the porcupine," Colonel White said. "Sharp spines all over it. No one bothers it."

"I doubt you'll be bothered either," Vicky offered.

"In a pig's eye," Mary spat. "We lose the Navy and we lose the high ground. Are we going to lose the Navy?"

"Not if the Navy has any say in the matter," Vicky said, but aware of how insecure any meeting might be, she named no names.

Mary, the new-made colonel, didn't look all that reassured.

Most of the remaining attendees were businesspeople, with only two women among them. Two were farmers who also had large ranching spreads in the valleys beyond the hills. All wanted to know what Vicky knew of matters on Greenfeld and how those would impact them.

Vicky answered with a shrug. "If this were a fairy tale, I'd say my father was under the spell of a witch. Unfortunately, this is no fairy tale, and what we are seeing is a middle-aged man making a fool of himself with his new, much younger bride. The Bowlingame family in the meantime is taking full advantage of his distraction to grab for power and wealth. You are lucky to be this far out. It's worse closer in."

"And I hear say that you talked the mayors into us making ourselves a target," one of the ranchers said.

"I've suggested that you expand your sphere of influence to include all the resources you need to make a successful go of it in the present circumstances," Vicky said. "I don't know who said that 'No man is an island,' but you know you aren't. You, sir, grow cows and crops. They feed the hungry city. You get wondrous things like the clothes on your back and those nice boots on your feet. You want to make a go of it on your own?"

The man raised his glass in salute and took a sip of the fine liquor. "I do like the finer things in life."

"For others out there, it's not a case of the finer things in life, sir," Vicky said, taking the offered opportunity to drive home her point. "There's not enough of any of the basic things they need for daily living. Not even food. People are literally starving to death. I saw it when we passed through their systems headed out here."

Vicky paused, hunting for a conclusion. "We built a civilization to provide us with the things that make life worth enjoying. Now that civilization is tearing itself apart at the seams. Civilized people count on each other for the basics of life as well as the luxuries. All that has vanished for a lot of people. Together, we can bring it back to them."

Vicky glanced around the room. "You here on St. Petersburg can do something about it. Not for everyone, but for some. Do you really want to turn your back on a starving child?"

"That's a strange argument coming from a Peterwald," an older man, his paunch hanging over his belt, said. He'd been introduced as George Gatewood, an industrialist.

Vicky nodded. "I'm hearing that a lot. It kind of surprises me, too."

That brought a round of silence, but it was an expectant silence.

"I don't know why my dad decided to send my brother to the Navy. All his upbringing had been business, but there was Hank one morning at the breakfast table in a Navy commodore's uniform. I thought he looked so handsome and grown-up. We women have a weakness for guys in uniforms, don't we?"

Two of the women present nodded agreement.

Mary's grin was almost a leer. "A regular chick magnet."

Vicky went on.

"Six months later, my brother was dead. I spent much of the next year trying to kill the woman I thought had killed him. You may have heard about her? Princess Kris Longknife."

"You tried to kill her?" Mary was impressed.

"I tried. You may have noticed, she's kind of hard to kill."

There were nods.

"Then Dad shipped me off to the Navy, too. He didn't say why. But there was no commodore's uniform waiting for me. I was an ensign. A boot ensign."

Vicky eyed Mary.

"You can't get much lower than a butter bar LT," the woman agreed.

"I learned basic things like how to shine my shoes. Dress myself. Keep my uniform shipshape. I learned to stand my watch and pull my weight. Not much weight at first, but more as I learned the Navy Way."

She let her eyes rove around the circle. There was a lot of skepticism there, but maybe some belief. Some trust.

"There's more to the Navy Way than shining shoes and getting your gig line straight. There's things like duty and honor and professionalism. I hadn't heard much about those things growing up in the palace. I learned it from Admiral Krätz."

She paused. "And if I didn't get it right, I got the toe of his boot up my ass."

That brought a laugh.

"Up your Imperial ass?" Mary asked.

"For him, I don't think there was anything Imperial about my rear end," Vicky said. "I was a boot ensign, and my ass belonged to him.

"It was an entirely new sensation for me."

That drew another laugh. Vicky let them enjoy it before she went on sardonically.

"And then there was Princess Kris Longknife. I kept running into her. A very strange woman."

That drew nods all around.

"You went with her out there," Mary said, motioning with her drink to the ceiling and the dark, star-speckled sky beyond.

"Yes, I went out there with Princess Kris Longknife in the Fleet of Discovery. And yes, I'm one of the few survivors who made it back."

"How?" Mary demanded.

"More luck than any human had a right to, that I'll tell you. Luck and some folks who were willing to fight to the death so that we might have even a slim chance of making it back here to tell the rest of you what's out there."

Mary took a drink from her glass. "Sometimes it's like that."

"And you have to learn to live with it," Vicky said, then went on.

"Maybe I've seen as much dying as I care to in one lifetime." Vicky discovered the words as they fell from her tongue. "Maybe it terrifies me that we're falling apart at the seams when something like what we fought up there might drop into our sky tomorrow. I'll let the historians decide for me. What I do know is that you here and the Navy up there have a chance to make it better for some folks who didn't do anything to deserve what's killing them."

Again, Vicky let her eyes rove over her listeners, polling their souls. Now she saw understanding. Maybe not acceptance, but understanding for why a snake-in-the-grass Peterwald was trying to grow two hind legs and pass for human.

"We can make a difference. Why the hell won't we?"

A bell rang. A voice announced. "Dinner is served."

CHAPTER 11

THE Grand Duchess Vicky Peterwald found herself seated not at the head of the table, or its foot. Instead, she was directed to a chair in the middle of the table.

It took her about two seconds to figure out why.

The guy with the big belly was seated directly across from her. The skeptical rancher was at her right elbow. Just about everyone Vicky would count as not yet sold on her idea was in the nine seats within easy listening of her.

Mannie was at the head of the table, barely within earshot. At the foot was the other rancher. The commander was at his right elbow.

Dinner was served, but it quickly became clear that Vicky was the main dish everyone was interested in.

"When did you meet your stepmom for the first time?" Big Belly asked.

Vicky took a moment to think. "I don't remember ever meeting her before I was summoned home to offer my fealty. That was when I wanted to chase after Kris Longknife and her Fleet of Discovery. I'd expected more questions from Dad about where Kris was going and the royal city charter I'd signed off on with Mannie, but Dad just kind of waved his hand, and I was out the door a-running and not looking back. Foolish me."

"Was that when the assassination attempts started?" The question came from Mary. She'd been seated at Mannie's left elbow. Apparently, she wasn't someone Vicky needed to sell.

"That's hard to answer. Kris Longknife figured the first assassination attempt was aimed at her. I later met a guy who assured me I was the target. Who knows? Then bombs started going off on the *Fury*, and there was no question someone didn't like me."

Vicky paused to raise a finger to her lips and appeared to think. "I wonder who?"

The entire table enjoyed the laugh.

"You were summoned home to Greenfeld after that Discovery debacle. How did you manage to get away from that cesspit?" Mary asked.

Vicky's face must have showed the pain because the laughter ended abruptly.

"I almost didn't. And it cost a good Marine, my escort and guard, his life," was all Vicky managed as her throat tightened up.

The room fell even quieter.

"You're tough on men, huh?" Mary said.

"I seem to be," Vicky admitted.

"I'm still here," the commander said, raising a glass in salute to Vicky from where he sat.

Vicky awarded him a smile as she raised her glass to him.

The rancher didn't let that go on for too long.

"Tell me. You say you've seen what's happening on the planets out between us and Greenfeld. Can all the stuff we've got to spare add up to spit in the bucket for them?"

Vicky nodded at the question. "It's hard to tell. A lot of famines start when there's *almost* enough food. When the first panic hits, hoarding starts, and food that might help a lot winds up in the storehouses of a few. If we eliminate the panic, maybe . . ." Vicky trailed off. She had no ironclad guarantee to offer.

The questions ranged across a gamut of interests. A younger woman wanted to know just how daring the fashions were at the Imperial court this year. Vicky supplied a "Very daring," and tried to dodge away.

Big Belly didn't allow the dodge. "Strange. The Empress pretty much makes the calls for all fashions in that madhouse. You'd think, what with her belly swelling, she'd want all the pretty young things covering up, wearing something like a balloon. Very strange that she's got them all parading around as eye candy for her husband."

"I kind of had the same question when I was at court," Vicky admitted.

"It's almost as if someone is setting someone up to be caught in the wrong bed by a jealous husband," opined the industrialist.

"What could a jealous husband do if he found his wife under the Emperor?" a woman asked. "He'd have to just close the door and pretend he never saw what he saw."

"Your husband might," the rancher said, "but someone with a temper might not do the smart thing."

"I don't know if you just insulted me or praised my husband," she said.

"I ain't exactly sure which I just did either," the rancher said, as the room laughed.

Which left Vicky wondering just how stupid her dad was.

That got interrupted by a question about the Fleet of Discovery. "Were you all ready to cut bait and run for home when you spotted that monster ship?" came from the young businesswoman to Vicky's left.

"I think everybody was," Vicky said. "Before Kris Longknife disagreed."

"I saw that first news conference you made," Mary said. "My compliments on how well you pulled off that dress."

"She didn't pull it off. Somehow she managed to keep it on. At least most of it," came from someone down the table, who appeared to be having trouble holding his liquor.

"Are you asking if I really think Kris Longknife seduced the admirals?" Vicky said, stripping the matter bare.

"You seemed to hint strongly at that," Mannie said.

"I wish I hadn't," Vicky said, and found herself using her fork to move early potatoes around her plate beside her untouched steak.

"I was there," Vicky finally said. "Kris Longknife was on her flagship, the *Wasp*. The other admirals were on their flagships as well. The decision to run turned into a determination to fight without anyone's leaving their ship. All she had was words, and she turned us all from cringing cowards into Sailors demanding the first place in the battle line. I don't know how she did it, but she did."

Vicky put her fork down. "I wish I'd played the record of that council of war instead of playing games."

"Why'd you do it then?" Mannie asked.

Vicky shrugged. "I was a long way from home. I didn't have any idea that Imperial ships were out there hunting for me. I had no idea how many assassins were lurking for me on the long trip home. I had a problem staying alive, and I made a bad choice."

"We all do that, sometimes," Mary offered softly.

Vicky looked up. "Now is not a time to make another one. People are going to die. People *are* dying. I hope we'll make the right choice this time."

Dinner broke up shortly thereafter. Mannie excused himself, saying he needed to stay for further discussions, discussions to which Vicky apparently was not invited.

The commander escorted Vicky to the six cars that would caravan her back to town.

In a moment, all six of them roared into the darkness.

CHAPTER 12

VICKY settled into the plush leather seats of the limo. She was cold.

She pulled her legs up and wrapped her arms around them. She was colder still.

Commander Schlieffen took off the wool uniform coat of his dress greens and wrapped it around her. Her teeth began to chatter.

"Will you hold me," Vicky said, and didn't care about the pleading in her voice.

Gerrit slid close to her and put his arms around her. Softly, he tried rubbing her arms. Her teeth kept chattering, but it didn't seem to get worse.

Vicky spread her body out on the seat. He settled between her and the cold night air and cuddled close.

She began to feel warm again.

"Thank you. I don't know what's come over me," she said.

"Shock. You were under one hell of a lot of pressure."

"It was a dinner, for Christ sake."

"You were selling them on saving thousands, maybe millions of lives."

"Kris Longknife sold people on saving a planet. I try to

save a couple of thousand and come down with the shakes. And I don't even know if I sold anything to anyone."

"You sold me on flying a wreck of a shuttle down here to give you a chance to make your pitch."

"You said flying it was no trouble," Vicky shot back.

"You knew I was lying through my teeth."

Vicky had to admit she had. "You flew a shuttle and walked out to face them. I get taken to supper and have to answer a few questions, and I'm shaking like a leaf."

A particularly bad shiver rocked her body.

"You're too hard on yourself," Gerrit said. "And you don't know how tight that man, what's-his-name, is with the princess?"

"Jack," Vicky provided.

"You don't know how tight Jack had to hold her to get her through the shakes after it all."

Vicky considered that idea. She shook her head. "They aren't that close."

"I'm glad we're this close," Gerrit said, and tightened his hold on her.

Vicky caught sight of a red glare through the car window.

Then her world exploded.

CHAPTER 13

THE rocket-propelled grenade must have had a double charge. The first explosion threw the car into the air.

The second explosion shot a stream of molten metal through the cabin, wiping out the wall between Vicky and the driver. His body burst into flames

He died before he had a chance to scream.

Commander Gerrit Schlieffen's body protected Vicky from the spatter. He uttered one sharp cry of pain before he locked his mouth shut.

Then the car hit the ground and bounced.

Gerrit was thrown off Vicky and against the shattered partition.

He groaned and seemed to lose consciousness.

Vicky knew his back wasn't right, and his left leg was bent all wrong.

The Grand Duchess once again found herself struggling with a safety belt. It came free just as the car settled to the earth with a groan.

Then the automatic weapons fire started. Lots of people were emptying their magazine at something.

In Vicky's personal case, bullets slammed into the armored

glass above her head. It held—for the moment, but it was bending in, and large cracks were showing.

Very soon, someone would be firing an automatic weapon through that window.

Vicky was unarmed. Maybe Princess Kris Longknife could hide an automatic under her simple black dress, but this Grand Duchess hadn't.

With one glance, she spotted Gerrit's automatic in a shoulder holster. It was in her hand a second later.

About then, the armored window gave up its pretenses and fell at her feet.

Outside, in the night, a man in a black mask and black clothing struggled to pull an emptied magazine from his assault rifle and load another.

As taught by Gunny, Vicky aimed the automatic with both hands. She leveled it at the gunner's face and fired once. She brought the weapon down from its recoil and fired a second time.

Both took the attacker in the face.

It was hard to tell with the mask, but he seemed very surprised to be shot.

That was okay. Vicky was quite surprised, too. For someone who had been shivering only a minute ago, she was holding her weapon quite steady.

Now there was more automatic weapons fire. The reloading must have been completed.

Vicky waited, her own automatic aimed at the empty window.

But now the noise of the night was changing. While most of the shooting before had been on full automatic, suddenly there was another brand of shooter out there. Now a single shot, followed quickly by a second joined the fusillade. There were more of those quick, staccato shots and less of the fully automatic riffs.

Then, for one wonderful moment, there was total silence.

Gerrit groaned. His head lolled on his neck.

"I need a medic," Vicky yelled.

"Medic needed." "Medic" was passed up some line.

Vicky didn't know whether other people needed medics or if that was just her request being passed along. She was not willing to wait in line tonight.

"This is the Grand Duchess, and my protection needs a medic. Now!"

A woman in the dark green uniform that Vicky had seen patrolling around the estate appeared in the blasted window. Her rifle was held high and aimed at the sky.

"The medic's coming." Her eyes took in the commander. "Oh shit. We need more than a medic. Sergeant. Get a medevac headed this way. Now!"

CHAPTER 14

THAT night would forever be a blur in Vicky's memory.

Medics arrived and cautiously surveyed Gerrit's injuries. Their faces showed more concern than Vicky wanted to see.

A helicopter beat its way into the field on one side of the ambush site. The assailants had fired the rocket from the trees on the other side. They'd launched their assault from there, too.

Maybe they'd thought they could complete their slaughter before the gun trucks trailing a mile behind the convoy arrived.

Or maybe they didn't know about the reinforcements.

Either way, all eight of the gunners died on the spot. So did way too many in the escort cars.

Colonel Mary White braked to a halt just as the chopper arrived.

She surveyed the wreckage of the failed attack and shook her head.

"They should have rocketed the passenger compartments. They went for the agents and drivers instead. I think they wanted to survive this night," she spat as it began to rain.

The colonel turned to Vicky. "So you lived, and a lot of good men and women died."

"It happens that way too often around me," Vicky bit out.

A moment later, the medics began extracting Gerrit from the limo. "Don't bend the back," was whispered softly.

"Bend the leg if you have to, but not the back."

Now Vicky found herself shivering.

A medic brought a thermal blanket to her and offered to take away the blood-splattered uniform coat. Vicky pulled it closer.

The blanket went over it.

The chopper lifted with Vicky and Gerrit aboard, along with two horribly burned agents who were still breathing.

One died screaming halfway to the hospital.

Vicky trailed Gerrit into the emergency room as far as they would let her. When they shunted her aside, she took a chair in the waiting room, staring blankly at the door Gerrit had disappeared through.

She didn't notice the guards until a woman with captain's bars gently lifted the automatic out of the pocket Vicky had stuffed it in when she began to feel safe.

The captain clicked the safety on, then handed the weapon off to a police officer.

"Is that evidence?" Vicky asked dully. Her brain didn't seem to be engaged in anything. Anything but watching the door with Gerrit behind it that never opened.

"I've been told there will be a hearing," the police officer replied. "Not to establish any guilt, Your Honor, but to figure out how we screwed this one up so bad."

"I paid a visit. Someone tried to kill me. Good people died in my place," Vicky muttered, distracted only a bit from her vigil. "That's the way it always happens."

"Yes, ma'am," the police officer said.

The captain brought Vicky a cup of warm coffee. Black, sugared sweet and strong. "The colonel says you didn't eat much dinner."

Vicky sipped the hot liquid and winced at its taste. Under the captain's eyes, she took another sip. "I talked a lot. Grand Duchesses seem to do that a lot."

"All of them?" the captain asked.

Vicky shrugged. "I don't know. I've never met another Grand Duchess. Now of princesses, I know at least one. She talks way too much as well."

Vicky considered what she'd said for a moment, then added, "Only she talks better. People do what she talks them into."

"Hmm," the captain said, and settled into watchful silence beside Vicky.

Time passed. Maybe Vicky dozed. Maybe she didn't but stayed in a haze somewhere between asleep and awake.

She did notice that somehow the room had sprouted a forest of armed men and women. Uniformed police. Agents who had the hard look of men who defended people with their lives and had close friends who had lost their lives to that duty. Military police.

Vicky had to visit the restroom. Six women escorted her in and waited while she did what she could.

As Vicky settled back into her chair, a chair that was in the same place as the one she had left but seemed to have been replaced with one a lot more comfortable, she turned to the captain.

"Guards guarding the guards?"

"No one should have known where you went last night. At least, no one who wasn't with you. Someone leaked. Now we don't trust anyone."

"Sorry about that. It's the money. My loving stepmama really wants me dead."

"All the way out here? Hell, lady, when did you arrive?" the captain asked.

"Yesterday afternoon?" Vicky guessed. "Don't take it too bad. The money is hanging out there all the time. Local players spot me and see lots and lots of commas in their next paycheck."

Vicky paused. She knew her thinking was muzzy. "I think all that keeps me alive is that they jump at the chance and don't really staff it out."

The captain's face was grim. "There might be some truth in that. This is our first major assassination attempt since we set ourselves up to run our own show. You talk like it's something that happens to you every day."

Vicky found herself laughing. It was dry and half-insane. "At the palace, we had four in one day. Maybe it was three. I forget."

"How do you stay sane?"

"Am I?" Vicky answered the question with one of her own.

After that, Vicky must have fallen asleep. Her next recollection was waking up with her head on the captain's shoulder and drool dripping from her mouth onto the poor woman's uniform.

Vicky sat up straight and tried to wipe the woman's shoulder clean. It looked better after a few swipes.

Glancing around, Vicky asked, "How long was I out?"

"Almost three hours. They've got a bed ready for you."

"Thank them, but no thanks. Was there any report on Ger . . . the commander?"

"No one's come out that door," the captain said.

"Well, seeing how we've slept together," Vicky said, "I'm Vicky, sometimes called Victoria, the Imperial Grand Duchess of Peterwald."

"I'm Captain Inez Torrago. Rangers. Your Honor."

"It's Your Grace the first time you address me. Ma'am or Commander after that. I wish we could have met under better circumstances," Vicky said, and stood, stretched, and marched for the door.

The Ranger captain followed.

Vicky pushed the door open and took a peek. Medical gear. Lots of it.

And a nurse who immediately headed for her in full and high dudgeon.

"You can't be here."

"I'm the Grand Duchess Victoria Peterwald."

"I don't care if you're Mary, Queen of Scots. You're not hurt and not medical staff. Get back on the other side of the door before I bust your head."

"I'm game," Vicky said.

"Head trauma goes to another unit. You can't get in here that easy."

"What does it take to get in here?"

"I'll see if one of the doctors can spare you a moment. Now get back where you belong."

Since the nurse was now nose to nose with Vicky and looked mean enough to break a head or three, Vicky retreated.

"Would you have defended me from a head-breaking?" Vicky asked the captain as she withdrew back to her chair.

"Interesting question," the captain said, apparently giving it serious thought. "I'm not sure whether my duty would be to help her bust you one or defend you. I think I'd have tossed a coin on that one."

"Heads you bust me, and the coin has two heads?"

"Something like that. We haven't had that many Imperials out this far lately. Kind of hard to figure out how to treat one of them just now." The words were hard, but the hint of a smile softened them.

Vicky settled back in her chair. "I'm properly put in my place. Damn, how busted up was Gerrit? How long can it take?"

The captain offered no answer. Vicky hadn't expected one. Her own conclusions were bad and getting worse.

Damn, if he hadn't been taking care of my shivers, he'd have had his seat belt on.

Another hour passed at a glacier's pace. The captain sent a uniform out for sandwiches. Vicky played with the ham and cheese on rye more than she ate it.

Then the doors opened, and a woman in scrubs came out.

Somewhere Vicky had heard a Navy corpsman say that they always sent a woman doc to deliver the hard news.

Vicky stood and prepared to hear the worst.

CHAPTER 15

T HE young woman approaching Vicky was almost tiny. However, her informal medical garb could not hide the power and purpose with which she moved. She had a medical-records board in the crook of her arm.

"You are?" she inquired curtly of Vicky.

"Vicky Peterwald," she answered.

"The Imperial Grand Duchess, Victoria of Greenfeld," the Ranger captain corrected.

"Hmm," the doctor said, making a notation on her board. "And you are related to the patient how?" came out cold and fast, from having been said far too often.

"He's sworn to give his life to protect mine," Vicky fired back with meaning.

"Oh. No box to check off for that, but I believe that I can knock something together for our Patient Privacy Office."

"How is Gerrit?" Vicky demanded, having been stopped by as many bureaucratic roadblocks as she could handle for one night. Morning. Whatever!

The doctor raised an eyebrow at the way Vicky used Gerrit's first name. "Commander Schlieffen is in bad shape," she said. "We expect that he will live, but he will need extensive additional care to recover from his injuries, and his recovery may not be to his former levels."

"How badly is he hurt?" Vicky demanded.

"We've handled most of the minor cuts and burns from the RPG attack," the doctor said. "It's his back and leg that are the real problems."

"Back and leg," Vicky repeated.

"His back was broken. The break is in the lower part of the back. He has control of his hands and arms."

"But his legs?" Vicky asked. She could not make herself ask about his other valued attributes below his belt. His ability to give and take such pleasure. His driving force pounding between her legs.

"We have managed to stabilize the break and are doing all we can to see that there is no further damage that will lengthen his recovery or make that recovery less than full."

Vicky weighed all the dodges in that statement. Thank God the woman hadn't retreated behind medical jargon and technical mumbo jumbo. His lower back was broken. Not some medically exact statement like a T-2 or L-50 break that told a layman exactly nothing. Vicky knew what she'd been told and could feel the full impact of those words in her gut.

"And his leg?" Vicky finally asked.

"His femur was shattered in several places. We are stabilizing it, but first we had to stop the bleeding. We've succeeded. We can begin trying to piece the bone together, but the break is complex and very near the groin. If I had all the equipment I had five years ago, it would not be a problem, but now, with so much of our modern gear off-line for lack of spare parts or consumables, we will have to do this the old-fashioned way."

"What are you getting at?"

"Trying to repair the bone is a chancy process with possible extreme damage to flesh and arteries. He could die. It might be safest to amputate the leg."

Vicky took that blow in the gut. She'd heard Sailors from backcountry planets talk about a mule kick in the stomach; now she felt one full up.

Vicky found herself retreating to her chair. She sat in it sideways, trying to force her brain to think.

Gerrit might lose his leg. Would he rather lose his life or his leg?

Again Vicky saw Admiral Gort sprawled out, facedown on the deck, his blood and brains spreading out from the bullet he'd taken that had been aimed at her.

Would the Navy officer rather have lost a leg, the use of his lower quarter, and returned to his wife? Or would he rather be facedown in gore rather than live the rest of his life as half a man?

Would the angry widow have preferred that human fraction to the body in the flag-draped coffin?

Now Vicky realized why the doctor had asked for her relationship to this man. Did a few wonderful hours passed in passionate embrace qualify her to make this call? A crippled life or quick clean death.

"He's Navy, isn't he?" the Ranger captain asked. "Could he get better care up on the station?"

"Yes," Vicky demanded, whirling in her seat to face the doctor.

"Possibly. Assuming we could stabilize all his issues and the lift up to orbit didn't kill him or wreck everything we'd done for him."

"Computer, get me Admiral von Mittleburg."

"It's awful early in the morning," the doctor said.

"Mittleburg here," her computer announced.

"Admiral, Commander Schlieffen has been seriously hurt in defense of my life."

"How bad?"

"Doctor, can you release the official report?"

"To a doctor."

"If you can't pass it through me, transmit it direct to the duty team at the station sick bay," the admiral said crisply.

Three computers swapped addresses and authorizations, and the commander's medical records were beamed up to the doctor on duty.

"That's a bad one," a new voice observed on net. "What do you plan to do?"

"We think we can stabilize his back so that a year or two of treatment and rehabilitation should return him most of the use of his lower quarter. It's his leg. There are a lot of pieces.

We've just gotten the bleeding controlled. If we amputate it now, could the Navy clone him a new one? We sure can't these days."

"Doc?" the admiral said. "Would he be better off up here?"

"No doubt, but what would a launch to orbit do to all the fine work the good doctors down there have done?"

"Would it help if you had some of our gear down there with you?" the admiral half asked, half ordered.

"I can give you a list of our off-line equipment and the parts we need to get them up and running," the Sevastopol doctor offered.

"Send us the list," the Navy doctor said. "I'll have my med techs and supply technicians go over it with me."

"Your Grace," Admiral Mittleburg said. "I see you've had a full evening. I'd have called you myself except I'm just now getting the report of the attack. Heads are going to roll."

"Don't roll them on my account," Vicky said. "Gerrit took the blast for me. Other than my pride, I'm unhurt."

"I don't think you have any reason to be concerned about your pride. I understand that you've done quite well for an uninvited visitor they threatened to shoot down."

"May I ask how you know?"

"I had a copy of your meeting with the mayors on my desk after supper, and I read the one concerning your other meeting before I went to bed. Well played."

"Again, may I ask how you knew, sir? Someone leaked my travel itinerary, and that's how we got bushwhacked." Vicky was going into a slow burn.

"Commander Schlieffen sent it all along to me. I assure you, up here, it was my eyes only."

"Oh," Vicky said, burner going out.

At that moment, she realized just how tired she was.

Vicky took a moment to settle deep into her chair. She really was exhausted. If Gerrit was stabilized, maybe she should think about some time in that bed the hospital had offered.

The doctor's conversation with the Navy doc topside was putting a happy smile on her face.

Vicky allowed herself a smile.

A nurse dashed through the door and up to the doctor to whisper words in her ear.

The doctor's face lost its smile, and she whirled to race back through the doors.

Vicky glanced up at the Ranger. The captain's face was that blank one officers were trained to wear when the battle goes suddenly and badly wrong.

Vicky didn't care what the Navy expected. She leaned over to rest her face in her hands and tried not to cry.

But wasn't very successful.

CHAPTER 16

O N the sunny ramp at the spaceport, Admiral von Mittleburg offered Vicky his arm. She took it gratefully.

A week ago, his admiral's barge had led a trio of landers
down into the bay. The longboat on the right had held a quarter
of the doctors, technicians, and supply yeomen from the station's sick bay, along with a major chunk of their medical stores.

The longboat on the left had held a company of Marines.

No one questioned their right to land that morning.

Admiral von Mittleburg had led the charge of medical personnel into the room where Vicky still waited for word about the
commander. While the station's senior surgeon moved swiftly
through to merge his team and equipment with the best the
locals had to offer, the admiral took a good look at his Grand
Duchess.

"You're out of it, Lieutenant Commander," he said, invok-
ing Vicky's Navy rank. "Walk with me."

A junior Navy officer could not refuse a walk with an admiral. This walk ended back at Vicky's suite, with two female
Marines undressing her and a medic giving her a shot.

She got one glance out the window at the rising sun before she
slipped into unconsciousness. The next thing she remembered

seeing was the afterglow of the setting sun as she rose, muzzy-headed from her bed.

Bathed, cleaned, and dressed in a proper uniform, she was soon dining with the admiral in the hotel's best restaurant.

The admiral ordered. That gave Vicky a chance to take in her new protection detail. Greenfeld Marines had now been added to Sevastopol Rangers, agents, and uniformed police.

The place was rather crowded even though it had a strange lack of clientele.

The admiral put down the menu as the waiter retreated with their order. "I expect that you will eat your vegetables," he said.

"How is Gerrit?"

"My answer to your question depends on your assuring me that you will get a filling and healthy dinner under your belt. I'm told you ate little of last night's dinner."

"Did the commander report that, too?"

"He was very worried about you."

"And then I gave him more to worry about," Vicky said, and tried not to follow into the dark place that thought led her.

"He did his duty to you. You did your duty to Greenfeld," the admiral said cryptically.

"He did his duty to keep me alive," Vicky conceded. "What of my duty?"

"I believe that your questions about that are best answered by the mayor."

Vicky glanced up to find Mannie, the mayor of Sevastopol, rapidly closing on their table. He gave her a shallow bow from the waist and settled into the empty seat between Vicky and the admiral.

The waiter returned. "My usual, Tony," sent the waiter back where he came from.

"Will someone tell me how Commander Schlieffen is doing?" Vicky demanded.

"I'm waiting for her to promise to eat her vegetables," the admiral put in.

"I agree. She must take care of herself. She's going to be a very busy Grand Duchess for the next couple of months."

"Will someone tell me about Gerrit before I scream!" Vicky

raised her voice enough to make it clear to the men that hers was a serious threat.

"Doctor," the admiral said, signaling to a Navy medical officer who had been seated at a distant table.

In a moment, the officer was at Vicky's other elbow. "The commander came out of surgery four hours ago. He is still in recovery. They managed to limit the progressive irritation to his spinal cord. However, they were not able to save the leg. It was removed above midthigh."

"Oh no," Vicky said, her hand rising without thought to her lips.

"The medical facilities on Bayern are equal to the best in Greenfeld," the admiral began. "They can handle his rehabilitation and clone a leg for him as well."

The admiral dismissed the doctor.

"In two or three years," Vicky observed dryly, as the medical officer walked away, "he'll be as good as new."

"He is alive," the admiral said with equal aridness. "That is more than the last two officers who got close to you can say. Three, if we include Admiral Krätz."

"I certainly had nothing to do with his death," Vicky said defensively.

"You wanted to go out stargazing. He took you. He died. One follows from the other as surely as day follows night."

Vicky had no answer to that.

"Your Grace," Mannie began, "I would like to personally apologize for the attack on you. We thought our meeting was secret. We thought your security was sufficient."

"It was for me," Vicky said. "Just not survivable for those providing it."

"Yes," Mannie agreed.

The waiter brought water and tea for all three and retreated.

"So," Mannie asked, "is this eat-your-heart-and-liver month, or can we discuss what we decided last night? I wasn't sure which way it would go, but after we got word back that someone had considered you worth throwing a hasty ambush at, a lot of my people got their backs up, and everything kind of fell into place. We folks in Sevastopol don't like it when strangers send us a message to butt out."

Vicky took a deep breath, letting the storm of emotions swirling around her come in and get out. When she could speak, she asked the mayor, "What fell into place?"

"We haven't quite figured out what to call it. The Grand Duchess Victoria Humanitarian Outreach Fund was voted down because it would enlarge the target that you clearly seem to have on your back. Moreover, we don't want to put a target on our planet. The final vote was to give it no name. It's just The Initiative."

"The Initiative?" Vicky said.

"Yes. We've got a pretty good idea of the wreck that is Poznan and Presov, thanks to your report. We've traded with them before, so we know what they usually need. We think we can have four boatloads of survivor biscuits baked up and two boatloads of spare parts, consumables and expendables, packaged up in a month. Maybe three weeks depending on the bakers' schedule and us laying our hands on parts and gear scattered all around our planet."

"That fast?" the admiral said.

"Our inventory has been getting way too large. That worried plant managers. It wouldn't be too long before we had to start laying off workers. On the other hand, our inventory of what we need to keep things working was getting way too low. No feedstock and spare parts means workers get pink-slipped just as often as when the inventory has filled up the warehouses."

He eyed Vicky. "It turns out the Grand Duchess of this Empire can be right. Lots of us wanted to do this. We just didn't have the spotlight. None of us had the chance to say it out in front of everyone where they'd have to listen to us. You did. Those of us who were looking for a venue jumped right on your bandwagon. I must say thank you, Your Grace."

Vicky considered several replies, and settled for, "You are very welcome."

"Now," Mannie said, eyeing the admiral, "what can you do to protect these six very luscious sitting ducks? I'm told there are pirates out there."

"I promised them a cruiser and a battalion of Marines," Vicky said, hoping everything was not about to come tumbling down.

"You'll need two cruisers and their longboats to help with the unloading," the admiral said. "I can loan you my two best. Take good care of them. Most of what I have beside them are in desperate need of yard time."

"I can't promise the pirates won't make a pass at them," Mannie said.

"Pirates don't faze my cruisers. It's going up against other cruisers, or worse, battleships."

"You think the folks that ruined the Grand Duchess's drive home last night might have bushwhackers that big?" The mayor seemed shocked to be even asking the question.

"I wasn't expecting a squad of gunners armed with anti-tank rockets last night," the admiral answered.

"Clearly, no one was," Vicky said. "What about my Marine battalion?"

"I'd go with a regiment if I could," the admiral said. "I can get you one battalion reinforced with armor as well as a light Marine battalion. The only other Marine battalion I have is so green, I really don't want to put them out in a shooting gallery just yet."

"Armored," the mayor said. "We're there to deliver survival biscuits, not gold bars. Aren't tanks a bit of overkill?"

"Overkill, hopefully not," the admiral said. "Let me rather say overawe. I don't know what arms the locals will have at hand. After last night, I'm not willing to bet that what they have right now will be what they have in a month or so. If someone's throwing a knife fight, take a pistol. A gunfight, take a tank. If it gets any worse, we've got lasers in orbit. As I see it, being the biggest bastard in the valley keeps it from being the valley of death."

Mannie weighed that for a long moment, then nodded. "You may have a point."

"So, Mayor," the admiral said. "You've got a battalion of Rangers. Good men and women from out in the backcountry. We'll need to be rounding up a lot of folks who have been driven out to make their way or starve. Any chance you could loan The Initiative your light-infantry Rangers?"

The mayor leaned back in his chair to glance at the Rangers and their automatic rifles interspersed with agents, cops, and now Marines in dress black and red.

"I can't ask you to provide the tanks in this knife fight if I'm not willing to provide the scouts under the bushes. Admiral, you've got yourself a deal."

The two shook hands.

Steaks, red potatoes, and mixed vegetables arrived.

Vicky made sure to ostentatiously down two forks of mixed vegetables before she touched her steak.

The men shared a chuckle.

Two days later, Vicky finally managed to visit Gerrit. He was heavily drugged, but he smiled when she took his hand and ran her thumb over his palm.

"More promises?" he managed to get out through cracked lips.

"As many promises as you want," she answered.

"It will be a while before I can take you dancing." It took him a while to get the words out. She kept gently stroking his palm and listening.

"You will have the first waltz on my dance card when you do," Vicky answered.

His eyes nodded more than he did.

Then they closed, and he drifted back off to sleep.

Vicky waited until she was sure he was asleep. Then she waited a bit longer until the tears stopped running down her cheeks.

With intent, she wiped them away, then stiffened her back and marched for what she knew must be done next.

Now, a week after the attack, Vicky waited on the space-shuttle apron, her hand on Admiral von Mittleburg's arm. She was out of uniform and wearing the red power suit.

With armor inlays.

The ambulance carrying the commander was the largest they could find. They had practically entombed the man to make sure that the tension wires they had attached to his body would not be knocked out of kilter on the ride to the shuttle.

What they'd do on the ride up was too frightful for Vicky to contemplate, but it involved a tank of water and something like a pair of waterbeds with him in between.

"Are they sure they can do this?" Vicky demanded in a whisper.

"The doctors say he has healed enough and that this rig

will keep everything stable. Do you want to check the math yourself?" the admiral asked.

Vicky's expertise in math barely extended to counting her change.

The shuttle taxied out to the ramp, then held for a moment while a landing craft, tank, motored out of the bay. It was the first one down from the *Crocodile*, a Landing Assault Transport that had just arrived from Garnet. It was not only the transport for the Thirty-fourth Armored Marine Battalion, but it would also be taking on the First Sevastopol Rangers. A company of them were forming up on the tarmac to await their ride.

Vicky eyed them, then asked the admiral to excuse her for a moment. She hitched a ride on a ramp truck over to where the commander of the Ranger company stood.

"Inez? Is that you?" Vicky asked.

Captain Inez Torrago came to attention and saluted Vicky while a sergeant called the entire company to attention.

"It's me, Your Grace."

"We meet in much better times," Vicky said.

"The Second Rangers is taking over your guard detail. They're almost as good as the First."

"I'd expect nothing less from Colonel White," Vicky said.

"Brigadier General White," Inez corrected Vicky. "She got her star when they reorganized us into a Ranger regiment and brigaded us with two other infantry regiments. Only six battalions all told now, but the recruiters are busy looking for eager young kids who want to see the Empire. Or maybe just what's over the next hill."

"You may be a while coming back to St. Petersburg," Vicky said.

"So I heard," Inez admitted. "Somebody's got to keep an eye on those planets we're going out to rescue. It would be a shame to let that itchy Empress get her hands on what we've pulled out of the fire."

"You shouldn't have to hang around out there too terribly long," Vicky said. "No doubt you've heard the rumors that the other provinces are raising battalions of their own."

"Damn straight of them," the Ranger allowed.

"Well, I'll see you on Poznan," Vicky said.

"Or maybe Presov," the captain added with enthusiasm.

Vicky left the captain to her troops and walked back to where the admiral stood. The shuttle with the commander and little else motored out into the takeoff area of the bay and began its acceleration.

"That closes one chapter," Vicky said, then glanced back at the Rangers. "And those will be the next."

"Yes, Commander," the admiral said. "Now, may I introduce you to your new permanent Navy escort?"

"Escort, sir?"

"Yes. You broke the last two. Here's your third. Do try to go easier on him."

CHAPTER 17

━━━━

STRIDING confidently toward Vicky was a Navy commander in undress greens. He looked tall, strong, and handsome, with a self deprecating grin that almost left him boyish.

He saluted the admiral, then offered Vicky his hand.

She did not take it.

"I don't need another escort sacrifice," Vicky snapped.

"I believe you do. Commander Franz Boch, this is the Grand Duchess Victoria. Vicky to her friends."

"So Gerrit told me," the fellow said, smile still there.

Vicky decided to squelch it fast. "Commander, the last two men who got too close to me ended up dead or broken. That doesn't include the two dead admirals."

"I know, Your Grace. Gerrit told me a lot."

"A lot," Vicky said through a scowl. How much danger would a man risk for a chance to get laid?

"He warned me you can get shocky when you've been under a lot of stress, and that I should keep a thermal blanket handy or be prepared to surrender my coat."

"You know Gerrit?" Vicky said, only half a question.

"We were roommates at the Academy and shared rooms

aboard several ships as junior officers. We know each other very well."

"How well?"

The commander looked at Vicky with the most open face she had ever encountered. "He told me you keep your promises."

"You'll be getting no promises from me."

"No problem, Your Grace."

Vicky spun around to face the admiral. "Where does the Navy get these lemmings, so eager to die?"

"I do not know, Your Grace, I'm just glad that Greenfeld still has a few. Maybe enough to get us through these times."

Vicky raised her eyebrows at that bit of philosophy and stormed off to where a limo awaited her.

The commander managed to get there first and open the door for her.

She settled in with an ungracious "Thanks," and suppressed the urge to tell the driver to move on while the commander scrambled around the car to his own door.

Somehow, she kept her mouth shut. As he settled in beside her and buckled up, he asked, "Where are we going?"

"I've been asked to chair a meeting of The Initiative. It appears that some things were not fully considered the night I was almost blown up."

"How interesting."

"Can you fly a shuttle?" Vicky snapped.

"Yes, Your Grace."

"Fly a spaceship single-handed through jumps?"

"It would depend on its size and equipment, Your Grace. A Revenge class battleship might be a bit much to handle single-handedly."

"Do all Navy commanders come equipped with a weird sense of humor?"

"Most that I've met, Your Grace."

"Quit 'Your Grace'ing' me."

"Yes, Your Grace," came out with that boyish grin.

"I'm Vicky."

"I'm Frank, more often than not, though a few still keep the 'Z' sound and make it Franz."

"What do you want me to call you?" Vicky said, then realized she'd left herself open for some bedroom reply."

"Frank or Franz, whichever rolls off your tongue easier . . . Vicky," he said, testing the last word and finding it . . . acceptable.

Vicky decided he might be a keeper. "I hate to be made a fool of in public. If you think you have a better idea, hold on to it until we can talk it over in private. Exception to that is when you're in the command chair of a shuttle or ship. You call the shots there. I listen and do what I can to help."

"Gerrit told me how that worked out well for you two."

"I don't know what else Gerrit told you, but I'm drawing a new line. You'll have your quarters. I'll have mine. I will make you no promises."

The grin was gone from Frank's face. A look of puzzlement replaced it. Then enlightenment.

"Ah, so it was that way."

"What way?"

"I beg your pardon, ma'am. There were things that Gerrit got quiet about. Evasive. Him being very good at evasion, I didn't figure out what they were. I think I've got a better understanding now."

He paused as if to choose his next words as carefully as one might choose a next step in a minefield.

"Commander Schlieffen told me nothing about any personal relationship that he and you might have had. If you think that I accepted this job with any expectations of any relationship except a proper professional one, or that which a subject might have with his Grand Duchess, I wish to correct that now."

He eyed Vicky for a moment, then let his gaze fall to the seat between them.

Good! Vicky thought. *That's cleared up.*

Probably.

The rest of the drive was a silent one.

CHAPTER 18

Vicky had often joked that her education at the palace had included little beyond needlepoint and the Kama Sutra for both offense and defense. The joke had been bitter . . . and true.

Hank had gotten all the business training from the time he was six. He'd learned the ins and outs of manufacturing, markets, and trade.

Of course, then he'd gone to the Navy and gotten himself killed.

Vicky had gone to the Navy with nothing much at all. Less than nothing. Admiral Krätz had made it clear to her that she had a lot of bad habits, and he intended for her to break them.

After she got caught in a paint locker with a really cute ensign, the admiral had taken her out back for a tanning. His words, not hers, and brought back a young Vicky with a vow of chastity.

She had managed to live with it about as long as the admiral managed to survive her.

The Navy had taught her to stand a watch, shine her shoes, and do a decent job of analyzing a problem in gunnery.

Unfortunately, the problems Vicky faced now had more to do with markets.

Once again, she was learning.

She had seen planets starving and come up with a solution not all that different from the times when she'd shared out stolen cookies with her five-year-old playmates. Of course, it had been a bit easier, then.

Today, she sat down with people who saw a trading-and-marketing system that had choked up and needed to get moving again. They were older, but the hunger in their eyes wasn't that much different from her five-year-old friends.

"Those crystal miners," a gruff fisherman said. "You can't offer them survival biscuits. They risk their life to harvest that stuff. They know its worth. They're gonna want fresh shrimp and lobster."

"Steaks, hams, and good frozen fruit and vegetables," a rancher added.

"Some of those miners follow religious dietary rules," another put in. "I've got the mutton they'll want."

"We'll need a refrigerated cargo ship," Mannie concluded. "Is there one laid up in orbit?"

"Commander Boch, will you check on that?" Vicky said, glancing from her seat at the head of the table to where he sat behind her.

"Already on it, Your Grace. The *Frozen Christmas Goose* has been laid up for three months. I've got a call in to its skipper to see if he can raise a crew and get his ship up and running in three weeks."

There was a beep. The commander glanced at his wrist unit. "He says, 'Hell yes, or he'll push the old girl out of orbit himself,' Your Grace."

"I think we have the ship you want," Vicky said.

"There are three other refrigerated cargo ships trailing the station," the commander added. "They've been parked longer. If the *Goose* won't run, one of the others will."

"Good," Mannie said. "Sevastopol is loading out most of the first fleet. If we make it happen, there will be more following us."

"If I get my hands on that market, those latecomers can sing for their supper," the rancher growled.

"Assuming we don't lose our shirt," the fisherman pointed out.

"No risk, no bucks," was the rancher's final rumble.

Vicky was hardly needed for the rest of the meeting. There was a lot of talk about spare parts and raw resources likely needed by the fabricating mills on both Posnan and Presov. The people around the table had streaming databases of what those planets had usually ordered before trade collapsed. They were ready to supply those needs again.

The difference between what had been done in days gone by and what would be happening if Vicky got her wish to start trade again was one single word. Money. When credit had dried up from the central banks on Greenfeld, managers found they could neither sell their products nor buy critical spare parts or raw feedstock to support production.

When enough businesses fell into this vicious cycle, everything collapsed.

Trade for this initial round would have to be handled strictly on a barter basis. If you want what the trade fleet brought, you'd have to offer something in return. If St. Petersburg offered enough of what they wanted, and they had what the people around this table wanted, trade would start up again.

If not, the collapse would continue. Only this time, there would be no hope at all.

A lot depended on the men and women here at the table guessing right and putting the right product on the four ships the Navy would escort.

Five now that the *Frozen Christmas Goose* had been added.

About halfway through the meeting, Vicky began to get a bad feeling.

"How much of these ships' cargo holds do you plan on filling with your goods and gear?" she put in when the room fell silent for a moment.

"We don't know exactly what the crystal miners will need. It's better to take extra cargo than discover we don't have the right part to get a mill up and running when we get there."

"And how much of the cargo space will that leave for humanitarian supplies?" Vicky shot back.

"There will be space for some."

"How much?" Vicky bore in.

"Maybe a third. Maybe less."

"No," Vicky snapped.

"What do you mean, no?" the rancher shot back.

"Half of the cargo is for survival rations," Vicky said flatly.

"You can't be serious about that?" had way too much skepticism in it and maybe a bit of "little woman," cut off just in time.

"You give me half the cargo by cubic meter, or you can get some other figurehead to open the next meeting."

"You're willing to risk that we won't have a critical part?" one industrialist said, incredulously. "This whole effort could collapse for want of a nail, as they say."

"Poznan will collapse completely if we don't feed the workforce that's been driven into the badlands to fend for themselves. We need to feed those starving to death quietly in the outback, where no one has to look at them."

"She has a point. Fabrication mills don't run themselves. The more skilled the worker, the better," the fisherman agreed.

"Right now, too many of those workers have been driven away from the plants. You may have the part in storage, but if they can't find the worker to install it, what good is it?" Vicky demanded.

"That's the likely situation on Poznan. Presov may be in better shape."

"Presov is only a few short jumps away," Vicky pointed out. "You need one spare part, you make a call back to St. Petersburg and have it sent out on the next ship."

"They'll charge an arm and a leg," an industrialist pointed out.

"And you won't charge the same arm and leg if you find out that you hold the kingpin for that whole arm of industry?" Vicky asked.

The man reddened but made no answer.

A call went up to see if some more ships could be quickly made ready for the fleet.

Vicky had to smile.

Kris Longknife had put together a Fleet of Discovery. She hadn't actually commanded all of it, but she had admirals following her corvettes around in their mighty battleships like puppies after their mommy.

Vicky was putting together a Fleet of Desperation. If she was lucky, she'd have maybe seven or nine worn-out and ill-crewed merchant ships.

But unlike Kris Longknife, Vicky would know what she was heading into. She'd have spare parts and survival rations in place and not have to wait for her grandfather to dump some Hellburners in her lap.

Interesting difference.

Of course, Princess Kris Longknife had known how to buffalo admirals and get them stampeding in the direction she wanted.

This Grand Duchess just hoped she could get these businessmen, intent on their own self-interest, to deliver enough stale biscuits to starving people on the verge of cannibalism.

Vicky considered the comparison of missions between her and Kris Longknife and found it well balanced.

Yes, Kris Longknife's mission was a hell of a lot more than Vicky's. But then, Vicky's skills and experience were a hell of a lot less than Kris's.

Vicky shrugged. No doubt Kris had started out smaller, too. If Vicky had the time, she ought to reread Princess Longknife's file with an eye toward her younger years.

Then again, Vicky was too busy learning and doing to waste time reading files that usually missed the main point anyway.

The meeting ended with no further surprises. Vicky's fleet had grown by three ships. That had to be good.

CHAPTER 19

━━━

"**W**HERE do you plan to get money for three more ships?" the station manager exploded when Vicky had him called into Admiral van Mittleburg's office to discuss the latest changes on what was actually being called the Fleet of Desperation.

Take that, Kris Longknife, Vicky thought with a smile.

"You've got the ships trailing the station," Vicky pointed out. "Certainly the crews are around here someplace."

"Not on your life. Do you think I wanted a lot of out-of-work sailors lying around my station? No way. I shipped them dirtside as fast as I could. They're gone. They aren't available."

"And the eight crews we do have?" Vicky asked.

"I found odd jobs for the best of them. Got rid of some of my less-than-satisfactory station workers. I can't say that I'm glad to have them shipping out on your ships, but they're here for you."

The admiral glanced at Vicky and grinned.

"And where will you get replacements for the hands that ship out?" Vicky asked.

The admiral nodded, and if anything, his grin got bigger.

"I'll put some feelers out dirtside. Feelers, mind you. I

don't want every dog-eyes swabbie hitching rides up here on every empty seat a shuttle has to offer."

"If you won't announce the extra crew slots," Vicky countered, "I will. Or you can give me the name of a couple of good skippers, and I'll have them put together the crews we need."

The station manager scowled at Vicky. No doubt, he was getting kickbacks from those he'd given jobs. If she took over hiring, he'd be out of that revenue stream.

The station manager gave her "that look." It was a good thing she had plenty of experience being the little girl in the room. The room with Daddy. The room with Hank. Hell, just about any room in the palace.

Strange, I haven't seen that look since I joined the Navy. At least not to my face.

"Little lady, you let me handle the ships, and you can go look pretty," the station manager actually said.

"You are talking to your Imperial Grand Duchess," the admiral growled.

"Let me handle this, sir," Vicky said, and stood to look down on the station chief.

"Captain," she said, giving the station chief his highest honorary claim. "You will need Navy reaction mass to get these ships away from the station. You will, no doubt, need some assistance from the Navy ship maintainers available here. They are very busy, but I'm sure I can get them cut loose for a bit. You are going to need a hundred different little items to get those ships away from the pier, and half of those will, no doubt, only be available in Navy hands."

The station chief blanched as Vicky laid out the long list of things he'd have to scrounge to get just these eight ships ready to pull away from the pier. No doubt, he never expected a "little lady" to have any idea of what it took to get a ship ready for space.

Thank you, Admiral Krätz, Vicky prayed.

"As *Imperial* Grand Duchess, I can grease the skids for things that need to cross the line between the Navy and civilian world. Between Navy accounts and civilian accounts, I can sign documents to lend materials in both directions and have the values settled later."

Vicky paused to make sure it all sank into his thick skull.

"You can find yourself doing this a really hard way. You can find someone else doing it, or you can play ball with me. Which is it?"

It didn't take him long to see which side his turkey was buttered on. "Whatever you say, Your Majesty."

"My father is His Imperial Majesty. I'm Your Grace, or ma'am, the second or third time you chance to address me."

"Whatever you say," he stuttered.

"What captains do you have for my eight merchant ships?"

Vicky had watched the dickering that morning around the table, putting her oar in the water only when she had to to make sure the water was still there. Now it was her turn to try her hand at dickering.

The station manager had picked four captains to start with and the ships they'd most recently skippered. Admiral von Mittleburg brought up problems that his maintenance people had identified with two of the ships.

Two ships were substituted for them along with the three more dry-cargo freighters added and their most recent captains contacted. Very quickly, they were recalling their old crews and moving them all toward the station.

One of the ships dropped earlier was added back in when it proved to be in better shape than the one initially nominated for the eighth ship. That ship had a major reactor issue buried in its records. There was no yard at hand to mend that problem.

The *Frozen Christmas Goose* did turn out to be the best refrigerated ship.

The haggling went on into the evening. Ships that had gone out of service needed maintenance and spare parts to bring them back. Who would pay for them?

Vicky ended up on the net, talking not only to Mannie but several other mayors. The idea that 100 percent of the profits from this first cruise would go to Sevastopol started to look more like 60 percent.

The swapping back and forth ended in time for Vicky to enjoy a pleasant supper with the admiral.

"You assumed a lot of power today," he noted over the first glass of wine.

"Did I assume too much?"

The admiral pursed his lips and eyed the commander, who

had stayed at Vicky's side through the meeting. He had said little and done a good job of fetching facts when they did not prove to be immediately in evidence.

"Would you prefer if I left, sir?" the commander asked.

"No. You're more likely to be the one dead before either I or the Grand Duchess encounter that grim fate."

The commander flashed that boyish grin. "I wouldn't be too sure about that, sir. By my count of them that hung around the Grand Duchess here, to date it's two admirals dead. Among the JOs, one captain is, alas, gone to his reward, but one commander has managed to stumble from the field bound for rehab."

The admiral raised both eyebrows. "You have a strangely optimistic viewpoint."

"Us field grade types can easily fall into that error, sir. We've survived our time as junior officers, and we have yet to discover the full burden of command."

As much as she didn't want to, Vicky found herself liking Frank.

"As I was saying," the admiral continued, "you are assuming a lot of power. The situation is so bad that if someone doesn't stand in the middle and let all the lightning strike her, we are not likely to get any power at all."

"I find that image, ah, burned into my vision, Admiral," Vicky said.

"The question that many will ask is this: Are you assuming power to make good possible, or are you taking this power as the beginning of a power grab?"

Vicky listened carefully, measured each word, then sighed.

"No doubt, there will be those who see what I am doing only from their own perspective. The people who want to seize absolute power will assume that any use of power by anyone else only siphons it away from them."

"What do you assume?" the admiral asked.

Vicky twirled her wineglass and studied the eddies in the liquid. Then she put it down.

"As strange as it may seem coming from a Peterwald, I want to save lives. Save as many as I can. I want to get markets flowing that will improve the lives of millions of others. Yes, Admiral, I know there are other games afoot. I grew up in the palace. I found games in my morning cereal."

Vicky considered what she'd just said, then chose her words carefully.

"I know games, and I know what is real. Starving to death is as real as it comes though I suspect it doesn't come all that much to those of us who have never missed a meal. Please, sir, let me do this one good thing. Maybe the only good thing I've done in my whole life."

She paused, then added after a moment. "Maybe the only good thing I will do in my life."

"So," the admiral said, "let's get across this bridge before we talk of burning any others."

"Let's build something," Vicky said. "Who knows, maybe we won't have to burn anything."

The commander raised his glass. "What do you know? I'm working with an optimistic Peterwald."

CHAPTER 20

━━━

T HE new commander turned out to be right. Vicky and everyone else who thought eight drifting hulks could be converted back into working merchant ships in three weeks were very much the optimists.

Two ships were dropped from the fleet and three more added over the next four weeks as fitting out turned into more "fitting" than "out." Only when all nine ships were declared ready and safe for space did the work of loading them with fuel, food, and various kinds of spare parts begin.

Vicky worried that every second's delay meant little children starving to death. They haunted her dreams.

Then she discovered that delay could have benefits.

The small tramp freighter *Doctor Zoot* docked at the station, and Vicky found she had visitors.

Kit and Kat showed up, with Mr. Smith and Maggie in tow.

Vicky was delighted.

For all of five seconds.

Then paranoia kicked in.

"How did you know where I was?" she demanded of Mr. Smith.

"None of *us* knew *you* were the pot at the end of the rainbow," he assured her. "The Navy asked me and these two gorgeous and diminutive assassins if we wanted to stay in the palace. What with you gone, it was getting rather boring. Hardly anyone was being murdered. A whole day might go by with only one new body, and it was hardly ever anyone we knew or cared about. So I said, yes, I'd love a free ticket to where I might have a better chance at snagging a job."

Mr. Smith actually grinned. "It turned out that the Navy was negotiating a ride out with Kit and Kat as well. We didn't know we were headed out together, or headed here until, well, we were headed here."

"Maggie?" Vicky asked, turning to her oldest and best friend.

"I was spending my hours working in the palace infirmary," Maggie said.

"And keeping us apprised of the odd assassination," Mr. Smith added.

Maggie made a face. "I made no secret that I hated life in the palace and wanted to return to St. Petersburg. Passage was arranged. Imagine my surprise at the first meal to find these three seated at my table. There is no escaping the punishment for my many sins," she said, eyes raised heavenward.

"I'm glad to have you back," Vicky said, hugging the doctor who cared for her, really cared for her, in her youth. "I hope you'll come with me."

"Where are you headed?" Dr. Maggie asked.

"There are two planets where civilization has broken down. They're past food riots and just short of cannibalism, or at least one of them is."

"Eew," Kit and Kat said, making faces.

"No doubt, they'll need a doctor," Maggie said.

"The Fleet of Desperation leaves as soon as we can get it all together," Vicky said. "We should have sailed yesterday."

"The Fleet of Desperation," Mr. Smith said. "Are our chances any better than Kris Longknife's Fleet of Discovery?"

"I'll know more about that in a month or so," Vicky admitted.

"So you're just as optimistic as last time," Mr. Smith said, with as inscrutable a shrug as you could expect from a part-time assassin/full-time spy.

"Pretty much," Vicky admitted.

At least with her four friends, time passed a bit faster. Mr. Smith made it easier for Vicky to keep her vow of chastity toward all things Navy. He didn't keep her from riding those who would have slowed down loading, but he might have contributed to her not chewing off any heads.

So it was that Vicky learned something from her two assassins.

That evening after supper, when Vicky was considering roaming the piers to see how the second shift was doing and knowing she could add nothing of real consequence to the effort, she noticed the two of them playing a game.

One would handcuff the other and hide a hairpin on that one's person. The cuffed one would have to find the hairpin wherever it was, then get out of the cuffs.

The two of them were always out of the cuffs in under a minute.

Vicky watched them for a while, concluded she knew how it was done, and stepped forward.

"Can I take a try at that?"

"But of course, mademoiselle," Kat said, and, maybe too eagerly, cuffed Vicky's hand in front of her.

"Give me the hairpin," Vicky said.

"Ah, but that is part of the game," Kit said, and did something behind Vicky's back. "Now find zee hairpin," the assassin said with a wicked grin.

The two of them had made it look easy to twist around and retrieve the pin. Five minutes later, Vicky had turned herself into a pretzel, and the pin was still eluding her.

Kat took mercy on her, but five more minutes later, the cuffs were still on.

Kit showed Vicky how it was done.

Next round, Vicky rubbed her head up against the wall, knocked the pin out, and was free four minutes later.

She was down to two minutes when Mr. Smith showed up and dealt himself into the game. He beat the two assassins' best time.

Then the game took an interesting turn.

Vicky was none too sure exactly how it happened, but somehow she ended up cuffed to the bed by her right hand and left ankle. Naked.

"Where's the hairpin," she demanded.

"You'll get it in time," Mr. Smith assured her.

It was a very delightful evening. Vicky was thoroughly and pleasurably exhausted before Mr. Smith gave her a good-night kiss and somehow slipped the hairpin from his mouth to hers, then said his good-byes to the other two and left Vicky to free herself while the two diminutive assassins did their best to distract her.

CHAPTER 21

Six days after Vicky's security team showed up, she was on the bridge of the Imperial heavy cruiser *Attacker* shortly after it jumped into Presov space.

"Who the hell are you?" demanded the first message from the planet that had once produced a quarter of the Empire's crystal.

The skipper of the *Attacker*, a small, dapper man, handed the question to Vicky with a raised eyebrow.

"Hello, I am her Imperial Grace, the Grand Duchess Victoria of Greenfeld. I am leading a trade delegation and convoy of merchant ships from St. Petersburg. We would like to reopen trade with Presov."

As expected, there was a long break between Vicky's answer and the next response.

"You sure you're not a damn invasion fleet? I'm making out what looks like two Disdain class cruisers and an Anaconda class attack transport."

Vicky was in civilian clothes, her red power suit. It was easier to come the Grand Duchess if she didn't display lieutenant commander stripes. She centered herself on the camera, rested both hands on her hips, and leaned into the camera, all business.

"When I passed through this system six weeks ago, you looked in bad shape and headed for a whole lot worse. We didn't know when we got here if there would be normal trade options or if we'd have to use Marines to guard our goods from theft and rioting. Our next planned stop is Poznan, and when we were last there, it already *was* a mess. We expect to have to protect ourselves while we hand out famine rations."

Vicky paused to let that sink in. "As for the cruisers, you may have heard there are pirates out this way. Ten loaded cargo vessels are a tempting target. No doubt the cruisers will help honest men stay honest."

Vicky turned to Charles Vickun, the senior member of the trade delegation. "You want to send them a list of some of the product we have available for them?"

He dispatched a message with a carefully chosen database of goods. Later, Vicky would discover just how carefully they had been chosen.

The next message was very terse. "Come on down."

CHAPTER 22

T WO days later, Vicky pulled herself down into her place
for dinner with her nine-member trade delegation and the
eleven representatives of the Mine Manager's Cooperative.
The dinner was in the wardroom of the *Attacker*; the cruiser's
chefs had outdone themselves despite the lack of gravity.

Marines in dress black and reds, sidearms in evidence,
served as waiters.

Milton Adaman, the president of the Mine Manager's Co-op,
eyed the weapons from where he sat across the table from Vicky.

"Do you think those are necessary?" he asked.

"We live in troubled times," Vicky answered evenly. "We
are transporting a fortune in foodstuffs, spare parts, and light
equipment. The famine biscuits on Poznan may be the difference between life and death for them. So, yes, we are careful.
We intend to deploy the Thirty-fourth Armored Marine Battalion on Poznan along with Sevastopol's First Rangers. The
Fifty-fourth Light Marines is assigned to ship duty on the
cruisers. If we need some ground security here, a couple of
their companies should suffice."

"We have mine-security personnel and local police," Milton pointed out.

"Yes, *you* have them, sir," Vicky said, pointedly. "*We'd* like to have some skin in the game to keep honest men honest."

"About honest men's honesty," he said. "It seems to me that in times like this, with belts cinched in as tight as they are, it might get hard to figure out just where honesty lies."

"That's a rather vague statement, Mr. Adaman," Vicky answered. "Would you care to explain to me what you're getting at? It only seems a riddle to me."

"What's the honest value of an item when one side of the market has a gun and the other side has, shall we say, a very empty stomach?"

"Ah," said Vicky. "I think I understand your meaning now. However, we have the recorded value of the last shipment of raw crystal that arrived on St. Petersburg, seven, no eight months ago," she said, glancing at her chief trade delegate. Charles was on her left.

Commander Boch, complete with Sam Brown belt and weapon, was dining at Vicky's other elbow and almost across from Milton.

That fact was not lost on the mining man.

Milton nodded. "So you have a potential value for our side of the trade. What about the price of the food you brought?"

Charles now jumped in. "We've had our problems, too. Prices for food on St. Petersburg have jumped fifty percent in the last six months."

"Fifty percent!" was somewhere between an echo and a shout from down the miners' side of the table.

Vicky had seen Kris Longknife negotiate with balky or troubling people. One thing Vicky noticed was how Kris kept a wide table between potentially violent parties. Tonight, Vicky had the miners on one side, the trade delegation on the other.

This matter was something Vicky had foreseen. She moved quickly to soothe. "I imagine your production has suffered dislocations as well. We might consider increasing the value of your crystal over old crystal by forty percent."

She'd run that number by the trade delegation. There was a lot of grumbling, but they finally agreed to 40 percent as a starting offer.

With some major grumbling from those who wanted to start at 50 percent . . . of the old price.

"We get forty percent allowance for inflation while you get fifty percent?" said Milton, looking up and down his side of the table. "Where's the honesty in that?"

"It's open to discussion," Vicky said, tasting her soup. "This is a delicious bisque. You might want to enjoy it while it's still warm."

The dickering went on around the table as the mine managers produced the last delivery of food, some six months ago, and the prices they'd paid then.

At the end of the haggling, there was a deal. The miners would sell their new crystal for 50 percent over the old and buy their food at 50 percent above their last order.

"Do you have any crystal to sell?" the trade rep asked as the haggling wound down.

"We've got plenty," Milton said with a scowl. "The next pickup ship isn't due here for two months. They should have been here last month, but they seem to have problems getting out this far."

"My question is," a mine manager near the center of the table said, "how do we pay them when they get here? Yes, it's nice to eat. This meal is the best I've tasted in months, don't get me wrong. But we have to pay our taxes and make a payment on the mines' mortgages. How do we do that?"

"They aren't bringing you food and spare parts," Vicky pointed out.

"But we have to pay our taxes, and if we don't meet our mortgage payment, someone will buy us up for pfennigs on the mark."

"Can't you produce enough in the next couple of months to meet your fiduciary obligations?" the senior trader asked.

The mining bosses around the table just shook their heads. "Production is way down. Half our gear is broken and off-line. You can't cut crystal with broken crap."

"Charles," Vicky said to her senior trade advisor, "didn't you provide them with a list of the spare parts and light equipment we brought?"

"I thought food was their main concern?" he said with a smooth smile. Butter would have melted in his mouth.

"We did bring spare parts and other products, didn't we?" Vicky asked, her voice letting the full power of a Grand Duchess out.

"We might have, Your Grace," came from what she'd considered *her* side of the table.

Someone apparently considered the negotiations about food and crystal as only a children's game, or maybe as a warm-up to the serious haggling over the prices for the spare parts.

Clearly, the ranchers and farms representative didn't see it that way.

Neither did Vicky. She leaned back in her chair. "I was led to understand that you passed that list along with the first transmission."

"It may have gotten cut off," Charles said with a notable lack of sincerity.

Vicky considered what lay before her . . . and didn't much care for it. She would have to speed this up or face a long, boring evening.

"Well, Charles, you will need to do your trading here quickly. Aren't *your* spare parts on the ships that have *our* famine rations?"

An oily smile vanished. Possibly he spotted her rare use of the Imperial we. "They are, Your Grace."

"I'll be taking those ships out with me tomorrow morning. Afternoon at the latest. Children are starving on Poznan."

"But if you take those ships with you, we won't be able to deliver the spare parts that are on board them. The next trade convoy will be here before you get those ships back."

"You might want to consider that and get your bargaining over quickly," was all Vicky said.

Now it was the miners across the table who grinned happily. As dessert was served, a second round of haggling began. Vicky did her best to stay Navy bland as she seethed inside.

Don't you dare play games with me, buster.

The prices for the spare parts were settled on before the Marines served coffee and brandy.

The Mining Operators Co-op officers' talk at the table now sounded confident they could buy food and parts from this convoy and still have enough product in their strongrooms for the tax man as well as the mortgage.

Vicky let Mr. Smith escort her to her room with a smile on her face and a happy song in her heart.

CHAPTER 23

IT was good for Vicky's new reputation that she sent Mr. Smith off to his own quarters before she settled in for the night because at 0200, the commander knocked on her door.

It still took her a bit before she could face him with a "Yes?"

"Your Grace, you have a message from something calling itself the Miners Union, and the Independent Mining Guild, and the Facilities Management League, and the Communication Workers Union, and about a dozen other things like them."

"Unions?" Vicky almost spat the word. That was the way Daddy said it. Like a curse word, only worse.

"Because of the value of crystals," Vicky's computer put in, "the workers in the crystal-production process have been more successful in organizing without the Imperial forces stepping in to resolve labor disputes. In many mines, that process has been reversed during these troubled times."

The commander quickly went on. "It seems that the Mining Co-op managers we met with this evening are interested in doing that here on Presov."

"And that's a problem for me how?" Vicky said.

"The management cartel has just hit the shift coming off work at midnight with a fifty percent cut in the going rate for crystal delivered to the mine head, Your Grace. They've also doubled the price of food in the cafeteria," the commander said.

"That must be nice for somebody," Vicky observed, still not sure of the problem.

"Assuming there isn't rioting and destruction in the mines," the commander said.

"We made our deal with the managers. Of what concern is that to us?" Vicky asked.

"The Navy likes to say it pays a living wage to the workers on our colonies. At double the prices for food but half the pay for production, I'm not sure that's a survivable wage, much less livable."

Vicky began to see the problem. "So what's the use of us opening trade routes again if the mine managers clog them up on the ground? And if the workers aren't paid enough to buy the ranchers' beef from St. Petersburg, what does that do to the ranchers' markets?"

Vicky sighed. "We could be going through all of this only to have it collapse at our feet, again."

"I wonder who makes all the money under this scheme?" the commander asked no one. But it was a good question.

Vicky glanced at the clock. "It seems a bit late for us to go play twenty questions with the Mine Managers Co-op. Frank, do you think the workers are awake at this hour?"

"They did send us this message."

"Can you land a shuttle down there?"

"Without a doubt."

"Land a shuttle without our being met by our friendly mine-co-op security thugs?"

"The communication workers' union did manage to get this message up here without interception or interruption."

"Tell them to start warming up a shuttle and make sure we can talk to whomever we want to talk to. I'll be dressed in fifteen minutes."

"I will have the shuttle ready to drop then, Your Grace."

CHAPTER 24

FIFTEEN minutes later, Vicky met the commander at her door, only to find Captain Inez Tarrago of the First Rangers as well as another captain of Greenfeld Marines present.

Vicky eyed the collection. "Did you skip anyone?" she asked the commander.

He made a point of appearing to think for a moment. "I might have missed a few. Do you plan to have the union folks in for dinner? Should I rouse the cooks?"

Ignoring his humor, they quick-marched for the drop bay. Two bosuns had a longboat ready to go. It was brimming with Rangers and Marines before Vicky got there.

Vicky settled herself into a seat and gave the commander a grin. "Gee, I think this is my first drop mission with Marines. I'll have to write Kris Longknife all about it."

"Assuming you survive."

"She always does," Vicky pointed out, optimistically.

"You're not her," the commander countered.

The two captains of infantry eyed them uneasily.

"Are you two married?" Inez asked.

"No!" Vicky spat.

"No offense intended, Your Grace. It's just that you two seem to enjoy arguing enough to be married," the Marine captain provided, right on the downbeat.

Before Vicky could manage a comeback, the shuttle dropped free, and the bosun hit the brakes hard.

A few Rangers looked a bit alarmed, but the Marines seemed to take it in stride. A few glares from their NCOs settled the Rangers without a word spoken.

"Where are we landing?" Vicky asked.

"There's a small strip outside the main mining town. The chief bosun at the controls assures me they can land short of the cow pasture at either end."

"And someone will be waiting to talk to us?"

"That's the latest rumor coming in on this secret side net."

Vicky found braking was throwing her sideways against the commander. He reached over and cinched her in tighter. He might or might not have copped a feel while doing it.

Vicky ignored the matter.

Besides, she kind of liked the feel of his strong hands.

I made a resolution, she reminded herself.

And why should this be the first one you don't break? didn't have an easy answer.

On the ground, the commander held Vicky in her seat while the Rangers and Marines deployed, in that order.

"Is there a problem?" Vicky demanded.

"None so far," the commander reported.

When he decided it was safe for her, he let her unbuckle her harness and march determinedly from the longboat.

The scene that greeted her was interesting. She stood in a valley between rugged, yellow ridges. The uplands were stark rock, bare of all but a few smudges of lichen and moss. The lower levels of the ridges, however, had some kind of low trees and brush covering them. Vicky could make out pigs and goats roaming the forbidding landscape.

The valley floor showed bare and yellow in places. However, years of human waste had turned most of it to brown soil covered with growing crops or grass, with sheep and small cows roaming it.

Vicky sniffed. She was surprised, knowing the mixture of

sewage, rock, and dust that went into this soil, at the fresh, growing scent that filled her lungs. *We humans go where we will and bring the smell of Earth with us.*

That was all the time she had for philosophy. A klick away from the lander, with a lot of armed troops in between, huddled several dozen civilians. No doubt, these were the people she'd come to meet. As she got closer, she could make out details. They were a mixed lot, young and old. Men and women. The one thing they shared was their clothes.

They were durable, well-worn, and visibly patched.

As Vicky strode toward them, an old man and a young woman came forward.

Vicky greeted them with, "I am Her Imperial Grace, the Grand Duchess Victoria of Greenfeld. Call me Vicky," and offered her hand.

The old man stepped forward and shook it.

"You was supposed to kiss it," someone shouted from the crowd behind.

"Either is acceptable. I kind of prefer shaking," Vicky said. Actually, she loved to have her hand kissed. Guys usually took the chance to do nice things with their thumbs to her palms.

You're a businesswoman this morning. Stay focused, some other self scolded.

"Why all the guns and stuff?" came, again, from the mob.

"She's the Grand Duchess, you doofus. Her new stepmom wants her dead. Don't you follow anything on net?" a woman's voice answered.

"So that bit of palace intrigue has made it out even to here," Vicky muttered.

"We may be out here, but we aren't totally in the dark about news from the bigger sphere," the young woman said, dropping something that might have passed for a curtsy at the palace.

From a cute three-year-old.

"If you'll come this way, Your Grace," the man said, and pointed toward a dimly lit hall of crude construction.

The Marines closed in on Vicky. The Rangers began to disperse under whispered orders from their officers and NCOs. Her commander's frown lines stayed deep. He might have talked Vicky into this little visit, but he didn't look all that happy about it.

The hall was made of thin plywood held up by rough-hewn two-by-fours. Mud bricks provided some insulation and protection to the outside. Windows had plywood shutters. It must get rough out here in the winter. Around the hall were plenty of buildings a lot smaller and with more mud bricks and less wood. Vicky would never have thought people could live like this.

There was a long wooden table down the center of the building. Its plywood was dinted and dinged, with undetermined stains and the occasional carved word. Benches lined both sides of the table. A single rough-worked chair stood at the head of the table.

Vicky was directed to it.

Once she was settled, with her commander and a Marine captain standing at her back, there was a long round of introductions.

The old man was Gus. He spoke for the Guild of Independent Prospectors. The woman was Molly. She spoke for the Tinkers Group.

Vicky lost track of the introductions after that. COMPUTER, RECORD ALL THIS AND BE READY TO GIVE ME A NAME IF I NEED IT.

YES, YOUR GRACE.

The room fell silent after the last name. That pause stretched and folded into a nice bow, so Vicky tossed out her first question.

"Who *are* you people? I thought everyone worked for the mines. Tinkers? Independent Prospectors? How do you fit into the big picture?"

"Think of us as the mice hiding in the walls," Molly said.

"Not all of us," Gus said with a cough. "Some of us are independent contractors to the co-op. Others, well, we're the people that don't exist on the record."

"Excuse me," Vicky said, "but I don't understand matters any better now than when I asked that question."

Molly glanced at Gus, then said, "Most of the crystal that is taken out of Presov comes from the hard rock mines. The companies drill deep underground, find a vein, and extract the huge crystals that industry needs. Us, or the independent prospectors, go out and find crystal veins on the surface. Others pan for it. The smaller, water-polished crystals are used for art or musical instruments."

"I think I understand what you're getting at. But what's a tinker?" Vicky asked.

"I guess you'd call us craftsmen, but we kind of prefer tinkers. We get a lot of tinker's damns from the prospectors," Molly said with a lovely smile. "We're the people with the fast fingers and good eyes that keep a prospector's gear working long after the co-op would have scrapped it. Hell, much of what they use, they take from the co-op's scrap heap and have to pay a sweet price for it, I'll tell you."

"Is there much scrap these days?" the commander asked.

"Damn little," Molly said. "And they want an arm and a leg for it. Half our group have been hired by the co-op of late. Even their mechanics and machinists can't keep the crap they've got up and running."

"So you live off the table scraps of the co-op," the commander said.

"Pretty much. You get banged up and hurt in the mines too bad to work for the co-op, you likely get a job with us. You complete your contract with the co-op, you take the ride home or use the ticket as a grubstake to go prospecting for yourself."

"Where do you get your food? Supplies? Where do you sell your crystal?" Vicky asked.

The commander rested an affirming hand on Vicky's shoulder. A quick squeeze, and it was gone.

He likes me, some little girl in a swirly dress cheered.

He likes what I'm saying, the desperate Grand Duchess shot back.

It's good to have another human being affirm me, Vicky concluded, then concentrated on the answer to her question.

"If you're desperate for money, you sell to the co-op. You take what they pay and pay their prices for what you need," Gus said.

"If you're not desperate," Molly said, "you hold out, swap among us, and see what you can get when the ship comes."

"The tax ship?" Vicky asked.

"Of late, that's about all it's been, but before, it brought supplies. Most went straight to the co-op, but the captain and crew knew we were here. They'd bring along their own bit of trading stock. Dry goods, spare parts, and gear. We'd trade with them.

We sold our crystal for a bit more than the co-op paid. Some stuff fetched quite a bit more. They gave us a decent price for what we needed."

"When someone needed a major item, they might give the captain something on consignment. He'd get his take from what he sold it as, and we'd get what we needed such as a new buggy or a small dredge."

"We bought our own reactor once when Abby brought that big hunk of black back from wherever she found it," came from down the table.

"You trade for all your food?" Vicky asked.

"We grow our own rice and oats," also came from down the table. "We've got our own hydroponic truck gardens. Some you can even raise out in the open if we get a bit of rain and decent weather."

"How's the co-op taken to that?" the commander asked.

"Lately, they been confiscating any food they can get their hands on," Molly said.

Vicky let the quiet grow around that statement as she thought. Getting this expedition off to a late start was looking more and more like some laughing god's idea of providence.

"We added a small freighter to our fleet at the last minute," she began, describing the tramp that had brought Kit, Kat, Maggie, and Mr. Smith out to her. "It is one of the few still making the rounds out here. When the skipper heard what we were up to, he asked to tag along. He had to throw together a cargo quickly. It's mostly stuff on consignment. Some of it is luxury stuff. Fine wines. Coffee. Chocolate, both in confections and in the raw."

Vicky could hear mouths salivating.

"But most of his cargo was a consignment of dry goods and canned goods along with some small motors and spare parts."

"That's what we need," Molly said.

"He may have to take your crystal on consignment," Vicky pointed out.

"So long as he delivers some of that food and parts for us to use now, I'll risk the trade," Gus said.

Vicky made the call to the *Doctor Zoot*'s skipper.

"I got a drop ship I can use to get a couple of containers'

worth of stuff down there in the next two hours," Captain Spee announced. "I'll need help getting more of my stuff down."

"I'll arrange for the *Crocodile* to loan you a few LCIs," Vicky offered.

"That would be good."

A nod to the commander, and he was on his commlink, making it happen.

CHAPTER 25

══════════

As the sun came up, Vicky was out on the tiny apron of the hardly larger runway. At her elbow, Captain Spee watched as locals examined samples of his cargo: bulging sacks of rice, corn, and wheat; cans of meat and fish, vegetables and fruit-juice concentrates. A lot of people were eyeing them hungrily.

But it was the crates of spare parts that were the center of interest.

Several locals had gone over the stock of parts, under the close watch of a half dozen merchant sailors who had dropped down with their captain. Now the skipper asked to see samples of the crystal they had available for trade.

"It's not much to look at," Gus said.

"That's why I hired a crystal mechanic on St. Petersburg when I heard where the next leg of this trip would take me."

A tiny civilian stepped forward, a huge pair of goggles on his forehead. He reached almost reverently for the first offered crystal with long, thin fingers. Then he pulled the goggles down to cover his eyes and did some sort of adjustment to the side of them that changed their color. Only then did he lift the crystal to the early rays of the sun.

"This is a good piece," he muttered half to himself. "All the sharp edges have been smoothed. Note the way they've been evenly worn down," he said to no one in particular. "Flutists will pay a high price for this. Forty to fifty thousand marks."

The captain was quick to step on that. "From which I'll have to subtract fees for transport and profits for at least three middlemen. Twenty thousand is the most I can offer."

"One middleman should get it to a fine musician, and he will pay at least forty thousand for it. Maybe more," Gus said. "We do follow the market out here. We'd be giving it away at thirty-five thousand."

Vicky wondered if every scrap of crystal would have its own dickering and failed to suppress a yawn.

"There are five large vehicles coming up the road from Emerald City, fast," Captain Torrago reported on net.

"Who's in them?" the commander asked.

"Hard to tell. Windows look thick and darkened."

"Mine-security people?" Vicky asked.

"No doubt. Surprised it took them this long. What do you want, Your Grace?"

"Peace and quiet," she muttered. "Captain, can one of your Rangers stop them?"

"Stop them how? Stand in the road and maybe get run over, or should I try putting a bullet in their tires or radiator?"

"I don't want to damage stuff they can't replace," Vicky said. "Try having someone stand in the road friendly-like."

Two minutes later, the Ranger captain reported. "They damn near ran her down, Your Grace. Is it time to shoot the tires?"

"Let's try something short of that before we do," Vicky admitted.

"I can put five Rangers in the road armed with guns lowered."

"Try that. If they blow by them . . ." Vicky paused and weighed what she was about to say. "If they blow by them, shoot out the tires."

"Roger that. Make one more attempt to stop them, with guns showing. If they run them down, this time we shoot out the tires."

"Affirmative," Vicky said.

"Your Grace?" came from the Marine captain beside her.

"Yes."

"There are Marines out covering the approach road with the Rangers."

"Inez, wait one on that last order. Are there Imperial Marines with you?"

"We got a couple."

"You got my Gunny," the Marine captain pointed out.

"Yes, I do believe I've got one big, mean mountain of an NCO out here in Marine combat dress."

"Include him in the roadblock," the Marine captain said. "I got twenty that says he should be enough to block the road all by himself."

"I don't gamble," came from Inez, on net. After a pause she added, "on open official channels."

"Captain Torrago," Vicky said to the Ranger skipper, "if they come near to running down the Gunny, let the Imperial Marines shoot out the tires."

"Do you think they can, Your Grace? These cops ain't coming at us slow."

"Also, Your Grace," the Marine captain put in, "I have two sniper teams in place. If they can't put a hole in one of those tires, the Ranger captain can have my next paycheck."

"That is definitely a bet I'm not taking," the Ranger answered. "I've seen them practice with my best. Hell, Your Grace, I didn't even know they were in the field."

"Captain," Vicky said lightly, "please keep the Rangers advised when your Marines chance to share a battlefield with them."

"Won't happen again," the captain said, just as lightly.

"Well, while we were talking, Gunny took the road with two Marines and three of my Rangers. All weapons were aimed high, but the locals got the message. All vehicles have stopped."

"That's good."

"Gunny reports the cops demand you let them through."

"Inform them that they are entering a security zone around the Grand Duchess and will have to request admission through proper channels," Vicky said.

The Marine captain beside Vicky looked fit to bust a gut.

The locals looked on in a mixture of terror and shock.

Well, nobody quite knows what to make of a Grand Duchess.
They all waited for the next move.

"They tell me that Milt Adaman, president of the Mine Manager's Co-op, is headed out here. He demands to see you."

"Tell them that is the wrong form of address," Vicky said.

The locals quit breathing. Gus started to open his mouth, but Molly placed a restraining hand on his elbow.

Curious are you to see how this plays out. Well, so am I.

The pause in communications went on long enough that the locals had to start breathing again. Captain Spee asked for another sample of their crystal, and they began to examine it and dicker.

Things were almost back to normal.

"Your Grace, the president of the Presov Mine Manager's Co-op requests the honor of an audience with you at your earliest convenience."

"Much better. Tell him I'll meet with him . . ." Vicky waved across the landing field at the log building where she'd first met with the locals.

"The Unified Guild Hall," Molly provided.

Vicky passed that location on and broke the commlink. She began to walk across the wet grass toward the guild hall.

Well, the dickering is over, and I know the value of a Grand Duchess today.

CHAPTER 26

"WHAT the hell do you think you're doing, young lady?" the president of the Mine Manager's Co-op roared.

Since he'd insisted the room be emptied of the locals before he entered, he couldn't be playing to any public.

Vicky wasn't either.

"Captain, I believe this man needs a lesson in court etiquette."

"Sergeant," the Marine company skipper said curtly.

The sergeant, who had been escorting the president as he approached the Grand Duchess, switched his rifle from port arms to a swift stroke to the gut.

Milton Adaman bent in half over his stomach. The security men behind him went for their guns. Marines in the room swiftly leveled theirs.

Rent-a-cops changed their reach from their weapons to the overhead.

"You can't negotiate with these people," the president got out through clenched teeth as he still struggled to raise his eyes from the deck.

"Strange," Vicky said. "I spent most of this morning doing just that."

"The trade delegation cut its deal with us. We bought all the cargo on the ship you brought with you . . ."

"You bought the fresh food and spare parts on nine of them. The tenth is different," Vicky snapped, cutting him off. "The *Doctor Zoot* is an independent trader. Its captain is doing his own marketing and trading."

Mr. Adaman managed to straighten up.

"What are your plans, Mr. President?" Vicky said. "If you cut the prices you pay the crystal miners and double the cost of their food, just how do you think they'll manage to pay for the food we just shipped in from St. Petersburg? You can't feed them famine biscuits."

"Pardon me, Your Grace," Vicky's computer said, "but we are in receipt this morning of a bid from the deputy vice president for administration of the co-op to buy all the famine rations."

Vicky arched an eyebrow. "When did that come in, computer?"

"At exactly 0800, Your Grace."

"The first order of business," Vicky said.

"It's business," the president bit out. He was still struggling to catch his breath.

"Business for you. Profits for you, but a lousy situation for the ranchers and farmers who sent me here. If they can't find a market for their fresh meats and produce, what good is this trade mission?"

"That's their problem," the president said.

"Yes, that is their problem," Vicky said softly, mulling it over as she spoke. "However, their problem just happens to be mine this morning. Tell me, Mr. President, based on the prices we worked out yesterday, how much food do you want delivered today?"

He said nothing to Vicky.

"I see," Vicky said. "Computer, talk to me more about the food order that just came in from the co-op."

"They are offering to sell all their crystal at the agreed-upon price. They want all the spare parts and gear, but only about a quarter of the fresh food. They want all of the famine biscuits. Communications passing between members of the trade delegation is such that I expect them to accept the offer."

"Computer, inform the trade delegates that the famine

rations are not for sale. They belong to me, and I'm not selling them."

"I have passed your statement along to them. They would like to meet with you."

"No doubt they would," Vicky said, then whirled on the commander. "I know this breaks your heart, Commander, but I'm leaving you in charge down here while I go topside. I suggest you keep the Marines and Rangers out and the riffraff away. Do anything you have to do to expedite trading between the independents and Captain Spee."

"Yes, Your Grace."

He trailed a bit behind as Vicky fast-walked for the door of the guild hall.

"And try not to start a war while I'm gone," Vicky added.

"Oh, but it would be such a short one," the commander answered through a grin that was all teeth.

"Yes. Most likely," Vicky agreed, "but what would I do with a crystal mine?"

"You couldn't do much worse than these thugs are."

"Ah yes," Vicky agreed. "Now, Commander, think peace and prosperity, or some such thoughts. I've got to get topside and open bargaining on a new front. You know, Frank, I think we got snookered last night."

"Looks like it," he said. "But the nice thing about having heavily armed Marines at your beck and call, Your Grace, is that you get to reopen negotiations just about anytime you want."

He turned back to the president.

"Sir, would you like to share a fine cup of tea with me?"

"Tea! Why would I want a cup of tea with you?"

"Because, sir, you will not be going anywhere very soon. Captain, would you please have these men disarmed and their commlinks removed."

"Sergeant, you heard the commander."

Vicky smiled as she left the building. The commander seemed to be developing just the kind of people skills she needed in a chief of staff.

CHAPTER 27

"SWEET Jesus! We've been taken for a bunch of green-horns!" Mr. Vickun shouted when Vicky laid out the latest turn of events.

"Thank God we didn't sign anything," observed his number two.

"We did shake hands on it after the third round of champagne," a third pointed out.

"I'm glad the second deputy assistant vice president for odds and ends, or whatever, jumped the gun this morning," the one woman in the delegation said. "When would we have heard about this otherwise?"

"I talked about heading out with the famine rations as soon as I could," Vicky said. "No doubt, the flunky was afraid the food for the peasants might get away. Then they'd have to give them a shot at the good stuff."

"Or starve them," Mr. Smith said. Somehow, the spy had inserted himself into the discussions. Vicky found herself wondering whether if he'd been there last night, all this could have been avoided. No question Mr. Smith had a corkscrew for a brain, but sometimes, when dealing with certain types, a cork-screw came in handy.

"Is their purchase request as small as I heard?" Vicky asked.

"Yep," said the man representing the ranchers. "They cut way back. I was looking at making a counteroffer. Lower. Much lower, to get more of this stuff off the ships. It's not like we can keep it in storage forever. If we take it back to St. Petersburg, it will wreck the market."

"Who's the industrial honcho here?" Vicky asked.

A young man raised his hand.

"Not one spring. Not one nut. Not one bolt drops out of orbit until this food issue is resolved, and resolved in our favor," Vicky said, putting some of that newfound Grand Duchess power behind her words.

"Do you think we can raise our prices for these parts and light machinery?" the young man asked. "Now that the glow has worn off the rosebud, I'm thinking we let them drive us way too low last night."

Maybe I don't have as much power as I thought.

"Am I the only one who thinks there are a lot of people looking back at last night's discussions and hunting about for fine print to twist to their advantage?" Mr. Smith asked.

"There is no written contract. There is no fine print for anyone to examine," Mr. Vickun pointed out.

"Yes, indeed. Yes, indeed," said Mr. Smith.

Which left Vicky wondering what exactly the spy meant by that.

What she did know was that she was about to take her entire team down to the guild hall and have a completely new game played out with all the bargaining chips out on the marred top of that wooden table.

CHAPTER 28

VICKY had read a few books on economics and the workings of the market. She'd read them after she ended up in the Navy. She had little else to do with her evenings after Admiral Krätz caught her in the paint locker the first time and sentenced her to a nunnery, or the Navy equivalent.

She was not unfamiliar with the concept of markets. Dad had been known to mention them from time to time. Usually it was in the context that "The damn market will do what I tell it to do."

The books in the *Fury*'s library introduced Vicky to an entirely different idea of a market. It was interesting, rational, clean . . . and maybe quaint.

What Vicky was seeing of the market today was down and dirty.

Once her commander got word of what Vicky intended, he enlisted the locals into rearranging the room. Now there were three tables in the shape of a U.

Vicky had the old table and her old chair. She imagined that was an honor.

The locals had knocked together two tables to form the legs of the U. In the case of the independent guild reps, their table was of rough, new wood complete with splinters. So were the benches they sat on.

The table the co-op managers sat at was knocked together from old slabs of wood, in some cases complete with visible rot. So were the benches. Every once in a while, a manager would tip a bench over, sending two or three of his cohort sprawling on the floor.

If there was any doubt at all about where the power lay, one only had to glance at the Marines and Rangers arrayed against the walls, their rifles at parade rest.

The rental cops had been sent packing. Both Marines and Rangers guarded a roadblock well down the road. Mortars and antitank guns covered it with clear intent. A co-op chopper had lifted off a couple of hours ago. It had landed immediately after being painted with a laser targeting device from the ground and threatened with laser fire from the cruisers in orbit.

Even to Vicky, the president looked cowed.

"You're telling us we have to buy your fresh meat and produce and we have to shell out enough wages to our employees so they can buy them from the company store." He didn't quite spit out the words.

"Now that we've had a chance to examine your system of company stores," Mr. Vickun said, "we're not at all happy to be selling to them. You don't pay your workers an hourly wage. Instead, you put a daily value on what they cut out of a crystal vein and bring to the surface. That daily variable is what you expect them to live on."

"It's our business model. It's worked fine for years," Mr. Adaman muttered as he worried a particularly rotten section of the wood with one finger.

"Back then, you weren't halving what you paid and doubling the prices at the store," a man at the new table shot back. He represented the mining workers union; he was missing an arm and part of his foot. He did odd jobs for the guilds in order to eat and served as union man when he could find miners to talk to aboveground in the evenings.

"I'm not talking to that layabout," Mr. Adaman shouted.

"But *we* are," Vicky said. "And we, for one, are finding those talks quite enlightening."

"He's a liar."

Vicky shook her head. "Let's cut the name-calling and stay focused, or this could take more time than I care to give you. For now, there are still ships full of foodstuffs, spare parts, and famine rations in orbit above our head. Come this time tomorrow, I intend to be boosting those ships for the jump out of this system. Children are starving to death. Those famine biscuits could save lives."

"We're offering to pay you for them," a junior member of the co-op said.

"They aren't for sale," Vicky said.

"Why not?"

Vicky turned to eye the senior member of her trade delegation. He answered for her.

"Because we won't sell them to you even if Her Grace weren't so adamant that we give them away."

"Why won't you sell them?" demanded Adaman. "We're offering you good crystal for them."

"Because we don't own them," Vicky shot back. "They were paid for by churches and collections in schools and I don't know what all. I came here to sell beef for crystal. You've got crystal. If you want to sell me your crystal, you can damn well buy the beef."

"We don't want your beef."

"You mean you don't want to pay your workers enough that they can afford to buy our beef," a rancher snapped.

"It's the same thing."

"No, gentlemen, it isn't," Vicky said. "Your crystal has only the value that we place on it. If you choose to slap a beggar's wage on the stuff at the mine head, that's your choice. But the crystal in your warehouse doesn't pay you a pfennig until a ship comes by to create some value for it. As much as I hate to say it, you are free to turn your workers into beggars, serfs, or peasants. But it's also our choice whether or not to do business with you."

Vicky paused and eyed the mining boss hard. "We choose not to."

"You've got to! You need our crystal!" Adaman almost screamed.

"Yes, St. Petersburg needs crystal. Computer, raise Captain Spee."

"Yes, Your Grace."

"How's your trading going?"

"Very well. I've acquired just about all the crystal they have at present. I've off-loaded a quarter of my cargo."

Vicky gave the startled Mr. Adaman a smile she hoped was pure venom before asking. "What do you plan to do with the rest, Captain?"

"Well, now that the independents have more of their rigs in running order, I suspect they'll be headed out to prospect for more crystal. I intend to leave behind a factor and supplies on consignment. I'm teaming up with a victualer here. As they bring in more, we'll sell more. I figure after I finish my trip back to St. Petersburg to service that market, I'll come back here, pick up another load, and swing around a half dozen planets. If they're still up and running, they'll need the crystal. We will move the trade to meet the market."

The skipper sounded quite chipper.

"That's the way it's supposed to work," Vicky said, eyeing the president.

He was frowning down at the plank again, but his fingers weren't worrying the wood. Now they were making circles.

"No. No you wouldn't!" The union rep was dragging himself up on his half foot.

"Won't what?" Vicky asked.

"It won't work the way it's supposed to work, Your Grace." The man was shouting now.

The managers from the co-op were looking uncomfortable. They couldn't seem to find anyplace to rest their gaze. The local independents were downright terrified.

"Why won't this work the way it's supposed to?" Vicky demanded of the union representative.

"Because the second your ships aren't up there with their lasers trained on him, he'll have his bullyboys over here. They'll drag every gram of food out of this village. Wreck every house if they have to. Kill anyone who gets in their way."

"Is that right?" Vicky demanded.

"Of course not," Adaman's words assured her, but his body language screamed "You bet I will."

Vicky shoved her chair back from the table.

"Captain Spee, are you tracking this?"

"Yes, ma'am. The local I'm dealing with has suddenly got very uninterested in our deal. So much so that he's running. The ones I've traded with are suddenly showing a whole lot less enthusiasm. Your Grace, could you leave some armed guards behind to protect my trading post?"

"I'll get back to you on that," she said, and turned to Mr. Vickun. "Can you make a bargain with anyone who would rewrite it the second you're out of town?"

The delegate scowled and shook his head. "They didn't wait for us to get out of town, Your Grace. They rewrote it between last night's champagne and this morning's first light. There's no telling what they'll do once we actually turn our back on them."

Vicky leaned back and eyed the co-op managers. "Yes, no telling," she said softly, then found a question coming to the fore that really puzzled her.

"What's in this for you?" she asked the manager.

Every one of the managers kept his head down. None would meet her gaze.

"What's in this for you?" she repeated. "Mr. Smith, help me out here. In two months, there's a ship coming with a tax collector and maybe a mortgage collector. What do they get by doubling the cost to their workers and halving their pay?"

"It seems to leave a lot of money somewhere on the table," the spy said. "It leaves me wondering where that money ends up. Whose pockets will it line?"

"If they don't pay the mortgage, they could lose the mines," Vicky said slowly. "If they don't pay the taxes, the Emperor would take the mines."

"Or the Imperial revenue collectors might sell the tax debt to a tax farmer," Mr. Smith pointed out. "If he paid the king his tax, he'd get to keep the crystal mine lock, stock, and barrel. I wonder which is the cheaper way of getting the shaft."

"Or who gets them either way?" Vicky said, ignoring the rude joke. Instead, her thoughts were going in so many directions, her brain felt like spaghetti.

"You'd have to look at the banks that hold the mortgage," Mr. Smith offered in answer to her question.

"Computer, can you access any information on the mortgage holder of these mines?"

"I am sorry, Your Grace, but that information is not available."

"Even from the Presov net?"

"Not on the public net."

"However, either way, the shareholders of these mining companies suffer irreplaceable loss, don't they?" Vicky said, eyeing the managers. Were a few of them starting to tremble?

"It would seem that way," the computer said.

"Let me review what we know," Vicky said. "There's a lot of potential money to be had by lining someone's pockets here and now at the mine operations."

"So it would seem," the spy said.

"And when the tax ship comes, these managers will, no doubt, have first-class accommodations to wherever they wish to go, taking their lined pockets with them."

"No. No! You got it all wrong," the president insisted.

"How?"

He said nothing.

"Computer, get me the JAG officer on the *Attacker*."

There were a lot of confused looks around all of the tables.

"Lieutenant Narvld here. How may I help you, Your Grace?"

Hmm. On one of Kris Longknife's tiny corvettes the JAG was a lieutenant. On a big Greenfeld heavy cruiser, the JAG officer was the same rank. That had to say something about the different level of respect for law that existed on Wardhaven and Greenfeld. Vicky put that aside for later.

"I need legal advice," she said, trying not to smile, "concerning the fiduciary responsibilities of corporate officials."

It was hard to tell if the look of shock and surprise on the president's face was greater than the sound of it from the lieutenant.

"I don't get many requests on that topic here aboard ship," the Navy officer said.

"I don't expect so," Vicky said. "However, if I were to level such charges against some officials here on Presov, where would they have to go to be adjudicated?"

"Presov is not a sovereign planet. It has no legal system in place. The nearest court would be a court-martial here on the ship."

"And if the Navy didn't want jurisdiction?" Vicky said.

"St. Petersburg is the nearest fully sovereign planet, Your Grace."

"So, we'd have to take them off to St. Petersburg and turn them over for trial there."

"That's what I'd suggest."

"No. No. No!" was coming from the president before the lieutenant rang off. "Forget our latest offer. We'll buy all your damn food. We'll sell you the crystal at only twenty-five percent above the last sale price. Tell us what you want, and you'll get it."

Vicky stood up. "Too late, gentlemen. Not to put too fine a point on it, but I don't believe a word you say. Any word you say. I also don't trust you to run these mines in a fashion that will make them prosper and continue to provide St. Petersburg with both crystal and a market. Captain, remove these men to the *Attacker*'s brig."

CHAPTER 29

═══

THERE were a lot of shouted threats that changed nothing as the Marines frog-marched the former managers of the mining co-op out of Vicky's presence. She spent the time drumming her fingers and eyeing the table that held the independent guild and union reps.

"Who runs the mines?" Vicky finally asked when things quieted down. "You, Molly? You, Gus? You, the guy missing an arm?"

The man stood. "If it pleases Your Grace, I'm Bartholomew O'Shannon. I was a fitter in the mining co-op before my accident. I can't run a mine."

"Your accident?" Vicky said. "I've heard management's perspective on that. You want to give me yours?"

"Yes, Your Grace. The gear they gave me to work with was shit and damn near killed me. They said I was screwing around and damaged mining property. They docked me my ticket home and said it didn't cover the damage. I got mad, and I did what I could to organize as much of a union as I could. It wasn't much."

"Who could run the mines who isn't on my list of people I'm dragging off to face a judge on St. Petersburg?"

Between the dozen of them still connected with the mines, they rattled off eight names. All were foremen at one level or another.

"Tell them I want to see them," Vicky said, then thought better of having people made to stand out at the mines. "Oh, do any of you see the need for the security police?"

"Most of the regular cops are decent types," O'Shannon said. "Well, as decent as they can be. Someone has to see that a miner on a bender gets a tank to sleep it off in. The mine-security men, now, there's a different breed for you. You're welcome to them if you can find any use for 'em."

"It would be interesting to see how they'd fare if we turned them loose to root hog or die," the commander said, showing a dark side Vicky liked.

"But they are comfortable applying violent solutions to their problems," Mr. Smith pointed out. "You might not be happy with the hogs they rooted with."

Vicky mulled that over and found it wise advice. "Captain, have a detail go into town and collect the brown shirts. Tell them they've got an all-expenses-paid trip to St. Petersburg, where they can look forward to new career opportunities in fast food."

"Captain, you might better grab them first before you enlighten them about their career prospects," the spy suggested.

"Sir?" from the Marine captain was directed more at Vicky than her secret-agent man.

She nodded. "Good idea. Collect them, then have one of your guys read them their fortunes."

"Will do, Your Grace," and the captain nodded toward a lieutenant, a big sergeant, and several even bigger trigger pullers.

Vicky found herself waiting for what would happen next. Fifteen minutes later, a rig arrived with four supervisors. They seemed unsure of why they were here. Vicky chose to observe silently as they talked quietly with some of the guild folks who knew what had happened thus far.

Vicky got lots of furtive glances and raised eyebrows. When the commander offered them coffee, they showed enthusiasm for it, leading Vicky to suspect even lower management had been on thin rations lately. The wait stretched for another ten minutes before a second rig arrived with four more supervisors. Vicky let them get their briefing from their own types and the local guild. She measured some surprise, some quiet consternation, but no shock.

Has the top management been so bad that their downfall is no surprise to their middle-management types?

Vicky called the new meeting to order.

"As you no doubt have learned, there are openings at the top of the Mine Managers' Co-op. The previous holders of those positions are now headed to St. Petersburg under guard to face charges of fiduciary malfeasance. It has been suggested to me that you eight might be the best people available to step into those shoes. Persuade me."

The six guys and two women eyed Vicky, then eyed each other. There was a bit of whispered table talk before one balding man whose clothes hung on him as if he'd recently lost a lot of weight stood up.

"I take it that the managers' unilateral decision to halve the price they paid for crystal at the mine head last shift change and immediately double the cost of food in the cafeteria and commissary didn't go over so great with you, Your Grace."

"When people shake my hands on an agreement, I really don't like the idea of their renegotiating everything about their agreement behind my back. Especially when I can't see where all the money is going. Do I make myself quite clear?"

"Completely, ma'am," the man said.

"I am here, representing an effort to reopen trade between St. Petersburg and Presov. Posnan is next on my to-do list. We've got food and spare parts. You've got crystal. I think we can all benefit and profit from trade between us. Some people, no longer present, seemed to think they could take most of the profits and leave little or no benefits for anyone else at the table. What's your take on this?"

"You'll excuse me, ma'am, but no one has so much as asked us what we liked and didn't like about matters here at the mines for quite some time. This is kind of a big lump of crystal to dump in our laps. How much time can you give us to come up with new management proposals?"

"You've got a good point." Vicky turned to the commander. "Please get me the CO of the Fifty-fourth Light Marines on the horn."

Then she turned to the head of St. Petersburg's trade delegation. "Mr. Vickun, how many of your traders would be willing to follow their goods down here and set up some sort of a trading post? They'd trade their stock for crystal as it became available. It might be more time-consuming, but after what we've seen in the last few hours, cutting out the middleman might not be so bad an idea."

"Most of them, I think," he said. "This has been an education for me, and I'm thinking your idea will look better and better to my associates the more we think about it. However, I'm also kind of thinking that we don't want to wake up to a knife in our hearts some morning or be beaten to a pulp as someone tries to run off with all our trade goods."

"I expect that you can count on the Navy to assure that the company thugs enjoy the hospitality of a cruiser's brigs or maybe the very empty hold of a freighter."

"In that case, it might work out best if we took the time pressure off this situation, Your Grace."

"Let's do that."

"Colonel Hilni here, Your Grace," came from Vicky's commlink.

"Colonel, I'm dirtside talking to a lot of new and interesting people. The trade delegation is undergoing a change of plans and looks much more interested in setting up a trading post than in selling everything today and sailing away with the fleet."

Vicky paused to watch people nod, not just among her own people but among the locals as well.

"That's a lot of expensive goods and gear they're planning on leaving," the colonel observed.

"And the rule of law has been a bit tattered of late in these parts," Vicky added for his consideration.

"Am I detecting a need for some security for the trading post?"

"It certainly seems that way to me. Hopefully, it will be temporary, just until the past panics and new opportunity for snatch and grab lose their attraction."

"I think that a company of Marines billeted in the warehouse district and doing a bit of friendly patrolling might be just what you're asking for, Your Grace."

"Please make it happen in the next twenty-four hours," Vicky said.

On the shuttle taking her back to her flagship, Vicky finally had a moment to catch her breath. She'd almost blown it, but she'd managed a pretty decent recovery.

She shook her head; growing up in the palace, she'd seen some pretty shoddy deals go down. She'd seen them but always as the cute kid in a new dress. She'd seen them from the sidelines and, more often than not, not really taken them for much.

Now, she was the Grand Duchess, and she was in the middle of it all. She couldn't afford to let herself sink back into the role of a sweet girl on the sidelines. This time, the powers that thought they had it all had screwed up on their timing. This time, she'd caught them.

She shouldn't count on the bad guys making mistakes and helping her out. Next time, she'd have her eyes open and be on the lookout for the rigged deck. After all, she was the Grand Duchess now. She was the power.

She was for now, assuming she didn't let it go to her head and join the bad guys.

Vicky shivered. Her stepmother was about as bad as they came. No way would she become like Stepmommy dearest.

Unless she had to to stay alive.

CHAPTER 30

THIRTY-SIX hours later, a somewhat reduced Fleet of Desperation jumped out of the Presov system. Vicky chose to leave four freighters and the *Frozen Christmas Goose* behind in orbit around Presov under the protection of the *Biter.* Captain Spee of the *Doctor Zoot* had completed his trading and was running for St. Petersburg with the first load of crystal. Aboard her under heavy guard were the former management of the mining co-op.

Now, Vicky led the four freighters with the most famine rations as well as more generic spare parts toward whatever awaited them at Poznan.

Because of the many unknowns ahead of them, the *Attacker* was cleared for action, and the *Crocodile* assault landing ship was combat loaded with the Thirty-fourth Armored Marine Battalion and St. Petersburg's own proud First Rangers.

Somewhere of late, the Grand Duchess Victoria had come to doubt that the universe was a nice place. The initial reports when they entered the Poznan system did nothing to change her mind.

"Silence. Dead silence," the captain observed as he stood

his bridge, the Grand Duchess at his elbow. "No radio traffic. No radiation at all."

"They had a fusion reactor for their space station," Vicky said. "I think they had one for their largest town."

"Yes, Your Grace," the captain agreed. "They *did*. Now those reactors are as cold as a tax collector's heart."

"Or my beloved stepmother's," Vicky added, not quite under her breath.

Beside her, the captain made an effort not to hear that. Vicky could almost hear his effort, it was such a strain.

Vicky turned to her brain trust. "Commander Boch, Mr. Smith, Doc Maggie, I'm open to any thoughts you may have."

For a long moment, they didn't have any.

Finally, Mr. Smith cleared his throat. "I can't say that there's much in the literature about a civilization going downhill, but there's been a lot of science fiction or horror speculation about just this sort of thing. Local power generators could provide a few centers where a level of technical comfort might survive while all those around them reverted to wood fires for cooking and warmth. What does an infrared scan show you about the heat budget of the planet?"

The captain turned to his team on sensors. There was a flurry of activity followed by the duty officer snapping to attention and reporting. "There do appear to be several low-order heat sources that match the fingerprint of internal-combustion power generators."

Mr. Smith smiled as the captain turned to him, and said, "Good call."

"Unfortunately for the generator owner, there's not much you can do with them once you run out of gas. Did Poznan have much of a hydrocarbon-refining base?"

There was a lot of looking around at each other on the bridge, but no one seemed to know where to get an answer to that question. There were disadvantages to the high level of confidentiality Greenfeld law and practices gave to just about all data.

"Computer," Vicky said.

"Yes, Your Grace."

"What can you tell me of Poznan's petrol, oil, lubricants, and natural-gas industry and reserves?"

"There are several proven fields that can be exploited, but the need has been low. One small refinery has been built to meet local needs."

"Please give the sensor team its location," Vicky said.

The sensor team began a frenzy of activity that ended just as quickly as it began.

Again the duty officer snapped to attention. "Captain, the refinery is not active."

"No surprise there," Vicky said. "Let's just hope we packed the spare parts needed to get it up and running again."

The planet kept its secrets as they made their final approach. The ships went into orbit close aboard the space station where Vicky and her earlier commander protector had gotten critical repairs made to the *Spaceadler*. Without those repairs, Vicky never would have made it to St. Petersburg.

No one was getting anything repaired at that space station now. In fact, no one was doing much of anything. It, like the planet below, was silent, cold, and dead in space.

A squad of Marines were sent to investigate. "It's cold inside, Colonel," their sergeant reported. "We got an atmosphere, but until someone takes off the chill and gets rid of all this water dripping off the ceiling and walls, you have to keep your suit on."

The captain of the *Attacker* sent an engineering team over with his three best chiefs. It took most of a day, but they got the reactor back up. That only started a cascade of challenges that required a major draw on the ship's supplies to get the life-support system back into working order.

While the Navy attacked problems on the space station, Marines concentrated on surveying the planet below. Signs of life were most easily identified at night. After dusk, the hills in the hinterland west of Kolna lit up with dull little fires. What was truly appalling was the frequency of such fires in the suburbs of Kolna, the one large city on the planet; there were even small cooking fires in some of the streets in the center of town. Well before midnight, all the fires had burned out, leaving the planet dark. Darker than any inhabited planet Vicky had ever seen from space.

They spent an entire day searching for any sign of traffic before they spotted a pickup truck making its way slowly into town. When they zoomed in, they found it pulled by two horses.

Its load was sacks of produce, but hardly enough to fill half the truck's bed. Unfortunately, their orbit carried them over the horizon before they confirmed its destination.

That night, they concentrated on Kolna, trying to find generators and any steady electric lights they might feed. Everyone couldn't be going to sleep that early.

They spotted nothing.

The planet kept its secrets even as the station became operational enough for the ships to dock and take on some semblance of gravity.

Inez Torrago bearded Vicky over dinner that evening. "Tomorrow morning, at 0530, the sun will come up on Kolna. I want my Rangers down there."

"Only if you'll take a company of tanks with you," Vicky said.

"What do I need with those awful things?" the Ranger company skipper asked, making a face at the thought.

"You want them because I don't want to win a firefight. I want to avoid one. I want to trade with people. Dead bodies don't have all that many needs they want to trade for. You understand me?"

"Are you coming with us?" Inez asked.

Vicky glanced around her table. Mr. Smith seemed suddenly totally involved in his salad. Commander Boch made a face. Doc Maggie said, "Can I take my medical bag down with me?"

"We have our own medics," the Ranger put in.

"You have medics, I'm a doctor. I'm also a doctor who hasn't had a patient in way too long. Certainly there are sick people down there in need of my help."

"And if you want peace done right," Vicky said, taking a moment to pat her lips with her linen napkin, "it's best you do it yourself. I'll go with you."

"Your Grace!" the commander said. The words were few, but the meaning was loaded.

"Don't 'Your Grace,' me," Vicky snapped. "I want to talk to the people down there. I can't do that from up here, not with everything closed down."

"As a matter of fact," Mr. Smith said, in a matter-of-fact way, "you can. All you need is this intrepid woman to take an operational commlink down there, and you can talk all you want to whomever she gives it to."

"Assuming she doesn't shoot them first," Vicky said.

"Assuming they don't shoot *at* me first," the Ranger captain said.

"And don't tell me," the commander said, jumping in, "that they won't shoot at a Grand Duchess. Who's to say they won't shoot first and check your credentials later?"

"I'll just have to be careful," Vicky said.

Commander Boch scowled as he rose from the table. "I'll go advise the Marines that they've got a drop mission tomorrow morning. Full kit and one Grand Duchess."

"And at least one load of starvation rations," Vicky put in.

"They can come down after we land all the Marines the *Crocodile* can land in one drop," the commander spat back.

"One load of rations," Vicky demanded, locking eyes with her commander.

"One load or what?" he snapped.

"No what," Vicky answered, her voice even enough to be measured against an iron-straight edge. "We came to help. It won't do any good to tell starving people that. We have to show them from the beginning."

The spy and the two warriors locked eyes with Vicky. She did not blink.

"Her Grace has a point," Mr. Smith finally drawled.

"Let's hope she doesn't get it between her shoulder blades," the commander said, but he went to do her bidding.

CHAPTER 31

N EXT morning, the Imperial Grand Duchess, Lieutenant Commander Victoria of Greenfeld strapped herself into her seat in the *Attacker*'s captain's gig. She was in full Marine battle armor. How it had come to pass that some Marine armorer had knocked together a set of combat gear that fit her hips, waist, and boobs, Vicky could only guess. However it happened, Vicky had a full set of battle rattle.

What she'd come to think of as her staff sat around her. The commander in undress blues and Mr. Smith in his usual black suit were across from her. Maggie, with her doctor's kit taking up the aft storage bin, was beside her. Kit and Kat, also in black, occupied the seats behind her. Two industrialists sat across from her diminutive assassins, holding tight to their computers with their long lists of available spare parts and assemblies.

Eight big Marines in full play clothes filled up the rest of the gig's seats.

Vicky's team was the last away from the *Attacker*, behind four longboats loaded with two platoons of light Marines. Eighteen LCIs and a half dozen LCTs had dropped from the *Crocodile* minutes ahead of them, loaded with companies of the Thirty-fourth Armored Marines and St. Petersburg's First Rangers.

The ride down was no more bumpy than any Vicky remembered. They began landing at Kolna's abandoned shuttleport at one-minute intervals.

No doubt, per the commander's orders, the captain's gig was last.

Initial reports said they'd seen nothing and no one. The real encouraging words were that no one had fired at them, either.

At least not yet.

Then the reports were modified.

As the Rangers secured the apron, a half dozen starving and ragged children wandered out to beg the troopers for food.

Vicky had no doubt that it was an almost automatic reaction for some of the Rangers to share out portions of their battle rations to the kids. No sooner had the children torn into the offered food than equally desperate adults showed themselves straggling forward from the hangars and terminal.

"We got about thirty pretty bad-looking folks on our front, split about evenly between adults and kids. They're begging for anything we can give them," came from Captain Inez Torrago. Her Rangers had claimed and gotten the right to the first half dozen landing craft.

"Do you have survival rations?" Vicky asked.

"After what you said last night, I had each of my troopers load out two bags of the things. There are more in crates in the back of the landers that we're about to off-load. I had to hold back a fire team from each platoon, so I had lift to carry them."

"You did good, Captain," Vicky answered. "Hopefully, those rations will come in much more handy than the four extra trigger pullers you left behind. Begin distribution of rations to individuals. Try not to let anyone walk off with a bag. We don't want to start riots or hoarding."

"Aye, aye, Your Grace, Ranger One One Six out."

Vicky smiled at the commander.

"You win this one," he said. "Want to bet me this is the easy part?"

"No bet," Vicky said.

The day would prove that a wise choice, but like most days, the full evil apportioned to it took a while to show up.

Then again, problems didn't take any time at all popping into view. The landing craft, tank, had hardly come to a complete halt when the unloading hit a snag. One tank and three infantry vehicles proved balky. They had to be pushed or towed out of the loading bays before the LCTs could continue with cycling back up to orbit for another load.

As the infantry trotted to take up their assigned positions, mechanics cursed and struggled to get recalcitrant machines to do man's bidding.

A few of them, that was. Most of the contraptions proved quite biddable. Five tanks and nine infantry carriers rolled off the landing craft and headed out to provide backup at the front gate or just formed a loose circle around Vicky to assure that her day only went so far sideways.

One infantry carrier turned out to have an air force. It launched a drone that circled the strip and gave them the first high-resolution picture of their surroundings.

"Those buildings over there," Vicky said, pointing at what she took for a warehouse district to the south of the runway. "Are there people in them?"

The drone quickly gave pictures in the affirmative. Worse, some of the kids who had finished their first meal since forever were straggling their way across the runway, no doubt to spread the word there was food available. They did this even as landing craft taxied clear of the unloading area to form a line to take off back to orbit.

Now there's an accident waiting to happen, Vicky thought with a scowl.

"Can somebody get some troops and food over to those warehouses?" Vicky called. The skipper of the Marine company shouted orders, and two of the working infantry vehicles came to life and rolled for the runway.

Only then did Vicky see that each tank and infantry rig had landed with a nifty one-axle trailer strapped to its back. Once it was pulled down and hitched to the rear, it allowed the armor to tow a squad of Rangers and/or food supplies.

Such a team of mechanized infantry and Rangers loaded with starvation rations drove for the warehouses. Another was soon dispatched to what looked like a housing complex to the east.

Things were going so well that Vicky hardly noticed it when her day went to hell.

"We got two guys bicycling into our perimeter," the Marine sergeant reported from their outpost on the road approach to the spaceport. "What do I do with them?"

"Find out what they want," Vicky said.

She spent the next couple of minutes talking with Inez and the Marine company skipper about sending some of the Marine tanks and infantry fighting vehicles up the road toward town with a load of famine biscuits to see how that would work.

While they talked that through, several irrepressible scarecrows stood at her elbow and thanked her profusely.

"It's been hell, here, ma'am, hell," mumbled one man in rags that failed to cover much of him. "No job. No food. My wife, she can make a soup of grass and bark. When we're lucky, we find a book. Their bindings make good eating," he told Vicky.

"Could I have another one of those cookies?" a child begged.

Vicky gave her a starvation biscuit from the bag she'd swung at her own belt before boarding the gig this morning. The girl began to eagerly gnaw on it. The kid was of that age where she was missing her two front teeth.

"You know, you could have your mommy cook that in a mush if you're having a hard time chewing it," Vicky said.

The kid turned away, as if afraid that someone might take the biscuit from her, and kept on gnawing.

The commander gave Vicky a raised eyebrow.

Yeah. How hard is it going to be to help these folks?

Vicky was still mulling that question over as the morning's first major problem cycled toward her on two rickety bikes.

Pedaling with little skill and even less coordination were two men. Both sported the machine pistols preferred by State Security, but neither wore the black uniform. That was no surprise considering what Vicky's dad had done to that previously-so-useful bunch of murderers.

These riders had their weapons slung over their shoulders and their hands on the handlebars. Since half the Marines in sight had them under loose cover, the pair were careful to keep their hands clear of their weapons and make no sudden movements.

They came to a halt a good hundred meters from Vicky. One was balding, the younger one had a mortal case of acne. The elder handed his bike off to the younger, fingered his weapon for a moment, then let it dangle free as he began stalking toward Vicky.

Several Marines moved quickly to block his way.

"Who's in charge here? They's got to talk to me. They's owes me money!" he demanded for all to hear. He looked around to take in the fleet of assault craft, now empty and slowly taxiing around to the other end of the runway for takeoff.

"Yous can't take off until yous payed me the landing fees, the ramp fees, the takeoff fees, and the air-traffic-control fees."

"Did you notice any air traffic control on the way down?" Vicky asked Commander Boch.

"Nary a word from the flight deck," he answered.

"Bring that clown over here before he gets himself killed," Vicky said.

"Who's yous?" he demanded as soon as he was presented to Vicky and her staff by two Marines, one of whom now had the fellow's machine pistol swinging at his belt. "Yous owes me money."

"I might ask who you are," Vicky shot right back.

"I'm the grand vicar for transportation, that's who's I am. I collect the duke's taxes for the use of his roads and runways. You's using them. Yous owes me."

"And you'll pass these fees right along to the duke," the commander said.

"Yeah. You's the guy in charge?" he said, clearly not impressed by Vicky. Maybe it was the armor. It couldn't be that she was a woman.

Yeah, right.

Either option, Vicky didn't much care for this dud.

"Big mistake, old man," Commander Boch said. "May I present you to Her Imperial Grace, the Grand Duchess Victoria of Greenfeld. Be careful, she's a real duchess."

The guy didn't seem all that impressed. "I thought she was dead, her stepmum and all."

"Nope," Boch said. "Not even close."

"Well, what's she doing out here?" he said, the look on his

face going from skepticism to belief quickly followed by consternation and open panic. He might have bolted, but the
Marines grabbed his elbow before he could turn to run.

"Now, about those fees you were yelling about?" Vicky said.

"Fees, oh, yes, fees. I begs your pardon ma'am, but I gots
to collect some fees. The duke, he heard the booms your jets
made, and he said to me, Jake, you go get the fees from thems
that are using my runways. I gots to get some money, ma'am."

"What say you that we go talk to your duke about these
landing fees," Commander Boch suggested.

"Really, you don't need to bother yourself. Yous just pays
me, and I'll go take it to the Duke and yous can go on about
your business."

"How much do *we* owe *you*?" Vicky asked, all cookies and
cream.

"Ah, let's see. Yous gots a dozen landers there."

Vicky counted two dozen, but she wasn't about to correct
the man's math.

"Landing, ramp fees. How long was yous parked?"

"An hour or so," Mr. Smith put in, a smile on his face that
was more evil than anything else.

"Oh, I gots to charge yous for the whole day. Can't charge by
the hour like some cheap hotel for streetwalkers, now can I?"

"Certainly not," Vicky said with deadly cheer.

"Takeoff. Air control while yous in our spaceport's air-
space."

"Yes, you have to pay those tower operators," Vicky said,
eyeing the tower and seeing only broken windows and no evidence of controllers. The guy followed her eyes to the tower. He
blanched but went on.

"Can't charge yous a pfennig less than sixty thousand marks."

"Hmm," Vicky said with a light frown. "That's a bit steep.
There any chance we might be able to trade you something
worth that much? Currency is in short supply."

"What do yous have in mind?" was all eager and no smarts.

"How about Marine field rations? Private, could you hand
me your lunch?"

"Ma'am, it's chicken loaf with lima beans," the Marine
said, clearly pained at the thought of anyone's actually eating

it. No doubt, he'd pissed someone off mightily to have it foisted off on him.

"I'll take it," the grand vicar said, grabbing for the offered meal box.

"How much of a discount do we get?" Vicky asked.

"Yous gives me sixty of these, and we'll call ourselves even."

"Sixty," Vicky said, eyeing the commander. "You drive a hard bargain. You going to carry all sixty of these on your bike there?"

The guy took in the measurements of the box, eyed his dilapidated bike and its twisted wire basket, and recognized the problem. "I'll have the kid carry the rest of 'em."

"What do you say that we carry them in to the duke?" Vicky said. "I'd like to meet the guy, and it would be a shame if you got jumped on the way back into town."

"Oh, no problem, yous don't have to do no nothing."

"We insist," Vicky said. "I'll even have you ride along with me."

"Ride?"

Vicky waved for an infantry fighting vehicle. Its motor roared to life in a cloud of smoke. Its tracks clattered as it turned in place toward Vicky.

The local looked like he'd seen a dragon.

Then three tanks fired up, and the ground rumbled as they, escorted by six infantry vehicles, ground their way toward the exit from the spaceport to the road into town.

The poor man collapsed in a dead swoon.

"Do you think he'll recover in time to tell us where we're going?" Vicky asked no one in particular.

"I can show you," a young woman said, stepping forward. Barefoot, she looked in need of a bath. Her scant clothing might have been alluring if all the skin it revealed wasn't bruised and encrusted with dried cuts and sores. Vicky could count every one of her ribs.

Mr. Smith, the only one who'd dropped today wearing civilian clothes, took off his coat and gallantly offered it to the young woman.

"You know where we can find this duke fellow?" Vicky asked.

"I know his place. I was there just last month, when his trusty Hussars dragged me in there to be raped for a couple of days."

Vicky's grin got tight and vicious. "I think you're just the one to introduce us to this bad actor."

CHAPTER 32

"**Y**OU ready to show us where this duke hangs out?" Vicky said as she joined the young woman in the last of the infantry vehicles heading into town.

It had taken longer for the operation to get underway than Vicky wanted, but the time had been put to good use. They'd managed a shower for the poor girl. Maggie had dressed most of her wounds and given her a shot for a roaring urinary infection. The lead shuttle down for the second drop of the day brought a new set of clothes.

"You're my guide. How you look reflects on me," Vicky had said.

Given a choice of something feminine and something military, the woman had chosen khakis.

She looked longingly at the Marine rifles around her. Vicky made a mental note to herself to keep the woman away from any loose weapons. Vicky might need her as a guide, but clearly, she was a bomb waiting to explode.

While the young woman looked much the better for the delay, the real reason for Vicky's needing four hours to clear the spaceport was the commander's insistence on getting more troops on the ground.

The second delivery had been a bit more widely spread.

Word was getting around that there was food at the spaceport, and people were struggling to make their way there. The drone take showed scarecrows barely able to put one foot in front of the other, some not even able to do that, only dragging themselves along as they crawled. Still, they struggled out of their hiding places and onto the road.

Vicky ordered a tank and two infantry rigs down the road and halfway into town to meet them. After some discussions with Maggie and Mr. Smith, rules were set.

"Only three biscuits per person. No more, no less," Vicky ordered on net. "Don't let anyone get away with more. Tell them this is only for today. There will be food tomorrow. We don't want anyone hoarding what they get today, and we don't want anyone getting killed for three lousy famine biscuits."

In most cases, people were gobbling down their three biscuits before they got five feet past the trooper issuing them. In a few cases, where someone wanted to take something home to a wife, child, sibling, or parent who couldn't make it to the rations stations, there had been violence as they made their way to wherever or whatever home was.

If the attack took place within sight of the Marines or Rangers, they shot, and they shot to kill.

If anyone got robbed of their rations, after a few of those incidents, it didn't happen in range of Marine or Ranger weapons.

"This place is sick," Maggie said, tears in her eyes, as the first story of a mother struggling home to her children having her head beaten in came over the net.

For the second drop, three of the shuttles didn't land at the spaceport. On the other side of town, among the rolling hills, there were three lakes. There was risk involved, but B Company, First Rangers dropped a lander in each bit of water. There, they set up camp and began handing out ration biscuits.

The sound of their landing and taking off was all the advertising anyone on that side of town needed.

Vicky eyed the drone take and found that small clumps of people who had already started the long struggle from the western hills quickly turned and struggled toward the sound of the shuttles.

There was no doubt in Vicky's mind that way too many of

those who drew food at the lakes would never have made it to the spaceport.

The drone made a pass over Kolna, both coming and going to the western hills. Each time Vicky studied the pictures. When it made the return flight, the young woman, washed, medicated, and alert, was at her elbow.

"There," she said, stabbing at the screen, "that's where that son of a bitch has set himself up. It used to be Government House. He calls it his palace. His Hussars are barracked in the bank next door. They have horses. They're stabled next door in what was the City Library."

"That's a shame," Maggie said.

"Not all that much of one," the woman said, her voice dull, devoid of feeling. "The books that we didn't eat, we burned. It got awfully cold last winter."

"We've got a lot to learn about this place," Vicky muttered to herself.

"Let's make sure we don't get killed learning any lesson, shall we," the commander said. "You remember what happened to the curious cat?"

"The same thing that happened to my brother when he thought he knew all there was to know," Vicky said.

One stupid, dead Peterwald in this generation was enough. Somehow, she'd have to learn and survive the learning.

CHAPTER 33

THE drive into town was an education.

In so many ways, Kolna looked like any other medium to large city in the Empire. The streets were wide, not so much to improve traffic flow but to make it harder to barricade them during a rebellion.

Daddy had told Vicky that once. He hadn't mentioned the reduced street traffic in his Empire. Vicky had had to go into Longknife territory to discover what a traffic jam was. No, the idea of people rebelling and blocking the streets or dodging down narrow streets to elude the law was something seared into her dad's mind.

Thus, the streets were wide. Vicky could have paraded all four of her tanks side by side down Prosperity Boulevard and still had room to spare had she so desired.

Instead, her tank commander kept his monsters spread out in a loose column, with infantry vehicles providing wide escort. The Rangers rolled along in trailers behind the tanks and infantry rigs, their eyes roving and alert.

For now, their rifles were down, but that could change in a second.

Vicky stood. She'd ordered the left half of her infantry

fighting vehicle's roof unlocked and swung up and over so she could stand and see what there was to see.

Beside her, the commander was having a fit. He whispered something to Kit and Kat, and they now stood close to Vicky, but they were hardly tall enough to get in the way of any bullet fired her way from a rooftop.

At the moment, the commander and Mr. Smith were engaged in a scowling contest. No doubt the commander felt the spy should be standing at Vicky's shoulder, ready to block a shot with his body.

Equally, there was no doubt that Mr. Smith had reviewed his contract and found no obligation to do so, either in the large print or the fine print.

Vicky ignored her staff and concentrated on what there was to see and what it might tell her.

Here and there, a handful of people would come out of hiding to see what the noise was about. At least one Ranger in each trailer was tasked with tossing ration biscuits their way.

Their reaction puzzled Vicky. She would have expected them to cheer or shout their thanks. They did scramble for the bars in the dusty streets, but they did it in silence.

"Do you think they're afraid to draw a crowd?" Vicky muttered half to herself.

"They could be," Maggie offered in answer. "They don't want to attract someone who might snatch the food out of their mouths. Worse, they don't know if there's more food where that came from, so they're keeping quiet about it."

"No share and share alike, huh?" Vicky said.

"No. Sad to say, when you're this close to starving to death, there's not much room for kindness."

Vicky nodded but said no more. She knew that her doctor friend had struggled on St. Petersburg, even to the point of having to pay to be smuggled into Sevastopol.

Did it get that bad while you were on the run?

Vicky kept the question to herself.

Most of the buildings showed peeling paint but were otherwise untouched, as if their owners had gone off for a holiday and would be back soon. Most doors were closed. Possibly locked.

There were exceptions.

On one corner, a store had been ransacked. Its door had

been smashed in and torn off the hinges. The large, plate-glass windows were broken and the inside hastily pillaged. Glass lay scattered in the street.

The tank treads made quick work of the glass. It shattered to powder under the first treads' passage and made not a sound as the others came up behind.

Other buildings had burned. There was no way to tell if the fire was the final stage of looting or just an accident that happened when desolate wooden fires got out of hand in buildings never intended for live flame.

The thought that sent shivers up Vicky's spine was the math that kept spinning around and around in her head. Normally, a city had thousands of people per hectare. Hundreds lived on every street.

Few blocks had more than a dozen people struggling out to scramble for the food Vicky's troopers tossed as they passed.

"Where *are* all the people?" Vicky whispered.

No one offered a reply.

That question hung in the air as their armored column rumbled into Government Square. The square might once have been a lovely place. If anything, it looked even more the worse for wear than the rest of the city.

In front of Vicky, an entire city block had been devoted to a park. In the center of what might have once been a fountain stood a large bronze statue. No doubt, it was her grandfather or great-grandfather, depending on who had been alive and arranged financing for this planet's start-up.

There had been trees in the park once; the stumps showed where they'd been cut down. Dozens of lovely horses struggled to graze on what might once have been grass but was now more dirt and weeds.

Facing the square directly across from where Vicky's task force was entering stood an impressive four-story-tall white house. Or it had been. It once had a wooden fence in front of it, but most of it had gone into someone's fire. Sections of iron fence had been dug into the lawn. They would have given a stronger "keep out or else" signal if most of them weren't slumped over at odd angles.

To either flank of the big white house were the bank and

library Vicky had been told about. The bank had snipers hurriedly taking up stations on its roof and upper windows.

The bank was the source of some of the iron-fence sections that now festooned the approaches to the white house. They'd been taken from a half-meter-high stone wall.

Between the low stone wall and the intermittent iron fence, Vicky figured any defense might slow her Marines and Rangers for all of fifteen seconds.

She could almost hear her troopers licking their chops at the thought of taking down these duds with guns.

To Vicky's right was the library, now a stable. Several grooms were hurrying horses indoors. The horses were lovely animals. Dad loved horses. He could talk for an hour about Friesians, Lipizzaners, and Clydesdales.

That was what Vicky saw. A dozen horses of various proud breeds were being trotted away by running grooms eager to get them out of the line of fire. More were racing to get the ones still grazing in the park.

"Where did he get those lovely horses?" Vicky muttered.

"He stole them," her young woman guide said. She'd been huddled in the forward corner of the track, almost curled up upon herself. Now she stood up and took in all there was to see.

"He killed the owners. Several of their daughters are locked up in the white house."

Vicky was taking a distinct dislike to this guy.

"Do they eat any of the horses?" Mr. Smith asked.

"Oh God, no," the young guide almost gasped. "He says he'll eat the grooms before anyone touches those horses."

"That's horrible," Doc Maggie said.

Vicky made a face. "I think my dad would agree with his priorities."

The commander raised an eyebrow but said nothing.

"It kind of explains how you got into this mess," Mr. Smith said.

The commander elbowed him.

"Don't look at me that way," the itinerant spy said. "I didn't swear allegiance to the nutcase."

"Enough!" Vicky snapped.

While her staff discussed culinary preferences, the skipper

of the Marine armor had been going about his business. Two tanks left formation and rumbled their way over to face the bank that had been turned into a guardhouse. One took a hard right and stopped in front of the tall, once-gleaming office building that still had its glass windows intact. So much so that the only weapons on display from it were being brandished by snipers on the roof.

No doubt the tank's long gun could not be brought to bear against them, but the machine gun atop the turret could be and was.

The two infantry tracks that escorted that tank had their guns aimed high as well.

The third tank and a pair of infantry rigs laid track for the library, now a stable.

On all three buildings, the snipers and gunners who had been so boldly waving or aiming weapons a moment before took the measure of this newly arrived force . . . and blanched.

Quite a few must have suddenly felt the urge to hit the head, because in only a few seconds, there was a lot less hardware aimed down.

Vicky raised her commlink. "Captain, could you take this rig around to the front door of the white house? Oh, and lose the tank."

There was a pause, then, "Are you sure about the tank, Your Grace?"

"I'm sure."

There was another pregnant pause. Vicky heard the commander's commlink buzz.

"Don't answer that, Commander."

He didn't.

Finally, the Marine company commander said, "If you say so, Your Grace."

"I think I did."

Vicky's and one other infantry track rolled over to the front of the white house. They stopped, facing a portico that covered the entrance to the building.

For a long moment, nothing happened.

CHAPTER 34

A short man in a most curious uniform strutted out onto the balcony. Following him were four men with machine pistols. They looked at the tanks, and they looked at their guns. Then they didn't look all that confident.

They might be smart, Vicky wondered about the other man.

He seemed quite taken with himself. His uniform was a crimson coat with gold dripping from just about every place the wild male military mind had ever thought to hang it on a uniform. His hat was also red, a fore and aft affair trimmed with even more gold. The britches were cream, ending high with white silk stockings.

"Where did that outfit come from?" the commander muttered under his breath.

"The last production by the Kolna City Opera Company was of *Aida*," Vicky's native guide provided.

Vicky raised an eyebrow at that. "Suddenly you know a lot more than I was led to expect."

"That's because you didn't expect much from a starving woman in rags."

"I admit to the fault."

"Cindy, I was told you'd run away," the man in the absurd uniform said.

"I guess I didn't run far enough," Vicky's guide answered back.

"You'll always be welcome at my dinner table," hinted at a lot more than just his table.

"I doubt I'd get past the guards."

"You really should have left the dinner knife for the steak and not my throat."

"I only regret I missed my mark."

"So who have you brought to visit me this time?"

Vicky wondered how long this talk would take to get around to her. Most conversation usually did bend toward her when she was present.

"I have the honor of introducing you to Her Imperial Grace, the Grand Duchess Victoria of Greenfeld, and her army," Cindy said.

"Aren't you going to introduce me?"

"Your Grace, this is Herbert, one of my rapists."

"Cindy, you wound me to the heart," Herbert said, clasping a fist to his chest where, depending on whose point of view was taken, he might or might not have one.

"Dhimitër," Herbert continued, "have the courtesy to introduce me to this fine example of a grand lady."

A large man, both tall and rotund, stepped onto the balcony. His head was shaved, and his mustache and goatee were well manicured. He was dressed in a long black robe, also likely of operatic origin though Vicky couldn't place the character who had worn it and didn't feel the need to ask. He sported a silver chain of office, which, Vicky strongly suspected, was costume plastic.

"I have the honor of making known to you," he said in a full-throated baritone, "His Majesty, the Grand Duke Hieronomo, Lord of All You Survey and Law of the Land." And he bowed to him with a flourish.

A sycophant of such high caliber Vicky hadn't seen since leaving the Imperial court. How could her dad or beloved stepmom have missed hiring this guy?

"Herbert, last month you were just a duke," Cindy said dryly.

"But I hadn't *known* you," he answered with a smirk.

Vicky hadn't thought when she hired her native guide—no Cindy—that her history with the local potentate or warlord or whatever would become a distraction from getting her mission done.

Then, on reflection, what exactly was her mission now that she had to consider this new twist? An opera buff with ducal delusions and a predilection for raping his dinner guests?

Time to think on your feet, girl.

"I'm glad to make your acquaintance, Herbert," Vicky said. "I'm here on a mission of mercy. We've brought famine rations for distribution to the starving populations."

"Why that's a fine idea. Why don't we discuss it over dinner? I am told that I set an outstanding table. We can work out the fine points of how my army will distribute this food you're donating to famine relief."

The commander threw Vicky a cautionary eye. Caution that Vicky did not need.

Cindy had only horror in her eyes as she turned to Vicky.

"I have a better idea. No doubt the chefs aboard my battleship in orbit can set an even finer table. Why don't *you* come up to the station? We have it operational, and we can discuss the food distribution with all the technical support we might need. It would be a shame for something to fall through the cracks, now wouldn't it?"

The man laughed. It was not a nice one.

"So you don't want to eat my food any more than I want to eat yours."

"Not one bit," Vicky said with a shake of her head.

"Well, my army will do the distribution of the food," he said, cold stone in his voice.

"My Marines and Rangers have already begun the distribution and are having no problems."

"On Poznan, my army controls everything. Your strangers could find themselves in trouble and not even know what happened before it hits them."

"Please don't say that too loud. My Imperial Marines might take umbrage at such an idea," Vicky said, buffing her fingernails.

"You have been warned. This audience is over," Herbert said with a theatrical flair, and turned to exit, stage right, off his balcony.

For a long moment, there was silence.

"You going to level the building?" Mr. Smith asked. For once, the look in the commander's eyes showed full support for something from the spy.

"No doubt, my dad would," Vicky said, considering her options and their outcome.

"No doubt," the commander agreed.

"What do you say we don't and say we did," Maggie said.

Everyone gave Maggie a puzzled look. Even Vicky.

"Let's not do it, but later we can say we did," the doctor said by way of explanation.

"Why would we do that?" the commander demanded.

The doctor just looked at Vicky.

"We are not going to do it today. And it doesn't matter what we say tomorrow. Captain," Vicky said to the company commander of the heavy Marines.

"Your Grace?"

"Conduct an orderly withdrawal."

"Ma'am, we have some grooms from the stables asking if we have any food they might have. They've heard we're handing out stuff to eat."

"Have the Rangers make the usual three-biscuit issue."

"And if they want some for their horses?"

"Please," Cindy said. "They've got my horse and my sister's pony."

"If we feed horses, will there be enough for the people?" Maggie made haste to point out.

Vicky took a deep breath and turned to Cindy. "If you had three starvation biscuits, would you share them with your horse?"

"In a switch of her tail."

"Issue six bars to the grooms. Three to any other goon that asks us for food. Withdraw the tanks to the next block and hold for ten minutes while half the tracks distribute food."

"What do I do with the other infantry rigs?" the captain asked.

"Spread them out, two to a street, and distribute rations."

"And if we take fire?"

"Return it heavy," Vicky said, tasting the blood in her voice.

"Aye, aye, Your Grace," said the captain, then, a moment

later added, "Ah, Your Grace, what do you want me to do with that fellow who was demanding landing fees?"

"Is he still with us?" the commander asked.

"We tied him up and tossed him in a track. He's been amazingly quiet ever since, but now I've got a sergeant asking what we want to do with him."

"Drop him off here," Mr. Smith said. "He can explain this all to Mr. Duke, grand or otherwise."

"He's begging not to be left here. He wants to come with us."

"Suddenly he knows which side his bread is buttered on," the commander said. "He picked his side long ago. Toss him."

"He's done us no great wrong," Maggie said. "You dump him here, and he's a dead man for sure."

Vicky eyed the spy. He shrugged most expressively and made to wash his hands of the matter.

"Captain, dump the guy two blocks from here. He can decide where he goes from there," Vicky said.

The withdrawal from Government Square was slow and orderly. It was also peaceful.

Vicky glanced back at the white house as they motored from the square. Behind one window, she might have caught the glint of gold.

She swore she heard the gnashing of teeth.

CHAPTER 35

"LET'S talk about what just happened," Vicky said on the drive back to the spaceport.

"Why didn't you blow that ass away?" the commander demanded.

"Why don't you hold that thought," Vicky said. "Cindy, why didn't you tell me what you knew about Herbert?"

"You didn't ask. You didn't even ask me my name," the young woman almost but didn't quite spit at Vicky. Clearly, she was holding on to her temper with her fingernails.

And ready to take those claws to anyone who gave her an excuse.

"Yes, you and I were on different tracks, and I didn't ask you for more information than you were willing to give, even your name," Vicky conceded, softly. "You looked in pretty bad shape, and maybe I wanted to get that trip downtown that you were offering before you fell apart. My mistake. Now, could you please tell me what I need to know about this planet? How did you get into this mess?"

"I don't know," the young woman said, settling back into her previous seat in the corner of the infantry fighting vehicle.

Vicky sat down across from her.

The staff quickly arranged themselves in the fighting compartment. The commander and Mr. Smith were to Vicky's left. Maggie sat next to Cindy with a comforting and mothering arm over the young woman's shoulder. Kit and Kat took seats on either side of the compartment, quiet, but ready to spring into action.

Cindy began to cry. Maggie and the commander produced handkerchiefs. The young woman took Maggie's.

"What went wrong on Poznan?" the woman repeated, then looked across at Vicky. "I don't imagine you'd be very happy if I said the Emperor screwed up."

"But I'd understand," Vicky said with a shrug. "My father's midlife crisis is causing the Empire a whole lot of trouble."

"But you want to know how it went wrong on this particular planet, right?"

"Kind of. I'm here with food and some spare parts. If I knew what happened, I might be able to help you make it better."

"Can anyone make it better? My dad tried, and look what it got him?"

"Where is your dad?" Maggie asked, saving Vicky from asking a question that might well bring on Cindy's final collapse.

"Safe, I think. He has a hunting lodge well back in the hills. There's a lake he liked to fish. When he gave up trying to make things better, he and Mom took off for there with my little sister."

"Why didn't you go?" Vicky asked.

"I have a girlfriend. I wanted to take her with me up-country. I tried to save her and got caught myself," Cindy said, ruefully.

"How did things go bad?" Mr. Smith repeated. "For the entire planet?"

Cindy sighed. "Dad said he wasn't getting spare parts. He needed motors to keep the oil wells pumping. Pumps to keep the pipelines moving the crude to the refinery. In the refinery, he needed just about everything. Then everything quit coming. First, his credit dried up with the big, offworld banks. After that, he couldn't get the parts he needed shipped in. He managed for a while, using the local fab mill, even machine shops and craftsmen, but they needed materials to make the parts that were broke.

"Before long, special materials quit coming from off planet, and we only mine pretty basic stuff here, and not a lot of it. Besides, our fabricators were pretty basic. You want a ton of rebar to reinforce a concrete wall or pipe, we can make that. You want the specialty steel that goes into a twelve-inch pump, and you can sing for it. More and more often, Dad couldn't make all the pieces come together. Dad knew a lot of guys who were having it just as bad as him, or worse."

The woman looked at Vicky, all the despair of her world in her eyes. "Then Herbert started meddling. I don't know how he got his hands on the guns left behind when the State Security went down. The Marines who came here to close down State Security took the men away. Dad said they were supposed to take the guns with them, but when they marched off with the survivors from State Security, the ones that didn't die in the firefights, the guns weren't accounted for."

"That happened a lot," Vicky said. "That was not one of my dad's better ideas."

"Well, suddenly Herbert had guns and confiscated trucks. Suddenly, he's telling everyone that *he* will provide security. He didn't say from what," Cindy said with a bitter laugh.

"One lunchtime, my father was holding a meeting with the fab managers and craft shops, trying to figure out who gets what little we had left, and Herbert crashed in with all his gun-toting goons and announces that my dad and all the rest of them were plotting against Posnan. He hauled them all off to jail, and there they sat until they posted bail."

"What happened when they did?" Vicky asked.

"He let them go, but that bail bond took about every spare mark Dad had. For most of the other people, it was the same. Now they were trying to run things with little or no cash. Can you imagine how that went?"

"Downhill in a hurry," Vicky said.

"Yes. And then Herbert took it in his head that the farmers were holding back on us city folks. Not bringing their crop to market. So him and his bullyboys go charging out to the country and started ransacking farms. The poor farmers were having enough trouble keeping their equipment up and running. I know. My grandparents worked a farm out in the country, and they were telling us every weekend what wasn't working anymore. So now the farmers have goons turning everything upside down looking for hoarded crops and making a wreck of everything."

"And when Herbert collected the food?" Vicky asked.

"He paid in a script the bank was now issuing. Script that quickly wasn't worth the paper it was printed on," Cindy answered.

"Nothing got better. Everything just went from bad to worse. Herbert was on Dad's neck to increase gas production when all it could do was drop lower each week. He accused Dad of sabotaging the economy, called him an enemy of the state."

"Is that when he ran?" the commander asked.

"Not exactly. Dad could see it coming. He ran when he still could. No, that was what Herbert told me after he caught me. Before he took me to his, you know, bed."

"That was when you tried to kill him?" Vicky said.

"It took me a few days to work up the courage or give up all hope. I don't know which."

"Could you get me to your dad?" Vicky asked.

"Why?" came out with terror in her eyes.

"I, too, need to get the oil refinery working, and the power and water and sewage going. I've got Navy techs in orbit and four ships with spare parts and small machinery as well as famine rations. We can just feed people, or we can help people get the wheels of civilization working again."

For a moment, there was hope in Cindy's eyes. Then it went out like a snuffed candle.

"Herbert won't like that," she said.

"I really don't care what Herbert does or doesn't like," Vicky said, and was surprised at the steel in her voice as she said it. "I let him live today. What happens to him tomorrow depends on what happens tomorrow."

"He raped me," she spat.

"Then he should face a judge for that crime," Vicky said.

"There are no judges on Poznan."

"Not today, but in the backcountry with your dad, I'm sure there are a few."

"Yes, there are."

"Let's make Kolna a city that has courts again," Vicky said.

Maybe the tight little smile that creased Cindy's lips had a glimmer of hope in it . . . with a huge twist of vengeance. "Yes, let's."

CHAPTER 36

"I guess that answers my questions," Commander Boch said, as Maggie took their exhausted native guide off to find a place to rest.

"Not really," Vicky said, eyeing the new tanks coming off the landers. This was the third drop of the day, and these were the last of the company of eighteen tanks the Thirty-fourth Armored Marines had.

Vicky smiled. *I have eighteen tanks. Herbert doesn't have any.*

That loadout included two carriers with four drones. Vicky ordered one drone tasked with keeping an eye on Government House along with its other duties. Then, her commander at her elbow, she went looking for the headquarters of her rump brigade.

The Imperial Marine lieutenant colonel was, of course, senior to the St. Petersburg Rangers light colonel. For now, that was not a problem.

Someday, it might well become one.

The problem they all faced today, however, had their full attention: the correlation of space to available forces. Even if they borrowed the two companies left on the *Attacker* from the Fifty-fourth Light Marines, Vicky still had less than two thousand troops to both feed people and keep an eye on the operatic drama queen's armed thugs.

"I don't want them to get a free swing at either a Marine or a Ranger," Vicky said.

"The best way to do that is to withdraw all our troops to an armed cantonment," the Marine light colonel said.

"But the starving people can't all walk in here," Vicky said. "We also don't want a huge refugee camp on our doorstep. That would provide too many opportunities for mischief. No, we need to deliver the food to where the people are hunkered down and starving."

Both colonels stared at the generated overhead map of the city projected on the table in front of them.

"He's ready for a machine-gun fight," the heavy Marine battalion commander said. "We have armor. He's going to have a hard time going up against that."

"Unless he has antitank rockets or even Molotov cocktails," the Ranger said with maybe a hint of a grin. "This is an urban area. They'd be tossing those on you from rooftops as you drove by."

"That assumes two things. Rockets and gas," Vicky put in before her two battalion commanders invited each other out for a duel to prove their particular point of pride. "He got his hands on State Security machine pistols. Anyone ever see a State Security goon with an antitank rocket?"

Heads shook around the table.

"And we just finished debriefing the daughter of the local refinery owner," Vicky pointed out. "They haven't produced a new drop of gas for several months. We spotted heat and light sources when we jumped into the system. Have we spotted any power generators since we went into orbit?"

"Are you thinking they ran out of gas as we were on approach?" the Ranger colonel asked.

"It's not an impossibility," Vicky said.

"Tonight should tell us," the Marine colonel said. "As you requested, we will have a drone watching the opposition's so-called palace all night."

"That would tell us a lot about his forces," the Ranger colonel said. "My Captain Torrago has an idea she wants to float.

We don't want to sit on our hands too long. That would surrender the initiative to him. Not a good idea."

The Ranger captain had been hanging back against the wall of the headquarters. Now she stepped forward. "Those horses we saw today. Assuming opera buff is out of gas, they are his only transportation. If we can take them away from him, he'd have to walk his machine pistols to our tank fight."

She nodded toward the heavy battalion commander as she paused to let that idea sink in. "And if we empty the stable of horses, he has no use for stable grooms. They become just another batch of mouths to feed, and he doesn't look like the type to keep mouths around that aren't earning their keep."

"So if he fires his grooms," Vicky said, "we get a whole lot of hungry mouths at our gate that know a whole lot about what's going on around the palace."

Vicky smiled at the Ranger. "What do you have in mind, Inez?"

"A horse raid," the Ranger said through a grin that knew no bounds.

Much later, as Inez left to organize her little raid, Vicky stepped outside the command post. The commander followed.

"You want to ask your question now, Commander?"

"I thought you might have answered it earlier, but the more I listen to you, the more puzzled I get. Before, I wanted to know why you didn't kill that idiot when he pranced out on his so-called palace balcony. I know your father, our Emperor, would have."

"Like he killed General Boyng and all his State Security organization."

"Yes."

"And that has turned out so well for us," Vicky observed in full sarcasm.

"There is that. So, why did you let him live? It's the kind of thing Kris Longknife might have done."

"And you're wondering whether, if you stop a bullet headed for me, are you saving a Peterwald or a Longknife?" Vicky smiled as she said that.

"You've hung around that woman a lot over the last couple of years," the commander said. "Are you going to start applying Longknife solutions to Greenfeld problems?"

"Do you think Longknife solutions might solve some of our Greenfeld problems?"

"Frankly, no, Your Grace."

"It took guts to say that. I like that in the guy who's hanging at my elbow."

"We aren't discussing me, Your Grace. We're discussing where you're rummaging for solutions to our Empire's problems."

"I'm not rummaging in a Longknife bag," Vicky said. "I don't know where I'm going to pull my next solution out of, but Kris Longknife is a Longknife, and they do things their way. I'm a Peterwald. We do things differently. Some of my father, the Emperor's, latest solutions have brought more problems with them than the ones they were intended to solve."

"You've noticed that?"

"And so have you, and so has just about everyone I've talked to in the last forever since I got out of the palace one step ahead of an assassin. No. Correction. The assassins caught me. I was just lucky enough to beat them to the kill before they did me the honor."

Vicky looked across the spaceport. The sky above Kolna was clear of smoke. There were a few clouds. As the sun sank lower, they became tinged with pink, silver, and gold.

When Vicky spoke again, it was as much to herself as to the commander. "Herbert lives because I chose to let him live. My father would have killed him where he stood. That was a good enough reason for me to let him live through his little drama. Now, I let him live until I come up with a nice way to separate him from his thugs and their guns."

She glanced at the commander. He was listening intently. "If I'd blown Herbert away, his thugs would have grabbed their guns and run. Then I'd be stuck sending Marines and Rangers out to chase each of them down. For now, I've got them where I want them. Tomorrow and tomorrow and tomorrow will each offer me ways to solve my problems. I'm patient. I can wait and see."

Vicky shrugged. "And I can always send in the tanks tomorrow."

Darkness fell quickly, and no lights broke it, not even around the camp. The recently-thrown-up temporary buildings were all blacked out. Where troops moved, they did so with night vision.

Because Vicky was looking for them, she could just barely make out four trucks across the field. They had come down with the last drop of the day. Electric, they rolled silently out the gate, showing no lights to the night.

Vicky turned to the commander.

"Shall we go back inside and watch the fun?"

"It beats any other show in this burg."

━━━

CHAPTER 37

THE plan for the raid had been hastily thrown together, building on what was already in place.

After Vicky returned from the so-called palace, she'd dispatched reinforced platoon-sized task forces around town to distribute food. Each consisted of two tanks and a couple of squads of Marines and Rangers. The Marines rode in four of their armored infantry fighting vehicles and the Rangers rode along in the trailers with the food. Three of these food-distribution points were about evenly spaced along the south side of town.

The drone coverage showed that they'd drawn starving people like magnets. People from inside hobbled out to them. People from farther out of town staggered in toward them.

With any luck, that would leave the farthest road around Kolna devoid of eyes. The sensor team on the *Attacker* continued to report no activity on the electronic spectrum. If it wasn't Marine or Ranger, it didn't squeak.

Opera Buff would have no warning before Rangers were all over him, eating his lunch.

The Rangers on the four electric trucks moved quickly and

quietly around the outskirts of Kolna. They arrived at their jumping-off point well before midnight. There, they paused.

The plan was for them not to start into town until 0100, and to be at their target at 0230, the deadest time of night.

Inez changed her plan.

Instead of standing around in their trucks for an hour or more where they might be spotted and the wrong word carried in to town, the Rangers moved off immediately. The Rangers began silently to infiltrate up the main south boulevard that led into the center of the city. Scouts afoot checked block by block, found it clear, and advanced the trucks. This went on for the next two hours. Without surprises, they covered the five miles into the city center.

"We've got the library in sight," Inez reported. "No lights visible from our side."

"We see no lights from the overhead," the Ranger battalion commander responded.

Vicky stood looking over his shoulder. The feed showed the four buildings around the central park. There were plenty of thermal images of human bodies in bed where they belonged. There were a few not in bed, but those on guard duty hadn't moved for at least the past hour.

"Stay sound asleep," Vicky whispered. Then frowned. "Do we have any images of the horses?"

"Sorry, Your Grace, but the horses are on the ground floor, and someone made that library out of local rock. We can't get past the second floor on it."

Vicky considered that and found it acceptable. "How's the bank?"

"It's locally made concrete. Maybe the contractor went a bit light on the stuff. We're getting down into the basement with no trouble."

Vicky shook her head, ruefully. Was graft and corruption the national pastime in her father and grandfather's worlds?

That was something to think about when she had a lot more time on her hands.

The drone take drew back. Now Vicky could see the Rangers making their way stealthily up to the library.

"We've found a guard," Inez reported. "He was sound asleep.

We've bound and gagged him. It might have been better for him if we slit his throat."

"When you get the horses running, you might want to cut him loose to run, too," Vicky said.

"Copy that," Inez said. "We'll see what we can do, Your Grace, but no promises."

"Your troops come first," Vicky said.

At her elbow, the commander covered his lips with his hands. "You going soft?" he whispered.

"They are all my subjects," Vicky answered softly. "Somewhere I read that royalty is supposed to concern themselves with the lives of their people."

"You didn't get that in a book from the palace," Commander Boch said.

"No. It was from a battleship's library, I think."

On-screen, the horse raid was fully underway. Vicky had watched enough movies to have some idea of how this was supposed to go. This one wasn't at all like the ones she'd watched.

In the stories, the raiders were usually Native Americans, but Vicky had checked, and all tribes where horses were available tended to do a bit of horse stealing. *Take that Kris Longknife*. The movies showed the raiders coming in shouting, scare the horses and stampede them, usually through the local village—dumb tactic—and off into the dark.

On-screen, the Rangers led strings of horses quietly out of the library and toward their trucks. Some were even saddled.

"Did Inez recruit her Rangers from the ranchers?" Vicky asked. She was pretty sure of the answer, but she asked anyway.

The Ranger colonel had to tap his database before he answered. "Yes, Your Grace, they were all ranch hands or rancher's kids. We call Captain Torrago's company the Rough Riders."

"To their face or behind their backs?" the commander asked.

"Either way. They're quite proud of their horse skills."

On the drone take, they were putting those skills to good use. Now mounted, they led strings of horses up the road and out of town. A last squad of troopers jogged from the stable; a civilian ran with them. They made it to the last truck and piled in.

Together with trucks rolling slowly and horses trotting alongside, the raid headed south into the night. Behind, it left a whole lot of gun-toting thugs none the worse, and none at all aware that they'd just had a major coup pulled off on them.

"Don't you love it when a plan comes together?" the Ranger colonel crowed.

"Well done," Vicky said. "We'll have to strike a medal to commemorate the great, silent Kolna Horse Raid when we get back."

The Marine colonel had been quietly watching as matters developed. He didn't seem as happy at the success of his light infantry comrades as Vicky might have expected.

"There'll be hell to pay tomorrow morning at my food out-posts when those thugs see what's missing."

"But they'll need most of the morning to walk out to them," the Ranger said, still quite happy with the night's work.

"But the food outposts are the closest," Vicky said, "and it will be their hide that Herbert tries to take it out of. The Heavy Marines get the horse-raiding medal, too. Put everyone on alert come daylight, but it may take a while for anything to develop. Keep the drones on them."

"Aye, aye, Your Grace," came from two colonels. They saluted.

Vicky returned the salute. She couldn't remember another time that anyone had given her a salute quite as meaningful as those two officers had.

As an ensign, she'd saluted her seniors and returned enlisted salutes. It was required. It was Navy.

But this one. This one had a whole lot of difference in it.

She relished the afterglow as she walked slowly to her quarters.

CHAPTER 38

VICKY'S quarters were spartan at best and still smelled of the plastic bag it had exploded from. There was a small sitting area with a tiny bathroom off to the right. Sharing that wall was an even smaller room with one bunk bed. Mr. Smith and the commander took it.

To the left was a somewhat larger room with two bunk beds. Vicky took one of the lower ones. Maggie took the other lower. Kit and Kat pulled the thin mattresses off the top bunks and put them where they wanted them.

Kit lay down blocking the door. Kat was closer to Vicky's bed but solidly between her and the door.

"I may need to go to the bathroom during the night," Maggie said.

Kit pulled a knife from her boot and laid it under her pillow, beside an automatic. "Be careful waking me," she simply said.

"Me too," Kat added, arranging her own arsenal.

"I may piss my bed," Maggie concluded with a wry look at the two.

"Crew," Vicky said, "let the lady through if she needs to go."

Both of them got angelic smiles on their face as they said in disturbing unison. "Yes, Your Grace."

"I'll get a can or something from the mess hall tomorrow," Maggie muttered.

Despite the portents, or maybe because of them, the night passed quietly but quickly.

Dawn was barely showing in the small windows of the quarters, high up near the roof, when there was a knock at Vicky's door.

"Who is it?" she called.

"Commander Boch. I have a runner from the command post. They think you might want to see what's developing."

"This early?"

"No rest for the wicked," he said through the door. "Or is it no rest *from* the wicked."

Kit and Kat were out of Vicky's way, rolling their bedrolls aside as she headed for the door. As she opened it, she said, "I think we qualify for both."

The commander blocked her way.

"Lieutenant Commander, you are not properly dressed for the morning," he said.

Vicky turned to find Kit and Kat holding out her body armor, top and bottom.

With a scowl, Vicky returned to her room and let her minions tie, clip, and otherwise strap her into her armor. "I've got to get some of that spidersilk underall armor that Kris Longknife has," she growled, as Maggie handed her a helmet.

"It's only available in Longknife territory," Commander Boch reminded her.

"Order some."

"There is the currency exchange problem at the moment."

"Damn it, ask King Ray, or what's-his-name, Grampa Trouble, to loan me a pair."

"I'll see what I can do about getting a begging-bowl request out through channels."

"Damn the channels, write it up from me personally. Kris loves her Gramma Trouble. Send the letter to her."

Dressed to her subjects' pleasure, Vicky made it to the command center just as the sun was coming up. The place was abuzz.

During the night, apparently, a couple of more LCT drops had come in. The command center was now four temporary buildings, blown up and linked together through large arch-ways in the middle of each long wall.

The colonels occupied one of the center modules. They looked like they had gotten little sleep; two rumpled cots in the back of the room attested that they'd gotten some.

The Ranger launched into a briefing as Vicky came through the door. "At 0400, someone missed the horses. Quite a few of the grooms were roused out of bed, lined up against the wall, and shot."

The large screen that now held central place beside the passageway into the next building came to life. Vicky watched as the slaughter of the grooms took place.

"Damn," was all she could say.

"Not all the grooms got popped," the Marine colonel said. "Notice the ones racing out the back."

"How'd they miss the honor?" Mr. Smith asked.

"No one really cared," the commander said, darkly, and pointed at the balcony of the palace. There, a lone figure stood, watching the murder.

"Herbert," Vicky spat.

"It was like that when the Navy and Marines were ordered to land and uproot State Security," the commander said. "We had overseers assigned. We called them political commissars . . . never to their face. They wanted to see people lined up against the walls and shot. They didn't care what rank they had or how important they were. So long as they were in the black uniform, they wanted to see them shot."

Vicky shook her head, incredulously.

"Later, we found out that most of our commissars were drawn from the managers of Empress Bowlingame's brother's banks. They were good at keeping count. Not so good at knowing the value of what they counted."

The room met the commander's observations with silence.

The Marine colonel was the one who finally spoke. "Whatever went down, we'll know soon enough. Most of the grooms who got away won't quit running until they reach one of our outposts. As soon as they calm down enough to talk, you'll know."

"We knew we had a bad actor. Cindy told us," Vicky said. "Now we've seen it for ourselves. I take it that you have your outposts on alert."

"We've doubled the guard, but we're letting the remainder sleep. Today looks to be a tough one."

"No doubt," Vicky agreed. "So, where and when do you think he'll come at us?"

The two colonels took a moment to think before saying anything. Vicky liked that.

The Marine colonel went first. "We have tanks. Herbert doesn't. He'll want to get his hands on one of ours."

Vicky turned to the Ranger, expecting disagreement.

"I agree. Tanks are big and sexy. We have them. He doesn't. He'll want one." Then he shrugged. "Or at least want bragging rights that he destroyed one."

"So he'll hit the food-distribution outposts around the edge of town," Vicky said. "You think he'll leave the Rangers alone out by the lakes in the hills?"

"The Rangers are probably safe up there," the Marine said. "It's a long walk to get to them. My troops, however, one way or another, he will hit." The last words held the finality of death and taxes.

"Is there anything we can do to make them more secure?" Vicky asked.

"Short of pulling them back to the spaceport and locking down the approaches? No, Your Grace."

"And since I insist we distribute food to the starving, that is not an option," Vicky said with a firm but cheery smile.

The Marine just nodded. "No use bringing all that nice heavy metal here if all we do is just sit on our diddies and shine it. We'll keep the drones up. With any luck, they'll see what he's developing. We can react a whole lot faster than he can act."

He broke into a wide grin and glanced at the Ranger. "After all, all he can do is walk."

They both enjoyed a laugh at that.

Two hours later, it didn't seem quite so funny.

CHAPTER 39

⸻

VICKY was headed for the newly installed mess hall when the horses came in. The trucks hung back in the rear, but the Rough Riders were solidly in control as the herd of horses, stallions to the right, mares to the left, trotted onto the grass between the hangars and the terminal.

"Computer, get me Inez," Vicky ordered.

"Good morning, Your Grace," came quickly in a cheerful voice. Vicky would bet her entire fortune that some company commander was mounted up and riding herd herself.

"What took you so long? I figured you to be here before daylight."

"We dared not push these horses too hard, Your Grace. They're in pretty bad shape. We were all surprised at how little hay and fodder there was in the stable we got them out of. We had to get them out of town to some decent grazing and let them eat a bit. Also, they needed water. There wasn't a lot of water in the stable where they had them."

"Herbert couldn't feed or water them, but he wasn't about to let them out of his sight," Vicky concluded.

"A really sicko, that man. How long you going to let him keep breathing our air, Your Grace?"

"I haven't quite decided, but he's got two solid strikes against him and working on the third."

"It can't happen soon enough, as far as I'm concerned."

"As much as I hate to tell you, you need to find some local horse people to turn those critters over to. You got a war to win, Captain."

"What'd you say, Your Grace? I think my mount just stepped on my commlink."

Vicky closed the link with a smile.

It was nice to do some good.

And it got nicer.

A familiar figure in khaki was just coming out of the mess hall. Vicky was glad that Cindy was drawing mess privileges along with the clothing. She, like everyone on this planet, needed to put on a few pounds.

Then there was a shriek of joy that must have carried across the entire spaceport.

Cindy took off running toward the herd. Somehow, she managed to run and whistle at the same time.

Among the horses, a roan mare pricked up its ears at the whistle and took off at a delighted gambol for the running girl. They collided, with the girl hugging the horse, and, so help me God, the horse hugging the girl right back.

Cindy had filched an apple from the mess. No doubt she intended to have an apple in her pocket until she was reunited with her horse. Now she produced it.

The apple vanished in three bites.

The roan was followed closely by a cute Shetland pony. It nuzzled into the pair and got a hug, too, but no apple.

That was remedied quickly as a Marine came forward. Exactly why he had taken an apple from the mess wasn't clear, but it quickly earned him the undying gratitude of a pony and a girl.

Vicky tried to pass the happy tableau by, but Cindy caught sight of her.

"You rescued the horses," she cried. She was crying, and if it was possible, so was her horse.

"We rescued them. There's a military advantage to putting Herbert afoot."

"But you rescued them. They look like they were starving."

"I'm told by the officer who led the rescue that they were. We'll see to feeding them. Do you know anyone who might help?"

Stupid question.

"Can I? I've seen a few people I used to ride with. I can find them. We'll all help."

"You do that," Vicky said. "That will allow us to concentrate our Rangers on keeping Herbert in line."

"Forget keeping him in line," Cindy snapped. "Just kill him,"

"We shall see what we shall see," Vicky said, not quite willing to commit herself to a funeral.

Cindy threw herself on her horse bareback and rode over to join the Ranger wranglers. Inez waved at Cindy. It was clear the local woman had just been hired for a job she'd do for free.

"That went nicely," the commander said. "I'm hungry."

"Let's eat," Vicky answered. "There's no telling when someone will ruin our day."

"Or us ruin theirs," the commander answered with way too much cheer for such dark words.

CHAPTER 40

VICKY was finishing up a breakfast that, while it might not be up to Navy standards, was warm and filling.

Enjoying a final cup of coffee, she allowed herself to people watch. In this case, it was Marine and Ranger watching. They were intent, attacking their meal with a rapid, methodical approach that they, no doubt, would take to their jobs.

There were a few Navy types thrown in who took to their meals with less intensity than the ground pounders, possibly because the food wasn't up to shipboard standards. Lost in the sea of green, gray, and blue was the rare civilian in newly issued khaki shirt and pants.

Apparently, Cindy wasn't the only civilian to earn mess privileges. While this handful appeared a bit dazed, they attacked their food with the ferocity of feral dogs.

More civilians would need to be signed on for jobs. There was no reason for a Marine or Ranger to stack their weapons so they could hand out ration biscuits. If they didn't have enough volunteers who could be trusted, more would have to be found.

God knows, there seem to be no other employment opportunities for locals other than gun-toting thug to a delusional duke.

Vicky had to wonder what kind of pay a minion of the duke collected.

The thought brought a sour taste to her mouth.

A runner appeared at her elbow, saluted, and said, "The colonel sends his respects and requests your presence in the command center, Your Grace."

Vicky returned his salute with one hand as she put down her coffee cup with the other. She did a quick assessment of the metadata behind the runner's comments.

So it seemed a Grand Duchess outranked colonels now. She chose her reply with that in mind.

"Very well. Give the colonel my compliments and tell him I will be there shortly."

The runner was off for the door even as Vicky got to her feet.

"It appears that Herbert is making his move," she told the commander.

He nodded agreement as he stood.

Vicky would have loved to race the runner to see who could get to the colonels first. However, Admiral Krätz had taught her that a Navy officer never runs, and a Grand Duchess never even thinks of it.

However, a Grand Duchess can do a very fast walk.

As Vicky got to the door, she noticed that a lot of Marines and Rangers were rising from only half-eaten meals and heading out right behind her.

She wasn't the only one who knew the clock was already ticking for his or her day.

As Vicky walked briskly across the apron toward the command center, she found herself musing.

I'm not supposed to run because it will scare people. But my runner can run and, as best I can see, scare everybody just as much. Someone has missed something.

This was, no doubt, something she'd have to think about in her plentiful spare time.

If she ever had any.

She entered the command center and quickly joined the two colonels staring at their battle board.

"By the way, gentlemen, I do have a commlink. You might have used it to get me here quicker."

"We don't know for sure that Herbert doesn't have a capacity to eavesdrop," the Marine colonel said. "Sending runners is not only traditional, but a good way to avoid giving out intel we don't want to part with."

It's also a good way to get you some time without me looking over your shoulders, Vicky read between the lines but did not say.

"What do we have?" she asked.

"You are looking at what appears to be Herbert's first move of the day. Shortly after you left for breakfast, his henchmen started rousing civilians from wherever they were hunkered down in town. We had a drone make a low pass. It got fired at but not hit. It appears that his thugs are yelling that there's food down the road and rousting people out to go get chow."

"What if they don't believe there is any food or don't want to leave?" Vicky asked.

"They're shooting people."

Vicky winced. This Herbert was a really bad actor and getting worse.

"Which of our food outposts are they headed for?" she asked.

"All three, it appears," the Marine answered.

Vicky spent a moment watching the visual on the screen. Several groups of people with the rough constituency of mobs were moving down nearly a dozen streets, possibly more. Even people on the roads over from the ones with gunmen prodding mobs along with promises and threats were struggling to make their way along as quickly as they could toward the suburbs.

"I guess there was a reason people yesterday kept quiet about the food or only went to tell their family or friends. Now that a lot more know, there are a lot more of them moving," the Ranger colonel said.

"When they hit us, it's going to be a god-awful mess," the Marine colonel pointed out. "Lots of desperate people going for too few food-issue lines."

"Can your computer give you an estimate of how many people we have coming at us versus the amount of food we have?" Vicky asked.

"We're running that count, Your Grace. So far, we've got ten times as much food as we need to feed them."

"So panic is more of a problem than food."

"It seems that way, Your Grace."

"So, let's get the food out there for everyone."

"Huh?" came from both colonels.

"This isn't a fight, at least not yet. People want food. We want to give it to them. Right?"

"Yes, Your Grace," from the Marine had a lot of question in it.

"Let's get the food out front. Let the people have the food. Are there any civilians who can issue the famine ration biscuits?"

"I don't know, Your Grace, we haven't looked into that," the Marine said.

Vicky made a face. "We will, right after we survive this little trick. Colonels, get your troops to load out the boxes of famine biscuits. Think of the boxes as mines. Put food mines out in front of your positions. I'll bet you those boxes do a better job of stopping these people than actual mines would."

The Ranger colonel looked intrigued. The Marine colonel looked like he had a bad attack of gas.

"Your Grace, how are we going to limit them to three biscuits a day?" he demanded as mildly as a colonel could of his Grand Duchess.

"We aren't. Not now. Not today. Not this morning. So some folks get a few extra rations. It doesn't matter. What we want to do is stop the mob before it hits your defensive line."

The Ranger colonel was almost laughing. "Strip the punks of their human shields. Have the starving multitude drop out of their charge to grab for food. That sounds like a plan to me," and he began talking on his commlink.

The colonel commanding the heavy Marines still seemed nonplussed. "Okay, your Rangers get the food out front, and I'll have my heavies cover you."

There had been some grumbling about mixing the two commands. Now, Vicky was glad she had both of them and their different mind-sets out there on the line. Between the two, they just might make this assault on her food stations peter out before it got anywhere.

While the two of them concentrated on their present problem, Vicky brought up an unused battle board and tasked it for the problem of the western hills.

Most people had headed west when they discovered the normal food-production chain had fallen apart. There were farms all around Kolna. Vicky had had those farms photographed and the resulting pictures run through the appropriate agricultural analysis.

There were crops in the ground, but they weren't going to be bountiful.

There were also a lot of guards protecting those crops.

Hungry townspeople had been shunted farther to the west, to the hills where there might be something to eat.

Analysis of that land showed it picked clean. Vicky had asked to have the analysis applied to the land farther to the west. There wasn't a lot to eat there, either. You had to go quite a bit farther west, up into the higher foothills, before you saw much decent eating.

There were people there. No doubt the strong and hearty, or the ones who were smart enough to leave first. Now, their smarts might be the death of them.

Vicky measured the distance from where the edible land was and where her three food stations had been set up by the Rangers. A lot of people would die trying to walk back over the desolate land if Vicky didn't establish food stations along the way.

As soon as the matter with Herbert was settled, Vicky would have to concentrate on those western hills.

Oh, right, Cindy's dad was somewhere out to the west. What could Vicky do to get him back here? She needed him and likely a lot of the people who could make Kolna work again.

"We're starting to have problems," the Ranger colonel advised Vicky.

The Grand Duchess of Greenfeld turned from her future problems to study the trouble coming at her today.

CHAPTER 41

VICKY watched as the starving masses struggled from the streets into the open spaces where the Marines and Rangers had set up the food-distribution depots.

In all three cases, the Marines had literally circled the wagons. The four infantry tracks were in a rough semicircle with their wagons. The two tanks completed the laager by closing the rear. All six of the heavy metal brutes had turrets, and all six were trained on the streets that would disgorge the mobs coming out from the city.

Scattered out well in front of the armor were pairs of Rangers with open bags and boxes of famine rations stacked in front of them.

It would be a shame if the Rangers had to resort to using the bags as cover to shoot from.

That wasn't in today's plan.

The middle food-distribution site was the first one to have a crowd arrive.

When the starving masses saw the food bags, those who could began hurrying for them. That was when the Rangers shoved over the bags, spilling their contents on the ground in front of them.

With a shout, the mob broke into a run.

The Rangers backpedaled for the next batch of piled food. They took up positions behind them and watched as the first line of food bags and boxes was engulfed in a mass of starving, desperate people.

It was not pretty. People were knocked over in the rush. Others stumbled over them. Many went down and were trampled. And that was before anyone got to the food.

Then it got worse as people grabbed for biscuits and struggled to get away with what they had. Others fought with them, kicking and scratching to steal one little morsel.

But not everyone lost all presence of mind. There were those who saw the next line and went wide of the first bags and the fight raging around them.

Maybe they were slower. Maybe they were weaker than the others. Either way, they walked wide of the mess and approached the Rangers more cautiously.

The bags and boxes at the second line were spread out wider. They invited people to form lines, and folks seemed to naturally do just that.

An officer with a bullhorn now got into the act.

"We have plenty of food for everyone. Come up and take three ration biscuits for today. We'll be here tomorrow. Get three and step aside for the people behind you. If you share and share alike, it will go a whole lot better than that first mess."

People formed lines. Rangers picked someone to stand over each bag or box, handing out the food. It wasn't always the first person there, but it was always an early arrival.

Vicky watched as the food-distribution process settled down to something a whole lot smoother at the second line than at the first. Even some of the duke's thugs stood patiently in line, their guns slung over their shoulders. They eyed the Rangers and their rifles at the ready, and kept their eyes down. Like docile children, they took their rations and followed the others in turning away to wolf down their food.

"That can't be what Herbert wanted?" Vicky said, giving voice to her puzzlement, puzzlement likely shared by the silent colonels beside her.

"And I had two rescue task forces already rolling," the Marine colonel said. He moved the battle board to show where two teams of similar size, two tanks and four tracks, were rolling up a side road from the spaceport to the threatened food outposts.

"Is there anything happening on our front?" Vicky asked.

"We haven't spotted anything," the Ranger colonel said. "There are people moving toward us, but nothing like the situation to the south."

"Show me," Vicky said.

They zoomed in on the road leading into town. There were a lot of walkers. The news about the food out here had to be catching on.

"We'll need to get the food out for them," the Ranger said.

"These seem better dressed than most I've seen," Vicky said. She had the picture zoom in more. It got too grainy, so she pulled out some. Still, despite the growing heat of the day, quite a few of the people walking down the road had coats on, or blankets thrown over their shoulders.

"Did I just see a gun?" Vicky asked.

"Backtrack, computer, scan the picture for weapons."

"I identify three people carrying weapons. I identify five people carrying weapons. I identify twelve people carrying weapons," the computer reported.

"Terminate search program," the Ranger colonel growled.

"We have a problem here," Vicky said.

CHAPTER 42

THE two colonels got busy ordering their troops into positions to defend the spaceport. The two detachments of reinforcements were ordered back. While they talked into their commlinks, Vicky examined where the best place was for her.

She left the command center.

"Where are *you* going?" the commander demanded.

"Where I can see what's happening and maybe make something better happen," Vicky said, looking around the port.

"If I ordered you to stay inside?" the commander only half asked.

"I'd ignore you."

Outside, Vicky picked up Kit and Kat.

"She's gone crazy," the commander muttered to them.

The two assassins just fell in step behind Vicky.

Around Vicky, it was chaos. Or so it would appear to any observant civilian. Vicky had no problem picking the order out of the disorder.

The Marines were standing to, getting their tanks and tracks ready for action. The Rangers were joining them, but several climbed around on the trailers hitched to the tanks, checking the food loads.

The Marines were eager to cut loose of the trailers. The Rangers, for their part, were pointing to the farther end of the port and demanding a lift. From the looks of it, *their* orders were to deploy another food-based minefield.

For a moment, Vicky considered charging back inside and knocking two colonels' heads together, but the problem between laagering the tanks up and getting food out was resolved as she watched.

While the tanks got rid of their trailers and headed off to firing positions, several of the tracks took off with their loads of food for the parking lot in front of the terminal.

Vicky was about to follow them when Cindy rode up on a lovely black Friesian.

"What happened to your horse?" Vicky cried.

"It needs more time to graze. Blacky, here, was Herbert's favorite mount. He's well fed. What's going on?"

"Gunmen are headed toward us on the town road. There are hungry people mixed in, but there are a whole lot of gunmen."

"And if they start shooting, a lot of innocent bystanders will die," Cindy finished for Vicky.

"You got it in one," Vicky said.

"You're putting food out for the people," Cindy said, standing tall in the saddle to watch what was happening down the road.

"We hope to get the people to stop at the food. With any luck, they'll take to the ground when the shooting starts."

"What if a lot of people took food down the road and stopped all of them before they got here?"

"The gunmen wouldn't be happy."

"The gunmen are hungry, too," Cindy said. "You feed them, and they might be open to anything you suggested."

"Something like that happened at the other food sites this morning, but there were a lot more hungry people and a lot fewer gunmen there."

"Well, let's see what we can do about getting more people out there among the gunmen."

"Is that wise?" the Grand Duchess asked.

"Do you want a bloodbath?"

"No," Vicky said. "I don't think it would be good for Kolna or its people."

"Me neither. Let me see what I can do," and Cindy kicked her horse to a trot.

Vicky found herself the observer as two quite different plans came together.

Three, if she admitted that the Rangers and Marines were playing different games themselves.

The Marine tanks formed a line in the space between the terminal and the hangars. Several tanks disappeared around the front of both sets of buildings to extend that line. The infantry tracks delivered the trailers and Rangers to several rough lines across the parking lot. Once those were unhitched, the tracks and their infantry withdrew to join the tanks in a deadly defensive array.

The Rangers off-loaded as much of the food as they could while keeping a wary eye on the approaching crowds out on the roads. Unloading sped up as more and more civilians from the apartment buildings to the north of the spaceport and the warehouses to the east joined the Rangers around the trailers.

Off in front of the apartment buildings, more people milled about in a growing mob. Cindy circled them on her Friesian like a sheepdog out to win a blue ribbon. That crowd grew both as more joined them from the apartments, but also as some who'd been helping the Rangers unload took off, lugging food sacks to the waiting crowd.

Some ration biscuits got gobbled up, but more than Vicky expected stayed ready in hands.

At the moment of Cindy's choosing, the mob headed down the road, following their mounted guide like an army behind its equestrian general.

Vicky asked Kat to rustle her up a mount of her own, but her minion instead came back with the two colonels. Between the six of them, it was somehow settled that Vicky would not get closer to today's hot business than the line of tanks.

"What are we now, a democracy?" Vicky spat, but it did her no good. She was outvoted five to one. The two colonels and the commander were no surprise. But Kat and Kit going against her!

Voting should be banned.

But what Vicky did see, even if it was from a distance, was quite a show.

The two mobs met about a thousand meters forward of the

farthest line of ration bags. The mobs collided, mingled, and became one milling collection of humanity.

It quickly boiled into one mob that didn't seem all that interested in going anywhere.

This confused state of affairs lasted for a couple of minutes as food was passed around from those who had it to those who desperately wanted it.

While that went on, nothing much happened.

Then the guns came out.

Someone fired a long burst in the air. Then someone fired a second long burst, and there were screams of agony.

Like a wave, the mob went to ground, leaving several standing. Many of them were waving guns. Several more were bringing them out. There was a lot of shouting, then more bursts of automatic weapons fire.

Try as Vicky might, she could not make out what they were firing at.

However, from among the Rangers came a ragged staccato of single shots. The Marine tracks added short bursts from their chain guns.

The results downrange were immediate and horrible. Where the Rangers' snipers picked off a gunner, the man dropped. When a Marine 20mm cannon took out a gunman, blood and body parts flew in every direction.

In a blink, no one was left standing.

"Somebody out there can learn," the commander said from beside Vicky.

"Get me a bullhorn," Vicky ordered.

"Your Grace," the commander said. "You'll make yourself a target."

But Kit had already scrambled up on the tank next to them and was returning with a mic. "Key it that way and several tanks will make sure everyone hears what you say," the tiny killer told her.

Vicky took the mic and keyed it. "This is Your Grand Duchess, Victoria of Greenfeld. I've brought food for all of you. I promise you that there will be jobs for all of you soon. To those of you with guns, I can offer you a job distributing food, but only if you turn in your guns immediately. This is an offer for this morning only. You can turn in your guns, get a job with us, or you can hold on to them—and risk having to fight my Marines and Rangers later."

Vicky paused to let her words sink into minds that were dense in the best of times and likely starving in the moment at hand.

"You've seen what they can do. Now the choice is yours. Make it quickly."

In front of Vicky, men were scrambling to their feet, rifles or machine pistols held over their heads. Quickly they made their way through the still-prone crowd to the first line of Rangers.

The Rangers checked the guns, safetied most of them, and sent them farther up the line to Marines who were now ready to take the weapons in return for sacks of biscuits.

Cindy, who'd never dismounted through the entire affair, now trotted up to Vicky.

"You know, of course, that a lot of women will want to press charges against those pieces of crap for what they've done."

"I know," Vicky said.

"So, what are you going to do?" the young woman challenged her Grand Duchess.

"I'm going to keep them close where I can see them, for the moment," Vicky said, "while you get your father and his friends back in here from the hills. I'm sure he can find us some judges eager to restore the rule of law. Then, I assume, matters will take their natural course."

"Good," Cindy said, uttering one word that Vicky had never heard carry so much venom.

CHAPTER 43

THE afternoon saw Vicky buried up to her eyeballs in adminutiae to the point where she found herself looking back on the near battles of that morning with fondness.

Her one break from paperwork was provided by Herbert himself.

He somehow took it in his head that he could ride out to the spaceport with two of his most trusted henchmen and carry out his own attack where his minions had failed.

He had three horses that the raid had missed because they were grazing behind the palace that night. Now he and his two biggest, baddest thugs rode them.

The drone take caught him before he was two blocks from the palace even though he was keeping to side streets.

People began gathering around him before he'd gone four blocks.

He tried to outrun them, but his horses were spent before they put spurs to their flanks.

He tried to shoot his way out, but he only had so many bullets and people would flit into view, then drop out faster than he and his panicked gunmen could react.

His horse didn't take well to all this. It reared, and his poor horsemanship was revealed to all as Herbert slid off its hindquarters. The horse wisely bolted, leaving the scene before Herbert could pull himself off the ground and dust himself off.

He called for one of his trusty henchmen to give him his mount.

His trusty henchmen were already retreating at a gallop.

Herbert whirled in place, firing his two six-shooters at shadows.

A rock hit him, likely thrown from the upper window of a house.

More rocks flew. He went down.

Then the people closed in.

Vicky ordered the drone view moved to somewhere more important to the mission.

Later that day, two emaciated skeletons each brought a pearl-handled six-shooter to the spaceport. They offered to turn them in for jobs.

They were hired on the spot. Vicky found this out when the colonels offered her the six-shooters.

She gave one each to the colonels as trophies of this fight.

Vicky now considered her main job to be getting Kona back to some shade of normal. She could feed people for a month, maybe two. What she needed was people to do what they'd done in better times.

She tried to jump-start the economy immediately by giving people jobs distributing food. Others were sent as a kind of town crier to shout job opportunities to those in line for rations. Vicky found some of the skills she needed among the starving people, but most of those left in town were those who had been too weak or unwise to flee.

So Vicky went hunting for Cindy. "You going to live on that horse?" she asked the young woman.

"You mean I can't," had a shy smile behind it.

"You're the only one I know that knows where your dad is. I got a Ranger gun truck reserved to run you back up into the hills. I really need him back down here."

Clearly in pain, Cindy dismounted and joined the motor Rangers.

Vicky got a call as dark was settling in that evening. Cindy had indeed found her father's fishing lodge, and her family was safe.

Vicky talked to Mr. Arnsvider. He did have several of his business friends and associates close at hand. Many had their own places along the streams leading into a fine lake. Many had brought with them some of their most devoted or critical subordinates when they chose to run.

Most had cars, trucks, or all-terrain transport; what they needed was gas.

Vicky ordered a fuel truck to head out west that night. Next day, a convoy arrived at the spaceport. No surprise, Cindy shared a ride with Judge Valburg. He had taken two of his clerks to safety with him. He was eager to see his court back in session.

After dropping Cindy off, he drove straight to his chambers.

Now the LCIs and LCTs were dropping with supplies, spare parts, and small machinery. The emergency association of businessmen met with the businessmen Vicky had brought from St. Petersburg.

The bargaining was hard. Everyone needed everything.

Vicky sat in but avoided the temptation to step in. She'd seen just how bad she was at the business end of bargaining when she blew it the first evening above Presov. She promised herself that she would keep her mouth shut and ride to the rescue only later this time without making a fool of herself early on.

As it turned out, she didn't have to rescue anyone.

The factory owners, administrators, and managers of Kolna had a pretty good idea of what had to come first.

"We all want to get our businesses up and running again, yes. But we need water and power if we're going to live in our homes," said Cindy's dad.

"And sewage treatment about fifteen minutes after you get the water running," another added. "Oh, to take a dump in my own warm bathroom." He sighed.

Everyone laughed, but everyone agreed.

The operator of the fusion plant had a short list of what was necessary to get his reactors back up and a long list of what he'd really like to have.

The St. Petersburg men had most of the stuff on his short list. Vicky was able to get the rest released from Navy stores. Until the local could round up all his workers, Vicky arranged for Navy reactor specialists to be on loan from the fleet in orbit.

Two days later, the lights started coming on.

Not all. There were problems with the distribution network that would need some careful work, but at least most of Kolna had lights that night.

The waterworks went through a similar process. St. Petersburg had sent the consumables to get water purification going again. The waterworks needed repairs, but there were plenty of welders and small-machinery mechanics either looking for work or available aboard the ships. Water came on.

Several sections of town with electricity didn't get water and vice versa. Vicky sighed. "What do they call it in Longknife space? Murphy at work."

"I believe in Greenfeld, we call it sabotage," the commander grumbled.

"Maybe we need a better sense of humor for our beloved Greenfeld," Vicky countered.

The cargo of the four freighters was quickly transported down into the empty warehouses, with the ready help of the *Crocodile*'s landing craft.

At first, the Rangers did guard duty, but Kolna had a police force, and the many unemployed cops were eager to get it working again. Sadly, they found the chief of police and his wife murdered in their home. Likely, they were the first of Herbert's victims. The police chief's friends remembered that he'd been proud of a glass display on his wall of two pearl-handled revolvers that he said came from old Earth, where an ancestor had been a Texas Ranger.

Among the weapons collected from hungry thugs were police automatics. They were returned to the recovering police force. The rifles were mostly taken from farmers and ranchers up-country. These folks usually came in to claim their guns even as they trucked the extra hands they'd hired for security back into town to see about their old jobs.

The machine pistols from State Security were placed under lock and key. No one wanted them issued, but no one wanted them destroyed, either.

How they'd end up wasn't something anyone wanted to address at the moment. It didn't seem to matter; they recovered very little ammunition for the machine pistols.

When the *Biter* arrived with the next four freighters, Vicky was ready to take this half of her Fleet of Desperation back to St. Petersburg. The *Crocodile* stayed in orbit to help with the unloading, but Vicky wanted to return to see how matters were developing on what she was now thinking of as home.

The first fleet had carried goods and gear, much of it to be given away. Vicky was heading back with plenty of equipment orders from Poznan, accompanied by loan papers already filled out. Poznan now wanted to buy what St. Petersburg had to offer *if* the money could be found for loans so they could pay for it.

Vicky wondered how much a Grand Duchess's encouraging word would be worth. She dearly hoped that she wouldn't be required to cosign the loans; she was not at all sure she could stand surety for an entire planet's needs.

All that was in the future. For the moment, the *Attacker* was headed home from a job well done. Vicky asked and was granted permission to stand the bridge watch as the *Attacker* made its jump out of Poznan system.

It wasn't a Kris Longknife thing. No, not really. It was just that it had been a long time since Vicky stood a watch on the *Fury*. Who knew what the future might hold? She really should have a solid feel for how a warship got around in space.

Tomorrow might hold many surprises. Someday, Vicky might have to fight a ship in space.

This jump was taken very carefully. The cruiser was dead in space, the freighters strung out behind her, as the skipper of the *Attacker* went through his prejump checks.

Having a Grand Duchess at his elbow seemed to make him loquacious. Vicky had seen the *Fury* go through jumps many times under Admiral Krätz's watchful eye.

But he had never explained what he was doing.

Captain Bolesław explained every part of his routine, and Vicky listened with her computer on RECORD so she could listen to it again until she had it memorized.

Maybe I'm not the only one who thinks it would be nice if a Grand Duchess knew how a warship goes about its business.

As the final step, the captain ordered everyone to tighten

their seat belts. "Some captains take their ships through a jump with them standing around, gawking. I remember the old ways. 'Get your ship ready because you can never tell when you'll be in a fight on the other side,' my first skipper insisted. We young ensigns thought he was a Nervous Nelly, but let me tell you, you really don't know what's on the other side of that jump."

Vicky tightened her seat belt.

The jump buoy went through to warn the other side to keep their distance.

They edged through the jump at a few kilometers an hour.

There was that moment of disorientation, as the stars wavered and changed. Then there were new stars.

And something else.

"What the hell is that doing there?" the captain blurted out as he hit the general-quarters button on his command chair.

CHAPTER 44

EVEN as the *Attacker* beat to quarters, the ship was rocked by laser fire.

The hull-breach alarm sounded as the cruiser spun up quickly to the normal battle defense of twenty revolutions a minute, intended to spin the damaged hull armor away from any searing laser hits.

And the *Attacker* had taken hits. Damage control boards to Vicky's left lit up with flashing red lights showing where the cruiser had been hit fore and aft.

"Forward batteries. Fire," Captain Bolesław ordered, and the lights dimmed as the forward 8-inch batteries responded. At least two of the twin turrets fired. The third had been nailed by incoming fire and was one of the red flashing lights that Vicky struggled to ignore.

The hostile ship, no more than twenty thousand kilometers off their port quarter was quickly pinned by all four 8-inch lasers. For a long moment it just hung there in space.

Then it vanished.

Oh, there was a roiling cloud of hot dust and atoms where it had been, but of the ship, not a shred of evidence.

"What, in the name of all that's holy, was that?" the skipper demanded.

A picture of the vaporized ship appeared again on the screen. Slowly, the sensor team replayed what had just happened, then provided in rapid fire, their analysis.

"It's a small ship. No larger than a schooner or corvette."

"Pirates use them a lot."

"It's got four 18-inch pulse lasers. You can see them firing."

"It had no squawker. There's no way to tell who it was or where it came from."

Vicky scowled; she knew damn well where it came from.

She and the commander exchanged glances. Stepmom had struck again.

And the bitch is getting bigger and badder.

What wasn't clear was whether or not she'd missed this time.

The *Attacker* had been hit aft and hit bad. Her reactors were damaged and going critical. If the snipes lost their battle with the superconductors, the demons that took ships between the stars would exact their price.

And their price was your life and soul.

"Is there anything I can do to help?" Vicky asked.

"Keep your seat belt tight, Your Grace. There is nothing any of us up here on the bridge can do right now but pray. Are you good at that?"

"Not very."

"You might get better." Captain Bolesław's suggestion was just short of an order.

Vicky remembered to breathe and look calm. That was what the captain was doing. Vicky glanced around the bridge. There were youthful seamen and ensigns struggling for the first time with the prospects that their young lives might be ephemeral.

Here and there, older chiefs and commanders went about their duties as calm as on any other day. That was the image Vicky must project. She wore the stripes of a lieutenant commander. She warned Admiral Waller when he had rushed her promotion that she didn't think she was ready for the extra thin stripe.

Today, you show if you've earned it, little Victoria.

Vicky waited; others had things to do besides look calm. Calm was the only job for her at the moment.

On the board to her left, some of the flashing red went to yellow.

Then it got exciting.

The first freighter came through. It was almost on top of them and coming fast.

Captain Bolesław shouted orders and the *Attacker* used its maneuvering jets to zig right as the big freighter rolled left.

Just barely, the ships did not crash together. Even a kiss aft might have been the jar or knock that lost the fight the engineers were slowly winning.

Reminded of the tiny fleet behind them, Captain Bolesław used what little he could coax from his maneuvering rockets to increase the drift of his cruiser from the jump point.

When the next freighter came through, they had a less hairy time of it.

"Can we render assistance?" the skipper of the second freighter asked.

"Just stand clear," was simple in its clarity. If the *Attacker*'s reactors blew, there was no need for two ships to go up with the one.

The freighter skipper remained on-screen for a few seconds longer, then he turned away, and the screen went blank. He had a second question. He had it but he didn't ask it.

Does the Grand Duchess want to run away to someplace safe from harm?

Likely he would have worded it a bit differently. Maybe in some delicate way that would save her a shred of pride.

It would still have been . . . what?

An insult. *Yes.*

Just what her dad would have been screaming for. *Oh, you bet.*

Vicky didn't like where these thoughts took her.

Her dad was her father, and she had to respect him.

Her dad was her Emperor, and she owed him her allegiance and her life.

Her dad was Greenfeld, and he was making a wreck of the place. Or at least he was letting his young bride make a wreck of the place, which was the same thing.

Now the target Stepmother had painted on Vicky's back was huge enough to snuff out the lives of an entire heavy cruiser's crew.

While others went about their duty to God and Country, trying to save their ship and their lives, Vicky Peterwald, Imperial Grand Duchess of Greenfeld, stayed calm and quietly contemplated treason.

CHAPTER 45

━━━

THE *Attacker* limped into High St. Petersburg station late and slow.

The last freighter, the *Proud Hussy* out of Port Royal, had stayed with her for the rest of the voyage, standing by in case the captain ordered the *Attacker* abandoned. That assumed that anything that went wrong in engineering did so slowly enough for the skipper to order his ship abandoned.

No one aboard really took a deep breath until the *Attacker* was along the pier and the reactors doused. Likely for good.

"She's a good ship, but where will they find a pfennig to repair her these days?" Captain Bolesław almost moaned to Vicky as they shared wine during her last supper aboard. If it was possible for a hardheaded ship driver to be brokenhearted, he sure sounded the part.

Vicky loaded her computer with a copy of the brief battle and everything the sensors had picked up on the attacker during the fight. Her temper flaring, she marched for Admiral von Mittleburg's station office.

"Would you care for a glass of wine?" the admiral said as she charged, unannounced, into his office.

Unannounced, but maybe not unexpected.

"No, thank you. I'd much more prefer to know who the hell let that ship get into our space and where it came from."

"Sit down, Commander," the admiral told Vicky's trailing escort. "Take a load off your feet, if not your soul. Would you care for wine?"

The commander accepted the offered wine with a "Thank you, sir. I am told that your father keeps the best vineyard on Bayern."

"As did his father and his father before him. Vines are delicate things. They grow better with age. Like Grand Duchesses, don't you think?"

"I think this one is aging well, Admiral," Vicky's watchdog reported.

"I'm glad that I'm still aging, considering that the Navy can't keep a pirate out of the commercial space ways," Vicky spat. She hated to be ignored, and ignored she most definitely felt at the moment. Instead of taking the offered seat, she paced back and forth. She was a tiger looking for something to devour, and the admiral was at the top of her dinner list.

"We are patrolling the commercial lanes as best we can with the resources we have," the admiral said, not at all defensively. "We just never expected a pirate to take on a cruiser."

"Well, one just did. Can't you protect my convoys any better than that?"

"We planned to protect you a whole lot better than that," the admiral said, swirling his wine gently.

"I didn't feel very protected."

"We gave you two cruisers," the admiral said, evenly. "Our plan was for the *Biter* to enter every jump ahead of the *Attacker*. Then you changed our plans."

Vicky was working herself up into a really fun rage. The air went out of it in a breath. "Oh," was all she got out.

She settled into the offered chair.

"I understand the urgency of your mission, Your Grace," the admiral said, "and none of us expected the mess we found on Presov. By the way, the people you referred to us for trial?"

"Yes," Vicky answered, expecting to lose more of her air.

"We've found out quite a lot about them as the prosecutors on St. Petersburg dug into their transactions and bank accounts. Quite a lot. Their mail will be sent a long time in care of some jail dirtside. And there are stockholder suits coming in just about every week. One has to wonder where all the money went."

"Are they talking?"

"Not yet. It seems they are expecting some pardon from the Imperial Palace."

"That will tell us a lot if it comes," Vicky said.

"Yes, but now, let us talk about how we keep one Grand Duchess alive. I apologize for sending you out with only two cruisers. We only had the two available. Admiral Waller sends his respects and informs me that the battleship *Retribution* has been ordered to St. Petersburg. It will always be available in the future for your use."

Vicky found herself rather empty of rage and rapidly filling with amazement.

The Chief of the Naval Staff had sent *his* respects to *her*. Admirals sent a lieutenant commander compliments if they noticed them at all. Commanders sent their respects when admirals deigned to grant them any attention.

Kris Longknife used to laugh that no one knew what to make of her princess thing, so she was making all she could of it. Apparently, Vicky wasn't doing too bad a job of making this Grand Duchess thing into something to be respected.

There was a lot she wanted to say. What she did say was, "A battleship?"

"For your exclusive use," the admiral pointed out.

"*Retribution*, that's quite a name," Vicky said, puzzled.

"Yes, it's one of the last produced before these troubled times. I'm told by Admiral Waller that your father, our Emperor, personally selected the name."

"*Retribution*?" Vicky repeated.

"I think your father intended to use it to settle some old score."

"Like the one he racked up with Wardhaven when he tried to level the place, and Kris Longknife blew away all six of his battleships."

"That was never proven," the admiral was quick to put in.

"I've talked with Kris and her staff. I know what they think. Oh, and I overheard Dad getting yelled at by Admiral Waller. Yelled at more than my father ever put up with from any man and let him live. I know where those battleships came from."

"What battleship?" her commander asked.

"It's way above your pay grade, Commander. You'll have to drink poison after this meeting is over."

"That's fine, sir. Might I have another glass of this delicious wine before the poison?"

"I'll take that as your last wish," the admiral said ruefully as he refilled the glass.

"I was kind of hoping my last wish would be for a lovely maiden to beg tearfully for my life," he said, casting gimlet eyes toward Vicky.

"I didn't know there was a lovely maiden on this station," the admiral said, but a smile was threatening to ruin any effect his words might have.

"Well, how about the supplications of a tired old lady?" Vicky offered.

"We don't have any of them aboard either," the admiral said, refilling his glass. "Sure you won't have some?"

Robbed of her anger and seriously curious about the wine, this time Vicky took the offered glass.

"This *is* delicious. As good if not better than any served in the palace."

"Don't tell your father. He'll confiscate it."

"Or my stepmom. She'll poison it," Vicky said, enjoying another sip.

"So, now that we've let wine soften our hearts, if not our heads," the admiral said, "what is your business on St. Petersburg?"

"I have a pile of orders from Poznan for everything from tractor carburetors to several types of specialty steels. I had no idea there were so many types of steel. It's as bad as ice cream."

"And likely as important to people of a certain age," the admiral agreed.

"Anyway, along with the pile of orders, I have a pile of loan requests from just as many sources. The businessmen I talked to don't want handouts, they just want a hand up. They all had good lines of credit with banks on Greenfeld before the banks suddenly quit lending. They're grateful for what we've sent them for free. Now they want to pay for the next round, but they need loans to get them started. Do you think the local banks on St. Petersburg can step up and fill the hole left by the Imperial banks?"

"That will depend a lot on what your friend Mannie can do, and you, Your Grace."

"How much can I push this Grand Duchess role?" Vicky asked, not expecting any answer.

"That is the question we're all waiting to see, Your Grace. You talked a whole lot of people into loading a Fleet of Desperation full of lousy food to keep a planet alive. By the way, how bad was it?"

"Bad," Vicky said, taking a sip of the wine. "A whole lot worse than we thought. I'll admit to you, I came back as quickly as I did because I'm a coward. I couldn't bear to be there when they started discovering all the children who didn't make it. All the grandparents who were lost in the great runaway. I dealt with businessmen who were looking for their workforce."

Again Vicky sipped the wine. "There were enough grown men missing. When they tally up all the wives and children who just disappeared . . ." She couldn't finish that thought.

Vicky might have drained the glass right then and there. Instead, she set it down gently on the table beside her.

"I understand that your doctor didn't come back with you," the admiral said.

"No. Maggie is a gentle soul who is in her element. You wouldn't believe what she's finding, though. I thought she'd have her hands full with cuts, bruises, and infections. Broken bones that weren't set right or not set at all. What acted as the local police were quite brutal. But she's loaded down with beriberi, rickets, scurvy, and other diseases I didn't even think existed anymore."

"Famines will show you the things we thought the human race was done with," the admiral replied thoughtfully. "I'm advised that the Navy's colonies have had very good crops this year. We'll be donating wheat, rice, beans, and other basic commodities by the shipload."

"Will we need to escort them?"

"Likely not, unless you want to go with them."

"Hmm, that is a thought," Vicky admitted.

Again, the admiral twirled the stem of his wineglass. "Has this changed anything for you?"

"Has any of this changed anything for the Navy?" Vicky asked right back.

The admiral remained silent.

Vicky listened to the old-fashioned chronometer tick off the seconds for a restful while, then ventured into mined waters.

"I am told there is a flag somewhere, hidden under the bed or up in the attic. I'm told that no one can decide if it should be taken out and waved."

The admiral pursed his lips but said nothing.

"I'm told there is a young woman somewhere that some people might want to wave that flag. Assuming they had it, of course."

Again silence.

"I find that a certain young woman is getting less and less reluctant to wave that nonexistent rag if it should ever be taken out of the closet and handed to her."

"But not eager yet," the admiral said.

"Let's say less reluctant," Vicky said.

"I'll keep that in mind and pass it along to anyone who might have that nonexistent heirloom in their closet."

Vicky stood. "Admiral, do you think you could loan me a barge and bosun to fly it? I'm reluctant to fly with this lush at the controls, but I feel a strong need to go dirtside immediately."

"I am *not* a lush," the commander said, standing on an even keel. "I was just anesthetizing myself for the poison to follow."

"Bad news, Commander," the admiral said. "That nonexistent fair maiden has put in a good word for you. The poison is postponed."

"Damn. I figured poison was the only way out of my present assignment."

"No rest for the wicked," Vicky said to her commander.

"But I haven't been wicked. Not even evil, sir. Truly. Just ask this fair maiden."

"It's got to be the wine speaking," Vicky said.

"Take him dirtside to sober up," the admiral ordered. "I don't want this lush befouling my station."

"Thank you, Admiral," Vicky said.

"I think the Navy needs to thank you, Your Grace."

"We shall see," Vicky allowed.

CHAPTER 46

═══════

THE ride down was smooth. This trip, no one threatened to shoot Vicky out of the sky. She took it as a good omen and concentrated on organizing her thoughts.

The time she spent figuring out how to arrange a meeting with Mannie was a waste. He was waiting for her with a limo before the shuttle made it up the ramp from the bay to the spaceport's apron.

"There's a meeting scheduled for ten minutes from now," the mayor of Sevastopol announced as he held the door open for her.

"Ten minutes?" Vicky said. "Isn't this a bit tight since I didn't radio ahead to tell anyone I was coming?"

"The business representatives from Poznan radioed in as soon as they entered the system. We know everything on their wish list and have copies of their loan applications."

"No secrets here," Vicky said.

"None needed. If you want to buy something, it's kind of silly not to ask the seller if he has it in stock, don't you think?"

"One might fear that they'd jack up the price if you let them know you want it."

"One might on Greenfeld, but this is St. Petersburg. We

have rather good records of what this item or that cost people yesterday and last week. We *want* to sell things today and next month. We don't have time for silliness."

Vicky mulled that over. The drive was short, and she was still thinking about it when they pulled up to the circle in front of a magnificent tower of steel, glass, and stone.

"Not your City Hall, today?" Vicky asked.

"This is business. We will beard the lions in their corporate den. The men and women you're about to meet are the most powerful industrialists and bankers on this planet. People from all over the Midland Sea have flown in for this meeting. It's not just Sevastopol you're dealing with this morning."

Vicky glanced down at her Navy undress blues with the few lonely stripes of a lowly lieutenant commander.

It may take a bit of work to make the Grand Duchess shine through.

The elevator took them to the top floor. The conference room Mannie led Vicky into was spectacular even by Greenfeld standards.

Glass gave a breathtaking panorama from the room's outer three walls. The ceiling was arched glass, inviting the sky to come down and sup with the powerful. *The panorama from here must be awe-inspiring at night.*

Don't gawk, girl. You may be underdressed, but you're still the Grand Duchess.

All conversation ceased as everyone stood upon Vicky's entrance. The chair at the head of the table was empty; with gentle pressure on her elbow, Mannie aimed Vicky toward it.

Vicky was halfway there when the silence broke into applause that continued until she took her place at the head of the table. She'd never been greeted with such a wave of approval. Vicky gave them her best Grand Duchess smile and sat.

The applause ended, and they all sat.

No one said anything. They just looked at her and she at them.

Mannie cleared his throat but didn't say anything.

Vicky took a deep breath.

"We want to thank all of you for coming here to meet with us on such short notice," Vicky said, laying the Imperial "We" on with a butter knife.

"We recognize some of you from our previous meetings and strongly suspect that all of you had a large hand in our effort to bring relief to Poznan and Presov. We can tell you that in both cases, your assistance arrived in time. Indeed, it arrived at a critical time before irreparable loss would have occurred. We wish to congratulate all of you."

Some of the men and women around the table smiled with satisfaction. Some, but not all. Vicky noted the number in attendance who let the praise wash off their backs like money vanishing into a corrupt politician's pocket.

This was not going to be an easy crowd to work.

"From your generosity, you gave enough to pull these planets back from catastrophe. We thank you, and they thank you. Now, they have sent representatives to reopen the normal course of business and trade between planets. They need to buy what you want to sell. However, in order for them to restart this process, they need to borrow money."

Vicky paused for a moment. Around the table, some eagerly leaned forward. Others sat back. Were they reluctant to get involved or just waiting to drive the hardest bargain they could?

"Only a few years ago, all of these businesses now applying for loans from banks in St. Petersburg were considered credit-worthy by Imperial banks on Greenfeld. At least they were before those banks quit loaning money. Now they are willing to focus their trade on St. Petersburg if your banks are willing to help them get that trade going."

Another pause.

"We, the Imperial Grand Duchess Victoria of Greenfeld, heartily endorse their requests to you."

There, Vicky had said all she could. Now she sat back in her chair and prepared to listen.

Dear Lord, but they had a lot to say.

With due respect, the two sides took turns presenting and reiterating their positions.

"This is just the chance we've been looking for to grow our industries," an industrialist would say. "We still are not up to full employment. We've got plant capacity that we aren't using. This is what we need to get us out of the doldrums."

That optimism, however, would be quickly countered.

"We don't have the money for this. After the last tax collector came through, we're just about out of Imperial gold marks. The St. Petersburg marks we're printing are no better than fiat script at best. If we expand the money supply too much, too fast, we'll have inflation. Maybe not runaway inflation at first, but it's a risk that's just waiting for us if we get this wrong."

Before that speaker even stopped talking, the next would be getting his oar in the water . . . or maybe slamming it over the last speaker's head.

"We're a long way from inflation. Where is the demand for things that can't be met with the goods available? You've got to have people waving money at you to get their hands on scarce resources or the too few goods before the market will let any seller start raising prices. Inflation is just you bankers' bogeyman, and, frankly, I'm not afraid of the dark."

"You will be if our economy overheats, and you get that excessive demand."

"Show me some demand."

"Gentlemen," Mannie finally said, "I'd like to introduce something else for our consideration."

"What?" came from several red-faced men at the table.

"Captain Spee, of the good ship *Doctor Zoot*, has been swinging around the planets in our jump group, selling the crystal he picked up on Presov."

"And stealing our market," someone down the table muttered low, but so all could hear.

"Can I bring him in? I think you'll find what he has discovered on his journey to be very interesting."

The captain was allowed in. He came to stand beside Vicky's chair. With a formal bow and a good heel click to her, he turned to the table.

"Ladies and gentlemen, thank you for allowing me to address you. I've just completed a voyage to several of your neighboring planets. Good Luck, Finster, Ormuzd, and Kazan have all, like you to a lesser degree, suffered from the breakdown in trade. I was the first ship any of them have seen in a year. They took my crystal, but all they had to offer were luxury goods and raw materials. What all of them needed were spare parts. None of them have any heavy industry. They need what heavy industry provides. They need to buy that, and, if they can, they want to buy some fab mills of their own."

He turned to Vicky with a nod. "You'll excuse me, Your Grace, but the colonial policies of Greenfeld stink. They stank before, and now what with credit dried up and trade going the way of the proverbial dodo bird, they stink to high heaven."

"Are those planets in danger of going the way of Poznan?" Vicky asked.

"Not this week. Maybe not this month, but, Your Grace, I am not at all willing to say what they will be like next year."

"More markets," an industrialist said.

"More demand. If it gets out of control, there will be hell to pay," put in a banker.

"Can we look at ourselves in the mirror next year," came slowly from an old man, maybe the oldest person at the table, "if we do nothing about this now?"

That brought the table to a long, meditative silence.

"Captain Spee, would you mention to those gathered here what Ormuzd gave you in trade for your crystal?" Mannie said.

"I got a consignment of rare earths. A nice balanced ton of all of them."

"What's your asking price?" came from down the table.

"What are you offering?" shot back the captain. "Ormuzd don't want marks, gold or any of that stuff. They have a long list of machinery and spare parts they need. If you want the dirt, you get me those parts."

"It's a deal."

"Rare earths?" Vicky said.

"They are critical ingredients to just about everything electronic," Mannie said. "Before the crash, Greenfeld bought all the rare earths Bayan Obo could produce and manufactured just about everything that used them. With a monopoly on the market, they priced them accordingly. We have a very small source of the stuff in the desert south of Moskva. We used it to develop our own little electronics industry. Not enough to be noticed by the powers that be on Greenfeld but enough to let us make a few things cheap and local."

Mannie looked down the table. Several men grinned proudly and nodded along with him.

"If we really want to build an electronics industry, and there is no doubt that we can, we'll need a lot of rare earths. Right now, the best source on St. Petersburg is way off in the eastern desert. To get there, we'd need to build a whole lot of infrastructure and somehow figure a way to bring water to the place."

The mayor paused.

"Or we could just start importing the stuff from Ormuzd and get the industry going now. No doubt, as our population grows, some of it will spread out into the eastern desert. Once that rare-earths mine isn't so way off and gone in the outback, we'll just naturally be able to exploit the stuff."

"Here, here," came from many at the table.

"It was fine for us to smuggle some cheap electronics into our economy," a banker pointed out, "but when things get back to normal, and we get Imperial inspector generals from Greenfeld looking over our shoulders, it won't be possible to hide a major, unapproved industry."

"And when are things going to get back to normal?" came from somewhere around the table.

"Never," came forcefully from several.

"Your Grace, this meeting must be very tiring, and I know you just completed a long and harrowing voyage," Mannie said. "Would you care to leave these fine people to their discussion of our planet's future?"

"Why thank you, Mr. Mayor," Vicky said, grateful for the hint. She wasn't so much tired as bored. She was starting to wonder if her dad didn't have something with his idea of just telling the market what to do and see that it did it . . . and she really didn't like the taste of that thought.

It was all too clear to Vicky that her dad's way of running things wasn't working out all that well, what with him busy in the bedroom and the Bowlingame mob doing what they pleased.

Vicky rose but did not turn to go.

"We are appreciative of all your great concerns, both for your proud St. Petersburg and those other planets that have been thrown on such hard times. You ask when matters may return to normal. We must tell you that we do not see that day coming anytime soon. We don't see it coming without even more disruption and pain. We hope that you will take it upon yourselves to alleviate as much of that pain and suffering as you can."

Now Vicky turned and let Mannie lead her to the door.

To her surprise, he led her through it and over to the elevator.

"You don't have to come with me," she said.

"You think I want to stay in there? They'll talk and talk for the rest of the day. Then, maybe about midnight, as they're yawning, they'll settle on something. I'll be there to make sure they settle on something the way I want it."

"And you're leaving now?" Vicky asked.

"To take a nap, so I won't be yawning later. Oh, and maybe talk a bit with you."

The elevator came, and they entered.

"Me?"

"How bad is it out there?"

"Worse than you want to imagine," Vicky said, and filled him in on some of what she'd seen. She finished her tale as they were crossing the foyer. "It was worse than I could take. I left before Poznan could start counting its dead."

Mannie shivered.

"It could have been us," he muttered, as the limo drove off.

"But you held together."

"We wouldn't have. Not without the city charter and the Navy work."

"I'm glad I let Kris Longknife talk me into signing that charter."

Mannie smiled. "I was flying by the seat of my pants that day."

"You flew very well."

Mannie seemed to like the taste of that, but he took the moment to hand Vicky into his limo, then joined her. When he spoke again, it was on a different subject. "I understand you were attacked on your return voyage."

"A pirate schooner or sloop or corvette came at us. We blew it to atoms, so we're not all that sure what it was or where it came from. Anyway, we got it, but it got us good. We weren't sure the entire way back that the *Attacker* would make it."

"About the *Attacker*. Will the Navy repair it?"

"Not likely," Vicky said. "They don't have the facilities on High St. Petersburg to do all that heavy repair work."

Mannie made a face. "Maybe they don't. Maybe *we* do."

"Maybe *you* do?" Vicky echoed.

"We have two repair slips on High Petersburg. They were

built to repair merchant hulls, but they're large enough to take in a heavy cruiser like the *Attacker*."

Vicky shook her head. "It's one thing to work on the light scantlings and engines of a merchant hull, another thing to tackle the heavy machinery of a warship or its 8-inch lasers, even less its heavy hull members needed to support the ice armor . . . and everything else."

Vicky started out sure of herself but was ending a lot less so. Mannie was smiling.

"We've got enough heavy industry down here that we could ratchet up the docks to do heavier work," Mannie pointed out. "We could make the upgrades to the docks as we make the repairs to the *Attacker*. Better yet, the upgrades to the yard and repairs on the *Attacker* would make a case we need for growing our heavy-industry base for generators, reactors, and 8-inch lasers, maybe larger. The bigger we grow, the more we can trade for."

They had arrived at City Hall. Mannie helped Vicky from the limo as she reflected on all that he had said.

"How would you pay for the dock improvement?" she finally asked. "No. More importantly, how would the Navy pay for the repairs?"

"That's the problem," Mannie said. "Your admiral is living pretty much hand to mouth, scrimping a bit here to add a little something off budget there. We're letting him run up a tab for food, so he can feed his extra Marines. Likely, he's using our free food to feed his Sailors as well."

"He can't squeeze a heavy cruiser's extensive repairs out of his food budget," Vicky said.

"But there is our tax account," Mannie said, with amazing ease.

"No one *ever* talks about taxes the way you just did," Vicky said, then added, "and stays out of jail."

"Yes, but to continue about our tax account." Mannie went on with a grin. "It's growing. Everyone is meticulously paying their taxes, using St. Petersburg marks, I might add, but no one has shown up in over a year to collect them. We don't have so many Imperial gold marks that it's worth sending a ship out to actually carry off a few bales of paper. Despite our many offers, no one seems interested in us just sending a draft payment through the mail, certainly if it's only backed up by our own script."

"Things really have broken down when paper and e-money aren't worth collecting," Vicky said, a frown growing as she entered the elevator.

"But the 'money' is there in the bank, going nowhere and doing no one any good. Actually, it's worse. It's a drag on the economy and causing a bit of *de*flation. If, however, it was spent here, on this planet, for goods and services *we* can provide, it would help whoever got those goods and services and boost our economy at the same time."

"Are you suggesting that you pay your taxes to the local Navy account, and Admiral von Mittleburg puts them to good use?" Vicky said slowly.

"Something like that," Mannie said, his face an unreadable mask now.

"My father, the Emperor, has never had the Senate make so much as a pfennig's change in his budget, but he does submit it, and they do rubber-stamp it. If the local admiral here started spending money that hasn't been through the appropriation cycle, some people might say that sounds dangerously close to treason."

"There is that," was the mayor's only reply.

The elevator deposited them on Mannie's floor. Vicky was still thinking as he guided her into his office and settled her on a couch before taking the chair across from her.

Vicky opened her mouth but was interrupted by her computer.

"Your Grace, you have a message."

"From whom?"

"I do not know."

Vicky frowned. So did Mannie.

"From where?"

"I do not know."

"When did you receive it?"

"I do not know."

Vicky frowned at Mannie. He just shrugged in puzzlement. "Deliver the message," she finally said.

"I cannot. It has visual content, and I do not have access to a screen."

"You can use the screen at my desk," Mannie offered.

Together they walked over to his work area and stood behind the desk, looking down at the screen inserted into its top.

"Computer, play the message."

The screen came to life.

"Hello, darling Victoria. Why are you avoiding me?" her very pregnant stepmom cooed.

CHAPTER 47

===

VICKY almost leapt away from the desk, but Mannie was in back of her. "Freeze playback," she ordered.

"Is that your stepmother?" the mayor asked.

Vicky eyed the stopped video. There was her young stepmother in all her pregger glory. The loose green gown she wore flowed over her distended belly. It couldn't be long now. The gown was cut low to emphasize her full breasts. Dad must be loving this.

But it was the smile, full of viciousness and venom, that held Vicky's attention.

"Yep, that's my loving stepmum. How did she get this message on my computer without leaving any tracks?"

"That shouldn't be possible."

"But she did, and it's here. Do you mind if I play the rest of it?"

"Do you mind if I call in my tech-support team?"

"I'd prefer dear loving Stepmum's words didn't get too wide a distribution until I hear them."

The mayor tapped several keys on his computer before saying, "Go ahead. The computer is closed down. Just using the screen shouldn't allow too much hidden in the message to get loose."

"You assume we know what my stepmom and her family can do."

"Sadly."

"Computer, play message again from the beginning."

"Hello, darling Victoria. Why are you avoiding me?" her stepmother repeated. "You're being a naughty girl," sounded like she was scolding a three-year-old.

"You can't get away from me. I know everything you do." Her tone was hard and vicious now. There wasn't even a hint of a smile on her face.

"If you think riding around in a battleship will protect you from my reach, think again. If you want to keep on breathing, get your ass on the next ship available and get yourself back to the palace, where you belong. You may not live very long here, but it will be a lot longer than you will out there."

The message ended on that note.

Vicky felt weak in the knees. Her throat was dry, and she wanted to cry.

So she walked slowly back to the couch, and asked, "Do you have a glass of water?"

Mannie brought one to her. As she drank, she considered her options.

Surrender. Run home and wait for some snake in the grass to kill her.

Fight. Grab that flag of revolution and start waving it like mad.

Keep on keeping on. Continue to build up the power base she was building until she had no choice but to rebel, and the people around her had no choice but to join her and do it with all the enthusiasm a rebellion needed.

Vicky smiled. Loving Stepmom was doing her best to get her to do one of the first two and stop doing the last.

That was a pretty solid vote for continuing down the trail she was going.

"Computer, call the commander and tell him to get the admiral's barge ready to return immediately."

"That is done, Your Grace."

Vicky found the off button on her computer and pressed it.

Mannie raised a questioning eyebrow, but Vicky went on now that she considered herself somewhat free of spying eyes.

"Ask your accountants to start looking into how to move the tax money into a slush fund the Navy can draw on without making the money actually disappear from the bank accounts it is in."

The mayor made a face. "Do you think our sneaky people can outsneak their sneaky people?"

"I don't know yet, but I'm going to look into getting us some reinforcements in that area."

"Okay."

"Now, about the *Attacker*. I like Captain Bolesław. I owe him and his crew my life. It would be a shame to leave them without a ship and the *Attacker* reduced to a hulk locked down to the station and good for nothing but barracks."

"That would indeed be a sad end for good men and their good ship."

"I'll broach your idea to upgrade your repair facilities to Admiral von Mittleburg and see what he thinks of the idea. About what those bankers were saying today. Spending money to repair the *Attacker* and start up trade with all those planets. It wouldn't cause your planet to be hit by runaway inflation, would it?"

"The taxes are deflating our economy as they go out of pockets and into bank vaults or computers or wherever money goes these days. We can fix the *Attacker* and maybe a whole lot of other ships and still have plenty left over to keep those other planets from falling apart. By growing them, we grow ourselves."

"I hope you're right. Now, I think I can walk again. Can I borrow your limousine to get back to the shuttleport?"

"And I will see that you have a police escort to get you there," Mannie said, giving Vicky a hand and walking with her to the door.

"You don't have to come with me. Don't you have a nap to take?"

"I can't sleep in here. My tech support will be tearing my computer apart," he said, turning to his secretary. "There may be something wrong with my computer. Have it turned over to the tech wizards for examination and get me a new one."

"Will do, boss," she said, and started tapping her commlink.

"I will not risk you, Vicky. You're the only Grand Duchess we have, and it looks like someone doesn't want us having you."

"Not if Stepmommy can help it."

They headed for the elevator.

"She mentioned a battleship?" the mayor said.

"Yes," Vicky answered. "I just found out a few hours ago that the Navy is sending the *Retribution* for me to use as my private yacht, what with the *Attacker* being nearly blown away."

"Your stepmother must have recorded that message a week ago, maybe longer."

Vicky raised an unsurprised eyebrow. "You could very well be right."

"So she knew about the battleship even before that ship attacked you."

"Even before *her* pirate ship attacked me," Vicky said, tasting the sound of it and finding it left her gut tight and her face determined.

"I remember being told when I was hardly out of diapers that the palace leaked secrets like nobody's business," she said.

"I wonder how we could put that to good use?" the mayor mused.

As Mannie personally turned Vicky over to Commander Boch, he said, "I had intended to invite you to dinner."

"We must do it next time I'm down here," Vicky answered. "Come back soon."

The admiral's barge was taxiing before Vicky found her seat.

CHAPTER 48

VICKY was quickly back in the admiral's day quarters. He did not offer her wine this time.

"We have more problems than I really want to contemplate," she said before she'd finished leading a parade of Commander Boch and Mr. Smith into his quarters.

"Do we really need this fellow with us?" the admiral said, eyeing the spy.

"Unfortunately, he's the fellow we most need. Admiral, do you have an old, off-net computer you wouldn't mind throwing out the nearest air lock?"

It took only a few minutes for one to be scared up. A second later, it was playing the Empress's message for all present.

"Where'd that come from?" Mr. Smith asked.

"My computer has no idea," Vicky answered. "It didn't know who the message was from, or where or when it even got the message, but somewhere between my leaving the admiral a few hours ago and attending a meeting with some very powerful businesspeople dirtside, and Mannie driving me around in his limo between the shuttleport and his office, I picked up that message without being any the wiser."

"Very good work," Mr. Smith whispered with respect. "Not your average delivery."

"Could this message have come attached to a knife in my back?" Vicky demanded.

"Very likely," Mr. Smith said, eyeing her, or maybe her computer, "but then, to put a knife in your back would have taken a very noticeable action. People who try to kill you tend to end up dead. At least when I'm around. Now about this thing. You just walked around or were driven by someone, and bingo, you've got mail."

"Any suggestion what we do about this?" the admiral asked.

"May I have your computer, Your Grace?"

With a scowl, Vicky surrendered her new toy. Made of the same material and matrix as Kris Longknife's famous Nelly, it lacked the spark that made Nelly what she was. Vicky was still unsure she wanted a computer with as much attitude as Kris Longknife's computer.

Right now, though, Nelly might have advantages.

The spy used the old Navy computer to access Vicky's new one. He studied whatever it was he got for a long ten minutes, ignoring the admiral's glower at being kept waiting.

Vicky considered dropping the next bombshell she had for the admiral but decided the room was much too crowded to discuss treason.

Finally, Mr. Smith faced his own computer toward Vicky's for a few seconds, then handed the computer back to Vicky.

"The message did nothing but deliver the threat and demand to you. There was a bit of a locator program along with it, but that is gone now. You may consider your computer safe to use. I might be able to protect your computer better, now that we know of this new threat, but I'd have to visit a small shop on Wardhaven."

"Would you and the commander mind waiting outside for a few minutes," Vicky said.

Both men raised an eyebrow at the demand, but they went where they were told.

Once the door was shut, Vicky asked, "What are your feelings about getting the *Attacker* repaired and back in full commission?"

The admiral raised an inquisitive eyebrow, but said, "I'd be very glad to have it. We're running short of good ships."

"What are your feelings about misappropriation of funds and a light touch of treason?"

Admiral von Mittleburg snorted. "I believe that you can no more commit a little bit of treason than you can be a little bit pregnant."

"Consider it a matter of perspective," Vicky said, and filled the admiral in on what Mannie had in mind for St. Petersburg's dormant tax accounts and budding ship-repair facilities.

"He's not the first one to look at those damn repair slips and see something more. I've got several ship maintenance officers who would love to add a few jigs and cranes to what we've got there. Does Mannie really think they can fabricate them in the mills they have down below?"

"He's pretty sure. Lifting them up here might take a bit of extra work. How long can you hold on to the *Crocodile*?"

"You noticed how helpful those landing craft, tanks are, did you?"

"Hard to miss," Vicky admitted.

"The problem, of course, is paying for them," he said, taking a seat behind his desk.

Vicky settled into the visitor's chair beside the desk. "Rather, paying for them and the source of the money not being remarked upon."

"Remarked upon and named treason."

"Precisely," Vicky said. "At least not in the here and now. Later, it may be the least of my sins, that nonexistent flag and all."

"It wouldn't stay unremarked upon for long if all it took was some stranger walking by the bank and suddenly, the bank's entire set of records is available for audit and review at some unpleasant person's convenience."

"Exactly. That's why I wanted Mr. Smith involved. I didn't just want his opinion of how much my own computer was compromised. We really need to know what else might be compromised and how to make sure they aren't."

Admiral von Mittleburg leaned back in his chair and stared at the overhead for a long moment, then closed his eyes. "I just wanted to command a warship in space. Do you know that, Your Grace? All I ever wanted was to be the captain of a cruiser. Then it looked like I could command a battleship, so I stayed in. Then they waved my own flag at me. I should have quit while I was ahead."

"You want to retire to your father's vineyard?" Vicky asked.

"I hated the place. Every summer, Dad would use his leave to take us out to the old place. His grandfather was still running it. Some kids love the dirt and sun. I hated it. What I did love was the shipboard experience getting out to Bayern but hated every minute I was there."

"And now?"

"I'd love to be there, just for an hour, with Grandpa," the admiral said with a sigh.

His eyes came open, and he leaned forward in his chair.

"First, we need to get better security around the banks. Do you think your Mr. Smith could arrange for that?"

"He can try."

"Can't ask for more. While he's doing that, maybe we could get the bank to arrange a loan. I don't know. Is my signature worth enough to upgrade two docks from merchant ship to heavy cruiser?"

"If nobody looks at the signature and collateral too closely."

"Keep it off the official books, yeah," the admiral said. "The *Attacker* isn't the only ship we need to put through the yards. The *Avenger* is barely safe for space, but if she got a couple of weeks of tender loving care, she'd be ready for just about anything."

"Two slips. Two heavy cruisers," Vicky said.

"Now, how do we keep you safe?" the admiral asked the thin air. "How did it come to happen that the commander was not there when you got this message? Was I mistaken, but was he just as surprised by your stepmother as I was?"

"Sadly, that was my mistake," Vicky said. "I felt safe on St. Petersburg. I had the mayor with me. I should have kept Commander Boch, Mr. Smith, and Kit and Kat close or closer. I will not make that mistake again."

"See that you don't. I'd hate to have to court-martial the commander for your mistake, you being dead and not available to face a court for your own shortcomings."

"Like being a head short," Vicky admitted drolly.

"Do you plan to respond to your stepmother's message?" the admiral said, changing the subject.

"That's one of my new priorities. If they can drop messages unknown into my mailbox, certainly I need to be able to return the compliment."

"Then I believe we need to get the gentlemen back in here."

"And have Kit and Kat bring me a change of clothes."

The admiral gave Vicky a jaundiced eye.

"I will not reply to my dearest stepmom in uniform," Vicky said. "She's likely to take the head off the nearest Navy officer in her rage."

"Good point."

═══ ═══

CHAPTER 49

MR. Smith was quickly given a list of Vicky's requirements for improved security.

"I don't want stray mail showing up without knowing it's arrived and where it came from."

"Very well," said Mr. Smith

"Assuming that anyone who could access my computer could also access any of the bank computers on St. Petersburg, I want them capable of shutting any such access down. I watched Kris Longknife and her computer open up our banking system like a filleted fish. I want it sewn up tight."

"A tall order, but possible."

"I also want you to deliver a message from me to my dearest stepmom. I don't want her to know she's got it until the agent delivering it is well away and safe."

"A return of the favor," Mr. Smith said. "I believe I know a small programming boutique on Wardhaven that might meet all your needs."

Vicky thought on that for a moment. "Admiral, is the *Spaceadler* still available?"

"I believe it is. That's one ship we were able to send through the existing space docks and have its reaction tanks recalked."

"Please arrange a crew for Mr. Smith to take him to Wardhaven."

"I'll need some money," the spy said.

"No," the admiral said, "you need some trading stock. I don't think anything that passes for money in Greenfeld is worth a tinker's damn in the U.S. However, I did manage to get several choice pieces of artistic and musical-quality crystal turned over to the Navy as payment for escorting the ships out safely and bringing them home again. I'll have them aboard the *Spaceadler* when you seal locks. My officer will be charged with either turning them over to you for trading or arranging to sell them on the Wardhaven market."

"Admiral, dearest, I fear you do not trust me," the spy said, striking a pose.

"And you'd be right," the admiral answered right back.

"Mr. Smith, I do trust you," Vicky said. "I'm going to trust you with a couple of messages. One is to Kris Longknife's Grandma Trouble. It's for her, or if she's not available, her Grandpa Trouble. You do know him."

"Like everyone of an age, I know of him. Sadly, I can't remember ever meeting him in the flesh."

"Well, this will be my introduction of you to him," Vicky said, handing Mr. Smith a data unit. "This is my personal plea to him for some of those spidersilk undergarments that have saved Kris's life a few times. I need a few pair for me, you, Kit, and Kat. The new kind that spread the hits over you a bit. Please don't slobber over the laser pics I provided of us girls."

"I not only will not slobber over them, I won't even look," the spy said.

"There is one more thing I want you to have. Maybe you can drop it off at Bayern on the way back in with the software that will allow its delivery to my stepmother."

"A message?" the spy said.

"My reply to her message," Vicky said.

"I will go about the business of getting away," Mr. Smith said, and left, with the commander at his elbow.

"Do you trust him?" the admiral asked, eyeing the door he'd just closed.

"No more than I have to, but in these matters, I must. Assuming you don't have a better idea?"

The admiral looked in serious pain. "Unfortunately, I know of no other way."

"Then, if you will allow me the use of your quarters for a few minutes, I need to change into something more appropriate for a talk with my stepmother.

The admiral did not seem surprised to be rousted out of his own space. "I'll be at dinner. You might join me when you're done." And with that, he left.

Kit unzipped the clothes bag Vicky had asked for.

"Are you sure, mademoiselle, that this iz ze dress you want?"

Vicky grinned at the little bit of nothing she'd worn when she was desperate to be noticed and to keep the television camera running and focused on her. This time, the girls had brought the thin blouse that was intended to be worn under it.

Vicky pulled the dress from the bag . . . and left the blouse hanging.

"It's exactly what I want my stepmom to see me falling out of."

In a few moments, Vicky was out of uniform and braless. In a few moments more, she was dressed, such as she was.

She let her eyes rove the room and settled on the settee in the admiral's conversation circle. She walked over to it barefoot and folded herself onto it, reclining in a most languid fashion.

"You ready to record?"

"If this is what you want to do," Kit said, and held up her commlink.

"Hello, Stepmother dearest. It was so good to hear from you. As you know, you continue to miss what you're aiming at. It's hard to believe that little old me is more than all your assassins can hit," Vicky said, waving a hand down her side, then moving quickly to pull her dress back in place as one nipple slipped out.

Vicky stared hard into the commlink. "Thank you for your most gracious offer of hospitality, but you know what it was like last time I visited. Dead bodies here. Explosions there. Your assassins just kept missing the mark and hitting innocent bystanders. I think I'll keep my distance for the time being."

Vicky glanced away, then turned back, voice as hard as she could make it. "Don't bother sending any more pirate junks to take a shot at me. I *will* have a battleship to look out for me, and

I *know* it will do the job very well. You stay in there, making the mess you're making of the Empire, and I'll stay out here, trying to mitigate the pain and agony you're causing. If you stay there, and I stay here, we are both likely to live longer. Ta-ta, until we meet again," Vicky said, waving at the camera.

As she did, both nipples slipped free of the dress.

"Mademoiselle, you are too too," Kit said.

"She is teasing a tigress," Kat said.

"And enjoying every moment of it," Vicky said as she stood. "Now, let us get me back in decent clothes."

CHAPTER 50

I T took most of what was left of the afternoon, but Mr. Smith was away shortly after supper in the *Spaceadler* with Vicky's message to dear young mom, her wish list, and an allotment of crystal to barter for the desired software. That done, Vicky found herself invited to the admiral's day quarters and included in a discussion with several ship outfitters and maintainers.

"Here's the list you asked for, Admiral von Mittleburg, for the minimum that it would take to upgrade those two slips so they can handle heavy cruisers," one commander said. "The list is long, but doable using St. Petersburg's heavy-fabrication capabilities, or so they told us when we asked for information."

"Will it use too much of it?" Vicky asked. "Some of the bankers are scared to death of sparking inflation."

"Have you ever met a banker who wasn't?" the admiral asked dryly.

That got a laugh from the Navy officers.

While they talked at length about whether they really needed this or that to make the docks into what they wanted, Vicky found herself with little to say and even less she could understand. She began fiddling with the comm station at her place around the admiral's conference table.

When she started, she had no idea where she was headed, maybe just scratching an itch that she didn't know she had. First, she brought up the planets that Captain Spee had visited when the *Doctor Zoot* made its hurried round-robin. Between them they produced a wide array of raw materials essential to the lifeblood of the Empire.

At least they had been deemed essential during the Empire's better days.

Vicky had her computer plug those resources into the St. Petersburg economy.

They fit nicely. They also fit nicely into Posnan's.

What was missing on all the planets was the big industrial base needed to convert those resources, the heavy fabricators. It was true that given enough time, St. Petersburg could make heavier and heavier fabricators, but it would be a whole lot nicer if she could just buy what she needed at the start.

Vicky found herself wondering if the admiral and his men weren't settling for too little. On further review, was Mannie looking at all the options the present disaster opened up to him and St. Petersburg?

"Admiral, if you wanted to make the generators, reactors, and capacitors for, say, the *Retribution*, where would you go to get the materials and fabs to make the tools you needed to make the tools?" Vicky asked, interrupting a conversation on just how little an upgrade they could make do with and still repair the *Attacker*.

The looks she drew from around the admiral's conference table were appropriate for someone who had just grown two heads. Maybe three.

The admiral looked around at his commanders and captains. Most just gnawed their lower lips. One spoke.

"Greenfeld and Kiel have yards with everything necessary to support the construction of battleships and other heavy warships," he pointed out.

"Such as the new Terror class battleships," Vicky said. "I understand a man is being brought in to command that first ship. A man not from the Greenfeld Navy."

That was met by silence around the table.

"And if we wanted to work on something the size of the *Retribution*, either to repair it, or maybe build a sister ship . . . ?"

Vicky asked, trying to be vague about what some might call treason.

The answer was a while coming. Several of the officers at the table silently polled each other. Finally, the one who'd offered the first answer spoke.

"Metzburg is the closest planet with that kind of heavy industry. Her and New Brunswick."

The admiral muttered something to his computer, and the bulkhead across from Vicky lit up with a star map. Both Metzburg and New Brunswick were about equidistant from St. Petersburg and Greenfeld.

"What are their recent economic circumstances?" Vicky asked.

Her computer answered, "Both are in recession. Their economies have shrunk for the last ten quarters by two to three percent on average. As much as five percent occasionally."

"Why?" Vicky asked.

"Imports are down. Several fabricators have closed down due to a lack of credit. Others lack critical resources. Even those still running are below capacity because they lack markets, both on planet and off."

"The same story we have been hearing all throughout the Empire," Vicky concluded.

"Apparently," Admiral von Mittleburg said evenly if not precisely.

"What are the critical failure points?" Vicky asked, then realized she was inviting her computer to talk through the night. "Cancel previous question. Do the critical failure points include crystal and rare-earths products?"

"Crystal fabrication takes place mainly on Greenfeld in the facilities owned by the Smythe-Peterwald consortiums. Repairs can be done almost anywhere, but the initial units come from Greenfeld. So does the miniaturized-electronics industry as well as power-generation facilities. They are an Imperial monopoly of the Smythe-Peterwald Holding corporations," her computer said, telling her what she'd learned at her father's knee.

"We hold the rest of the economy by the neck," he'd bragged. "If you have their balls clutched in your hands, their hearts and minds will follow." That had been Vicky's introduction both to male anatomy and mixed metaphors.

"Have the security firms of my dearly loved stepmum and her brothers set up shop on either planet?"

"No. There is much civil unrest, but so far the local officials have been able to avoid large-scale riots in the streets," her computer reported. It was as reliable a report as Vicky was likely to get in the empire.

"So there are likely small-scale riots," Vicky said dryly. Her smile was bitter.

The Navy officers sitting around the conference table were staring at her, as if trying to figure out a name for this strange and unheard of beast that had been dropped in their midst.

"What are you thinking, Your Grace?" the admiral finally asked.

"I am thinking that you are thinking way too small, gentlemen. I am thinking that we need to grab this bull by the horns. Rather than waiting for it to trample us and gore our guts out in the dirt, we should be grabbing its horns and twisting it around to gallop off to where we want it to take us."

"And that would be?" the admiral asked.

"Look what my stepmum and her robber-baron family have been doing. They are wrecking the Empire. However, as the Empire my family built goes up in smoke, they are pulling this and that bit of wreckage out of the fire and claiming it for their own. I say we should be looking for bits of their future plunder and grabbing it before they barbecue it."

Vicky stood up and strode around the table to the star map. "Metzburg and New Brunswick are hurting, but they are not burning. Not yet, at least. They have what we need here on St. Petersburg. Our little trade consortium here"—she jabbed at the six planets they had involved so far—"has what they need. What they need and the Navy colonies need, I might add. Despite the best monopolistic efforts of my ancestors, St. Petersburg has managed to manufacture some of what is needed to keep the larger economies of Metzburg and New Brunswick working during these hard times. If we swap them what they need for what we want, St. Petersburg grows, they stay afloat, and the raw-resource suppliers get the business they need."

Vicky made a face at the planets visited by Captain Spee. "I suspect my father's purchasing agents have been quite good at keeping down the prices of the raw feedstock they buy from them. If the value is allowed to float on a free market to what it's truly worth, they may be surprised at what they can buy."

Now, several of the Navy officers were staring at Vicky with their jaws hanging half-open.

"Gentlemen," the admiral was quick to say, "what you hear here, no doubt, you understand, will stay here."

"Can we do that?" one was heard to whisper.

"Keep our mouths shut?" his neighbor asked.

"No, damn it, I'm a Greenfeld officer, my right hand never knows what my left hand just did. No, can we do this trade thing?"

"Can we?" Vicky repeated the question, then answered it. "Yes."

"Are we permitted to?" the admiral said. "Likely, no."

"Will we?" an officer from the foot of the table asked.

"Why not?" Vicky answered.

The officers around the table looked at each other but did not gainsay her.

"Gentlemen, let us continue this discussion tomorrow," the admiral suggested, and, in a moment, only he and Vicky were still seated at the table.

"That was interesting," he said to Vicky.

"How so?" she asked.

"Well, for one thing, I've never sat at a table and had a Grand Duchess propose treason."

"I warned you I was close to it," Vicky said, not suppressing a smile.

"Yes, you warned me, but I didn't expect it so soon."

Vicky shrugged. "We can let my robber-baron in-laws plunder and destroy, or we can take action. My question to you is whether or not you think this action will work," she said, still eyeing the star map.

"You've got the best analytical computer aboard this ship," the admiral pointed out.

"Computer, will the plan just outlined work?" Vicky asked.

"Economically, it is very likely to succeed," the computer said. "Practically, it is a very complex proposed action plan, and there are several complications and potential failure points, but none that should prevent it from working. However, politically, there are several laws, trade restrictions, and other constraints of trade that seem to make this entire action plan something that cannot be done."

"So, nothing but politics to stop us," Vicky said, and tried to look as confident as her words sounded.

Inside, her gut was doing fifteen hundred revolutions a minute.

The admiral groaned. "I did want to spend a few good years retired and growing grapes, testing casks to see how the wine was maturing," he said.

"And I do want to see our beloved Greenfeld prosper," Vicky said.

The admiral met her firm gaze with level eyes. "Then let us see what we can do about both of our wishes."

CHAPTER 51

B Y midmorning, Vicky was back in Mannie's office. Only this time, she came as the full Grand Duchess. Well, the full Navy officer who was the Grand Duchess.

That morning, Kit and Kat had dressed her carefully in dress whites. It turned out that Vicky was officially attached to the admiral's staff, so a gold aiguillette was added to the left shoulder of her uniform. Her medals were few, but the golden starburst of the Order of St. Christopher, Star Leaper, made up for any lack with its weight. The few stripes of a lieutenant commander might be light, but it showed she worked for a living.

A ballroom gown had been laid out, but Vicky had sent it back to the closet. "These people remember when the Navy saved them from my loving stepmom's Security Consultants. I need all the good memories I can snatch."

Still, her appearance stopped Mannie in his tracks.

"Oh my Grand Duchess," he said. "Is this what you really look like?"

"Yesterday, I was underdressed. Today, I came prepared."

"I'm grateful for the vision, Your Grace, but you really needn't have. I have quite a deal for you," he crowed.

"I come with a better one to lay on the table," Vicky said.

With a puzzled frown, Mannie ushered Vicky to his couch and took his place in his usual chair. Two minutes later, Vicky was off the couch and showing him around a star chart. Five minutes later, he was out of the chair and pacing.

"Good God, woman, don't you ever think small?"

"I've thought small most of my life," Vicky admitted. "Small isn't going to cut it in the mess we're in. You can't cross a ten-foot-wide, thousand-foot-deep chasm in two five-foot hops."

"Not unless the last leap is a doozy," the mayor muttered. "But this. It's not a ten-foot hop you're asking for. It's a thousand-foot hurdle!"

"But it gets you what you want," Vicky said, pointing to the star chart. "Out here, there are dozens of inhabitable planets just waiting for Greenfeld to expand into. Where is the logical base for that expansion?" Vicky asked. "Here, on St. Petersburg. You could be the next Wardhaven, the mother of colonies, the supplier of goods and services that this whole new sector of Imperial colonies need."

She eyed Mannie. He was eyeing the star chart as if he'd never seen it before.

"You already had the initial market needed for your first growth spurt. The Navy needs everything for Port Royal. The five closest planets need just about anything you can fabricate and get to them as well as what you, in return, need to make it."

Vicky had her computer cascade the list of raw materials that each of the five planets provided, then opened a new window that cascaded their needs alongside that original list. Then she did the same for St. Petersburg.

Mannie nodded along as the matches became clear.

Then Vicky punched one more button and added Metzburg and New Brunswick.

Mannie whistled.

"You get much sleep last night?" he asked.

"My computer did all the work after I asked it the right questions."

"Do you always ask the right questions?"

"I rarely did until last night. I got bored during a meeting about upgrading the space docks to work on heavy cruisers. I scratched an itch I didn't know I had, and this is what came of it."

"Well, I can vouch that long talks about upgrading the yard and docks on High St. Petersburg can be boring," Mannie said, casting Vicky a whole new look.

Vicky found she kind of liked that different look in Mannie's eyes. It tasted of a job well done, and proud of it. She could really get used to it.

"You're right. We are thinking small, but small is the way we've been trained to think. Small and *legal*."

Rubbing his chin, he walked over to one of his office's large windows. Vicky joined him. Her eye was drawn to the larger tower, the one where they had met with the titans of banking and industry last night.

"Are they still in town?" she asked.

"Likely sleeping. We were up into the wee hours last night. No, this morning."

"You think you can wake them up?"

"Damned if I'm not going to give it a try. And any that blow me off, roll over, and go back to sleep will deserve what they don't get," he said with a boyish laugh. "Oh, Vicky. I had no idea what I was getting into the morning I ambushed Kris Longknife's truck. I figured I'd get her to get you down here to sign off on the greatest brainchild of my life."

"You did."

"No, Your Grace. I used a princess to hook a Grand Duchess, and now I'm riding a tigress who seems to know no bounds."

"We could all end up being hanged?" Vicky decided she should point that out. Mannie was being most manic.

"Yes, I imagine we could. Or we could save *your* Empire."

"I like to think of it as *our* Empire. To the Navy folks I talk to, it's theirs as much as mine."

"You keep this up, Duchess, and a whole lot of people will be thinking of it the same way."

Again, Vicky found herself feeling warmed by Mannie's words in a way that she'd never quite felt before. "We will have to talk about this more," she said, feeling almost shy before his approval.

"But first, we need to talk to some very important people who have no idea just how important they are about to become."

"Or very dead," Vicky added.

"The less we say about that, the better, Your Grace."

"Are you suggesting that I am wrong to think so?"

"No, Vicky," he said, using her given name for the second time. "I am suggesting that you are right. Oh so very right. These people will know how so very right just as soon as the words are out of your mouth. However, there is no need for us to belabor the obvious. Not when the obvious is what we intend to avoid."

"Very wise advice, good Mayor."

CHAPTER 52

VICKY found that the third time she presented her proposal for St. Petersburg's new future, it flowed smoothly into a natural structure. That was good. Its third audience needed to have it fed to them smoothly.

It did not go down easily.

She was hardly into her proposal before she was getting looks from around the table like she had never gotten before.

Half eyed her with eagerness, ready to follow her to hell and back. The other half clearly thought her mad and well gone around the bend.

"This treason is just plain suicide," one banker shouted into the silence when she had finished her presentation.

"Maybe it is suicide, but if it isn't, it's the future for my kids, grandkids, and their grandkids as well," followed on the heels of the first response.

Vicky sat down and allowed the initial reactions to gently wash around the room like a tsunami. By the clock, it took a full half hour for the waters to calm.

Finally, someone voiced an idea that captured unanimous consent. "Come on now, none of us here are innocents in the woods. We've all had our hands in a bit of smuggling somewhere in our lives. If we haven't actually done the smuggling, we've passed this or that trade off to someone who has. And you bankers, you've funded a few accounts here and there that didn't make any sense on the usual ledgers, now haven't you?" The speaker raised his hands in an expressive shrug. "We smuggle a bit of this or that to New Brunswick or Metzburg, and they smuggle what we want right back."

The room heaved a sigh of assent, and everyone smiled.

Until Vicky cleared her throat and said, "That confession of ancient sins sounds delightful, but it won't work. Not in the here and now."

She could not have unsettled the room more by lobbing a hand grenade onto the table.

"Hold it, Peterwald," snapped an attractive young woman, one of the few females present. She sported a bright red power suit and had been a strong ally of Vicky's until a moment ago. Now she was on her feet. "Did I miss something? Wasn't this your idea? Are you suddenly getting all Peterwald graspy at talk of a bit of smuggling?"

Vicky waited for the table side chatter to settle to a dull roar. "No. I still support the idea. However, you will not be able to implement it with a bit of smuggling here, there, or yonder."

"And why not?" the young woman demanded, hands on hips.

Vicky stood to face the woman eye to eye. "Because smuggling is out of the question. You smuggle a little bit of this or that by adding a few containers to this ship or that. You slip them through customs with a wink and a bribe, and all is well. Smuggling gets lost or hidden in the normal flow of trade. I'm sure you have noticed that nothing is normal about the flow of trade these days."

Many around the table mouthed a silent "Oh." The young woman actually gave voice to a squeaked one.

"The situation is even more complicated than that. We don't just have a lack of trade. We actually have ships in space with a clear intent to restrict trade and even blockade certain planets," Vicky said, going on in the face of growing amazement around the wide, gleaming conference table.

"My darling stepmama and the rest of the Bowlingame family are not just grabbing the fruit that falls as Greenfeld wallows through this autumn of its life but are actively shaking the tree."

The woman in red had collapsed into her chair. Vicky settled into her seat, refusing to tower over those around her.

"Last night, Admiral von Mittleburg shared some of the nastier sides of our present situation. As revenues have shrunk, so has the official budget. So has the budget of the Navy. Ships that still had several years of use in them have been laid up in ordinary. Some have even been sold for scrap to raise money, no doubt so my father could pay the stonemasons working on his palace," Vicky said dryly.

"The problem is, some of those scrapped ships have been showing up in the crosshairs of ships still serving our Empire."

Vicky paused to let that sink in. "Just last month, a Navy light cruiser found itself fighting a Bremerhaven class heavy cruiser."

That drew a gasp.

"Fortunately, the amateurs fighting the larger guns were less well trained and officered. The *Emden* left the pirate bloodied and glad to surrender. Navy intel is still going over the captured data, but they have a pretty good picture of what the pirates are up to and why. The only thing they haven't been able to get to the bottom of is the "who."

"What is going on?" Mannie asked in pure puzzlement.

"We are all suffering as trade shrinks," Vicky said. "But we are not suffering fast enough for some people's greed. These pirates have been unleashed to speed the decline of trade, and the Navy has been shrunk to cause the pirates less trouble, if not to fatten the pirates on the ships stripped from the fleet."

"Damn their black hearts," Mannie muttered.

"Yes," Vicky agreed. "Interrupted trade causes fabricators to close down. No work sends jobless men and women into the streets. Overburdened governments can hardly feed the starving. And when the hungry riot, the Security Consultants arrive with an offer to bring back law and order, but at a price. A very high price, because the vultures quickly strip off what is worth taking at a price that would have been thought a bad joke only a few months before. My in-laws are building themselves a private empire off the scraps they strip from the carcass that was our Empire."

Vicky paused, then made a sour face. "Did I mention that I do not like my new in-laws very much?"

"May I mention that I never had any love for any Peterwald?" the woman in red said.

"I have begun to see just why we are not loved," Vicky said. "The last few years have been an eye-opening experience for me, as the Navy showed me what had been missing from my training, and a certain Wardhaven princess rubbed my face in my own shortcomings. She also laughed at some of the more absurd aspects of what I had been raised to firmly believe in."

Vicky ran a worried hand through her hair. "It has been a tough time for me," she said, but then turned to face those around the table. "But a worse time for you and the Empire."

"You found out about this blockade gambit last night," Mannie said.

"Yes."

"But you still brought this idea to us this morning? I take it that you don't see the lack of the smuggling option to be a showstopper."

"No."

"How?" the mayor asked.

"We do for Metzburg and New Brunswick what we did for Poznan and Presov. We load a convoy with what they need and we can provide, then have the Navy escort it to its destination. If pirates attempt to stop us, the Navy blows them out of space."

"You make that sound simple," the woman in red said.

"It has been simple enough to work in the real world. I'm told simplicity tends to."

"But it lacks something," the woman said, waving a hand. "What shall I call it? Subtlety? No. How about secrecy? We fit out a fleet and parade it halfway into the heart of the Empire. Everyone will know what we're doing."

"And right now they don't already know it?" Vicky said, raising both eyebrows in mock shock.

"These consultations are secret," the woman snapped. "We swore it among ourselves."

"I have been a guest on your planet for only a short time," Vicky said, "and already there have been two attempts on my life. Just yesterday, a little note from my loving stepmom was slipped into my computer in a fashion that left the best security technicians dumbfounded. Do you honestly think that you can do anything without its being reported to certain circles on Greenfeld?"

The tsunami of shock, fear, and desperation smashed back into the room. It swept around the table before swirling into eddies of panicked conversation.

Vicky waited again for the waters to calm, then stood. "You have the same choice I have." She held up her fist. "One, you can wait for them to come for you." She raised her thumb.

"Two"—she jabbed her pointer finger out—"you can run away and hide and hope you are not worth the cost of hunting you down and hanging you."

She paused and emitted a laugh that came out sounding more like a cackle. "I don't have that option."

"Or"—she added her middle finger to the jab—"we can grab for something we want, that your planet needs, and make your future better than your past. We go for it and do our best to get away with it for as long as we can before anyone figures out what we're up to. And maybe, in the grabbing, someone we all love to hate will unbalance herself into a pratfall. Remember, those who hoist themselves up on the bodies of their innocent victims can fall a very long way."

Vicky let her eyes circle round the table. "Which will it be?"

The silence was hard and went long. Eyes flitted from one to another around the table as friends, allies, maybe even enemies silently took each other's measure and waited for someone to launch themselves into the long hush.

"It seems to me," the woman in red finally said, "that you have taken that second option. You fled Greenfeld to try to lose yourself on St. Petersburg. We are just about as far from the palace as you can go and still have indoor plumbing."

That drew a nervous laugh from around the table.

"I think I have a higher opinion of St. Petersburg than you may have," Vicky offered. "Yes, I fled here, but I fled to a planet that had the best industrial base I knew of."

"Knew of and owed you a bit of a debt," the woman shot back.

"Knew of and was in better shape because I had stuck my neck out and helped you when you asked for it."

"Helped us because a certain Princess Kris Longknife suggested you help," was sharp as any knife.

"Yes. I admitted that the last couple of years have been a learning experience for me. There's nothing wrong with learning from the best, even if they are one of those damn Longknifes."

Laughter softened the hard edge of the silence. Around the table, people turned to each other and whispered among themselves. Vicky could only hope they were not taking the counsel of their fears.

"How will we work this trade?" a man asked. "Ships showing up in orbit with a load of miscellaneous junk might work for planets in the depth of collapse, but I don't see Metzburg and New Brunswick in that shape."

"Many of you have business agents on those planets," Mannie put in. "Admittedly, we were limited to selling dried fruits and fine wines before, but we have agents, and we can have them quietly check into expanding the range of our product line to include dried electronics and fine crystal fabrications."

Again the room tasted the softness of shared laughs.

"You can have most of what we're carrying already sold before it arrives in orbit, and most of what you want built and waiting for us on the pier as we dock," Vicky said. "As quickly as we can off-load and onload, we'll be out of there and on our way back here."

"But you said our convoy could be fighting its way through a blockade of pirates with heavy cruisers. Some of us have heard about the *Attacker*. The pirates got it good," the woman in red pointed out.

"Have you heard of my new yacht?" Vicky said, most daintily. "Its name is the *Retribution*, and it sports 18-inch guns and three-meter armor."

"You call that a yacht?" the woman said, eyes wide.

"I'm a Grand Duchess. I do things a bit grander than most," Vicky said, grinning.

"I should say you do."

"What will happen to us if we start this new trade route?" a man asked.

"You will make enemies in high places," Vicky said, as offhand as she could manage. "Or should I say, you already have people in high places plotting your downfall and plunder. You will make them unhappy. Is that a problem?"

"Not in my book," Mannie said. Now it was his turn to stand. "For those of us living in Sevastopol, Greenfeld has kept us under its boot for a very long time. Sometimes harder than others, but there was never any doubt: We were the dirt. They were the boot, and they had the upper hand.

"Well, thanks to our city charter, we managed to soften the boot, but it was still a boot. Then things went to hell for some of you, but we down on the south coast managed to make lemonade out of those lemons. It was also nice to not have a boot on our necks."

He turned to Vicky. "I don't have a doubt that under any projected regime likely to take hold in the palace on Greenfeld, there is a boot in my future. Under the Empire I see in Vicky's eyes, there is no such boot. Not for Sevastopol. Not for St. Petersburg. Not for the Empire.

"I don't know about you, but I'm game for this chance for a change. I've had enough of boots; let's see what we can do about making our own future."

That got a few cheers from the table.

The woman in red stood silent, though. When the room grew quiet again, she shot a verbal dart at Vicky. "Do we need a damn Empire? What have the Peterwalds and the Empire ever done for us but keep that damn boot of yours, Mannie, on our necks. Put that in your pipe, Your Grand Douchessness, and smoke that."

Vicky couldn't say that she was surprised at the shot. She'd even found herself gnawing on that question quite a bit of late. Not while she was growing up. Not while she lived in the warm embrace of the palace. But fleeing from the palace had caused her to reflect, and in reflection, find herself questioning.

She examined the possible comebacks and found the first one the best.

"I'm not surprised at your barb, ma'am. I've found myself considering the same question as I dodged one assassin after another sent by the Empress. I think most of you were raised like me, to sing the praises of Greenfeld, and if it wasn't an Empire back then, it sure walked and quacked like one, or so it seemed to me."

She got a few nervous chuckles at that.

"I do not doubt that whatever we had is dead and gone. What we will have for your kids and grandkids and their grandkids will depend a lot on what we do here and now.

"Now, as for me?" Vicky laid her hands on the table and spread her fingers wide. "Princess Kris Longknife shared something with me that likely won't surprise any of you. She has no idea what a princess is worth. She isn't at all sure that the worlds need another princess, but she is one, at least for now, and she's willing to see just how high she can push up the value of a princess."

Vicky clinched her fists. "I don't know what a Grand Duchess of Greenfeld is worth, either. What I do know is that I've got the title, and I see things that need doing. So, right now, I will use my Grand Duchess card to get all I can for the good people who have paid too damn high a price for this Empire my father has declared.

Vicky chose her next words carefully. *I will not betray the Navy's trust.*

"If you feel that you can get some good for you out of me, I'm here to be used. If you have a problem with me, come, talk to me, and we'll see what we can work out. You don't have to be afraid of me. I am not followed about by an Imperial headsman. I have yet to order anyone's head off. Maybe I'm a fool, but I think this Grand Duchess is worth more on the hoof than hung in the closet.

"What do you say?"

"I think you are worth a try," Mannie said, right on the downbeat.

"It sounds worth it to me," came from another. "I'm game." "There's bound to be one good Peterwald in the bunch," seemed to fill the room.

The woman in red spoke last. "Yes. I do think we should give you a try." She paused for a moment, then went on in a businesslike fashion. "So, Your Grace, how do you propose we work this thing? Do we come up with a wish list and an offer list and send it off in the mail to our factors on those planets? I'm no expert on the Imperial mail of late, but that looks like a good way to wave a red flag, or worse, get our mail intercepted and never delivered."

"I couldn't agree with you more," Vicky said. "How about

you come up with your two lists and I see if the Navy has a light cruiser or destroyer going that way. We deliver it for you and make sure it gets where you want it to go."

"Having the Navy deliver it would also show the level of our support," Mannie pointed out. "This isn't just something a few, ah, intrepid souls are doing."

"A few intrepid, traitorous souls," the woman in red countered.

"Whoever is making the offer," Vicky said, "having the Navy behind it will make it more real. Especially since you're asking for heavy industry, the kind of heavy industry a Navy needs to get work done on its ships."

"I think that will work best," a banker said, eyeing the young woman in the red power business suit.

"If you insist, Preston," the woman said.

"Then let us begin composing our lists," an industrialist suggested.

"While others of us figure out how to pay for it," a banking type added.

CHAPTER 53

───

VICKY found herself ushered out of the meeting on Mannie's arm. Commander Boch rose quickly from his seat beside the door and opened it for them.

"Would you care for a late lunch?" the mayor asked her.

"It has been a long time since breakfast," she admitted.

Kit and Kat joined them from their monitoring posts outside the conference room, accompanied by four of Mannie's local security crew. As they waited for the elevator, Vicky cast a glance back at the door behind which the rumble of discussion was quite audible.

"Do we dare leave them alone?" she muttered to herself.

"Your father likely would not," Mannie said, "but do you want to walk in the ruts he left?"

"That doesn't sound like a good idea to me and likely is a worse idea to you, from the tone of your voice," Vicky admitted.

"Then what do you say we leave business to the businesspeople?" the mayor said with a confident smile.

"Will they leave politics to the elected officials?" Vicky asked, as they entered the elevator, trailed by their small army of guards.

"When they do a good job, we tend to leave business to

them. When we do a good job, they tend to leave us to our politicking."

"Tend?" Vicky said, both eyebrows coming up in a question.

"Nobody's perfect," he threw off with a casual wave of his hand.

"Or we wouldn't be in this mess, would we now?" Vicky agreed.

Mannie took them up to a restaurant in the penthouse. It was small and featured every variation on dead cow, by his own words, and plenty of it. "It's owned by one of the ranchers who outfitted your fleet with frozen beef."

"Vertical integration?" Vicky asked.

"Yep, he makes money out of everything but the moo."

The first taste of steak showed that he deserved every pfennig he made.

Mannie had seated Vicky in a quiet, shadowed corner. The commander and the two miniature assassins had the only approaches covered. They shared that duty with Mannie's foursome of security guards, but Vicky suspected that none of the seven was sharing anything with anyone.

The thought brought a smile to Vicky's face and a questioning glance from Mannie. She lowered her voice, and said, "Our guards do not play well in the shooting gallery with others, do they?"

Mannie and she shared a soft chuckle on that thought that they would not want to explain to their protectors.

"They *are* taking this protection job very seriously," Mannie said.

When Vicky said nothing but allowed her eyebrows to climb up in question, he went on. "You can't blame them. Two assassination attempts on you and that damn love note from your murderous stepmom."

Which raised a question for the mayor. Vicky spoke without reflection. "You afraid to be around me?"

There was a long pause before he answered. A pause that Vicky found discomforting in a way she was not used to.

"I have to admit, things are never boring around you," he finally said, looking down at his steak. "I kind of like that."

Vicky shared his chuckle. So. She was not boring. That was an interesting response from a man.

"I'll take that as a compliment," she said. It was strange, talking to Mannie like this. Strange and different. She had met a lot of men and taken them in a lot of different ways. Mannie was kind of hard to figure out how to take. Hard and challenging.

"A Grand Duchess must get lots of compliments," Mannie said.

"Yes, I hear plenty, but most of them aren't worth a pfennig to the mark. I kind of like the sound of yours."

Mannie mulled that over for a long moment before offering, "You must live in a very strange world."

"Deadly. Deceitful. Full of too much vanity and foolishness," Vicky provided. "Lots of bootlicking and backstabbing. You are an interesting change of pace and a pleasure to be around."

Now it was Mannie's turn to take time to think. "I haven't had many women tell me I'm a pleasure to be around."

"That can't be true," Vicky said before she gave his words a moment's thought.

"Actually, it is. Most women find me rather boring. Too focused on my job. I think even my mother wishes I'd take a long vacation. Meet some nice girl at a ski lodge or beach."

Vicky looked around at the nearly empty restaurant. "You're not likely to meet many ski bunnies here."

Again, Mannie chuckled. Vicky found she liked the sound of his laugh. "Nope, I've made it to this hardening-of-the-arteries phase without convincing a woman it would be a good idea to share her life with me. Then again, I could ask what a nice girl like you is doing all alone."

Vicky found she had to laugh at the idea of her alone. Her eyes swept over their guards, and he joined in.

"I find I have to be on my own, if not all alone. Most men who get too close to me end up dead or seriously injured. Oh, there I've gone and done it. No doubt you'll be running for the exit, now."

"Oh, so you don't want me running for the exit?"

"No, you see, I find you interesting, but I should warn you that my sins are many, and a full review of them all at one time would likely result in the loss of this fine lunch."

They applied themselves to said lunch for a few silent minutes.

When Vicky spoke again, she found herself falling back on the business at hand. "When I came into your office this morning, you said you had a surprise for me, then I surprised you."

"Your surprise was a much more fantastic one than mine," Mannie said, making as if to brush something away with his hand.

"But what was it?" Vicky said, plowing on.

"Last night, the industrialists all agreed that we can upgrade the two main docks at the station with fabrications from our industry. Surprise of surprises, the bankers came up with creative ways to finance the work. We should be able to start running heavy gear up to the station in a week. However, some of the completed space-dock frameworks and machinery are likely to be way beyond the lift capacity of our shuttles. We will have to put them together in orbit. That will take more time than if we fabricate them completely down here and fly them up. Can the Navy help?"

"Computer, when is the *Crocodile* due back?" Vicky asked, already seeing a solution to this latest problem.

It's fun having answers to people's problems.

"The second section of the convoy has started its way back to St. Petersburg already," the computer reported. "It should be here in four to seven days."

"That's when the Navy can begin lifting up your heavy stuff," Vicky said.

"And that will be when we have the first of the heavy stuff ready to lift," Mannie said, and had his computer send Vicky's computer the entire project plan for changing two docks on the station from nice-to-have to just-what-the-Navy-needed.

The maître d' approached them when the meal was winding down. He brought no check. Instead, he knelt beside them and met Vicky eye to eye.

"Your Grace, we are most grateful to have offered you one of our fine meals, you, the generous Grand Duchess. What you have done has left my daughter in tears and my wife but little short of them as well."

Vicky must have looked as puzzled as she felt, because he went on.

"When you first raised the question of feeding the starving, my daughter's heart was much moved. She and her classmates mowed lawns, washed cars, and baked cookies to raise money for some of the food you took to Poznan. In their name, I thank you, and I offer you this meal on our behalf."

Vicky found herself speechless.

"Why, thank you," was what she finally managed to stammer out.

"Please, Pierre, you must be paid for what you served us," Mannie said, offering the credit chit he had already pulled from his pocket.

"No, no, Monsieur le Mayor, when you are with the gracious duchess, your money will be no good in my establishment."

Mannie joined Vicky in speechlessness as they watched the retreat of the servitor.

"I've never experienced something like that," Vicky finally managed to get out.

"You'll excuse me if I say I never expected to see anyone on St. Petersburg react to a Peterwald like that either, but then, you have not acted like a Peterwald since the first time you set foot on our planet."

"I had a good guide," Vicky said, and blessed Kris Longknife, wherever in the galaxy she was.

Mannie leaned back and rubbed at the side of his nose. His eyes went thoughtful.

"Can I trust you when you look like that?" Vicky asked. "Just for future reference?"

"I don't know," Mannie answered in a distant voice.

"A St. Petersburg mark for your thoughts," Vicky said.

"It's either not worth that or worth a whole lot more."

"Share, Mannie. Share." She was surprised to find that she'd used his first name.

"The gracious Grand Duchess. The generous Grand Duchess. An interesting choice of words, don't you think?"

"Certainly not a choice of words that has been applied to a Smythe-Peterwald since, oh, way before the popes had armies."

"You've been around that long?"

"Longer, if you can trust my great-grandfather. He paid quite a sum to have a genealogist verify the family stories. The gal found a whole lot more than was recorded in the family books. I suspect she was a fantasy writer in her day job."

Mannie waved off this distraction. "The times, they are

a-changing, as the words go in some old song my grandmadre likes to sing. Change is not something most people like."

"I don't much like the changes coming at us," Vicky admitted.

"Yes, but we've got a lot of people who need to see change and accept it. Even pay taxes for it. Do you see my problem?"

Vicky winced. "Let's say that I don't."

"I need to make change more palatable," Mannie said, leaving the how and wherefore hanging unspoken.

"If people could see a Peterwald as a gracious duchess, as a generous duchess, they might find it easier to get behind those changes," she finished for him.

"If they actually got a chance to see that gracious, generous person in the flesh."

"Oh, my aching, shot-up butt," Vicky groaned

"Yes, like every sort of change, this has its minor down-sides."

"I consider getting shot a major downside."

"Yes," Mannie agreed. "Shall we forget this bad idea of mine? I get a lot of ideas. Way too many of them are eminently forgettable."

Vicky found herself reflecting on Mannie's idea. She'd never thought of herself as someone who was very likeable, but then, she'd never done any of the things she'd done of late. Would people follow where she led?

Vicky remembered some of the stuff she'd read in Kris Longknife's file. She'd led, and people had followed. Often to their death. But people still followed that woman. Stood in line to follow her.

Could I ever be the kind of leader the Wardhaven princess is?

For a moment, Vicky considered the talks that she and Kris would have when they got back together. There were quite a few things that Vicky would love to see the reaction to from that Wardhaven princess when Vicky told her what she'd done.

Helping haul two planets away from the abyss was something to be proud of.

It would be a shame to come this far and get too scared to go on.

It would be worse to get my brains blown out.

"How might we get some of the rewards that waving a

generous Grand Duchess might bring?" Vicky said slowly. "That assumes I don't get my brains blown out. That would, no doubt, ruin the entire effect."

"And ruin someone I'm finding most interesting."

"Mannie, you are saying the nicest things."

"And coming up with the worst of ideas."

"Maybe. Maybe not. Tell me, Mannie, did you call ahead and tell Pierre, that was what you called him?"

"Yes, he is Pierre, and if you are asking me if I let him know ahead of time, the answer is no. I may have dumb ideas, but I am not completely lacking in wits."

"So. Might I expect that some more of these spontaneous demonstrations might follow in my wake? Might we get some of the benefits if I just happened to be present when something nice happened without the downside of alerting my flock of waiting assassins?"

"Like visiting the county fair and handing out the blue ribbons for the kids' three-legged race without anyone's knowing you were going to be there?"

"The rewards might not be as high as we'd like . . ."

"But the risks might be a whole lot more manageable even if your stepmom keeps that bull's-eye enameled on your backside."

"Exactly."

"Let me think," Mannie said. "I get a whole lot of requests for ribbon cuttings, first-shovel liftings, tree plantings, and ribbon giving. How many times have I told my grandmadre that I'd love to have a king to take the easy stuff off my hands?"

"Easy stuff!" Vicky yelped, but softly. They were getting appraising glances from their shared guards.

"Not the stuff you've been doing, Your Grace, unless, of course, you've been cutting ribbons."

"The Navy had me standing too many watches to be much of a ribbon cutter."

"So, let's see what we can have you do to make folks a lot happier you're here with us."

"Yes, you look into that. I think I need to get myself back up to the station and let the admiral know that he's got some heavy lifting ahead and a chance to patch up one badly dinted heavy cruiser. Oh, and I also need to schedule a couple of ships for a fast run to Metzburg and New Brunswick. I can't be much of a Grand Duchess if I drop the ball on my coordination duties."

"Most definitely. You'd be a pretty okay duchess, but not a Grand Duchess," Mannie quipped.

"Are you always like this?" Vicky asked through a feigned groan.

"Pretty much, or so I'm told."

"It might explain your being single and all that," Vicky tried her own shot.

"Very likely," Mannie said sadly, "but it's a condition always subject to change."

Vicky laughed out loud. "Are you flirting with me? I should warn you, flirting is not something I've much experience with." Throwing men down and taking them by storm, yes, but not a lot of flirting.

Mannie shrugged enigmatically as he offered her a hand up from the table.

He delivered Vicky safely to the shuttleport and was still watching as the shuttle motored down the ramp and into the bay.

That was nice. Vicky tried to remember when the last time was that someone had stayed to see her off rather than turned away, glad she was gone.

She couldn't.

CHAPTER 54

VICKY often used shuttle rides for planning. This afternoon, she found herself forced into reflection.

It wasn't for lack of trying. She reviewed what she needed to talk over with Admiral von Mittleburg and found it short and easily organized.

That done, she sank into self-examination with unaccustomed speed.

What is going on between me and Mannie?

It wasn't that the guy was a hunk. She'd had a lot better-looking men in her bed. He wasn't even all that cute. No more than a few inches taller than she and with that bit of a paunch, he was the epitome of a desk-bound bureaucrat but hardly the guy a looker like a Grand Duchess would give a second glance.

So what is it about his smile that makes me feel all warm inside?

The business of the moment was throwing them together, but she'd managed to dodge a lot of men the times had thrown at her.

Dodged them or used them and tossed them aside.

Vicky whispered the word "used," aloud. It rolled off her tongue oh so easily. She'd used a lot of men. Hardly had her boobs and hips come in than she discovered the marvelous power they gave her over men and put them to good use.

Dad kept calling her his "nice little girl," even after she'd been caught in bed with several of the available studs. Come to think of it, he hadn't given up that "nice little girl" shtick until he shipped her off to the Navy.

Bedding the available beefcakes had gotten her what she wanted from the guys but not so much from her dad.

Interesting.

If I keep this up, I'm going to need a shrink to unsort my brain.

Maggie had been the only one she could talk to about things like this. *Where are you when I really need you, Doc?*

One thing was clear. Mannie was like no other man she'd had in her life. Mannie was passionate . . . not about her but about the world they could make happen together. Good things for his city. For his planet. For his people.

Was that what made him attractive? He was passionate about doing things *for* people, not using people *for* things.

And what are you doing? Vicky asked herself.

For most of her life, she'd been Daddy's little girl. Hank's little sister. *That* girl. *The* girl. She'd *been* things, not *doing* things. She hadn't felt passionate about anything. Not even passionate in bed.

Now, she was committing herself passionately to doing something for people. That felt like nothing she'd ever felt before. And somehow, Mannie was fitting her into his passions. That was leaving her feeling something for Mannie that she'd never felt for any man.

Vicky pursed her lips and mulled that over for a long while. The shuttle was matching with the station, leaving her still very much in need of exploring the full depth of this . . . something.

But when the hatch opened, she pulled herself up out of the seat before the commander could offer her a hand up and marched quickly for admiral's country.

CHAPTER 55

As Vicky expected, the admiral was meeting with his ship-repair specialists, trying to see what they could do to make the *Attacker* fit for space again.

"We need more yard for that," was the conclusion voiced by a commander as Vicky was ushered into the conference room by the admiral's aide.

"Then I think I have just what you need," Vicky said. "Computer, put the yard-upgrade project plan onto the admiral's main screen."

The large bulkhead to the admiral's right lit up with boxes and lists. In an instant, Navy officers were scrambling from their seats to study the displayed action plan.

"Good Lord," seemed to be the most repeatable response.

"Can you actually get this?" the admiral asked Vicky.

"This was what they decided to offer you last night," Vicky said.

"And they'll be taking it all back by tonight," one commander grumbled.

"I doubt it. I've got them all busy on another project," Vicky said breezily.

"What kind of project?" the grumbler asked.

"The one I proposed to the admiral last night," Vicky said, not willing to let that cat out of the bag until it was racing across space to the finish line. Not even among these Navy officers.

What had Kris Longknife said about paranoia keeping her alive?

Are all royalty paranoid? Vicky wondered. It took only a moment's reflection to decide that it was likely they all weren't. *Only the live ones.*

Some of the commanders eyed the admiral, but he stayed focused on the screen in front of him and said nothing.

Yep, it's need to know, and they don't need.

"Sir," a lieutenant commander who'd never taken his eyes from the screen said, "this might make my plan not only doable, but the best of the options we've been looking at."

"Refresh my memory, Eugene," the admiral said.

"If we upgrade D and E docks, we gain two slips that can handle anything. However, that's all we'll have. Yes, the other six slips can handle minor hull damage, but if you want to do anything with a ship's reactor, you've got to get it into one of these two, no matter how small the ship. If we upgrade B and C, we get them able to handle large cruisers while D and E can still handle your large merchant ships or Navy destroyers."

"Furthermore, we may be needing to refit some of the laid-up merchants, if I know what's coming our way," the admiral said, studiously not looking at Vicky.

"I agree with Commander Eugene," said a full commander who wore the gears of the engineering branch in place of the command star above his three stripes. "If we upgraded D and E, we'd either be storing the lighter cranes that we replaced or moving them to B and C. Better to do all the refurbishment on those two and keep the working docks working."

"Gentlemen," the admiral said, "I think you have your work cut out for you. We'll meet tomorrow at 0900 to review your implementation plans."

Dismissed, the commanders quickly departed to their duties.

"A good morning's work," the admiral said, offering Vicky a cup of coffee and directing her away from the table to his couch. He settled into the armchair across from her.

"Oh, that? It was just handed to me on a platter. It was what I dropped into their laps that got them all hot and bothered."

"And you dropped in their lap . . . ?" he left unfinished.

"What we talked about last night," and Vicky quickly outlined what could hardly not be called treason, if not against her father, the Emperor, most certainly against her stepmum, the Empress.

"And they took it well?"

"About as well as anyone offered a chance to be the first in line to be hanged," Vicky said with a dry chuckle.

"So they said no."

"Hardly. As we speak, they're making up lists of what they want to ship to Metzburg and New Brunswick and what they want in return. And if they get what you want, you can expect a very major upgrade to several of your slips."

"You are most persuasive," the admiral offered.

"The times are most persuasive. You can stand still and be run over, or you can start running and grab what's up for grabs. These folks are the naturally grabby type."

"God help us simple peasants when the grabby type are grabbing," the admiral said, and made it sound like a prayer.

"I'd never think of you as a peasant, and certainly not simple," Vicky said, hoping her eyes and smile were sparkling with good humor. A commander doesn't call an admiral a peasant, simple or complex, even a Grand Duchess commander.

"At heart, I find myself a simple farmer," the admiral said.

"Well, I need you to be an admiral for a bit more," Vicky said. "At least, I need you to loan me a few ships. The folks below are making up their wish list and *quid pro quo*, and they need to get it to Metzburg and New Brunswick without it being intercepted."

"They can't just send it over the net, huh?"

"Not and it have any chance of getting there," Vicky said.

"So they want to courier it out on one of my ships."

"You got it in one, sir."

"I expect they want to use their own couriers, too."

"They want to send along some folks who can start the negotiation balls rolling."

The admiral winced. "So I'm to have civilian passengers on my warships."

"Is that a problem, sir?" Vicky asked. She'd carried contractor personnel like Kit and Kat with her without questions asked.

"If I'm caught shipping folks around on my ships, even if they aren't talking treason, I'm guilty of all sorts of violations of rules and regs. That tends to draw attention we don't want."

"And we really don't want to be caught on something minor while we're doing anything that smacks too blatantly of rebellion," Vicky said.

"Exactly."

The two exchanged pained looks for a long moment as they contemplated how not to get caught.

Finally, Vicky shrugged. "About that flag someone might want me to wave," she said.

"The nonexistent one?"

"I'm about to do some flag-waving. Not that one, but one of the gracious, generous Grand Duchess type."

That drew her a blank look from the admiral. Vicky quickly explained how her lunch with Mannie had ended and what the two of them were looking at.

"That's dangerous. Likely deadly," the admiral said.

"No doubt it is," Vicky said, "but I can't wave any flag or gracious banner while hiding under my bed, now can I?"

The admiral scowled. "Point and match to you. I begin to think some of us may not have thought through all our moves."

"Rebellion not being taught at the academies, no doubt you can be forgiven missing a few of the finer points."

"Like trying to wave a banner without making a target of oneself," the admiral muttered.

"So, how do we do this?" Vicky said. "Mannie has made a good case that I am something that people might enjoy gathering around. Then again, those interested in plugging me and collecting my loving stepmum's reward will likely show up as well. We think that if we make me a moving target and one of opportunity, no plastering the town with posters of my itinerary, I might manage to dodge all the small-arms fire."

"I seem to remember something about surprise and stealth in some course I took in my younger and less attentive days," the admiral admitted.

"So we do that and let it be covered on the five o'clock news feed."

"That might work," the admiral allowed.

"You game?"

"You'll have to take your chances if you ever were to take out that only mumbled-about family heirloom and begin waving it. I think my associates had kind of assumed you'd be doing it comfortably and safely from the bridge of a well-protected battleship, but I think we have not made allowances for the need for a popular action to gather popular support."

He mulled the idea over for a long moment, then seemed to resolve his conflict. "I'll have some Marines made available to serve as your obvious protection. I'll see what I can do about finding you some less obvious protection."

"I think Mannie will be doing the same."

"He seems to be coming up a lot in your conversations," was not quite the inquiry of a worried father.

When have I ever had a worried father? Me, not Hank?

"He's the lead politician down there. He's my interface with the planet's business and finances. If I want something, it goes through him."

"And if I want something," the admiral said, "it seems to go through you *and* him."

"Something like that."

"I will see what I can do about getting ships that aren't likely to be snapped up by pirates," the admiral said, "and I'll see if any of my procurement officers might meet the expectations of the business interests. They have the advantage, at this stage of the game, of not shouting rebellion."

"And we don't want to even whisper that word, do we?" Vicky whispered.

"I don't think you can whisper the contents of this trading effort softly enough to not make it treason. Have you given any thought as to how you'll get the goods out and back safely?"

"I was thinking of using the *Retribution* for one of the escorts?"

"Your battleship! It's supposed to be here for your use, and maybe to protect St. Petersburg as well."

"I suspect that might be the idea," Vicky said, "but I do intend to be on my battleship when we make this trading swap."

"Nothing like a Grand Duchess to arrange a grand trade, huh?" the admiral said.

"Kind of like that. Also, if they've got all that future riding on those ships, we want to make sure it gets through. Someone else, no doubt, will want even more to make sure that it does not."

"Putting all your eggs in one basket comes to mind, but I don't know just how."

"We've only got one basket, sir. I say we protect it for all we're worth."

He blew out a worried breath. "A good point. Well, Your Grace, you have made a hash of my evening. I must go about retrieving some of the things I started that will not be finished and begin things I never thought I'd start."

He stood. Vicky did the same. He went to his desk as she headed for the door.

Supper that night was a salad built around locally grown greens, a mix of other things that had never seen old Earth, and topped with sprinkles that the wardroom signboard called shrimp. From the taste of it, it clearly hadn't swum in any earthly deep. Still, she found it tangy. No doubt, human taste buds had done their own evolution since leaving Mother Earth in the rearview mirror.

She adjourned to her quarters to find Kit already naked and ready to help her with her shower.

"I'll take care of myself, tonight," Vicky said

"Can I at least help you out of that dirty old uniform?" Kit pouted.

Vicky relented and enjoyed the feel of Kit peeling her out of her whites. Still, she made it into the shower on her own.

"What's happening to you?" she muttered to herself as she sudsed up quickly and attacked her own skin with a simple washcloth. "Have you been bit by the monogamy bug or something?"

She had been bit by something. Something named Mannie. Or something like the fellow she called Mannie. She didn't know him. She didn't know what he was like or liked, for that matter.

Still, he had a kind of respectable air; there was something so normal about him. The thought of his replacing the detached Mr. Smith in her bed with Kit and Kat flashed across her mind's eye . . . and flashed up TILT.

Somehow, the picture of Mannie sandwiched between her and Kit and Kat just didn't fit the way he went about his day.

She could be wrong. She'd have to find out.

She found herself giggling softly at the thought of them doing sex his somewhat stodgy way Monday, Wednesday, and Friday and taking her multiplayer approach Tuesday, Thursday, and Saturday. Sunday, they'd likely need for recuperation.

Vicky was smiling at that thought when she exited the shower. Kat was waiting with a towel. Vicky took it and dried herself off, then donned the offered sleeping silk pajamas. Again, without the offered help.

She returned to her bedroom to find Kit with several pairs of handcuffs dangling from her spread hands.

"Not tonight," Vicky said.

"Mademoiselle, have we offended you?" Kat asked.

"No, I just need time to think."

"Ze Grand Duchess needs more time with ze handcuffs, I think," Kit said.

"I don't think so," Vicky said, stepping aside.

"Maybe not all of them, cuffing you to ze bed," Kit said, "but you were not so sharp with ze handcuffs the last time you were in them that you do need ze practice getting out of them."

Vicky considered her pet assassin's argument and found she had a point. If she was headed out into the public shooting gallery, not all of what she faced would be bullets.

She held out her hands, and Kit slapped the cuffs on her.

And Vicky found herself frowning. She'd just washed her hair and all her hairpins were still in the bathroom. She suspected that she'd be tackled to the ground by the tiny duo if she turned her back on them. Where that would end would definitely be easy to guess.

She spotted a hairpin behind Kat's ear and grabbed for it.

Kat pulled away, but not quite fast enough.

"Good, my Grand Duchess, but not everyone will be as slow as my grandmere."

In a moment, Vicky was handing the cuffs back to Kit.

That was a mistake. She grabbed Vicky's right hand and swung her around, pinning her arms and cuffing her hands behind her back.

Vicky had half expected that move, at least once Kit started it. She had secreted her hairpin between two fingers and waited, doing a good imitation of bored while her security guardian got her where she wanted her.

"Now," Kit said, "are you still ze Grand Duchess, or are you ze helpless pinned butterfly?"

Vicky had always found working behind her back, by feel and touch alone, a whole lot harder. It took her a couple of minutes to get her hands free.

While she struggled, Kit and Kat hummed and did their best to look bored.

"Too slow, too slow," Kit was saying well before Vicky handed her the cuffs.

"Let's do that again."

Vicky was faster the second time.

"So, ze Grand Duchess can learn. That iz good. Now, ze bed."

"No."

"One hand only," Kat suggested.

"One hand," Vicky allowed. So one hand was cuffed to Vicky and one to the left post of the large bed. When Vicky reached for the cuffed hand, the two assassins latched on to her other hand.

"No. No, no. You may not let us cuff you like they would, but you must get loose from what they would."

Ugly memories of being naked and cuffed spread-eagle across a bed came back to her. She shivered in revulsion. She'd gotten out of the cuffs that night without key or hairpin. What were the chances she could use the same approach to the next situation like that?

Slim to none, she told herself. She'd read the file on Kris Longknife. No doubt there was now a file on one Vicky Peterwald. What had worked for her once wasn't likely to work a second time.

Besides, I still have nightmares about that time.

She likely could not go there again, and most definitely did not want to go to that place ever again.

"So, my experts in all things human and deadly, how do I get out of this?"

"It will never be easy," Kit said. "It iz not intended for it to be easy for you. But here, put the hairpin in your mouth."

Vicky did.

"Hide it well."

Vicky hid it between her left lip and lower teeth.

Kit forced her mouth open and removed the pin not at all gently. "That iz not well done. Do it again."

Now Vicky used her tongue to move it around in her mouth until it was between her right lip and her upper teeth.

"Go get it," she told Kit.

The woman forced Vicky's mouth open. "Nothing there," she muttered. "Raise your tongue."

Vicky stuck it out.

Kit grabbed it and none too gently pulled it out farther, then ran her fingers under the tongue. "Good. I did not see it when I pulled your mouth open. I did not see it under your tongue. I suspect it is hidden between your upper teeth and your lip, but I did not see it. If they are not too diligent, and most do not wish to risk the loss of a finger should you bite, you might get away with it."

Kit moved back on the bed and nodded to her fellow assassin. "Do not let go of her hand. Now, Your Grace, can you use your teeth to work the lock?"

It took three tries. Twice, Vicky dropped the pin onto the bed and had to turn herself into a pretzel to retrieve it. Twice, the lock defeated her lips-and-tongue-guided pin. On the third try, she was rewarded by a soft click, and the cuffs fell onto the floor.

"You are slow, and lacking in any finesse, but you will not likely starve to death if cuffed to a bed and left on your own," Kit concluded.

"We will sleep in the next room," Kat said, collecting the cuffs from the floor. "Let us know if you need anything in the night."

And with that, her two assassins by day, seductresses by night, padded out of her bedroom.

"Remind me to be more careful about pissing those two off," Vicky muttered to herself as she tried to find a comfortable place in her bed. A comfortable *alone* place in her bed.

"Mannie, if I've misread you, and you turn out to not be the upstanding, respectable, salt-of-the-earth type I'm taking you for, I am going to be so mad at you. You are going to get *so* familiar with those cuffs and all the things I and those half-pint-sized murderers can do to you."

Still, as she drifted off to sleep, it was just Mannie and herself in the bed.

And it was so nice.

CHAPTER 56

T HAT morning, the Gracious Grand Duchess Campaign got off to a great start. Once again, Vicky rode the drop shuttle in full, Her Grace, the Grand Duchess, Lieutenant Commander Victoria trappings of ribbons and gold on her gleaming dress whites that the warm autumn weather encouraged.

At noon, Mannie had her standing beside him digging the first shovelful of dirt . . . actually the first thirty-five shovelfuls of dirt . . . for a new business tower.

At three, she cut the ribbon to a very strange building. It seemed to be one floor, but that floor went up through twists and turns for a good five stories. Inside were over a hundred little boutique shops selling frippery of every description.

At six, there was the winner of a spelling bee to congratulate and all the participants to encourage. Vicky passed a few words with each of them and failed to spell any of the words they tossed her way. Several, however, wanted her to know how they'd helped raise money for the starving kids of Poznan.

Yes, Vicky was the caring, generous, and gracious Grand Duchess that they all wanted to see.

It took some getting used to. Not by the people; they loved

it. No, it was Vicky who needed time to get comfortable in these new shoes

It didn't always work out for her own self-interest. She ended up getting quite hungry as lunch somehow got skipped, and dinner was a long time coming.

Vicky tried to image her stepmother, or even her dad putting up with any of this. She couldn't. *Maybe I'm onto something here,* she reflected with a smile.

Three days of this around Sevastopol, and she was not tired of it yet.

Then her Marine guard officer pulled her aside just after she finished cutting the ribbon for a new wing of an expanded hospital. Mannie's senior guard was at his elbow. "We interrupted a woman trying to pull a pistol on you," he reported. "We took her down before she could get a shot off, at you or anyone else in the crowd."

"Did the newsies spot it?" Mannie asked.

"I don't think so, sir, but you might want to call in a few chits."

Mannie nodded. "I'll do that."

"It was fun while it lasted." Vicky sighed.

"Who says we're done?" Mannie said with a cat-that-ate-the-canary grin.

"They've spotted your pattern."

"So we expand our scope and break the pattern."

The next day, Mannie met her for breakfast in the station wardroom and told her where she'd be going that day.

"You haven't been to Moskva. It's a ways east of Sevastopol on the Midland Sea. They've got a harvest festival going today, the first of the season. Care to hand out the blue ribbons to some cowboys?"

"Will I have to kiss them, too?" Vicky teased.

Mannie didn't miss a beat. "They just might expect you to," he said with his full-face grin.

"You going to break their arm if I do?"

"Maybe I'll break your arm," he said, but his eyes sparkled.

Vicky couldn't remember when a man had cared about what she did or who she was. Plenty had cared about what she could get them. This tasted oh so different . . . and very nice.

"I don't think you'd hurt me," she said slyly.

"I doubt I could," he agreed somberly, then brightened. "But I'm trying to be unpredictable here."

The next day, he met her again at breakfast. "So, what are we going to do unpredictable today and where will we do it?" she asked.

"How about we hit the north side of the Midland Sea today. There's St. Petersburg to the east and Kiev to the west." He pulled a coin out of his pocket. "Heads we go east."

He caught the coin in his hand and flipped it onto the back of the other one. "It's heads."

"Tell me about St. Petersburg," Vicky said.

Before the breakdown, St. Petersburg had been the main industrial city of the planet. It had been hit hard when trade collapsed and had little other industry to fall back on. It could hardly feed itself. It had been a long, hard pull to recovery.

Mannie told her this as the shuttle dropped them into the wide bay that provided the shuttle-landing ground for St. Pete, as it was more often called. They'd just created a new farmers' market, so Vicky got to cut a ribbon at ten. At noon, Vicky was at a huge industrial park where a large plant had been divided up into several light-industrial concerns.

"I'm not sure it's safe for me to show my face around here just yet," Mannie said. "Sevastopol managed to buy up much of the content of this building. Huge presses and tool and dies came our way a couple of years ago for not much more than the price of scrap."

It turned out Mannie's sins were not forgotten. He took a lot of ribbing, but it seemed good-natured.

Vicky spent her afternoon at an apprentice graduation ceremony before attending an ice-hockey play-off so she could award the winning cup. They were back on the shuttle after a late supper of chicken and rice done up in a spicy fashion that Vicky had never tasted before.

Vicky managed to talk Mannie into staying the night on the station. Unfortunately, the admiral heard about it and assigned quarters to the mayor and his party before they docked with the station. Vicky watched as the mayor's security team and guards led him off to his room as if they had to protect him from her.

They weren't far wrong on that one.

They didn't flip a coin the next morning. There were several things going on in Kiev, and they hadn't visited it yet. As the shuttle dropped from orbit, Vicky watched Kiev come into view. It was also a seaside city, stretching around a bay. Off to its east were high mountains. Flowing through its middle was a wide river. To its west was a forested plateau. Its sandy beaches were white enough to make Vicky blink and look away.

"I could live here," she told Mannie. "Its weather is as warm and balmy as Anhalt on Greenfeld."

"Then I can see how green slipped into the name," Mannie said, looking at the verdant parks and tree-lined boulevards. "Still, I like our rugged hills and sun-kissed plains. They green up very nicely in the rainy season. Have you ever seen our rolling backcountry when it's aflame with wildflowers?"

"Not yet."

"I'll have to arrange it."

"Just add it to my schedule."

"In a random fashion, of course," he added with a grin.

Today's schedule included a high-school competition to see which school could answer the most questions the fastest. The poor young man who led the winning team turned beet red and stammered horribly as Vicky gave him the trophy and a peck on the cheek.

"But he was so vocal during the competition," Vicky told Mannie as they left.

"I bet his competitors wished you'd been asking the questions."

"Then one of the girls on the team would have likely beat him to the buzzer and gotten a buss on the cheek from you."

"Not likely. I'm not the gracious Grand Duchess."

An electronics-fabrication mill had just been completed. Although it was already online, Vicky cut a ribbon and officially opened it. She spent lunch talking with workers and designers who were putting together several of the upgrades going to the station yards. She thanked them; they seemed surprised that anyone from the Navy would ever do such a thing.

"Have we been taking too many people for granted?" Vicky asked Mannie, as they motored from the plant to a school honor assembly.

"You got a paycheck. What more do you want?" he growled softly. "I've known a lot of management types who had that kind of attitude. Not all businesspeople have the vision of those you've been meeting with."

"Still, workers are people, too," Vicky said.

"I'm glad you've discovered that. You may be the first Peterwald to ever entertain such an idea."

"True," she agreed.

The school had also been involved in raising money for Poznan. Going one better, they'd planted an empty field behind the school in Tridium grain and would be harvesting their second cutting this weekend. The next week, several classes would be devoted to baking their own biscuits for shipment to Poznan.

"We have a cookie press that imprints each cookie with GIFT OF KIEV HIGH," an enthusiastic girl told Vicky.

And to think, the scumbags on Presov had thought they could fatten their own bank accounts by buying up these kids' donations to other kids who were starving.

Vicky shook her head on that thought.

Later that afternoon, they visited a harvest fair. There were a lot of farms and ranches in the hills behind Kiev. In the past, Kiev fed St. Pete and got its consumer goods from there in return . . . at a high markup. Kiev was now meeting its own needs at a better price and selling its food where it could find markets. Kiev and Sevastopol had been the main sources of food for the trade fleet to Presov and Poznan.

The women from the farm towns up in the hills most certainly knew how to cook. Mannie finagled himself into a job as judge for the food tasting. Vicky had the honor of handing out the ribbons.

It seemed to work out well for all although how Mannie didn't end up with a stomachache amazed Vicky.

There was one contest she did judge for herself.

Members of the local Pathfinder Escadrille had recently earned survival badges for living off the land. Vicky was invited to taste their efforts and award the ribbons. She found the whole situation interesting. Father had renamed the Pathfinders; now they were Imperial Youth. At least that was what they were back on Greenfeld.

Here, there had been no change. Apparently, rebellion came easy the farther you got from the palace.

Among the young women Pathfinders, Vicky found herself feasting on salads. Every one of them was better than any she'd tasted in fine restaurants on Greenfeld. The girls were quick to point out that they had to find their ingredients at the end of a mountain trail, well back into the hills.

"You all made quite tasty salads," Vicky said, and had to struggle hard to find a reason not to award all of them blue ribbons.

She took their adult leader aside and explained her challenge. The young woman, only a few years older than her charges, produced a handful of blue ribbons and quickly got them stamped. Oh, and a silver pen was located, so Vicky could sign the back of each one.

The girls were giddy with delight. Vicky found herself just as giddy. *Why didn't Daddy ever take me and Hank to one of these?*

Sadly, she suspected she knew the reason. You made time for what was important, and neither his kids nor something like this ranked very high on his priority list.

The boy Pathfinders were a much easier, if a more squeamish decision for Vicky.

While the girls got to gather leaves, herbs, and spices, the boys were expected to bring home meat. Or in this case, a small thing with long ears. It wasn't an Earth rabbit, but it was close.

Four of them had done their hunting with twine traps. They skinned what they caught with their certified Pathfinder knife and either cured, stewed, or dried it using equipment from their fathers' hunting supplies.

Vicky tasted each and found them good.

Then she came to the last boy.

He looked quite scruffy, compared to the others in their best uniforms. His boots were well-worn and had likely never seen polish; his hair was a mess.

But his hands were busy.

He was making twine, using a sheaf of grass that lay on his table. He took time to show Vicky how to twist the grass together and make sure the ends were spaced so that they didn't end all at once. "That's how you get long twine out of a lot of grass that isn't very tall."

"So," Vicky said, "is that how you caught your bilbie?"

"Yep, I put some good seed grass out for it and it hopped right into it."

"Show her how you skinned it," the adult leader suggested.

Vicky tried not to flee at the thought of having to watch and listen as the young man killed and skinned her food, but she needn't have panicked. The boy had brought several stones as well as a monitor that played the scene as he first struck two stones together to get sharp fragments flying off from the two of them. On the screen, he wore eye protectors.

"Here, ma'am, Grace, you can try your hand at it, too."

The adult provided eye protectors all around before he was taken down by a wave of Marines, security agents, and diminutive assassins. The protectors took several steps back as Vicky tried her hand, knocking two rocks together. On the fourth try, she actually got a hunk loose from one of them. It was kind of large and very dull, but it was loose.

On her sixth try, the kid announced, "You got one, girl."

"I think I do," Vicky agreed. The chert was large, but sharp at one end.

The boy retrieved it from where it had flown, then showed Vicky how she could use it to cut the soft pelt from a bilbie. Vicky gave it a try, trying not to imagine what it would be like to do this to a living thing.

I doubt I could ever be this hungry.

The lad then showed her, again on the video, how he'd smoked strips of the raw flesh using a fire, stones, and a woven mat.

"That took a lot of work," Vicky said.

"I guess it did, Grace, but my old man says if a man can't catch and kill what he eats, he ain't got no right to eat it."

The other boys had no problems splitting up the lesser ribbons.

That was the last thing on Vicky's to-do list that day. However, as they were leaving, she noticed a full roar coming from their left.

"What's that?" Vicky asked.

"Haven't you ever been to a carnival?" Mannie asked, incredulously.

"Never, I think. What's a carnival?"

Mannie put his head together with her guards for a moment as Vicky eyed the source of the noise. There were brightly-lit-up rides and delightful smells. Oh, and plenty of laughter.

Mannie broke from the huddle to offer Vicky his arm. With her Marines trailing behind and a half dozen guards spreading out ahead, the two of them made their way into the bubble of delight and noise.

Vicky rode rides. Not the most interesting ones. Security put their foot down at the big wheel that took its riders up into the evening air. They also balked at any ride that involved whirling around at high gees.

"I think I've done all the high gees I care to for one life," she told Mannie.

"Oh, if you haven't ridden the Twister, you haven't taken gees."

The security folks shook their heads firmly, saving her from telling Mannie what it was like to flee across the whole length of the galaxy spinning and accelerating and hoping to dodge the next slashing attack.

With a sigh, Vicky took in the vicarious, commonplace, and not deadly excitement of those around her. Still, she had more fun with Mannie than she'd ever had in her life.

More fun than I've ever had with my clothes on or *off,* she had to admit.

Which was certainly food for thought.

The fun must have gone on for an hour or more. The day was just beginning to soften as evening approached on silken paws. Vicky knew it was time to go before her handlers insisted. She and Mannie made their way back toward the entrance.

They were passing along an avenue lined with entertainment opportunities. Up ahead, a woman was shouting at the men to take a chance, show their strength by pounding a huge mallet down on something that made another something rise. If you got it up to the top, it rang a bell.

Few of the men attempting it got it that far, but the woman waiting for them seemed to think that whatever their results, it earned a kiss.

There were ring tosses, ball tosses. Oh, and there was a shooting gallery.

A young fellow of maybe fifteen was trying his luck with an air rifle. He wasn't a very good shot. The young girl waiting for him couldn't have been more than eight or nine. A sister, no doubt.

For a moment, Vicky had a vision of her and Hank that had never been. Her eyes misted at the lost memory.

"Better luck next time," the booth's operator said in a voice that held no such wish.

"I'll get you a bear some other place," the boy said, dejected as he put the rifle back down on the board.

There was only one bear among the prizes. A huge pink thing, nearly as big as the girl.

"Kit, Kat, what's your shooting like?" Vicky asked.

The two women said nothing, but stepped up to the board that held two air rifles. Vicky rested a restraining hand on the young girl's elbow.

"I think I can get you that bear," the Grand Duchess of the Greenfeld Empire said.

"You can?" came with saucer-wide eyes from the girl and a sad sigh from the boy.

Maybe I'm stomping on what budding manly pride the kid has?

But the girl's eyes won.

The assassins began shooting. They went for the smallest targets, the ones on the top row.

Each of them missed her first shot.

"Sights are off," Kit said.

"Badly," Kat added.

Each took one more shot, now at larger targets.

"Mine shoots high," Kit said.

"Mine's off to the right," Kat observed coolly.

"You hear that?" Vicky said to the young fellow. "The gun's sights are off. It wasn't your fault you missed."

He took the absolution in with a puzzled look.

The assassins plumped down money for five new shots. The looks they gave the huckster were pure venom.

Wise man, he took their money and handed out the shots before retreating well away from the killers.

The two shot as one. Two horses collapsed from the top row.

Another two shots, and tiny ducks flipped over.

The next two rounds put down miniature deer. Fish of some sort on a spinning wheel rang as Vicky's two guards potted them. The last to fall were a pair of birds, eagles likely, that also swooped in circles.

Beside Vicky, the girl began clapping. The boy was smiling, too, as the guy running the rigged game brought the big bear over to the girl. She took it and seemed lost in its huge hug.

"You want somp'en else?" the guy asked.

The youth seemed puzzled by the question.

"You got a girl?" Mannie offered helpfully.

The kid's eyes lit up. He pointed at a tiger, not all that much smaller than the bear. With that in his arms he turned, with his sister, to face Vicky.

"Thank you, thank you, thank you," the girl gushed.

"Ain't you. I mean, *aren't* you the Grand Duchess?" the boy asked.

"Yes, I am," Vicky admitted with as cute a curtsy as she could manage in dress whites.

The boy's face went to somewhere south of shocked. Maybe appalled.

"Oh my God. Oh my God. Oh my God," the boy shouted. "Mom won't believe this. Dad won't believe this. Evie won't believe this."

"You don't have to tell them," Mannie suggested, an imp's grin on his face.

"Oh no! I *have* to tell them. Excuse us, I have to find Mom," the boy said, grabbed his sister's arm . . . and pink bear . . . and the two of them galloped off.

"I wonder if that story will make the evening news?" Mannie said.

Vicky watched the two kids go. If only it were that easy to make everyone happy.

Then she heard a loud pop. Two more followed in quick succession.

And people began to scream.

CHAPTER 57

SMOKE filled Vicky's vision. Through it, she could make out her security guards bringing their weapons out. Kit and Kat produced their automatics and whirled, looking for a target.

Vicky could see plenty of people, but no one within sight showed evidence of a gun except those who should have them.

Vicky drew in a breath, and choked on it. She tried to hold her breath, but there was something in her lungs that demanded she breathe. The second breath was worse than the first.

People along the midway began to collapse. Through the smoke, Vicky spotted the two kids. They'd turned back to look at the first pops. The girl wanted to run back.

Her brother was smarter. He dragged her away, away from the smoke, away from the danger.

Good brother.

A Marine was pulling a face mask from the belt pouch of his dress black and reds. He was trying, but he still fell to the ground, retching up his last meal, mask hung up in the case.

Vicky was racked by coughs that only worsened as the

salads and bilbie came up, flooding her mouth and clogging her breath.

She collapsed.

Somewhere, she heard sirens.

Help was on the way as darkness took her.

═══════

CHAPTER 58

THE taste of vomit was the first thing Vicky became aware of as she fought her way back to consciousness.

The taste of vomit and the pain of cuffs wrenched in way too tight on her wrists.

She stifled a scream, a croak, any voice, any action.

She listened. She felt.

She lay on a ratty carpet. She was jostled and bounced about as if on a rough road.

Carefully, she edged her hands up. The girls had put two pins in her hair this morning, one behind each ear.

The first one she reached for wasn't there.

She risked raising her head just a bit and felt behind that ear. Thanks to any heaven that looked after bad girls like her, the second hairpin was still there.

Carefully, silently, she pulled it out and slid it into her mouth. Despite the vile taste and dry lips, she tongued it into her right lip, the upper lip from where she lay on her side.

Vicky forced it back as far as she could without swallowing it.

It wouldn't do to have to wait for her hairpin to cycle through her alimentary canal.

Confident she'd done as much as she could for her future safety, Vicky mumbled, "Water. How about some water here?"

"Sleeping beauty rejoins the living," came from ahead of her.

Vicky managed to open her eyes through the gunk that glued them shut. It took several blinks before she could take in that she was in the back of some SUV or truck. To her back was a seat. The windows around her were blackened with paint. It still seemed to be night, though.

"Did you kill everyone?" she managed to mutter.

"No. Like you, they'll wake up only wishing they were dead. But unlike them, you are going back to sleep."

Vicky felt a sharp prick at her neck. She had time to draw in one deep breath before the darkness reclaimed her.

CHAPTER 59

═══════

VICKY'S dreams were horrible. From moment to confused moment, she couldn't remember anything, but she felt her heart pounding and terror coursing through her veins.

The horror of the dreams slowly melded into wild, clashing sounds. But the first sounds Vicky actually recognized were the chirping of birds and the soft hum of insects.

So I can hear.

She concentrated on hearing, but could catalog nothing but birdsong and different clicks, hums, and other things she suspected were more insects.

Even as she listened . . . and forced her face to blandness and her body to water limpness . . . she found herself taking in more of her surroundings.

She was cuffed, spread-eagle, to a bed.

Not again!

She redoubled her listening, trying to catch any hint of human presence.

Nothing.

But she could feel a soft breeze play across her face.

And caress her breasts.

And other things.

Handcuffed spread-eagle to a bed, naked! Again! Can't these people come up with some new ideas! What am I, trapped in a lousy movie!

Not that Vicky wanted to apply plan A to another pair of too-stupid-to-live scumbags.

Still, as much as she struggled to hear, there were no scumbags in evidence.

Vicky opened her eyes. They were gummy and stung from whatever had been used to put her and her security detail down. She blinked several times before her vision cleared.

There was not all that much to look at.

She was cuffed to a wooden bed. The walls were unpainted wood. There was a door of wood. Of furniture, there was none in evidence.

Her clothes weren't in evidence, either, although she couldn't see the floor very well around the bed.

That floor was also rough boards.

Until recently, Vicky had had no experience of wooden floors in wooden buildings, but she'd been in a lot of local schools of that construction. Schools and barns for harvest festivals.

She'd learned one thing about wooden buildings.

They creaked and groaned.

And when you walked across a wooden floor, it made all kinds of noises.

This house made sounds as the wind blew through the tree outside the open window, that same breeze that cooled Vicky's body. The house groaned as it bent and twisted in the gentle breeze.

None of those groans reflected the movement of a person or persons.

"Hello," Vicky croaked. "I really could use some water."

No answer.

"Hey, guys, I'm awake, and I'm just lying here naked. We might as well have some fun."

If that didn't bring guys running, they were deaf.

Vicky checked her upper lip. Her hairpin was still in place. She worked the pin around her mouth. The metal of it brought forth saliva; that, at least, was good.

But of other human beings, Vicky could hear nothing.

"Well, it looks like it's just you and me, babe," she said to her favorite friend in the world, her lone hairpin.

Still, Vicky delayed spitting it out. It would be just like her stepmom to hire from the smarter end of the gene pool this time. Hire someone who would let her get started on her self-rescue before bringing it to a roaring halt.

Vicky lay back on the ratty blanket and thin mattress and waited for them to pop out and surprise her. She spent the time studying the room.

It was primitive, leading her to guess that she was well away from anything called civilization. She twisted her head around, going for a better view out her one window, but the tree was still in full leaf.

She could see nothing behind it.

Getting tired of waiting, she tried another tack. "Hello. I need to go to the bathroom. You really don't want to clean up my mess, do you?"

That had gotten her leverage on her captors the last time.

It didn't even get her an echo today.

So, no rerun. What kind of new trick has Stepmommy dearest got up her sleeve today? Clearly, I have nothing up my sleeve.

Vicky eyed the cuffs. They weren't your standard-issue police cuffs. No, these were the fun types. Fur over soft rubber, they didn't cut into her flesh even when she pulled hard.

They also didn't loosen as she pulled.

"So, you don't want to leave my wrists all cut and bruised. What does that tell me?"

They wanted her body in good shape.

She eyed the ceiling. If there was a camera up there, it was too small for her to spot. Knowing her stepmom's tastes in entertainment, Vicky would bet all the money she had on her that Annah Bowlingame had ordered up a permanent record of Vicky's final moments for her to soak in if she didn't have some more recent atrocity to cackle over.

Vicky fell back on waiting. While she waited, she tried to estimate the time.

Her stomach said she was hungry. Way past any hungry she'd ever been in her whole pampered life. The light coming through the window seemed to be edging from morning to noon. Likely it was a good twelve hours since she'd been snatched.

"Admiral, Mannie, please find me," she pleaded to the thin air.

It was interesting that the Navy came first, ahead of Mannie. Interesting, but appropriate. The Navy had all kinds of search-and-rescue assets. Mannie was not only outside his own neck of the St. Petersburg woods, but hadn't had to use all that much security before one Victoria Smythe-Peterwald darkened his doorway.

She broke that worthless train of thought to listen intently.

The house made its usual soft noises, but nothing that showed a human treading its boards.

Vicky promised herself to start working to get out of here as soon as the shadow on the floor reached a certain bent nail.

Then she broke her own promise and began yanking on her cuffs and the bed.

The bed looked flimsy.

It wasn't.

The bed had four posts, but Vicky's splayed-out body and cuffs hadn't been able to reach that far. The headboard and the footboard looked to be about the same. There was a pair of rough-hewn saplings reaching across from post to post, reinforced by dowels that had been drilled through them. Vicky's right ankle and left wrist were cuffed to the main saplings. Her other cuffs were to the dowels.

Vicky tried yanking.

The cuffs might be padded, but the fur didn't keep it from hurting like hell when she applied all her strength to first one extremity, then another.

The bed creaked, moaned, groaned . . . and held.

"Hello, I'm trying to escape. I'm going to tear your flimsy bed apart," brought nobody running.

Having nothing better to do, and still not trusting her kidnappers enough to bring out her last, best hope, Vicky attacked the bed again.

She threw herself around it. She tried to bounce herself right out of it. The bed bowed. It bent. It wobbled.

But it held her.

"This is the least amount of fun I've had naked and in bed

in my life," she told any recording camera. "See, you bastard stepmom, I still have my sense of humor," she growled.

And threw herself back at the bed. Was one of the spokes coming loose? One of the dowels was certainly getting wobbly in its hole. Vicky had it twirling in the sapling, but it refused to splinter. Not even a little bit.

The bed twisted as she threw herself at first one edge, then another. The bed gave a bit here and a bit there, but its very weakness seemed to give it a strength all its own. Vicky could bend it to her will but nowhere near enough.

Somewhere in school, Vicky had read a poem about the mighty oak that got uprooted and blown down while the gentle willow bowed to the hurricane's blast and lived.

"This damn bed has too much willow in it," she grumbled.

"But it's got me," she said, with a half-insane giggle. Then she went back to trying to wreck it.

She and the bed had worked their way away from the wall. As Vicky twisted and turned, it went first one way, then the other. Vicky thought she might use that to her advantage, but the thought was one thing.

Finding that advantage was something else.

She was hungry. She was thirsty. She was working up a sweat that she couldn't afford, but she was damned if she was going to just lie here, waiting for some damn Prince Charming to come along and kiss her.

"To hell with your kiss," Vicky told that AWOL Prince Charming, "I want your water canteen."

Finally, Vicky decided to risk her hairpin. She worked it forward into her teeth and tried to stretch her neck to one of her wrists.

As she feared, she couldn't reach the cuff.

She stretched her neck for the other wrist.

No better luck.

"I'm cuffed, naked to a bed. I've got a pin to work the lock on the cuffs, but I can't reach the damn lock," Vicky said slowly, enumerating the full depth of her imprisonment.

A wave of helplessness swept over her, the likes of which she hadn't felt since Admiral Krätz forced her to listen to Kris Longknife as the Wardhaven princess enumerated all Vicky's failings in her attempt to assassinate Kris.

Vicky had felt like crying.

She'd been too proud to cry in front of the admiral and the princess then.

Now, she lacked the moisture to cry and couldn't afford to spare it if it came.

Vicky lay back on her ratty blankct and let herself wallow in the full hopelessness of her situation.

CHAPTER 60

———

THE Grand Duchess Victoria allowed herself a full two minutes of floundering about in deep despair. No doubt that was twice as long as Princess Kris Longknife would ever give herself.

"Kris, next time we get together to dish dirt, you must tell me how you keep so damn upbeat. Assuming you do," Vicky muttered.

Vicky took a deep breath and did something she'd rarely done before. She examined her options. They were few. She could somehow break out of this spiderweb of a bed, or she would die. Certainly, dying was what her stepmommy dearest wanted.

"You want me dead. You've already killed Captain Morgan and anyone who tried to help me that you could get your hands on." Vicky almost spat that last at the corner she was talking to. It had to have a camera pointed right at her, so that witch could cackle at Vicky's dying.

"But it's not just me dead, is it Annah. You want anyone who won't be your slave dead. That's it, isn't it? Wreck Greenfeld, reduce it to starvation and ruin, then offer the pieces a few scraps of bread and a chance to live if they do it under your yoke."

Vicky paused to listen to the echo of her own words. She'd said it. She'd said out loud what she and a whole lot of people were coming to realize but couldn't spit out. Couldn't say to anyone, not even themselves.

Vicky repeated it. "That's what this is about. You and your clan want everything. Every scrap of power and property. You want every human being in Greenfeld as your personal slave. I bet you really are setting my dad up to be found by some jealous man in his wife's bed. That's what you want. With Dad dead, that would leave everything open to you and your family of grasping thugs."

Vicky shook her head. "But you need me dead, too, don't you? Don't you?" Vicky screamed where she thought the camera was.

"So that's the way it is. It's you or me. You want me dead, and I have no intention of dying. Not until way after you."

Strange, even in her naked rage, even with her conviction of what her stepmother was doing to Greenfeld—doing to Vicky—she still couldn't say she'd kill her stepmother.

"Give me time," she muttered to herself. "I'm sure Step-mommy will come up with some new twists that will make me madder than I am now."

Now Vicky bent herself to busting out of the bed's tight embrace.

"I can keep this up a lot longer than you can keep me in this," she lied to herself and the bed.

The day was getting on to noonish and warm. She had the head of the bed pointed now at the door and was considering trying to upend it and see if she could work her way through the door and into whatever lay past it.

She examined that idea from several perspectives, including the one that had the bed upended and her hanging from one arm and leg or the other or sprawled naked and upside down, like a turtle, with no good handle on much of anything.

"We stay in the room," she told herself.

She rocked the bed. She got the posters thumping a tattoo on the floor. She doubted any four naked bodies had ever gotten a bed bouncing as wildly as she had this one all by her lonesome.

Still, the bed refused to weaken its grip on her.

"Well, I'm not going to stop my damn attack on you just 'cause you won't budge," she snapped.

She and the bed did another ten rounds before she paused for a breath. Then she did another fifteen rounds.

She was breathing hard, and sweat was running down into her eyes when it finally snapped.

The slat her left leg was cuffed to gave up the ghost, splintered into several pieces and fell away. Vicky finally had a leg loose.

She rejoiced for about a second, then scowled. There was not a lot she could do with just her left leg.

It would, however, let her get her head and the hairpin a bit closer to her right hand.

It did, but not all that much closer.

She softened her bite on the hairpin and slowly worked it out farther, praying her hold on the damn thing, either with her teeth or her lips, wouldn't fail her now. She stretched for her wrist.

She could just barely get the edge of the pin into the lock. She got it in. She got it moving a little.

And she lost the pin.

It took her a couple of minutes wiggling around in the bed to find the pin, but no matter how she tried to twist her neck, she couldn't pick it up again.

Near cross-eyed, she frowned at the hairpin, then decided desperate times called for desperate measures. Again, she began throwing herself from side to side. The bed bounced once, twice, then, with a mighty heave, it flipped over.

Vicky found herself facedown on the floor with the bed on top of her.

"Never tried it this way," she told no one in particular.

The pin had followed its own path to the floor. She had to do a bit of wiggling, nothing new for her naked, but under the bed kind of added a new twist to matters. Finally, she had the hairpin back in her mouth.

She also had a sliver of wood in her right boob and another in her tongue.

Vicky lost it all, big-time.

"Damn it," she shouted, "I'm a Peterwald. No one does this to a Peterwald. Certainly not someone who just slept her way into the family. Stepmom, you and me, we are going to finish this."

Vicky got the hairpin back between her teeth and took another try at the lock.

Close, but no damn cigar.

She tried again.

No way.

"Okay, we got the bed to give up some space before. Bed, you and me are going to twist as much as we have to."

Vicky worked the bed back up on its side. It was no easy thing with just one foot on the floor and the rest of her in the bed's clutches, but she managed to get it where she wanted it.

Then she shoved it up against the door.

Nothing happened.

About the tenth or twentieth time she hit the door with the bed, the lock popped open, and she found the bed headed into a hall.

That didn't do much for her, so she wedged the foot of the bed against the end of the door and started seeing what kind of leverage she could get on the bed between them.

The bed creaked and bent, but it did not snap.

Vicky alternated between shoving against the top of the headboard and pushing hard against its bottom. The wood did a lot of moaning and groaning as it strained against her efforts. Better yet, Vicky could feel the wood start working.

"Are you a loose bed?" Vicky asked. She knew she'd been a plenty loose woman. What she was now was a very hurting woman. She was feeling pain in places she didn't know a woman could or should.

She was leaning into the headboard, putting all the torque on it that she could manage, thinking she might take another try at seeing if she could reach the cuff lock . . . when the bed emitted a snap, and something came very loose.

The post had parted from the upper sapling. The slat holding her right hand came loose and the handcuff slid up and off.

Vicky had a hand free!

She only needed a moment to work the lock and free her other hand.

Now she lay with the bed on its side, her falling out of it, but her right leg still held up high in the air.

"I've had a few boys who would have loved to see me in this predicament," she muttered, and struggled to pull herself up on her one free leg. She was hurting. Hurting bad as she bounced on one leg to get herself in reach to work the damn cuff's lock.

When the last lock snapped open, she made a grab for the bed, then, putting it to the best use yet, settled slowly to the floor.

For a long moment, she sat there, cross-legged on the floor, her body shaking uncontrollably.

Her body was shaken, but she wasn't.

"I did it. I did it. I did it all by myself!" she shouted, over and over again.

When the trembling finally stopped, she used the bed again, this time to pull herself up. One of the slats would make a very nice spike in case she ran into any vampire that needed staking.

"It won't be much good against a machine pistol," she admitted, but considering her luck of late, she wouldn't bet against her running into anything.

The hall that had been so close but so far away for so long turned out to be only the walking space between the cabin's two bedrooms. The other room was as primitive as the one she'd been in. More so. The two pallets that lay on the floor didn't even sport a bedstead.

Down the hall was a common room that included a field-stone fireplace and a kitchen with a cast-iron woodstove and a metal sink.

There, glory be to one and all, was a water pump.

Vicky made a beeline to it. She worked the wooden handle on the pump, but only ugly noises came out, no water.

"Damn them," she said, then her eyes lighted on a battered tin can. She lifted it to her lips. The water within was scummy and hot, but it was water.

Vicky barely stopped herself before she gulped it down.

"You've got to prime the pump," Vicky said, remembering the words before she remembered where she'd heard them.

It was Doc Maggie who told her that. They'd been discussing economics and the need to put money in if you wanted to take money out. Something Maggie didn't think her father did often enough.

A young Vicky had asked what she meant. "Prime a pump?"

"You've never seen a pump, have you?" Maggie had said. "I doubt if any of you kids in the palace have ever seen one or likely ever will."

But Maggie had done an internship in one of the more primitive areas of St. Petersburg, and she had actually worked an old-fashioned hand pump.

Now, Vicky suspected that she was also in one of those primitive areas, and the metal piping with a long wooden handle very likely was what Maggie had been talking about that day.

Vicky lifted a metal flap at the top of the pump. Yep, it was damp in there. With a prayer to a God she knew nothing about, Vicky poured the water down the hole.

Then she again applied herself to working the wooden pump handle. For an agonizing moment, nothing happened. Then all Vicky got was a racket that left her even more thirsty. Finally, with a gurgle and a gush, water poured forth from the rusty mouth of the pump.

Vicky kept pumping with one hand. The other she used to catch and lift to her mouth cool, deliciously wet, water. She lowered her head and dunked it in the spurting stream of water. Only after she had refilled the metal cup did she use a cork stopper to plug up the sink. She filled it before beginning to wash herself all over.

There was a lot of scum she needed to be rid of. Some was on her skin. A lot more of it was out there, waiting for her.

"Speaking of waiting for me," Vicky muttered, and took a look out the window above the sink. She spotted a corral of rough-hewn logs, but it held no animals. There was a rusting old truck, but it was up on blocks, and its wheels lacked tires. Vicky was not likely to get a ride there.

She edged herself up to the other windows and peered out. There were wooded hills not too far away, snow-clad mountains in the distance. The meadow around the house was green and empty.

"Stepmom, you bastard, you really did intend for me to die of thirst," she concluded. She measured the thirst she'd felt before she quenched it at the pump, then multiplied it by several days.

"You bitch. I was toying with the idea of raising that banner of rebellion against you. Now you've bought it full price and full measure. Stepmom, only one of us is coming out of this alive, and it's not going to be you."

It was one thing to say that. At the moment, Vicky not only questioned her ability to kill her stepmother but kind of wondered at her chances of surviving the next couple of days. Hours even.

Being a hardheaded Peterwald, she set out to take stock of her empire. Hers was a bit smaller than her father's, and it looked to have even less to offer.

A visit to the rusting truck showed that it not only lacked tires, but the engine was long gone. Vicky could find nothing worth stripping from the wreck. Most everything that could be taken had been.

The corral was empty. Its split rails were lashed together with some sort of plastic binding, not even a nail for Vicky to arm herself with.

From the lack of any droppings, it had been empty for a very long time. The only things in it were some huge flying things that buzzed Vicky. She could swat them away. It was the tiny things that swarmed around her that annoyed her. They didn't bite but did seem attracted to the water on her skin.

She gave up slapping herself silly and did her best to ignore them.

The barn was no more generous than the rest of the ranchstead. There wasn't as much as a rusting pitchfork or a piece of broken leather harness. Even the few bales of hay were broken and molding.

In its shade, Vicky did discover gnats or mosquitoes that bit. She swatted them and was rewarded with bloody splotches on her skin.

The walk around the barnyard reminded Vicky that she never even went to the pool without sandals. She was very tender of foot.

A return to the house and a thorough search turned up nothing of her uniform. No panties or bra. Most especially, no shoes.

Sitting on the edge of the porch, she examined her options. Somewhere in her survival training she remembered something about staying put. Wait in one place for rescue. Now she recalled sorry tales of lost people and rescuers wandering around in circles and missing each other.

Missing each other until someone stupid was dead.

While the prospects of sitting still might be nice on her tender feet, this place had nothing to offer her but water. She could probably last without food for a week or two, but what were the chances that her assassins would come back sooner for her desiccated body?

Sooner than any rescuers?

That raised the issue, was the house transmitting her tribulations for someone to enjoy or only recording them for retrieval and later enjoyment?

"No way would Stepmommy dearest allow her Vicky darling to die in private."

If a shack like this one was transmitting live, it would have to attract attention. The Navy would not miss that. No, this place had to be off the grid.

She stood and walked into the middle of the yard. As she'd observed on her approach to the landing at Kiev, there were mountains to her east. Thus, there was likely a very wide river somewhere around here.

She shook her head. It could be to her east or west. They could have crossed it in the night. She could have been driven two, three, even four hundred miles inland during her drugged sleep. All she knew was that somewhere to the south was the Midland Sea, and the mountains were to her east. Her route lay south. How east or west she was stood as a question mark.

It would be nice to send out an "I'm here, come get me" signal before she started her walk. The question was, how subtle did she need to be.

"No, the question is: How do I do it?"

She returned to the corral. She thought she'd noticed some familiar rocks there. She found two that looked like flint. Try as she might, she could not get them to spark when she struck them together. Then she remembered. Sparks came not from flint on flint but from flint on steel.

She headed back to the truck. It had little to offer her, but she managed to work a few pieces of the rusted steel frame off the wreck.

With flint and steel, she headed for the barn. The place had seen better days. There was plenty of rotten punk, fortunately dry. There was also some straw that was less moldy than the rest.

It took her an hour, but she finally got a fire going. In a whole lot less time, the barn was fully involved, sending fire and gray smoke up to the heavens.

Vicky had heard somewhere about fire being used to make offerings to the gods. She hoped the Navy god was paying attention.

Of course, the stepmommy-bitch god might also be attentive to her prayers.

Vicky headed for the hills. Not the mountains east but the wooded hills to the west.

She was in the trees before the barn collapsed in upon itself. It was still smoking, though, and her hope for rescue rose with it up to the heavens.

CHAPTER 61

━━━━━

BEING tender of foot, Vicky tried to stay to the softer ground. Sadly, even she could see that she was leaving a trail. That would be good if Mannie was racing to her rescue.

If the Empress's murderers were ahead of Mannie, not so good.

Before too long, she came to a well-shaded stream; she waded into it and turned south. She stepped carefully to keep her balance, to avoid flipping rocks, and, very much to avoid doing a full flop in midstream. That would be a definite "hello" for those following her.

While she tried to stay invisible to overhead observation, she kept her ears peeled for the sound of helicopters. Her efforts to keep quiet didn't seem to matter much. She appeared to have the place all to herself. Just herself and the four-legged types that lived here.

In the undergrowth, Vicky found a reddish green leaf and gobbled it up with gusto, if not the proper spices, praising the Pathfinder girls with enthusiasm and precision. In the last few hours, she'd gained a whole new understanding of hunger. She'd have to see that another fleet of emergency food relief got headed for Poznan. It wouldn't be a bad idea to start a survey of the local planets, either. If she sent out scouts, they might find places that were even hungrier.

Being a Grand Duchess was fun . . . when she wasn't dodging her family's traditional values and assassins. The Navy had been an education. What she was getting now was something more than an education.

This was experience.

And this experience would be with her the rest of her life.

"And I'm going to have a long life," she told the sky, "unlike you, Annah. Unlike you, my grasping corpse."

The water was cold, leaving Vicky's teeth with a tendency to chatter. She balanced her passage south between time in the water leaving no trail and time walking carefully along the bank that very likely did leave a trail despite her best efforts. There were game trails through the woods. Paths the animals followed. They weren't wide, and she was getting all kind of cuts from the brush and thorns along the trails, but she used the trails to let her move quickly.

Evening came, and she dined on more salad greens before pulling up several handfuls of grass from a meadow and spreading it under a bush to make an if not cozy, then at least warm enough, bower.

In the night, she heard a helicopter pass overhead. With no way to tell if it was friend or death, she chose to lie low and wait for the morning. She suspected tomorrow would be very challenging, if not interesting.

She was up at first light; her hunger woke her as much as the dawn.

As she headed south, she kept an eye out for more of that salad she'd had for supper, but she spotted none. She picked up a rounded pebble from the stream. If she spotted one of those floppy-eared things the boys had killed, she was game for giving it a try even if the thought of cutting into one still made her squeamish.

She saw nothing worth making a throw at.

Before too long, though, she started hearing the sounds of unmuffled vehicle engines rumbling through the woods to the north. She quickened her pace downstream, trying to move silently, tracklessly, away from the sound.

"If I were Mannie, I'd be in a helicopter using a loud-speaker to tell me I was safe," Vicky muttered.

For now, she did not feel very safe.

The problem was that, other than fleeing, she couldn't think of any way to make herself safe.

While she puzzled over that problem, she fled like a frightened deer, of which there were several keeping her company. Being a battleship Sailor, she'd gotten few courses on dirtside survival and paid even less attention to the ones she was obliged to sit through.

"Dumb little shit," she chided herself. "In the future, I will not assume I know everything about my future."

She considered some of the things she'd learned from the Pathfinder boy. She'd spotted the tough grass that he'd used to make twine, but she doubted that a bit of twine would trap the booted feet following her. With only her two hands, there was no way to dig some of the traps she'd seen in vids.

"There's not much I know how to do with my own two hands and bare-ass naked," she finally concluded.

What she did know was that she'd become predictable—again.

She'd been moving south along this same creek, now widened into a stream, for most of yesterday afternoon and all of this morning.

"It's time to do something off my beaten path."

The stream passed through a rocky section. There was a touch of white water and some solid rock on her right. When she found the chance, she climbed up onto the rock and headed uphill, into more rocks. Even taking as much care as she could to avoid breaking a twig or twisting a bush, she knew she was leaving wet tracks. Fortunately, the day was warming up. Given an hour or so, the tracks would be obliterated by the sun.

She climbed, moving from rock to rock. She did not climb very expertly. She dislodged a rock here and there. One landed on her toe as it bounced off down behind her. She muttered a curse and kept heading for higher ground.

She froze when she heard the motors get suddenly louder. Through the trees on the other side of the stream, she could just make out three rigs. All were four-wheel-drive all-terrain vehicles. Each carried two men in tandem.

The one in back of all three had a scoped rifle at the ready.

Vicky melted into the shadows of some trees beside a rocky outcrop and kept climbing. The top of the ridge wasn't much farther. If she could make it over that, she'd have some pretty rough ground between them and her.

"Who knows, if I'm up here, and they're down there, maybe I can throw rocks at them." She made a face; Hank had always gotten the best of her in snowball fights.

She reached the ridgeline and rolled over it. A second later, a bullet whizzed by to the left of where she'd crossed.

She eyed the valley before her. It was rugged. It might be fun to hike with solid boots. Bare naked and barefoot, she winced at the thought. She headed off to her left, away from the stream, not dropping down, but staying to high and rocky ground.

Behind her, she could hear the roar of engines being pushed beyond their designed limits. She had figured the motor brigade would head downstream with the intent of doubling back, but from the sound of it, they were gunning their rigs right up the rocky outcropping.

Instead of having hours before they showed up, she might only have minutes.

Vicky hurried down the ridge, hoping to make it into the trees. She'd spotted a thicket. She might be able to squeeze herself in there. It would cost her scratches and blood, but she could go where they couldn't.

At least, not with their ride.

She made it to the trees a scant minute before an ATV gunned over the rise.

She turned to see just how she might wiggle her way into the thicket, then froze.

The beating of rotors filled the rocky vale.

Four choppers slid in, two on this side of the ridgeline, the other two on the other side. They were the standard passenger helicopter ubiquitous to the Empire. These had armed sharp-shooters riding their skids.

Vicky lost all hope. No way could she dodge them.

Then all three of the riflemen on the ATVs whipped their

rifles up, and the drivers pulled out machine pistols, all aiming for choppers.

Vicky took another look at the helicopters. Those were Marines riding the skids of one! Rangers on the other!

They shot first.

Vicky's pursuers got a few shots off, mostly at random and at the sky as they died.

Another chopper flared in to where Vicky had gone to ground. Mannie leapt from it before the pilot settled it in place.

His shout of "Vicky! Vicky!" were the sweetest sounds she'd ever heard.

Later, when she told the story, she'd say she raced into his arms.

Scratched, bleeding, and barefoot, the truth is, a girl doesn't race anywhere. What she did was make her way as carefully and quickly as the situation allowed.

"My God, Vicky, what did they do to you?" Mannie said when he got a good look at her. He had his shirt off in a moment. He did have a bit of a paunch, but Vicky only had eyes for the look on his face.

If ever she was to see what love looked like on a man's face, she was seeing it now.

"They didn't do anything to me," Vicky said, folding herself into the offered shirt and the open arms. "I think they were waiting for me to die of thirst before claiming the body. I don't know if they thought they could leave me dead somewhere else and write their own story about my death. Hard to tell. We'll have to talk to those who were chasing me."

She and Mannie turned toward the chopper. Commander Boch was rapidly covering the ground. "Are you okay?"

"I'm fine enough. I want to talk to those who were chasing me."

"You'll need a séance for that," he said.

"Dead?"

"Their desire to go down fighting was too obvious not to grant," the commander said dryly.

"I wish we had some of those sleepy darts Kris Longknife's troops have. Don't we have any rounds of something with less than lethal intent in this Empire?"

"I don't think so, ma'am. I'll look into it if you wish."

"I wish," Vicky growled. "I really wanted to see how they took to a couple of days without water."

"You are not a nice girl," Mannie said.

"You shocked?"

"Nope. I was contemplating doing worse."

"I think I like you," Vicky said, resting a hand on his knee where he sat beside her in the chopper.

"Commander," she said, changing her focus.

"Yes, Your Grace."

"I spent a miserable afternoon in a farmhouse farther up this stream. You should have no trouble finding it. It has a smoldering barn."

"Yes, Your Grace. We know of it."

"You spotted the fire."

"Of course, Your Grace."

"And you didn't come to my rescue?" was loaded with shell and grapeshot.

"I asked them not to," Mannie said.

"You what?"

"I thought you would want us to see who responded to the lure. They did, and we collected them. Sadly, dead, but we got them."

Vicky considered this. "So you used me as bait."

"As you would have used me, Your Gracious Grace," Mannie said, looking her evenly in the eye.

"And the admiral agreed with this idea?"

"So long as we had you under observation and a rapid-response team ready to come to your aid as soon as we were sure we had them all, yes."

"I can't fault his tactics. Only next time you do that, please have someone drop me a meal, shoes, some bug spray, and a nice book to read," Vicky said, dryly.

"If I could have, I would have dropped me," Mannie said. "You have been most fetching."

"I have been most naked. Did you like ogling my cut, splotched, and bare skin?"

"We watched you on infrared," Mannie said. "If you've seen one body on infrared, you've seen them all."

"You are a prude," Vicky said, trying to adjust his shirt to cover more of her scratched skin. "You are also distracting me," Vicky said, then changed topics.

"Commander, there is very likely one or more tiny cameras hidden somewhere in that bedroom I was locked down in. You can ignore the recording of my naked struggle. No. You *will* ignore my struggle. However, I want those cameras taken apart and examined with the best we have. I want to know everything that the cameras tell us about the people who set it up."

The commander spoke into his commlink. "It is being done as we speak, Your Grace."

"Good, now I need a bath, a meal, and a good night's sleep, not necessarily in that order."

Vicky could almost hear the commander's heels clicking as he sat at attention. "The Imperial Suite has been reserved for you at the Kiev Cosmopolitan, Your Grace. This helicopter can deposit you on the roof, just a short elevator ride down one floor to your rooms."

"Take me there," she ordered, then added, upon only a second's reflection, "Is it safe?"

"Your Grace," Mannie said, "I don't think a planet could be made any safer for you than St. Petersburg is now. Your abduction was the lead story on every media account. Your face has been shown in every home."

"On some planets, they'd print out a Peterwald face and use it for a dartboard," Vicky said, dryly.

"Not here, Vicky," Mannie said. "You know that big pink bear?"

"I dimly remember it," she allowed.

"Well, another girl, a teen with dreams of a career in the news, caught that whole shooting thing on her phone," Mannie told her. "Much of her footage was up close and personal before her older sister dragged her away. Still, she was walking backward, recording more as she left. So she caught the whole attack on film. All of her story, from pink fluffy bear to your disappearing in the smoke has been playing every fifteen minutes on every newscast on the planet. The people loved it, and they love you. It's gotten a lot of them mad."

Mannie paused to catch his breath. "It got us leads. We knew that two large black SUVs were seen speeding north from Kiev and took off into the backcountry. We couldn't track them. There seemed to be some sort of electronic spoof-ing involved. That's another thing the admiral wants to find out more about. Anyway, we knew you were somewhere up there and had surveillance working the area when you gave us a most definite, what did you call it, Commander?"

"A hot datum," the Navy officer provided.

"A very hot and smoking datum," Vicky agreed.

"As the planet's personal representative to you, Your Grace," Mannie went on, "I wish to be the first to apologize for this attack. I also wish to assure you that if there is any whisper of such an attempt in the future, it will be scotched at its first breath. We do not have much trouble with our criminal underground here on St. Petersburg, but we have received assurances from the highest levels of that underground, or maybe it should be lowest levels," Mannie clarified with a grin, "that no amount of money can be offered to any of their people to take a contract on you."

"Has my stepmother finally found a place where her tenta-cles cannot reach?" Vicky marveled.

"We certainly think so," Mannie assured Vicky.

The helicopter did indeed land atop the Cosmopolitan, and it was just a one-floor drop to her rooms.

Kit and Kat were already there, making sure the room was secure, laying out towels for her bath and checking out the doctor who had been waiting to examine Vicky.

Before Vicky could do anything, though, she had to lift Kit and Kat off their knees at her feet.

"We cannot express our embarrassment at our failure," Kat said.

"We should have been prepared for a gas attack," Kit added.

"No. It was not your fault," Vicky said, raising them back to their feet. "I made the mistake of being predictable. Kiev was the only city I hadn't covered. I always hit the harvest festivals, and I stayed too long at the carnival. It was as much my fault as anyone's."

"If I may interrupt these penitents," Mannie said, interrupt-ing, "Vicky, you had never gone down a carnie line like that. The people who actually did the takedown had used others to track you during the day. We never had a chance to see their faces in the crowd twice. There was no warning at all."

He shrugged. "They were good. From what I'm told from our examination of the bodies, none of the actual kidnappers were from here."

That gave Vicky pause. "There's so little traffic, how'd the Empress manage to ship her assassins in?"

"Little traffic is not zero traffic. We are looking into things and should know more by tomorrow. Now, if all is forgiven, can the doctor debug, delouse, and descratch the Grand Duchess?"

"Can you, indeed, descratch me?"

"No," the female doctor said, "but I can at least make you feel better. Now, who gets to stay for my examination?"

Vicky shooed Mannie out. No doubt by now he had seen all of her that there was to see, but familiarity bred contempt, and she wanted his memories to be of her vivaciously naked, not bitten, splotched, and scratched.

The doctor checked Vicky out thoroughly. When Vicky tried to refuse the rape kit, the doctor balked. "Were you unconscious for a part of your abduction?"

Vicky allowed that she had been.

"Then we check everything," the doctor snapped.

As it turned out, Vicky was right, she had not been raped. Considering what she did to her last rapist, no wonder Stepmommy was now giving more definite instructions on that matter.

Before the doctor finished, Kit and Kat were running Vicky's bathwater. That turned out to be providential. When Kit began to add oils and herbs, the doctor again put her foot down.

"Plain water until these scratches and bug bites heal. You will put these ointments on her cuts, abrasions, and the bleeding bug bites. I suggest you get her some silk pajamas to cover the ointment, or she's going to smear it all over her bed."

"I'll be careful," Vicky said.

From the looks she was getting from the two seductive assassins, they were already thinking up ways to include Mannie in their discreet play so as not to smear her medicated wounds.

The doctor must have mistaken the two for Vicky's nurses because she showed them how to dress her wounds and handed off Vicky's medications. "Her temperature is slightly elevated. Make sure she takes these on the prescribed schedule. Water. No milk."

"We will make sure she does," the two said as one.

They ordered in the prescribed silk pajamas while Vicky wallowed in the tub. It felt so good to get clean. She had the girls scrub her down twice and didn't complain when some of her sores bled. Or when some of their scrubbing got more than personal.

Dried off, the two of them insisted on sharing the duty of "greasing her," as Vicky put it.

Mannie passed the pajamas through the bathroom door and informed them that dinner was waiting.

Dinner was by candlelight. It was also delicious. Kiev was famous for its fisheries, and Vicky found herself enjoying every different kind of shrimp that had been imported from old Earth and adapted well to the clear waters off the coast. There were also steamed oysters. Mannie would have passed on the offer, but Vicky insisted they were delicious.

Kit's and Kat's eyes gleamed with expectation.

As soon as dinner was removed, Mannie made to remove himself as well, but Vicky held lightly to his elbow. "It has been rough. I would very much like not to sleep alone. If you could just hold me?"

"I believe that can be arranged," he said, softly.

Vicky shooed an incredulous Kit and Kat out to sleep in the sitting room and took Mannie to her bed.

He held her very close until she dozed off.

He was still holding her when she came awake in the night, screaming.

And he held her close, soothing her like a child, until she could again lose herself in troubled sleep.

CHAPTER 62

════

BREAKFAST was again served in the room. It came earlier than Vicky wanted, but it was accompanied by a fresh uniform. This time dinner dress blues. Somehow, in the search for her, her Order of St. Christopher, Star Leaper, had turned up as well as her computer.

"A minor member of the troop that snatched you snagged the medal and your computer. He had no idea what they would be worth, but he figured to make a little extra on the side."

Mannie shook his head and laughed. For this, it was unusually harsh. "The first pawnbroker he showed it to called us before the guy was out of his store. He didn't know much about the computer, but he'd seen the medallion on you in the news vids. We had the fool, and your computer and Order in hand, likely before they had you tied down to that bed."

"A lot of people were looking out for me?" Vicky said with amazement, tasting the words as much as saying them. She suspected it had been a long time since anyone looked out for a Peterwald. Likely well *before* the pope got himself an army.

"Since you've woken me at this absurd hour and are plying me with coffee, I deduce, even in my befogged brain, that something is going on today."

"Yes," Mannie said, with more enthusiasm than this hour deserved. "You are scheduled to meet with the Kiev City Council. They want to personally apologize for what happened to you in their city."

"That shouldn't take so very long," Vicky said, taking a sip of her coffee. Today it was dark and bitter. She liked it that way on certain occasions.

Like today, the first day of her life to be spent plotting the downfall of an Empress.

The first day of many.

Stupid woman to not just want me dead but the entire Empire on its knees before her.

Not going to happen.

"I'm afraid it won't be that simple," Mannie said, interrupting Vicky's reflections. "They've reserved the city auditorium for the meeting. It holds five thousand, and I understand there's talk of moving it to the city stadium, so they can fit in another fifteen thousand."

"They want twenty thousand people to watch them apologize!"

"No, twenty thousand people want to personally make their apologies to you."

Vicky found herself wondering if she'd traded one form of torture for another. "Will it involve shaking all twenty thousand hands?" she asked, raising a limp, bitten, scraped, and thorn-slashed paw.

"I think their applause will do," Mannie said.

Upon second reflection, Vicky decided today was bound to be better than the last one. She'd have clothes to wear and, no question about it, Mannie at her elbow.

Breakfast was cut short, so Kit and Kat could put Vicky through an abbreviated shower before greasing her down with the prescribed ointments and sliding her into her dress blues.

The drive to the stadium was blessedly short. However, the short walk from the car to the stage door on her scratched and blistered feet was barely endurable. Vicky was discovering that she needed a lot more rest before all the aches and strains would leave her alone.

She was still unprepared for what met her.

The applause as Vicky was ushered to center stage was

thunderous. Vicky took it all in with unprepared eyes and found herself weeping like a beauty-pageant winner.

Fortunately for her, she got to sit down while Kiev's mayor opened the proceedings. He made his apology brief. There was no doubt it was from the heart; tears streamed down his cheeks as he spoke.

Then it was Vicky's turn to accept the expression of regret. The applause this time as Mannie helped her up to the microphone rolled over her and would not quit.

Vicky stood there, wiping away tears and smiling, then wiping away more tears and smiling some more. Flowers fell at her feet. Not only bouquets of roses but small offerings of garden flowers and wildflowers, many brought up to the stage by little girls who attempted curtsies that would never make it at court but were surpassingly cute.

Vicky felt the applause hammer at her heart. She let it in. Never had she felt such feelings of approval. Such value. Such love.

"Thank you," she said, and found she'd only managed to whisper it into the mic.

"Thank you," this time came out loud, but was lost in the wash of applause.

She took several deep breaths. They were filled with the sweet air perfumed by the flowers and the roar of the people of Kiev.

From deep in her chest, she brought up the voice Admiral Krätz had forced her to find. The voice of command. This time her "Thank you," was just as loud as the applause.

It did not stop it. It rolled on and on, drowning her in its thanks that she was still alive.

Now two young people were ushered onto the stage. Vicky smiled as she recognized the girl even without her huge pink bear. Today, the two youths held flowers. They were simple bouquets of the kind a young boy might cut illicitly from a neighbor's garden so he could give his girl her first bouquet.

Vicky accepted the flowers and hugged the two kids, squishing the flowers between them. No doubt, her dress blues now showed streaks from yellow and lavender pollen.

The two children stepped back. The boy did a bow. The girl's attempt at a curtsy might have ended with her sprawled on the floor, but her brother spotted the impending disaster and grabbed her arm.

Vicky laughed. It was possibly the most heartfelt and joyous laugh of her many years of laughing on cue.

The applause showed no signs of abating. Vicky wondered how any pair of hands could keep this up.

Mannie stepped up to the microphone. "Her Grace has words she wants to share with you. Would you like to hear them?"

The clapping was replaced by a roar of "Yes," and, slowly, silence elbowed its way into the stadium.

Vicky found herself wiping away more tears before twenty thousand pairs of expectant eyes. She swallowed the emotions in her throat and spoke.

"I want to thank you for all that you have done to secure my safety," she said. No need for an Imperial and impersonal we. These words were personal, between herself and twenty thousand of her very best friends.

The applause leapt out again, pouncing on the silence and banishing it. Vicky smiled into it, wiped tears again and waited for her next opening.

The applause this time wound down before it became embarrassing.

"I know that many of you were involved in breaking the chains that held me captive. I thank you from the bottom of my heart."

It was some time before she could go on. Again, she had to wipe away tears.

"I know that no citizen of Kiev had anything to do with my abduction, and I want you all to know that I will always hold the people of Kiev close in my heart."

The applause exploded, spiked by whistles and cheers. There were shouts of "Yes" in the roar, as well as "Thank you" and "Our Grand Duchess," or maybe it was "Our Generous Duchess." Vicky couldn't make the words out clearly.

It didn't matter. These people were special to her, and she would remain special to them. Vicky waved. Standing before her, people waved back. Men and women threw kisses, and she blew them kisses in return.

The mayor of Kiev came to lead her away, and the cheering rose to impossibly new levels. Now Vicky did find she had hands to shake and hugs to exchange. The Kiev City Council was thirty strong, and each was there to say a few words of personal apology and offer the Grand Duchess best wishes in the future.

Offstage, there was a lineup of stagehands who wanted to offer their own heartfelt wishes that she might never come into such danger as she had now been delivered from.

Only then was Vicky able to make her exit, leaning heavily on Mannie's arm.

"I'm exhausted," she confessed.

"Great approval can be just as taxing as great censure," Sevastopol's mayor observed.

"It is, however, a whole lot more fun," Vicky said, allowing him a warm smile as he handed her into the limo that would take her to the spaceport.

Inside, the jump seats were taken by Kit and Kat, each close to a window. Between them was Commander Boch, looking very much like a man with a report to make.

Vicky settled deeply into the leather of her seat, allowed herself two deep breaths, finished with an exhausted sigh, and faced the commander.

"What can you tell me that you didn't know last night?"

"Quite a bit, Your Grace. There are people in custody who are talking so fast we don't have time to ask them questions. I can't tell if their verbosity is the residue of State Security's reputation or the sea change that has come over this planet's attitude toward the Peterwalds. Or maybe just one Peterwald," he ventured.

"It might be," Mannie added, "that our local organized crime has turned its organizing force toward the safety of the Grand Duchess."

"You know your organized crime?" Vicky asked.

"Certainly. They paid their tithe to State Security and did what we needed them to do. Some were just petty criminals, smugglers, black marketeers, the things that made a failing economy work. Others were less socially acceptable but met the appetites of the less virtuous."

"And this went on under State Security's nose?" Vicky demanded.

"Here and everywhere else, I suspect."

Vicky pondered that for a moment. "I never heard that from my father. I wonder if he knew. Which makes me wonder if State Security's private machinations were only minor games compared to what the Empress's family has now started."

Mannie said nothing but raised a quizzical eyebrow.

"Kris Longknife once challenged me on who was really running this Empire. I assured her it was my father. It seems I may have been a bit naive."

"We tell our young about a world we want them to believe in," Mannie said. "As grown-ups, we live in a world devoid of such illusions."

"So it seems. I'll think about all this when I have a spare moment. For now, Commander, what can you tell me about the plot that left me cuffed to a bed and dying of thirst?"

"You were correct yesterday to raise the question of how your attackers got on this planet, what with trade so limited and traffic between planets near nonexistent. We showed the pictures of the dead bodies around the station, and a tramp freighter's captain immediately identified them as the passengers he landed here a week ago."

"He was hired to bring them. Didn't that raise any questions?"

"Actually, the captain made the jump from Hobarton to here hoping to get a cargo of crystal assemblies he could sell on Metzburg. He'd heard we had crystal to sell. The 'lawyers' "—a sour twist Commander Boch made as he spoke the word put it in quotes—"said they had been retained by the home offices to aid the defendants of the Mine Manager's Co-op of Presov."

"Were they?" Vicky asked.

"Initially, it appeared so. They immediately dropped down and met with the defendants. Only later did we check on how that meeting went."

"And it went . . . ?" Mannie asked.

"Not well. They presented credentials introducing themselves as lawyers and told Mr. Adaman and his associates they were here for them, but, as the conversation went on, they seemed to lack any sort of grounding in the law. The Co-op had already retained some local lawyers here. The managers had been talking about their expectations of an Imperial pardon, but they also have heard tales of loyal servants hung out to dry. Anyway, our local lawyers listened to this new delivery and suggested to Mr. Adaman that he might want to continue to retain lawyers who understood the local law."

"Local law," Vicky said. "I wasn't aware that Imperial law was given to local accents."

"It may have just been our lawyers' way of suggesting that this new bunch didn't know their briefs from boxers."

It took Vicky a moment to catch the joke. It took the commander a bit longer to allow a smile. Kit and Kat totally missed it, but then, they were intent on what was going on around the limo. Vicky had a large escort this trip: Marine, police, Rangers. Still, her own assassins were taking no chances.

"So, what did our lawless lawyers do after talking with their so-called clients?" Vicky asked.

"They seemed to have disappeared. No net presence. We would not know where they booked rooms if the hotel manager hadn't come forward when you became the leading news topic. He recalled their rental of two black SUVs. This ability of strangers to drop out of sight is troubling," the commander admitted.

"Kris Longknife had problems with these types as well. Even her magnificent Nelly at times couldn't get through their jamming."

"More of what your Mr. Smith is trying to get a handle on," the commander said.

Mannie's eyebrows went up.

"We'll talk about it later," Vicky said. "Maybe."

"They hired local help from the crime syndicates to track you," the commander continued. "All of their contacts are now talking to us. The big picture we are putting together is telling, but the individuals knew next to nothing about what they were doing or why."

"Is this leading us anywhere?" Vicky asked, seeing a lot of data but not much information.

"Sadly, no," the commander admitted. "We did recover nano cameras. Several, from the room you were, ah, detained in. No one in the Navy has ever seen the likes of them. We started trying to examine one, and it went poof. As did the second. We are holding the other three for the return of Mr. Smith."

"Damn. I hate playing second fiddle in a tech duet," Vicky said.

The commander allowed a pained response. "It seems we are caught in just such a predicament. However, that crew from the Mining Management Co-op has decided that they have gotten all the help they are likely to get from their higher-ups and are singing like a bunch of choirboys."

"Is the song worth listening to?" Vicky asked.

"Most of it we already know. One thing attracted my attention. The top managers were bribed for the last couple of years not to increase production but to cause it to plummet."

"Restrict the amount of crystal coming to market?" Mannie almost sounded incredulous.

"Exactly. The Imperial economy needed more crystal. Someone was paying the producers to see that less was available for sale."

"Crystal is critical to just about everything we fabricate in the Empire," Mannie said. "Power, electronics, everything high tech needs some sort of crystal in it."

"And if it's not there, the entire economy crashes," Vicky said, drawing the obvious conclusion.

"My father's economy is not crashing because of a hundred different things. They are only symptoms of a single dagger stabbed into its heart."

"So it would appear," Mannie said.

"I wonder," Vicky whispered, "if they started this plan the moment my beloved stepmom caught the Emperor's eye."

"Or if that was part of the plan?" the commander offered.

Vicky shook her head at the sheer audacity of it all. Her father had been so confident in his power. Or so he had seemed to his little daughter. Had he been a fool the whole time? Was he the first of the fools, or had her grandfather and great-grandfather built their empires on the willing cooperation of men just as venial and corrupt as those who were finally grasping for it all while Dad lolled around the bed of that pregnant sow?

Yesterday, her stepmom's attempt to kill her had stripped all the blinders from Vicky's eyes. Yesterday, she'd come to the realization that the Empress's obsessive efforts to kill Vicky were only a part of an obsession that left the entire Empire in the dust and its subjects begging on their knees for any crust of bread the Empress and her family might allow them.

Now I have proof to back up my conclusion.

"Commander, tell the motorcade to speed up. Call ahead to the shuttle. I want it moving the moment I'm aboard. Oh, and tell Admiral von Mittleburg I'll want to talk to him the moment I'm back on the station."

"Yes, Your Grace."

Vicky leaned against the window and stared out at the prosperous city of Kiev. A city whose prosperity owed nothing to the Empire.

All her life, she'd been trained to never think of treason. To never even think of thinking about treason. Now, she opened her thoughts to rebellion. Her mind was hot with it.

She grabbed some figurative bellows and blew the fire hotter.

═══

CHAPTER 63

As soon as the shuttle docked, Vicky was on her sore feet and moving. She ignored everything that got in her way between the shuttle bay and the admiral's quarters.

Smart people took one look at her and got out of her way.

The admiral's secretary had the door open for her as she steamed in. "Commander, you wait here. Mannie, with me," she said curtly, and stormed in.

The admiral was meeting with his yard-improvement staff. They'd been warned of her approach. They stood aside to allow her entrance, then quickly fled the room.

"Admiral, we need to talk."

"I expected we would. By the way, Mannie, the work on the dock is progressing faster than any of my men thought possible. Thank you."

"We are glad to be of service to the Navy," the politician said.

"Mannie," Vicky said, "if you have any problems with a discussion that some might consider treason to my father, you should leave now."

The mayor grinned. "I've been waiting all my life for a chance to sit in on that kind of thing. Admittedly, I haven't done it yet, mostly for fear that half the people at the table would be in the pay of State Security."

"They likely would have been," Vicky admitted. "Admiral, are you in anyone's pay but the Navy?"

"You know I am not."

"Mannie?"

"I helped put them out of business on St. Petersburg, then I danced on their grave, and when no one was looking, I stood in a long line to piss on it, too."

"Then let us talk of how we may save the people who look to us for leadership. My most recent encounter with minions of my stepmother has clarified my thinking. What she wants is a wrecked Empire that she and her family may wander through and pick up select features to enslave to their will. I *will* save the Empire, though I have to admit that I have no idea what will be left of it when this cleansing tidal wave is done."

"That's wise of you," the admiral said. "You can throw a snowball off the top of a tall mountain. You can't tell what the avalanche will do at the bottom."

"But," Vicky said, fists clenching, "we have to stop them. We can't let them continue their campaign of destruction and enslavement of what's left."

"No," both the admiral and mayor agreed.

Vicky quickly told the admiral of the plot to wreck the crystal supply.

The admiral spoke to his computer, and the wall turned into a series of bar charts. "Those are the demands for crystal, five years ago for all the planets. The yellow shows demand, the red supply." Supply almost met demand.

"Computer," the admiral ordered. "Update charts to show the latest reports of the supply of crystal available to each market."

Only the Greenfeld bar showed supply meeting demand. All the rest showed available supplies as a small red portion at the bottom of a much larger yellow demand. Some of the markets had shrunk down to nearly nothing in just five years.

"You knew this?" Vicky demanded.

"The Navy is not blind. We knew the problem was there. You have just told me why. When you've got so much data coming at you, it's not always easy to see which cow is wearing the bell. Which cow is leading all of them down a path to destruction?"

"Crystal is the cow with the bell," Mannie whispered.

"Definitely," Vicky agreed, then found herself with a new question. "Show me the planets under the control of my stepmother's Security Consultants."

The admiral spoke to his computer, and several markets changed color from red and yellow to black and white. No surprise—there, availability of crystal almost met demand.

"Admiral, can you get this to the Navy high command? Also, until we get an answer back from them, may I suggest you assign a cruiser to the defense of Presov?"

"We'd also better escort any shipments of crystal from there to St. Petersburg," he added.

"Also, any crystal assemblies we ship out from here," Mannie put in. "We are at war. A war for crystal. Our economies need it as much, dear Duchess, as you needed water yesterday."

"Yes," Vicky hissed. "When does the *Retribution* arrive?" she said, switching to the practical.

"It is in system. It should dock later today."

"Mannie, where are we in our negotiations with Metzburg and New Brunswick?"

"The admiral was kind enough to loan us destroyers for high-speed runs to both planets."

"Last I heard, you were worried about having civilians on your ships," Vicky said.

"Some of the industrialists were found to hold reserve commissions in the Supply Corps," Admiral von Mittleburg said vaguely.

"But the good admiral still sent along his own men to observe our negotiations," the mayor observed downright aridly.

"We have their wish list," Mannie went on. "We're using a single use, throwaway cipher. Much of what they need we had expected and already were producing. Some needs are very specific, and we're working on them now."

"Where are all these trade goods?" Vicky asked.

"Some have been shipped up here on the LCTs that were carrying dockyard gear."

"They have been?" the admiral growled, storm clouds rising in his eyes.

"The dock gear is heavy, and leaves a lot of spare cubic meters in the LCTs empty," Mannie said. "The crystal constructions are light. You could fit a lot of them in a load before you added much weight."

The admiral appeared mollified, if not happy that something had been done in his domain without his blessing.

Vicky weighed all she knew and chose her course. "Have the *Retribution* ready to sail as soon as possible. Have all the crystal assemblies loaded into the available merchant hulls. Admiral, I'd like a cruiser to take the jumps ahead of us."

"You can have the *Rostock*, she just came in yesterday. It will add half a day to your trip, but I'd like you to go via Presov and drop off the *Kamchatka* there. She's cranky and old, but she'll provide them with a station ship and 8-inch guns to argue with anything that comes their way."

He spoke to his computer, and the wall screen changed. Vicky saw the Navy and merchant ships available to him. Some were marked for Poznan and already loaded with food, both emergency and basics. "I can have them swing by Presov on their way back and pick up a cargo of crystal," the admiral said.

"Are the mines that productive?" Vicky asked.

"Under their new management, and considering the prices the miners are being paid, along with the gear and victuals they now have, it's amazing how production has gone up. Skyrocketed, one might say. I think those scumbags rotting in jail below had to work mighty hard to screw that place up and earn their bribes."

It was clear he knew what he needed to do and was ready to do it.

"I better get myself packed for another trip," Vicky said, and dismissed herself. Mannie followed her from the admiral's quarters but did not make any attempt to enter Vicky's quarters across the passageway.

"I need to get below," he said, not looking her in the eye. "I've spent most of the last week, more, following in your footsteps. It seems I need to look to my business."

"Can't someone else take care of it?" Vicky asked, running her hand down his arm.

"You want to get away quickly. I need to make sure my

merchants know what is expected of them and how little time they have to make it ready. As they say, we in government don't make anything, but just let us drop the ball on coordination, and see who gets the blame."

They shared a chuckle.

"I'll be back soon," Vicky found herself promising a man for the first time in her life.

"I'll be waiting for you," she heard a man say, also for the first time.

They parted without as much as a kiss.

I *am changing,* Vicky thought. *I hope it's for the better.*

Then she submerged herself in the voyage that lay ahead of her.

CHAPTER 64

THE *Retribution* was away from the pier at 0600 the next morning. Following in her wake were the *Rostock*, *Kamchatka*, and nine freighters. Vicky spotted the *Doctor Zoot* near the end of the line. No doubt, the smaller one following in the *Doc*'s wake was the other tramp freighter that had happened into her merry affair.

Merry affair, no doubt, until Stepmother dearest names it treason. I wonder how many ships will follow in my wake when they know where I'm going and what I'm up to.

When Captain Etterlin asked if she had a fleet speed, Vicky answered, "Fast."

They departed the station for the first jump at one-gee acceleration. The flip at midcourse was a bit ragged. Vicky expected it of the merchant ships, but the three Navy ships didn't seem to do all that well among themselves. Captain Etterlin blamed the age of the *Kamchatka* and the inexperience of the *Rostock*'s skipper.

Vicky remembered how Commander Schlieffen had horsed the *Spaceader* around the *Rostock* as it stayed rock steady to cover her flight from High Greenfeld station. She didn't like what she was hearing from this captain but kept her own counsel.

Together, the convoy decelerated toward the jump, arriving at it at a near dead stop. The jump went smoothly, as did the next jump.

What they found after that jump was anything but smooth.

The Presov system was occupied. A pair of ships had themselves just entered the system from Jump Point Adele. That jump led deeper into the Empire. The two ships squawked as *Golden Empress No. 21* and *Golden Empress No. 34* of the Golden Empress Line. A query of Vicky's computer showed no such shipping line and no such ships. The specifics of the ship allowed, however, that they might have until recently been the *Imperial Red Star* of the Imperial Star Lines and the *High Ball* of the Humphrey Shipping Company.

They were making 1.5 gees for Presov.

"They will get there before us," Captain Etterlin advised Vicky.

"Then we will have to get there faster," Vicky said.

"Your Grace," did not hold either disagreement or agreement.

"You have high-gee stations aboard your ship, don't you, Captain?"

"Of course, Your Grace."

"Then I suggest you inform the *Kamchatka* to conform to our movements. The *Rostock* is to escort the convoy toward the next jump at one gee, and both your ship and the *Kamchatka* should prepare for high-gee acceleration."

"Your Grace, there is no way that old wreck can do more than one gee."

"Then advise the *Kamchatka* to follow us as soon as possible, and you get this tub underway. We are wasting time, Captain."

The captain looked a bit green around the gills.

"The *Retribution* has done high-gee accelerations, hasn't it?" Vicky asked cautiously.

"We did two gees for an hour on trials."

Ah. Vicky saw the problem. "Well, Captain, I was on the *Wasp* with Princess Kris Longknife when we were doing four gees and glad of it because the alien ships chasing us did not take prisoners. I suggest you advise your crew to prepare for three-gee acceleration in fifteen minutes and get ready to go about your business."

The man visibly swallowed. "Yes, Your Grace."

Around the bridge, Vicky spotted consternation among some of the senior officers. Several of the junior officers seemed hard put to suppress their glee. Chiefs eyed their officers. Ratings eyed their shoes as if wishing they were anywhere but here.

Vicky used her computer to tell Kat to bring her high-gee station from where it was parked in the back of her closet.

There would be hell to pay if it didn't work. Exactly who the piper was would remain open to discussion.

Fifteen minutes later, the *Retribution* began to accelerate. The chief boson at the engineering station called the rising gee count. "One point five."

Vicky's new high-gee station still smelled of paint and friction reducers.

"Two gees," and Vicky found herself being pulled back into the padding.

COMPUTER, she thought, using the skull harness Mr. Smith had fitted to her and that was supposed to let her talk to her computer in private. MATCH MY STATION TO THE ENGINEER'S MAIN STATION.

A moment later, the board in her high gee station changed. Vicky studied it for a moment. It had been over a year since she stood a watch in the *Fury*'s engineering spaces, still she spotted the important readouts. They were tending toward the yellow margins but still safe.

CAPTURE ME THE CAPTAIN'S BOARD, she told her computer. Her board adjusted itself. It still showed several of the engineering readouts, but now damage control was there as well as an overview of casualties.

Damage and casualties showed nothing.

Good.

"Two point five gees," the chief reported. Vicky spotted the change on the gee meter on her board.

"Two point six."

"Two point seven," from the chief brought a pained look Vicky's way from the captain. Their high-gee stations were reclining, leaning back to help the human body better handle the extra weight.

"Two point eight."

All the important engineering readouts were in the yellow, but well back from the red. Vicky remembered how the *Wasp*'s had run deep into the red as they fled for their lives.

But the Wasp *was made by Wardhaven. The* Retribution *may not be as well built as the* Wasp.

"Two point nine."

"Your Grace?" the captain said.

"Steady as you go, Captain," the Grand Duchess answered the unasked question.

"Three gees," the chief reported, finally.

Vicky checked her board. Nothing in the red in engineering, though there was creep on one of the reactors. Damage control reported one of the turret scantlings had deformed. Turret Dora would likely not be available. Five crewmen had suffered casualties: back sprains because high-gee stations did not perform to the manufacturer's guarantee.

The captain motored his high-gee station over to Vicky's.

"Your Grace," he whispered nervously, "we need to slow down to make repairs."

"Can your damage control parties correct the deformation below turret Dora?" Vicky asked.

Dismay showed on the captain's face. "How do you know about Dora?"

"I do. Now, can you fix it?"

"No, that will require yard time. Time in a major yard. There aren't any this side of High Anhalt."

Vicky saw no need to tell this captain that his ship was not likely to go to High Anhalt until a lot of water, milk, and blood had flowed under that bridge.

"If it cannot be repaired, I see no reason to slow down."

"But it may get worse. Other turrets may fail."

"Captain, I was told that the *Retribution* was one of the Empire's newest and best battleships."

"It is," would have had more pride in it if the captain's voice didn't have to allow for so much worry.

"Then let's see that we get to Presov before they do."

"May I ask why, Your Grace?"

"No, you may not," Vicky snapped the way Admiral Krätz had at her when she'd had the impertinence to ask the same.

The captain folded a lot faster than she had.

Who selected you to captain this ship? If this ship has no more fighting guts than you have, we are in trouble.

The proud battleship stayed at three gees. The hull showed no new weaknesses although there was a steady stream of reports about failed high-gee stations.

Vicky tried not to remember that her high-gee station was also her battle-survival pod, and, if Kris Longknife was to be believed, it was not her battle with her brother's first command that killed Henry Peterwald XIII but someone's sabotaging his survival pod that was the death of him.

The battleship creaked and groaned as it sped through space at three gees. The Empress's ships tried to take themselves up past the 1.5 gees they'd been doing, but one ship blew an engine off into space and had to slow down to 1.2.

The other ship pulled back to 1.5 gees and stayed there.

Vicky motored her station over to the navigator's post. The captain quickly came to park at her elbow.

"Navigator, could you please run me some course assumptions based upon all ships maintaining their present course and speed."

"Yes, Your Grace."

He must have had the plot ready. He tapped his board and plots appeared on the main screen.

"We'll be there two orbits before they arrive," Vicky observed.

"Yes, Your Grace, and if I may point out, we'll be on the far side when they make orbit."

"That is not what I want," Vicky said.

"May I ask what you do want, ah, Your Grace?" the captain said.

He was learning to ask nicely when he talked to his Grand Duchess; Vicky managed to turn to face him and awarded him a smile.

"We have only two Marine companies on the planet to protect it. Those ships could likely land two battalions of 'Security Consultants,' possibly more, and we'd always be on the wrong side of the planet to confront the ships that brought them."

The navigator's nostrils dilated just a bit. The captain looked like he'd swallow his tongue. If he had something to say, words eluded him.

Strange, he's the captain of this ship. I'm supposed to be just a passenger, and a junior one at that, yet he's letting me order his ship around and can't raise a question about what I'm doing.

On the other hand, I'm just as glad that he's keeping out of this.

"Navigator, what adjustments to our course would we need to make orbit with that first ship, the *Golden Empress No. 34*?"

The navigator tapped his board slowly under the weight of high gees. "I make it two point nine one for the rest of the way in. A bit of adjustment as we come into orbit should let us trail that *Golden Empress* by about a hundred klicks."

The navigator looked proud of himself.

"But the other ship could adjust its course," the captain pointed out.

"Yes, but we've seen what happened when they tried to jack up the speed," Vicky said. "They can slow down. However, they can't lay on even one-tenth of a gee more."

"I think she's right, sir," the navigator said to the captain.

"Watch your board carefully, Navigator," the captain shot back, and turned his station away.

Vicky gave the navigator an encouraging wink. He grinned. She turned away, back to what she'd come to think of as her station, just a half meter back from the captain's own place in the middle of the bridge.

CHAPTER 65

T HE *Retribution* made orbit exactly one hundred kilometers behind the *Golden Empress No. 34*. It wasn't for their lack of trying to dodge the inevitable. *No. 34* slowed, and slowed, then made as if to go for a higher orbit.

The *Retribution* might have a warped turret support, but it had a lot more energy to play with. When the *Empress* finally gave up and made orbit, there was one huge battleship on its tail.

"Battleship *Retribution*," came over the hailing net, "there is nothing for you here. Move along."

Grimly, the battleship returned silence.

"This is Commissioner Lanz. I hold a warrant from the Empress to reduce the striking workers on Presov. They have put down their tools and refused the lawful orders of their management. I command Security Consultants Group 121 and 122. We will set matters right."

"Put me on-screen," Vicky ordered, standing in her gee station, careful in zero gee not to drift off.

The screen came alive. Vicky found herself facing a middle-aged man of balding pate and nervous demeanor. He frowned at her, probably trying to remember where he'd seen her. She solved his problem.

"I am the Imperial Grand Duchess, Her Grace Lieutenant Commander Victoria of Greenfeld. And I know very well where the managers of the mining co-op are. I arrested them for taking bribes to act against the fiduciary interests of both their employers and their stockholders as well as conspiring to illegally restrict trade. The workers are working under new management I appointed. Rather than downing their tools, they are producing several times more crystal a month than they could under those now awaiting trial for their crimes."

Commissioner Lanz looked like he'd swallowed something both surprising and poisonous. After several moments of looking like a landed fish trying to gulp down air, he got out, "But I have my warrant. From the Empress."

"Who, no doubt, will withdraw it when she discovers she was misinformed."

In a pig's eye, Vicky did not say aloud.

"But right at this moment, I have my orders."

"And I am telling you that you will not land on that planet."

Now the landed fish found some sort of backbone. "I am under the Empress's protection."

"And the miners of Presov are under my protection. I might add that my protection includes a battalion of Marines on the ground with them and this battleship in orbit. Which protection would you care to rely on at the moment?"

The fish took only a moment to flop and slithered back whence it came. Without another word, the screen went blank.

"They are powering up their engines," sensors reported.

"Captain, will you please follow them as long as they are in orbit."

"Yes, Your Grace." He gave the necessary orders but motored his high-gee station over to Vicky's elbow.

"Would you have ordered me to fire on that ship?" he whispered.

"Do you think I am so foolish as to threaten what I would not do?"

The man leaned back in his chair. "So that was what the admiral meant," he muttered.

Vicky did not ask him to explain what he now thought the admiral meant. Since the poor captain had not been required to act on anything, he might still be allowed to clutch some shred of ambiguity from which to hang his peace of mind.

Let us see how much longer we can put off starting the rebellion.

The *Golden Empress No. 34* dropped down, then applied power and made a clean break from orbit. On Vicky's word—she still didn't like to use the word "order" where the captain was concerned, and no doubt he preferred it as well—the *Retribution* adjusted its own orbit and managed to stay in the planet's embrace.

They did prepare to receive the *Golden Empress No. 21.* It, however, chose to come in fast and low. After that pass, it swung out high, applied a lot of correction, and blew right out of orbit without completing one. Only when it was headed back to the jump did Vicky suggest that the *Retribution* join the two of them accelerating out.

The navigator had a course already in hand. "If we do two-gee acceleration and deceleration to the jump, we can catch up with the convoy just before they jump out of the next system."

"That sounds good to me," Vicky said.

"Make it so," the captain said.

"Captain, I need to send a message back to Admiral von Mittleburg."

"I imagine you do," he said, but for her ears only.

"I wanted your permission before I used your communications."

"Thank you," he said, and turned back to his duties.

Vicky encoded her message using a single-use cipher. She brought Admiral von Mittleburg up to date on what had happened. "I suggest that you arrange for the reinforcement of the garrison on Presov. I suspect this is just the first attempt to take the mines back. This is just my guess, but I wouldn't be surprised if not only the so-called scrapped ships are showing up either in her livery or as pirates, but if other merchant hulls that could be armed aren't also hauled in for merchant cruiser conversion. Please ask Mayor Artamus to examine with your yard managers the prospects for outfitting some of those laid-up merchant ships with armaments."

There, she'd said it. She was outfitting a fleet to fight the Empress's fleet.

When Empress and Grand Duchess fight, who is the traitor?

Only the history books could tell, and the winner would write them.

As Vicky headed for Communications to dispatch her message, she passed a door marked INTELLIGENCE CENTER. In all her time on the *Fury*, she'd never seen such a door. Clearly, Admiral Krätz had his source for intelligence, but it did not rate something called a center.

Vicky tried the door. It was locked. She waved her ID card over the admittance sensor. The door stayed locked.

So she knocked.

A second class petty officer, young for his rate, opened the door a crack. His eyes lit up as he recognized her, but the door didn't open farther.

"Lieutenant, the Grand Duchess is here," he called.

"Well, don't keep her standing in the passage. Open the door, Kelly."

The door opened only wide enough for Vicky to squeeze inside. She did, with a whole centimeter to spare. What she saw brought her to a halt as the petty officer closed the door. It locked behind her with a solid click.

The room Vicky found herself in was Navy gray, but very spacious in a non-Navy way. Its bulkheads were lined with computer stations, only half of them occupied, and black boxes.

The black boxes were what gave Vicky pause. The computers and communications gear aboard ship all bore manufacturer's labels with familiar brand names. Most owned by a Peterwald concern.

These black boxes were black and devoid of any markings. The Sailors hadn't even taped nicknames on them or operating instructions.

Vicky blinked and turned to meet the approaching lieutenant.

"I'm so glad you came, Your Grace," said the lieutenant, whose name badge identified him as Lieutenant Blue. Vicky wondered if that was any more his real name than Mr. Smith's. "You saved me from having to find you and introduce you to our setup here. We have some interesting intelligence for you. Would you care to sit down?"

Vicky took the offered chair.

"We were able to sync with the ship's main computer on that ship you talked to. I bet you didn't know that it wasn't christened the *Golden Empress No. 34*."

"Yes, it was originally the *High Ball*, of the Humphrey Shipping Company," Vicky said.

"So you do know."

"I know about the reflagging of those ships, yes. Do you know more than I do?"

"A lot more. We got a complete dump from the ship's main computer and from several others although there was at least one computer we could not so much as touch. I was warned to expect such things when around the Empress's handiwork."

"Yes," Vicky said. "I know about that. What did you find out from your dump?" she asked.

"Not all of the Humphrey Line's ships became *Golden Empresses*. The ships with the strongest scantlings, hull strength members, and reactors were ordered to the yards on Stettin. I checked. Stettin has the capability to make up to 6-inch lasers, although their 4-inchers for arming merchant ships are their most reliable product."

"Yes," Vicky said, "I know about Stettin. What I didn't know about was the shunting off to them of the hulls most ready to be made merchant cruisers. That's interesting."

"That was the news we found the most eye-catching," the lieutenant said. "There's a lot more. We also caught a full update on what's happening in the Empire, at least from one perspective."

"Yes, though perspective is such a malleable thing these days. Do you have a comm station I can use? I need to change the message I'm sending Admiral von Mittleburg."

The lieutenant looked pained. "Your Grace, we try to keep the equipment in here as separate from the rest of the ship as possible." Then his eyes lit up. "We do have one standard comm station. We wipe it after every use, though, and reinstall its system."

"Then that is what I would like to use."

Vicky quickly had her computer interface with the comm station, uploaded her message, and updated it to change her hunch to a very likely fact. She added, DEFINITELY HAVE

MANNIE LOOK INTO GETTING NAVAL LASERS MOVING UP TO THE STATION AND START ARMING THE BEST AVAILABLE MERCHANT HULLS FOR CRUISERS. WE WILL NEED THEM SOON ENOUGH. MORE TO FOLLOW FROM ANOTHER SOURCE.

Vicky then had the updated message recoded and sent.

"You will send a full data dump to me and Admiral von Mittleburg as quickly as possible," she told Lieutenant Blue. He'd been watching as words popped onto the commlink's screen but showed no surprise.

"Yes, Your Grace. As soon as we have something to show."

"Very good," Vicky said. She paused for a moment. The lieutenant showed no interest in showing her around his domain. Vicky considered asking but then decided she very likely knew more than he would tell her.

While the *Retribution* had sailed with a captain chosen with Imperial approval, Vicky would bet money she didn't have that this room had been outfitted after leaving Greenfeld. Quite likely at a Navy retirement colony that wasn't only full of retired Sailors.

The Navy knew it was behind in the computer, signal-snooping, and intel games. Behind, maybe, but it was playing its own game of catch-up. This room no doubt sported the best the Navy had in the game.

Vicky nodded. "Well done, Lieutenant. All of you, a job well done." And, having said all that needed saying, Vicky turned and left.

Just before the door clicked shut behind her, the room broke out in happy, confident talk.

So I leave behind me more folks happy to serve their Grand Duchess. I wonder how happy my stepmommy dearest's worker bees are?

Then Vicky remembered the ones who'd gone down shooting when the odds were impossible.

It's going to be a tough civil war.

CHAPTER 66

T HE *Kamchatka* and its lone merchant ship arrived at
  Presov before the *Retribution* jumped out of the system.
The two *Golden Empress*es were fully committed to their
jump by then. As planned, Vicky's battleship yacht caught up
with the *Rostock*'s convoy just before it made its next jump.
That allowed them to hold one gee as they crossed the last
system before their jump into Metzburg.

At the jump, no pirates blocked their way. The *Rostock*
jumped into the Metzburg system first; they sent no warning
back through the jump buoy. The *Retribution* and the merchants
followed her through.

In system, they accelerated toward their goal, with silence
their only companion.

Vicky was in her day quarters when intel reported that the
planet up ahead appeared normal. "They're going about business as usual. Strange they aren't trying to talk to the five-
hundred-pound gorilla in the room," Lieutenant Blue reported.

"I'll try to do something about my weight," Vicky said dryly,
while Commander Boch looked daggers at the lieutenant.

Lieutenant Blue smiled back, devoid of good sense and either
missing the meaning of everything or refusing to acknowledge it.

I may keep this fellow close, Vicky decided.

"Lieutenant, does intel have a station on the bridge?"

"No, Your Grace."

"See about setting one up. Say, next to sensors. I'd like to compare what the sensors see and what you see."

"If that's what you want, Your Grace."

"It is. I want you keeping track of things on any planet we approach. If you see anything that changes, especially regarding business and industry, let me know. If it's 0200 hours, let me know."

"Understood, Your Grace," he said, and left to fulfill her wishes.

"Do you trust that man?" Commander Boch asked.

"I trust him as much as I trust anyone," Vicky said. "Are we getting any reports from the men of business we sent out here first?"

"Nothing, Your Grace," the commander said.

"I do not like the taste of this. Tell sensors I want a report of every ship in system. Every reactor burning hydrogen."

"Yes, Your Grace," and the commander now left her.

Kit and Kat eyed Vicky. "You are getting bitchy. Would you care for a bath, and maybe a massage afterwards?"

Vicky knew where that would lead. Did she want to be satiated and satisfied or stay cranky and bitchy?

She chose the latter and dismissed the seductive assassins.

"Computer, show me everything we know about the industry of Metzburg again. I want to see what it produces. What it needs. How it can go to war."

The wall screen in her quarters began to cascade information.

Now, how do I bring it all together? Better yet, if I were my stepmother, how would I kick it all to pieces?

With a day of acceleration, a flip, and deceleration, they went alongside the pier at High Metzburg station early the next local day. No one on the station questioned their docking, but no one from the planet below sent so much as a greeting to their Grand Duchess.

Vicky took the beanstalk down into that continued silence.

She did not go alone. The commander had half a company of Marines around her, along with Kit and Kat. No surprise to

Vicky, but not to the commander's liking, Lieutenant Blue and a second class petty officer joined her collection, black boxes in hand.

The space-elevator ferry carried the kinds of workers, businesspeople, and travelers you'd expect. Vicky took over half the VIP lounge with her teams. The Marines took station at the exits.

That didn't stop customers from coming in for a drink and staying to talk.

Vicky exited the ferry to find that the ground station was as normal as could be. Of a welcoming committee, not so much as a gleam in anyone's eyes.

What if a Grand Duchess came to visit and nobody noticed? was not a thought she'd ever had, but she had it now.

The commander left to arrange transport and returned quickly. "There's a limo waiting for you, Your Grace, and transport for the Marines."

So there was. Out front, at the curb, waited a black limo and six black security rigs. There was also the Supply Corps commander who had been sent ahead.

"I'm the lead man the admiral sent with the first group on the destroyer *Viper*," the supply commander told Vicky. "I've set up a meeting for you. Sorry about all the secrecy, but no one trusts their commlinks these days."

"Understandably," Vicky said.

As they left the elevator complex, two police cars fell in line ahead of the Marines. Another two pulled up the rear. The convoy sped up but did not head into the city but rather turned outwards, toward rolling hill country. They drove for less than half an hour before turning into what looked like a working ranch with one huge mansion on a low rise.

The enormous central building looked like someone had crossed a massive box with a spaceship. There were angles and glass everywhere. In the middle of it was a lake with fountains everywhere. Raised in a neoclassical palace, Vicky found the effect . . . disturbing.

She waited in the limo while the Marines, Commander Boch, and Lieutenant Blue did a security sweep. The commander was back in fifteen minutes to usher Vicky through one mammoth, coolly impersonal room after another, footsteps echoing off marble walls. Finally, she was swooped up to a meeting room in a high-speed elevator of all glass, even the floor.

The room Vicky was ushered into was huge and cold. High glass walls showed a view that was both spectacular and intimidating. Above a long and wide marble table swept something like an airplane wing. From the screens spaced along its surface, the table might have been one huge computer.

Twenty men and women were widely spaced around its sides. The foot of the table was left open for Vicky. As she moved toward her place, the Grand Duchess quickly took in the people sharing the table with her. The faces raised to meet here were expected, with the usual blend of skin tones from olive to dusky. One was extraordinarily dark. Most were young to middle-aged in appearance, except the woman at the head of the table. She carried an unknown number of years with grace and poise. Her dress was a shimmering dance of crystal light that embraced the blue end of the color spectrum.

Vicky settled at her reserved place, then noted the lack of anyone else in the room who wasn't seated at the table. She turned to the commander. "Leave us. Take the lieutenant outside and see to it that this room is not disturbed or monitored."

His "Yes, Your Grace" and bow had obedience but no agreement in it.

No one spoke until the door was closed.

The woman at the head of the table broke the silence. "Your men may join our men, doing their best to see that these conversations are not distributed to the four winds. Personally, I doubt they will succeed."

"We do seem to face superior tech," Vicky admitted.

"Yes, *you* do," the woman agreed. "The day before your ship jumped in system, we all received a notice of unknown origin, warning us to have nothing whatsoever to do with you on pain of earning our Empress's severe displeasure."

"The Empress's displeasure. Not the Emperor's, my father's, displeasure."

"While he takes his pleasure with the Empress, who rules but her?"

"Yes," Vicky agreed.

The woman eyed Vicky as if to read her fortune on her

forehead. Dissatisfied with what she saw, she said, "What are you here to say that we risk so much to hear?"

Vicky cleared her throat and had her computer feed their computers the information the admiral had developed on crystal need and availability.

"I had thought," Vicky said, "that the credit disruption was the main cause of our difficulties. I had *thought* that a bit of manipulation of the planetary banks by the black-hearted Empress and her clan might explain the sudden lack of central credit from the Imperial-enfranchised banks on Greenfeld. That lack of credit certainly is *a* problem, but crystal is *the* problem."

"And how would you presume to solve this problem?"

"I now hold the crystal mines on Presov under my protection. Fabricators on St. Petersburg, fabricators that established themselves there without Imperial rescript or warrant, are ready to provide you with the crystal assemblies you so very much need. As production in the mines increases, no doubt raw crystal will come available to you as well."

"Assuming we dare to risk Imperial ire by developing an industry for which Greenfeld holds an Imperial monopoly," said the woman.

"Yes," Vicky said.

The woman emitted a sigh. Others around the table seemed to be barely holding their tongues. The woman silently surveyed the others, then asked, "But at what cost?"

"You can imagine what the cost might be if you go against the Empress, and your imaginings can be quite dark, no doubt. However," Vicky said, raising a hand with a finger pointing at no one, "what is the price for doing it the Empress's way?"

Vicky did not wait for them to attempt an answer. "On my way here, we stopped an effort by the Empress to retake the crystal mines on Presov."

There was a sudden gasp of surprise from people who had stayed bland-faced through everything thus far. Vicky went on. "We sent two Golden Empress Line ships on their way with a tattered warrant to return to the black-hearted Empress."

Vicky had been wondering what to name her stepmother. Annah preferred to name herself golden. Vicky would love to see her face when someone first let her know what she was called on the Grand Duchess's side.

"You can see from the chart that Minsk, Cologne, and Dresden now have all the crystal they need. They are all under the boot of the Empress and Bowlingame's Security Consultants. How are your family and associates making out there?"

Vicky paused only for a moment. "You *have* heard from your friends and relatives, haven't you? Well, even if they are not saying much, you have tried to talk to them. Sent them messages?"

"Businesses that are not held by Imperial corporations do not need to talk to each other to carry out their activities," the woman at the head of the table said with the sound of tired repetition in her voice.

"But your brothers and sisters are often the husbands and wives of those who run those businesses, are they not? I used to read the bridal registries as a young girl and dream. Have you not heard from your uncle or aunt, brother or sister? Has no one announced a new baby or pending nuptials? Has no one arranged a family reunion, or even shared a skiing vacation on New Alps?"

"Do you know something, or are you just filling the air with noisy speculation?" the woman demanded.

Vicky had watched the data cascade in front of her eyes. They'd been just cold names and numbers, reports and statistics. For this woman, they'd be flesh and blood. A family silent for too long was a growing chill around the heart.

"We stripped the *Golden Empress No. 34* of the content of its main computer in addition to several others. I have a report that brought me up-to-date on the official news of the Empire. What I found most scary was the private news, one commissioner to another. Foolish men brag . . . and often do it in easily broken codes."

Vicky said a few words, and her computer began to spew out the organized report that Lieutenant Blue's intel specialists had provided Vicky. At the time, they had just been the stories of wolves armed with Imperial warrants feeding on those helpless to protect themselves. Now, Vicky realized the full impact of her organizing the catalogue of crimes alphabetically, by family names. For her it had been a convenient way to get a handle on crimes that seemed to go on forever.

For those seated around the table, it made for an easy search for their own family's tragedy. Those who'd sat so quietly as the elder woman questioned Vicky now gasped and muttered curses.

"Can we trust this?" one young man demanded.

"Have you heard from your aunt lately?" an older woman snapped. "We knew they'd been strangely quiet of late. Now we know why."

"The lieutenant waiting outside can provide any of you who want it the raw feed he got from the *Golden Empress No. 32*," Vicky said. No doubt the Navy would be angry to have its capability flaunted so openly. Vicky would take that slap on the wrist when it came.

Today, she needed these people on her side.

The iron silence broke as people turned to each other, asking for whatever clarification might be found. Better yet, for anything that might prove that what Vicky had shown them was just another Peterwald lie.

A Peterwald bearing truth was a strange sight indeed. It took them a while to admit that what they saw from her was indeed true.

"Is there no court of law?" one man demanded. "If they actually bought my uncle out of his life's work for next to nothing, worse than nothing, there must be a court that will hear this crime." He had raised his eyes to the heavens, but he finished looking down the table at Vicky.

"Where Security Consultants hold Imperial warrants from the Empress, there are no courts to review their actions," the Grand Duchess responded, keeping her temper and voice ice-cold.

Angry, despairing words wound down to another hard silence.

"So. There is this. What would you have us do?" the woman at the head of the table asked.

"Nothing that you are not already doing. You run businesses. You employ workers, meet payrolls. Some of you manage the banks that are now financing the industries that are struggling to hold themselves above water. I stand behind St.

Petersburg's merchants, who want to sell you the raw stock you need to keep your plants running, your people working. That is all I came here today to do."

"And what will you come here to do tomorrow?" came back at Vicky from the other end of the table.

"Today has enough evil for the moment. Let us worry about tomorrow when it comes."

"But the Empress doesn't want us to have anything to do with you, either today or tomorrow."

"Did she say anything about the St. Petersburg merchants?" Vicky answered.

"A technicality, some might say," the woman in the shimmering blue dress shot back.

"Yes. And what court adjudicated differences over technicalities?" Vicky asked.

There was a long pause. Again, Vicky had the impression that the woman at the head of the table was silently polling the others. "We will need to talk on this," she finally said. "Can you rejoin us tomorrow?"

"Of course," Vicky said. Smiling softly, she stood and strode from the room.

CHAPTER 67

═══

H ER companions were waiting outside among a much larger group than Vicky expected. The commander from the Supply Corps stepped quickly up to Vicky.

"What did they decide?" he asked. It wasn't quite a demand. Not quite.

"Nothing," Vicky spat. "Absolutely nothing."

"Nothing!" the merchant in uniform squeaked.

"We will talk again tomorrow."

"Should I start unloading the cargo?" he asked

"Only if you are prepared to load it back up again, it seems."

"The meeting did not go well?" Commander Boch asked softly.

"It did not go anywhere," Vicky spat. "Enough of this in public. Am I to stay dirtside or go back to the *Retribution*?"

"Traveling is dangerous, but I am not sure I trust your safety anywhere but on our own ship," the commander said. The suspicious glance he threw those he'd been waiting with told Vicky more than his words. "We will talk more in the limo."

"Yes," Vicky agreed.

She seemed to exit the house faster than she'd come in, as if it had shrunk, or perhaps her feelings toward the people it held had gotten smaller.

In the portico, the limo awaited her with the black SUVs before and behind and Marines standing tall all around them. She headed for the open door of the limo. Before she had taken two steps, the commander put his hand on her head and forced her to duck down.

He low-walked her to the SUV behind the limo.

Vicky allowed herself to be moved by his will. The commander slid into the seat beside Vicky, his hand on her arm, pulling her down. He was as hunched down as Vicky. He rested his finger over his lips. *We will talk, but later.*

Already seated across from Vicky were Kit and Kat. Their small bodies showed hard and eager, like tightly wound springs. Their heads swiveled slowly. Their eyes took in everything and gave back nothing.

Orders were given. The click of Marine dress shoes on the stones showed they were obeyed even before doors began to slam.

The convoy gunned away from the mansion.

Vicky waited for an explanation.

"Lieutenant Blue's black boxes brought hints of matters not being as well as they should be. Our commander of supply had one of his contacts sidle up to him and suggest that he might not want to be in the same limo as you. He was assured that there would be business aplenty for him tomorrow but not if he got too close to you today."

"Nice of his contact," Vicky said, dryly.

"The Marines are on full alert. Lieutenant Blue is using everything in his command to give us warning."

"Who is in the limo?"

"Only a Marine driver in full battle armor. We brought down several sets."

"Is there a set for me?" Vicky asked.

"Sadly, there are none that fit a woman," Kit spat.

"Wasn't there a set of battle rattle for me on Poznan that you forced me into?"

"Sadly," Kat said, "that pirate destroyed the locker we stored it in on the *Attacker.*"

"I have got to get some of Kris Longknife's spidersilk undies," Vicky said. "Some for me and some for you two."

The two assassins showed no sign they'd heard her.

Vicky waited. She didn't have to wait that long.

As the convoy rounded a bend in the road, there was a huge explosion. The SUV Vicky was in shot into the lead and rocketed faster than the winding road really allowed.

After a moment, it slowed. "That was not much of an attack," the commander said.

"What was that bang, then?" Vicky demanded.

"A roadside bomb aimed at the limo."

"And that's not an attack?"

The commander shrugged. "I was expecting a full assault. You know, like the one that got your last escort."

Vicky gave him a dirty look, then got a different idea. "Let's go back."

"Your Grace, I'm not sure that would be safe."

"Someone just risked his life for me. I will see how he fares," she demanded.

The SUV found space and turned about.

"Besides, if this is the only vehicle leaving the area, doesn't that pretty well say who is in it?"

"I hadn't thought of that," the commander admitted.

"We are going to have to think of more things than we have in the past," Vicky snapped, as much to herself as anyone else.

What she found when she got there was a limo up a tree. The blast had hurled the long transport against a gnarled oak and wrapped it around its trunk. They were just cutting the driver out of the wreck as Vicky arrived.

"I'm okay. I'm okay," the corporal insisted. "Though it feels like I have a two-by-four up my ass."

He might have a lot of wood intimately involved with him. His armor made him look like a hedgehog, so many splinters stuck out of the protective plastic.

When he was finally out and lying down for the medic to check out, Vicky came to stand over him. "Thank you for your service to my life. It seems I need a medal for those who have placed their life between me and death."

"Between you and the black-hearted Empress," the corporal corrected his Grand Duchess.

"Did that room leak as bad as that?" Vicky said.

"I could tell just how badly it leaked," the commander said, "by those who laughed when you said that."

"Did Lieutenant Blue bug the room?"

"One of many."

Vicky paused to look over the scene. The limo was still up the tree, a total wreck. The backdrop, however, was gentle and bucolic. Now undisturbed, cows grazed in green fields or stood chewing their cud. The restful scene spread away to rolling hills.

Vicky wondered what it would look like in a year. Half a year? Next month, if her stepmother and family got their way?

"I don't think that meeting accomplished nearly enough. Commander, mount up the troops. We're going back, and we're not leaving again until our business here is finished."

CHAPTER 68

VICKY stormed through the vast rooms. She did not run. Marines may have had to hurry to catch up and form a phalanx around her, but a Grand Duchess does not run.

A Grand Duchess in full fury does not halt when foolish men get in her way. Her Marine outriders discouraged such fools and sent them on their way to cause other people trouble. Vicky did not bother herself with them.

She arrived back at the doors from which she had been ushered out without breaking stride. Two Marines hurled the doors open before her. She marched in, followed by most of her entourage.

Apparently, her approach had been so rapid that word had not gotten to the conferees. Silence fell on them like a hurtling mountain as Vicky quick-marched up to the table.

She eyed them all. "Which of you just tried to kill me?"

Her voice was low and deadly. The room plumbed new depths of quietude.

The woman in the shimmering blue dress at the head of the table stood up, her stance neither quelled nor belligerent but finely tuned somewhere in between. "I take it that someone *did* just try to kill you?"

"A roadside bomb wrapped my limousine around a tree. Someone knew I was here. Someone knew when I left. And that someone knew the only way I could take back to the space elevator and when I would pass their bomb."

"How could anyone have known of such timing and routes?" the woman said, honestly puzzled.

"Let me guess. Did you broadcast a notice about this meeting in all your media?" Vicky spat a broadside of pure sarcasm.

"For our own safety, we desperately wanted to have this meeting in private."

"You failed," Vicky shot back.

"So it seems," the woman said, her eyes roving the attendees. Few met her glance.

"Then, the black-hearted Empress knows you are here with me and, no doubt, every word said here will be reported," Vicky snapped. "So, shall we finish our business now rather than later? Metzburg can be an important trading partner for St. Petersburg, but it is not the only one we are talking to. After that attack, I will not waste any more of my time negotiating with you. Are you with us or will you open your hearts for my stepmother's dagger?"

"There must be another option," someone at midtable almost pleaded.

"You've talked for a week, Abe, and you haven't come up with anything more than that very same question," a young woman snapped. "It's time to fish or cut bait. I say we fish. Otherwise, we'll likely be cut up for bait."

"She has a point, damn it." "She's right, God help us," and "The Empress will have our heads on her mantelpiece," came in quick response.

Vicky listened to them but did not sit down. This meeting would not last that long.

"Okay, tell me again what you want us to do?" the middle-aged woman who sat at Vicky's left asked.

"We can provide you with electronic, crystal, and other miniaturized components that you need to keep your industry humming and your workers on the job. In return, you ship us what St. Petersburg needs to quickly grow our heavy industry."

"Why do you, I mean St. Petersburg, need heavy industry?

If we spur your growth, we're just cutting our own throats. Killing our own markets, aren't we?"

"If we followed that to its absurd end," Vicky pointed out, "St. Petersburg would not be shipping industry to the new colonies around her. They are hungry for industry. We are feeding it. You need to look to growing your markets, not grasping to keep what little you have."

"Spoken by a Peterwald with all your Imperial monopolies," was tossed from midtable like a hand grenade.

"I'm a Peterwald, and I'm shilling for St. Petersburg today. Shilling for their products that have no Imperial warrant and defy Imperial monopolies," Vicky snapped right back.

"Strange, that," a man's voice observed dryly.

"Yes, it is strange," Vicky agreed.

"You brought the goods we asked for?" the woman at the head of the table asked.

"Yes. And our escorted trading fleet is ready to carry away the heavy-fabrication plants we want for them. I know your inventory is full to the choking point. Do you have them ready for us?"

"My jigs are in storage on the station," one woman said.

"My heavy fabs went up the beanstalk yesterday and today," a man said.

"Then let's do business," Vicky said.

The woman spoke again. "I've ordered my station representative to start loading my consignment as soon as we review the delivery we were expecting."

"I'll order my man to do the same," the man said.

"Commander, is the cargo from all eight of our ships being unloaded?" Vicky asked the Supply Corps officer.

He spoke on his commlink. "It started fifteen minutes after you boarded the ferry for dirtside," he admitted, a bit taken aback. That hadn't been his answer an hour ago.

"Then it seems that the deed is done," the older woman at the head of the table said, and stood. "Your Grace, will you walk with me?"

Vicky strode to meet her and was led to double doors that opened onto an immense balcony. Vicky paused at the wide glass doors. COMPUTER, GET LIEUTENANT BLUE AND THE

MARINE SKIPPER TO ME. HAVE THE MARINES BRING THEIR
BEST SNIPERS.

YES, YOUR GRACE.

"Is there a problem?" the woman asked when she noticed
that Vicky was slow to join her on the terrace.

"Only for a moment," Vicky said.

Four Marines, long rifles held at the ready, double-timed
out onto the balcony. Lieutenant Blue was only a few paces
behind them. Commander Boch and the Marine skipper
brought up the tail of the parade.

"Commander, see to it that this balcony is secure. Lieutenant Blue, see to it that no one else hears our conversation,"
Vicky ordered.

"Yes, Your Grace," in three-part harmony greeted Vicky.

Lieutenant Blue, joined by his petty officer, set themselves
up at a marble bench and bent to their business. The snipers
distributed themselves around the edge of the balcony and
began covering the distance. Two more Marines joined each
sniper, one with binoculars, the other covering the close in as
the man with the long rifle covered the far out.

"Is it always like this around you?" the older woman asked.

"Only since I decided I didn't want to let my loving stepmom kill me."

"That is a sorry state of affairs," the old woman spat.

"A sorry state for state affairs," Vicky agreed. "Now, I
believe all my Marines are out of earshot. My signal intel team
is not waving madly at me, which I take to mean they are
happy with the silence. What do you wish to say to me?"

As they strolled together toward the edge of the terrace, the
woman said, "You and I both know that the steps we are taking
today are only the first. While I am old enough to know that
every journey begins with a first step, I am also wise enough
to know that a planned itinerary is an optimistic hope for the
latter stages of the journey. Still, it is well to have some idea
of where you are going."

"And you want to know where I am going? What I am
doing?"

"I confess to some curiosity."

"I am Emperor Henry's daughter and his loyal subject.
Does that surprise you?"

"No. But you say nothing of his present wife and Empress."

"I prefer not to."

"That is good, as far as it goes."

"That is as far as I choose to go today."

They strode to the end of the balcony. The older woman leaned against the rail; her gaze wandered the land before them. In the distance, rolling hills were covered with fir trees native to distant Earth. They looked no more than forty years old. Closer in, the land flattened, softening into pastures where cattle grazed or sought shade under wide-spreading oak trees. Directly under the edge of the wide terrace was a several-hundred-meter drop. In the gorge below, white water boiled over rocks, sending up spray.

The woman took a deep breath. Vicky did likewise. She breathed deeply of cool water, grass, and cows, with a hint of the distant firs.

"It's a lovely land," Vicky said.

"And you are asking us to take a tremendous risk," the older woman said. "Since it was settled, this planet has not seen the fire and ruin of war. What will it look like next year, or the year after that, after an army fights its way over it?"

"We of Greenfeld have no army," Vicky said blandly. "What army could possibly rape and pillage your lovely homeland?"

"Ha," the woman snorted. "We had State Security to keep us in line, or else. Now those wolves have their Security Consultants. An army by any other name is still an army."

"So you need an army to protect you from those wolves," Vicky said.

"But for us to raise an army is treason against your father," the woman snapped.

Vicky shrugged. "So you don't raise an army. The black-hearted Empress has raised herself an army by another name, and she seems to have successfully skirted that treason. Why don't you do the same?"

The woman turned her gaze from the distant hills to fix Vicky with a hard stare, but she said nothing.

Vicky raised a hand and ticked off her fingers one by one. "You have out-of-work young men and women. Left on their own, they are just the tinder that provocateurs need to start riots guaranteed to bring the black-hearted Empress's Security

Consultants down on you sooner or later. Then you do have an army loose on your lovely planet to wreak havoc and nothing to stop them. Nothing at all."

Vicky let those words sink in, then raised another finger. "But what if those out-of-work young people were put to work? What if they were out of the cities and busy from sunup to sundown?"

"How?" the woman shot at Vicky.

Vicky turned away to the view. "Your planet has many lovely vistas like this one, but much of it is still in need of terraforming. There are whole mountain ranges begging to have trees planted on them, rolling hills just ready for grass."

"There's never enough money to make this planet what we want," the woman admitted.

"But now you have out-of-work youths who you must get working, even if it's only backbreaking labor. I had my computer do a search last night for historical situations like this. In one of them back on Earth, they raised a Civilian Conservation Corp. Don't those words just drip of peace and harmony as they roll off your tongue? A corps of civilians working to conserve the planet. Almost as innocent-sounding as Security Consultants, don't you think?"

"Don't armies have corps?" the woman didn't really ask.

"Yes. Yes they do," Vicky answered, holding tight to the grin on her face. "In this particular case, the young civilians working hard out in the woods were supervised by officers and NCOs from their nation's army. Some were active duty and detached for this work. Others were recently retired.

"Now," Vicky went on, "I just happen to know where we have a supply of recently retired officers and NCOs. Even more, a lot of officers and noncoms are being RIFed out of the fleet as the Navy and Marines find themselves forced to trim their budgets, retire ships, and disband Marine battalions. I think we could get our hands on quite a few competent leaders for your civilian conservationists."

"Civilian terraformers," the woman corrected. "About this drawdown, I haven't heard of it. How's it going?"

Vicky suppressed a smile. If the woman was renaming the corps, Vicky had her headed in the right direction. Still, Vicky stepped away from that and followed the woman to the RIF.

"The Reduction in Force is not going well. The Navy gets smaller. Strange thing, some of those retired ships sold for scrap are showing up as pirates. Some are even crewed by officers and Sailors who got their pink slips just recently."

"So the Navy is being split," the woman said, "as the officers and crews are dumped on the beach. Those who can stomach working for that damn woman end up under the pirate flag, and those who can't are stuck seeing how long they can survive on unemployment."

"That's what we're looking at."

"And you want me to hire your laid-off Navy types to teach my young men and women to plant trees and what?"

"Am I correct that you are allowed hunting rifles?" Vicky said, knowing very well the answer.

"In our outback and gone, there are some really nasty critters that don't much care for us humans, except as dinner," the woman admitted. "Anyone who goes there better carry a rifle."

"So, if we're sending young folks out to terraform your outback," Vicky said, "it might be a good idea to teach them how to shoot. Shoot a rifle and hit what they aim for."

"Unlike the State Security boys who just sprayed everything and let the coroner sort them out."

"And, no doubt, like the Security Consultants do."

"So," the woman said, "our Civilian Terraforming Jobs Companions will plant trees Monday and Tuesday and spend Wednesday at the rifle range. What do they do the rest of the week?" There was a fey smile on the older woman's lips.

Vicky brushed a speck of dirt from the balustrade. "They might well go back to the mountain they planted on Thursday and figure out a way to dig in and defend it? Maybe spend Friday learning how to storm that defense?" Vicky said.

"I think our gun makers could well benefit from a contract for several thousand, maybe tens of thousands of hunting rifles," the woman said.

"And I think I know just the people to train your tree planters?" Vicky said.

The woman leaned on the stone balustrade. She eyed Vicky, then eyed the drop-off from the terrace. It was a long way down to the tumbling river below.

"It would be nice to be able to protect Metzburg, to stop the

Security Consultants from landing and making a mess even as they die," the woman said to the drop-off.

Vicky nodded.

"Could the Navy protect us the same as they protected St. Petersburg?"

Vicky shook her head. "Sorry, did I mention the fleet was getting smaller?"

"I think you did."

"But," Vicky said, and let that word hang over the gorge and the shadowed white water below, "if you are raising an army, by some other name, there is no reason you can't raise a Navy to defend this verdant land you call home." Vicky noted the curl of a smile her words brought to the woman beside her. "I have been told that Metzburg makes some very effective defensive lasers for merchant ships, 4- or 5-inchers."

"I believe that we do," the woman admitted.

"I've been told you might well be able to scale up your lasers to 6- or 8-inch."

"I expect that we have people who would love to try."

"I have an expert who can give you some advice on that. I couldn't help but notice that you've got a lot of laid-up merchant ships trailing your station."

"You don't miss much, do you?"

"What I miss, some smart people tell me."

"And you listen?" was dripping with skepticism.

"Not all Peterwalds have mud in their ears."

"I think you would be the first," the older woman answered.

"So I've been told by folks who were surprised by what I'm doing," Vicky replied.

The woman's eyes turned to the far horizon. "Our space yards on the station have had little business of late. They and their workers could be put to work arming those ships. And if we are asked, what would we call them, we nice, loyal, subjects who are not revolting."

"We have a long tradition of arming merchant ships against pirates. I'm told that the pirates are rather heavily armed these days. I don't think a 6- or 8-inch gun would be too much for self-defense," Vicky said with an air of innocence.

"I'm told by one of my designers that we could put a half dozen 15-inch lasers on an unused liner."

Vicky raised an eyebrow. "That might be harder to explain."

"We will need to keep very quiet about that," the woman said, a tiny smile dancing around the edges of her mouth.

"Shall we very quietly go talk with those who can make all of this peaceful, civilian work happen?" Vicky said.

"Yes, let us."

Vicky eyed the old woman. She was smiling now, and her eyes sparkled.

"Before you came into the room this afternoon," the woman said, "I doubted there was any hope for us. When you left the first time, I feared all hope was gone. When you stormed back in, madder than a wet hen, I thought I saw possibilities. Now, I see hope. Hope for me and my family. Hope for all the men who work for us. Hope for their wives and children."

Vicky tried to accept the words the woman spoke, but she could not. "Ma'am, I am just a survivor. If I hope for anything, it is to help others survive as well."

"Oh, no, young lady, you are hope. Hope for a future that will not be as good as our past but so much better."

ABOUT THE AUTHOR

MIKE SHEPHERD grew up Navy. It taught him early about change and the chain of command. He's worked as a bartender and cabdriver, personnel advisor and labor negotiator. Now retired from building databases about the endangered critters of the Pacific Northwest, he's enjoying some fun reading and writing.

Mike lives in Vancouver, Washington, with his wife, Ellen, and close to his daughter and grandchildren. He enjoys reading, writing, dreaming, watching grandchildren for story ideas, and upgrading his computer—all are never ending. He's hard at work on Kris's next story, *Kris Longknife: Unrelenting*, coming from Ace in November 2015, and *Vicky Peterwald: Rebel*, coming in June 2016, as well as other exciting tales in Kris's universe.

You can learn more about Mike and all his books at his website mikeshepherd.org; you can e-mail him at Mike _Shepherd@comcast.net or follow Kris Longknife on Facebook.

From national bestselling author
MIKE SHEPHERD

Kris Longknife
DEFENDER

Kris Longknife is back in the good graces of the brass—and to demonstrate that, they've promoted her to commodore. But no mission is ever simple when your name is Longknife, as Kris discovers when she has to make some difficult command decisions about her future...

• • •

Praise for the Kris Longknife novels

"Kris can kick, shoot, and punch her way out of any dangerous situation, and she can do it while wearing stilettos and a tight cocktail dress."
—*Sci Fi Weekly*

mikeshepherd.org
facebook.com/AceRocBooks
penguin.com

An original military science fiction novella from
MIKE SHEPHERD

KRIS LONGKNIFE:
Welcome Home / Go Away

A Penguin Group Special from Ace

Kris Longknife is back home from her galactic adventures, but her entire Fleet of Discovery has been annihilated. And the alien race that she fought has now declared war on humanity. Some people think Kris is to blame, and it may take more than the efforts of her war-hero great-grandfather to save her from the wrath of the angry—and frightened—citizens of her home planet!

• • •

Praise for the Kris Longknife series

"A rousing space opera that has extremely entertaining characters."   —*Night Owl Reviews*

"Kris can kick, shoot, and punch her way out of any dangerous situation, and she can do it while wearing stilettos and a tight cocktail dress."   —*Sci Fi Weekly*

Only available as an e-book!
Download it today!

facebook.com/AceRocBooks
mikeshepherd.org
penguin.com

M1140T1013

An original
military science fiction novella from
MIKE SHEPHERD

Kris Longknife:
TRAINING DAZE

A Penguin Group Special from ACE

Kris Longknife dodges assassins, gains an unwelcome
(though rather handsome) bodyguard, and puts together a
training squad to travel from planet to planet, preparing
crews for the newest, fastest, and deadliest fighting ship.

And, of course, nothing goes as planned!

ONLY AVAILABLE AS AN E-BOOK!
DOWNLOAD IT TODAY!

penguin.com
mikeshepherd.org

M931T1013